STARGÅTE
SG·1™

RELATIVITY

JAMES SWALLOW

FANDEMONIUM BOOKS

An original publication of Fandemonium Ltd, produced under license from MGM Consumer Products.

Fandemonium Books, PO Box 795A, Surbiton, Surrey KT5 8YB, United Kingdom

Visit our website: www.stargatenovels.com

STARGATE
SG·1

METRO-GOLDWYN-MAYER Presents

RICHARD DEAN ANDERSON

in

STARGATE SG-1™

AMANDA TAPPING   CHRISTOPHER JUDGE   DON S. DAVIS

and MICHAEL SHANKS as Daniel Jackson

Executive Producers ROBERT C. COOPER   MICHAEL GREENBURG

RICHARD DEAN ANDERSON

Developed for Television by BRAD WRIGHT & JONATHAN GLASSNER

ISBN: 978-1-905586-07-3   Printed in the USA

STARGATE
SG·1

RELATIVITY

Back in the tunnel-like corridor, Jack and Daniel made their way down the passageway. The alert sirens were sounding as the detachments made their way through the open wormhole to the Pack's rendezvous point.

"You think Teal'c might be right?" O'Neill asked the question without looking at the younger man.

"What, are we going to break out the thumbscrews, Jack?" The scientist pinched the bridge of his nose. "Come on, I mean 'forceful application'? He was talking about torture."

O'Neill shot him a look. "Teal'c's been on the wrong end of a Goa'uld pain-stick enough times to know what it's like, Daniel. And I had my fair share too. It's not something he'd say lightly."

"I can't believe we're even having this conversation." Jackson shook his head.

"I didn't say we were gonna stretch her on a rack, damn it!" The colonel's temper flared briefly. "But we might have to ask some hard questions. I'm thinking we could call in the Tok'ra, maybe use that mind-scanner gizmo they got."

"You say that like it's the gentler option."

Jack stopped and looked the other man in the eye. "Hey!" He snapped his fingers in front of Daniel's face. "Hey, Space Monkey! Look at me! What's goin' on? This woman lied her ass off to you, she tried to blow us all up, and here you are stepping up to defend her? Am I missing something?"

Acknowledgements:
Special thanks once again to Keith Topping, to Jo Walton and Steve Riley for friendship and l33t skills (Steve Riley is indestructible; you are not. Do not try to imitate him) and to Rachel Cooper for her generosity and enthusiasm.

Author's note:
The events depicted in *Relativity* take place toward
the end of the seventh season of Stargate SG-1.

CHAPTER ONE

The glittering flash came without warning, creating a watery glow in its wake that shimmered around the floor and the walls of the canyon. It caught fragments of crystalline mica and made them twinkle. In the dreary light of the day, the deep reds and burnt umber of the rocks were dulled, diluted by the sheen of fine, persistent rain. The glowing puddle of radiance set into the sheer side of the tallest rock face shone like a mirror made of ripples, held in place by a steel-gray hoop studded at regular intervals with luminous orange arrowheads.

Presently, a boxy mechanism on whining motorized wheels ventured through the circle, took the steps below it with robotic care and paused on the threshold. It offered telescopic arms to the sky, casting around with a stubby head equipped with digital abstractions of human senses. After a while it fell dormant and waited patiently, its job done.

The mirror flexed once again and figures in green followed the path of the machine. Four people, moving in a way that might have seemed casual to someone who did not know them.

She turned and flashed a grin as she stepped down the shallow stairs from the Stargate. "Well. No trees. That means you owe me lunch, sir."

Jack O'Neill grimaced as he took in the sparse landscape. "Yeah, okay. Fine. Easy bet. Just don't gloat, Carter. It's unseemly."

At his side, Daniel Jackson raised an eyebrow. "Unseemly?" he repeated.

"What?" O'Neill asked. "I'm reading a book on improving my word power. Don't take that from me as well."

From behind him, Teal'c came to his commander's rescue.

"I would doubt that this valley has ever seen vegetation of any kind, Colonel."

"Right now, I'd settle for some better weather." O'Neill took his sunglasses off the lanyard around his neck and peevishly put them inside an inner pocket of his gear vest. "Or maybe an umbrella."

"It's not that bad." Jackson adjusted the boonie hat on his head. "A brave man likes the feel of nature on his face, right Teal'c?"

"Indeed," replied the Jaffa, "but a wise man has the sense to get in out of the rain."

O'Neill pointed and nodded. "That's what I'm talking about." He stepped down to where Carter was studying the hooded monitor panel built into the back of the MALP remote explorer. There was a rushing whoop of air as the gateway's energy folded in on itself and vanished. Jack looked over his shoulder at the now-dormant Stargate. Most of the ones they found were free-standing but this one had been set into rock, almost like it had been embedded there. O'Neill was reminded of a fossil, fused into the stone.

He didn't have to look to know that Teal'c was already scouting the perimeter of the gate, or that Jackson was giving the dialing podium a once-over. They had been a part of SG-1 for so long now that they worked in easy lockstep, in a kind of team-player single-mindedness. Jack liked that; it was comforting, like a pair of good, worn-in boots. That sort of dynamic was what kept them together, kept them alive in even the strangest and most dangerous of situations. It was also the reason why, after nearly seven years, the members of the team had remained relatively unchanged while other SG squads had come and gone. *If it ain't broke, don't fix it.*

Carter glanced at him. "I'm going to go ahead and deploy the MP-UAV, sir."

"A-OK," he replied. "Go ahead, major, knock yourself out."

From the cargo compartment of the MALP rover, Carter recovered what looked like a cross between a laptop and the controller from a videogame. In moments, she had it booted up and running. A cylindrical container on the MALP's flatbed flapped open and something inside rattled into life with a noise like a swarm of wasps inside a tin can. She toggled a control and a fat torus painted in dark green leapt out of the canister and slowed to a trembling hover a few feet over their heads.

"What is that? Sounds like a lawnmower." Jackson frowned.

"It's a man-portable unmanned aerial vehicle," explained Carter. "Like the regular fixed-wing UAVs we use, but smaller. It's got a ducted rotor blade in there, cameras and sensors, solar-chargeable batteries. The army's been testing them for their Advanced Warfighter program, and I got a couple on loan."

"Looks like a flying donut," said Daniel.

"Mmm. Donut." O'Neill nodded sagely.

"I'll send it out to the end of the ravine." Carter worked the controls and the drone's motor changed pitch as it raced away. Over her shoulder, Jack watched the relay from the UAV's cameras to the monitor screen on the control unit. Sam clipped it to a brace on her webbing vest so she could walk around with the thing.

"Neat," he opined, and moved forward, his gaze ranging about to take in the whole of the box canyon where the Stargate was situated. In the distance, in the direction the UAV had flown, he could see odd shapes like shallow hills, and overhead nothing but slow-moving, heavy clouds, black with rain. "The army always gets the cool kit. How come we don't have anything like that?"

"We do have spaceships, Colonel," noted Carter dryly, "and ray guns and interplanetary wormhole travel."

"I mean besides those." He sighed. "Still. Better than being in the navy. All they have is that song."

Teal'c approached him. "I find no tracks in the immediate area, O'Neill. This gate does not appear to be in regular use."

"The rain could have wiped out any trails," offered Carter.

"See the shaping of the rocks, the smoothing? That's from water flow. My guess is that this place sees a lot of precipitation."

"Should have packed our slickers," Jack retorted. "Okay, let's do the exploring thing, then."

The team advanced along the canyon, with Daniel a few steps to the rear, panning about with his video camera. He gave an arch sniff. "Whose idea was it to come here?"

"Dixon," explained O'Neill. "He came back from that ice planet with a lead from the locals to this gate address, something about alien gizmos..." He threw a look at Jackson. "And ruins. I know how much you like ruins."

"I remember that part," Daniel nodded, missing the sarcasm.

"Why didn't Major Dixon take this mission then, sir?" Carter glanced up from the screen.

"His wife's having another baby. He's a good airman, but he's a glutton for punishment..." The colonel broke off as a diffuse flash of lightning flared overhead, followed rapidly by a low rumble of thunder. The tempo of the rain stepped up. "Why do we always have to walk everywhere, anyhow? I should get Hammond to get us some little jeeps. Maybe like those moon-buggies they used to have on *The Banana Splits*."

Carter's console chimed and she manipulated the controls. "Huh. That's peculiar."

"Got something?"

"The UAV has a short range ground-penetrating radar, the army use it for detecting buried landmines... I'm getting intermittent returns from the area up ahead, where the canyon opens out. It looks like it might just be metal strata in the rocks."

O'Neill frowned again. "Given our track record, let's not stray too close, huh?"

Carter nodded. "Yes sir. We should head this way, then."

The rain gave everything a fresh chill, but there was little wind. The walls of the narrow arroyo gradually sank down to reveal a large open plain formed from the same kind of porous, silicate-laced stone that surrounded the gate. Daniel took a couple of steps forward and stopped, blinking. From a distance, he had thought he was looking at regular hillocks, maybe tomb mounds of some kind; but as the canyon floor sloped a little, he saw the full dimension of what the objects were. "Spheres," he said aloud. "Whoa."

Scattered across the plain in what seemed to be a random pattern were dozens of huge stone balls of uniform size, easily forty, maybe fifty feet across. It was like an ant's eye-view of a pool table.

"This is a new one," noted Jack. "Did some giant kid leave his marbles behind?"

Carter squinted at the screen, wiping off a few stray droplets of water. The thin droning of the UAV's rotors carried down to them from where it orbited overhead. "There's a lot of them out here."

"Can you take that thing up higher, get a look down on them?" Jackson jerked a thumb at the dull sky. "There might be a pattern we can't see from the ground, like the lines at Nazca on Earth."

"I'll try," she said, "but the cloud base is pretty low."

"T," called the colonel, "You ever see anything like this?"

"I have not," replied the Jaffa, terse and to the point as ever.

Daniel was already leaving them behind, briskly marching toward the closest of the orbs. "Not Goa'uld in design," he said aloud, partly to voice his thoughts and partly to narrate the recording he was making. "They never stray from that pyramid look. Not Asgard either…"

"Daniel, wait up." O'Neill came with him, the P90 submachine gun strapped to his shoulder cocked and ready. "Let's not be too eager. This is a just a recon, remember? We take a look-see and then gate back."

"Yeah," Daniel wasn't really paying attention. Close up, he could see that the spheres were polished smooth and made from some kind of marble. He was willing to hazard a guess they weren't carved from any local rock, and they were too big to have come through the Stargate. There were lines of writing, little more than a couple of inches tall, layered in strings around the circumference. He ran his hand across the surface and felt a smile pull at the edges of his lips. There it was; *the thrill*. So often these days, Jackson found himself buried in databases and aged records as he raced against the clock to search for answers to some immediate threat, some deadly danger to life and liberty. Too many times, when he could step back and take a breath, he realized that he was turning into a *reactive* scientist, only making discoveries when events forced him to find solutions to problems, instead of learning for the sheer joy of it. He had wanted to become part of the Stargate program not because of the things he knew, but because of the new things it could show him; and with all the fighting and surviving in recent years, Daniel felt as if he'd lost sight of that.

But this... These orbs. They were unknown to him. He knew it immediately. He was going to want to come back here with a lot more hardware and a lot more time. "The writing on these things, if they're all covered with it..." He traced a line of text. "If there are hundreds of these spheres, it could be more text than the books in the Library of Congress..." *The thrill of discovery*; it tingled in the tips of his fingers. "These carvings are ancient..." Off in the distance, another flash-rumble of lightning and thunder rolled away.

O'Neill eyed him. "Is that capital-A weird alien Ancient or little-a just-kinda-old ancient?"

Jackson paused. "The second one. It's a runic design that shares a lot of characteristics with an early British and Irish written language called Ogham that features etchings or marks in pattern over a central median line, sometimes made with sticks or cut into stones—"

"Daniel," Jack halted him in mid-flow with a raised hand. "Remember that conversation we had a while back about the difference between what counts as *mission-critical informa-*

tion and *stuff that only Jackson thinks is cool*? Which is this?"

"It is cool," retorted the archaeologist, a bit too defensively. "And it might be critical later."

"You say that every time."

"How often am I right?" Jackson grinned a little.

"Occasionally," admitted O'Neill. He scowled and walked away. "You know," he threw over his shoulder, "you weren't this smug before you died."

Daniel set up his camera and began to film some of the lines of writing. "What can I say? I've picked up your bad habits."

"Wiseass," murmured the colonel, as Teal'c came closer.

The Jaffa gestured with his staff weapon. "The other spheres appear to be of similar form and design. Perhaps they are memorials."

"Like a graveyard?" O'Neill grimaced and looked at the wet sands beneath their boots. "I hope not. I have a thing about walking on dead folks."

"I have found no tracks around the canyon," Teal'c continued, "however..."

"Don't give me that arched eyebrow look," demanded O'Neill. "However what?"

Teal'c dropped to a crouch, examining the ground. "I considered Major Carter's comment about the rock strata. If she is indeed correct about the action of the rainfall on the landscape, then there should be no evidence of motion in the sands."

"What are you saying, that someone's been digging the ground up around here?"

He nodded. "There are signs, albeit very vague, of movement."

"We don't know anything about the tectonics of this place," called the major, catching their conversation. "What you saw might just be displacement patterns from heavy storm activity."

O'Neill's eyes narrowed. The man had a warrior's sense for the untoward that Teal'c found worthy of great respect, and he recognized it at work on the Tau'ri's face. "Carter," snapped O'Neill, "forget what I said earlier. Get your flyin' donut back here, close to the dirt. Give that underground radar a workout. Let's be sure what's down there before we go any further."

"Roger that, sir." Carter worked the controls on the remote console, and from the dreary sky the drone flyer swooped in, buzzing over Teal'c's head.

"There," he pointed, blinking as another flash of lightning lit the clouds from beneath.

"Got it." The major deftly steered the UAV into a low, swift pass over the area of the sands Teal'c had indicated. "I'm tuning the system to full gain… Reading those metallic clusters again…"

The Jaffa felt the faintest of vibrations through the soles of his combat boots, and threw a glance at O'Neill.

"That feel like thunder to you?"

Teal'c staff weapon spun around in an arc as he brought it into a two-handed grip. "No."

On the monitor screen, the blobs of color from the radar return refused to form into anything that looked like a coherent shape. Sam chewed her lip; she wasn't a geologist, this wasn't her specialty. As far as she could tell, there were big chunks of metal ore beneath the sands, in lumps the size of a Toyota. Inert and lifeless; at least until one of them moved.

Sensor glitch. The rational, detached part of her mind immediately supplied an explanation. *Check it again. Nothing to be alarmed about.* But that wasn't the part of Samantha Carter that she was listening too; there was the other element of her, the veteran of hundreds of off-world missions, the bit that knew the taint of danger in the air from too much first-hand experience.

She felt the shift in the sand beneath her feet and the rush of icy adrenaline through her veins. "Colonel—" she began.

The flash of light was so close and so harsh that it made her wince in pain, and Carter turned her head away, screwing her eyes tight shut. She saw only the purple after-image of it, seared on to her retinas. A streak of energy connecting the sandy earth with the torus of the UAV. She blinked the pain away and heard the coughing crash as the small drone exploded, scattering pieces of itself in a shower of plastic and steel fragments. The monitor screen in front of her showed the words *Loss of Signal* in angry red letters, and once again that rational bit of her was wondering how annoyed the US Army were going to be that she had lost one of their new toys.

All that fell away as the sands trembled and small mounds began to press up from beneath the level ground. Vapor from rainwater, flashed to steam, billowed and faded around a shallow crater near where the UAV had been obliterated.

"Was that lightning?" Sam heard Daniel's voice behind her.

"Lightning does not come from underground," Teal'c's retort was brisk.

With a swift motion, she let the dead weight of the control unit detach from her webbing vest and Carter's P90 came easily into her hands. From the blast crater a shape made of wet brass pushed itself up out of the clotted sand. Sam saw something that approximated a humanoid torso, but with four limbs emerging from the broad shoulders instead of two. It was a seamless thing that reminded her of an Art Deco sculpture more than a machine, and where a person would have had legs, the construct ended in a set of spinning wheels at canted angles. It was most definitely an automaton, moving with steady purpose, spitting out divots of mud as it climbed out of the earth. More of the things were emerging from the newly-formed mounds around them, blunt dome heads with actinic blue sensor monoculars casting about to find them. The one in the crater shifted and extended something that had to be a weapon barrel, the muzzle at the end still steaming from the blast that had brought down the UAV. Carter squeezed the P90's trigger and suddenly everyone was firing, the flicker of amour-piercing rounds sparking over the brass machines.

"Regroup!" shouted O'Neill, over the low shrill of blasts

from Teal'c's staff. "Use the spheres as cover!" He thumbed the selector switch on his weapon and sprayed a fully automatic burst of fire at the closest of the robots—that was how he was thinking of them, these big, brass Robby-the-Whatever rejects. The colonel took small comfort in the fact that they weren't much harder to put down than a Serpent Guard, but he was already mentally counting off the number of rounds he'd fired. He could see the problem coming; these things were popping out of the mud all around them, and there was no way they could tell how many of them were buried down there. More yellow darts of laser light screamed past him, cutting black streaks in the dirt, fusing sand instantly into twists of dirty glass.

"Must be some sort of defense mechanism," shouted Daniel. "Looks like we found the 'gizmos' Dixon was talking about!"

"Lucky us," Jack retorted. "Reloading! Carter, cover me!" He swapped out the SMG's spent ammo stick for a fresh one and backed off into the shadow of the closest stone sphere. Sam beat back a couple more Robbies and followed suit. The machines hesitated, as if they were reluctant to get too close to the stones.

"Colonel, we have to disengage. We don't know what we're facing here."

"Yeah, I reckon we've outstayed our welcome, don't you? We'll double time it back to the gate, laying down fire as we go."

"O'Neill." The tone of Teal'c's voice was enough to drain the energy from his orders. Jack looked in the direction the Jaffa indicated and his heart sank.

Across the mouth of the box canyon that led to the Stargate, there were a dozen of the battle machines, far more than the four of them could handle; and he could see others dragging themselves out of the dirt beyond those. "Ah, *crap*."

The machines turned their unswerving attention on the humans, and so none of them were witness to the new arrival at the Stargate.

An observer, had there been one, would not have seen the usual sequence of events; the lighting of the chevrons in turn about the ring, the roaring plume of exotic radiation. Instead, there was only the briefest of shimmers around the circumference of the steel-gray construct, a crawling net of blue-white sparks that extended out around the ring, pausing to touch something deep inside the Stargate's mechanism, then vanishing. In their wake, there came a peculiar hazing of the air some distance away from the gate proper, as if the light of day was being cast through a distorted lens; then the haze dissipated with a buzzing crackle and in its place there was a woman.

She coughed and spat, holding her chest for a moment. The transition was unpleasant, and she never got used to the feeling. She swallowed hard to force down the vomiting reflex and sipped at a plastic squeeze-ball filled with water.

Grimacing, she blinked at the rain and pulled the hood of her cloak up over a head of short, unkempt blond hair. The garment's coloration changed as she fingered the cloak's control studs at her neck. It shifted from tiger-striped jungle camouflage, to a torrid swirl of brilliant reds before finally coming to rest on something that approximated the shade of the local landscape. In the folds of the cloak, she paused to detach the cylindrical pod from her belt and turn it over in her hands. The device parted along its length to reveal a crystalline keypad and a small status screen. Power was low, she noted. This unit had been problematic before, one of the ones they had tried to repair back at the Holdfast, and it had a hard time maintaining a charge. Little wonder that she had materialized so close to the Stargate. She slid it shut and replaced it on her belt clip. There was enough energy inside for her to get back; but wasn't the point of all this that she wouldn't need to? If she did the mission right, it wouldn't matter.

Those had been the Commander's words, not hers. She pushed them out of her thoughts and moved out, staying low in a quick, loping motion. The cloak blurred about her, keeping her on the edge of visibility.

In her right hand she held her beam pistol, the folding stock extended and the digital-optic sight active. She gave it a quick double-check through the implant link; the emitter muzzle was tuned to the non-visible light spectrum, so any shots she fired wouldn't be seen by organic eyes. She didn't need to look at the weapon. The smart-chip in the control mechanism fed the raw data directly into the front of her thoughts. She felt the gun, understood the pistol like it was a part of her. All she needed now were her targets.

The box canyon opened out, and she kept to the shadows, coming upon the sounds of sustained gunfire and directed energy discharges. She checked her internal chronometer. The time index was wrong. They shouldn't have been shooting at each other yet, it was too soon! She was supposed to have arrived in time to scout out the area, lay the jammers, and get out.

She cursed under her breath, using a particularly filthy and heartfelt epithet she'd learned on Chulak. *But this is the problem with this sort of operation, right? And this is why I'm here, because these things never play out like they should, because you need an operative to be flexible and adapt on the spot.* She watched. A bunch of the guardian mechs had already started new lives as piles of scrap metal, thanks to a few hurled grenades from the four figures firing from the cover of a stone sphere. Peering through the gun scope, she panned the sights over the machines. These droids were canny in the up-close fight, something she remembered from first-hand experience, but they tended to become a little unfocussed in a shooting battle. The problem was, there were enough of them that sooner or later they would wear down the intruders with sheer weight of firepower. And again, here was another point where her intel had been wrong. The briefing said there were a dozen of the mechs out here, maybe less. She could see at least twenty of the tin-heads, not counting the ones that had already been put down. The scope swept over the mechanoids and across the wet sands to the figures by the marble sphere. She wanted to dwell on them, take a good long look at their faces, but that would have been a mistake. She didn't have the luxury of thinking of them as people; they were just elements in the assignment. Just pieces on the board, just units. *Like me.*

The mission was already coming to pieces and she'd yet to even make a move. The choice lay open in front of her; she could bug out and scrub the jump, go back to the gate and trigger the pod's return cycle, and no-one would know she had been there. But that would mean another window of opportunity sealed shut and blacked out, another roll of the dice coming up snake-eyes; and they were getting desperate now back at the Holdfast, as each missed chance and wrong step piled upon the last. She knew the theory as well as any of them. There would come a point—and she knew they were damn close to it already—when the pods wouldn't work any more, when it really would be too late to have any effect on things.

She had to try, at least. *Do your job.* The Commander's voice echoed in her head. *Everything else is secondary.*

It would take crackerjack timing on her part. She watched the play of the gunfight, letting the implant ease into control of her human reflexes and perceptions, letting it shift her into fast mode. The familiar cool rush of it came on strong as everything about her seemed to slow down. She saw where they were placing their shots from the P90s and trained the beam pistol to hit the same marks. With the discharge from the gun rendered invisible, by thought she set it to wideband mode and let the energy blasts streak out in a fan of lethal radiation. The kill shots merged seamlessly, and as one robot went down sparking and fizzing, three more erupted in flames alongside it. Anyone watching would think that the machine had caught its comrades in a backfire, cooking off their energy cells in a rush of detonation.

She did it again and again, firing in time with the machineguns or the whooping blasts of the Jaffa staff weapon. All she had to do was make sure that SG-1 got away, that they made it back to the gate before... Before...

The implant's time index pressed in on her accelerated consciousness. The window was closing. She had to get this done quickly, or it would all be meaningless. *More time! I just need more time-*

Then the sand around her began to tremble and shift. The implant burned her thoughts with a violent alert warning. There were more of the machines, and she was right in the middle of them. Her eyes snapped to the cloak's control brooch; the thing was working okay, but the droids weren't stupid. They might not be able to see her, but they were clever enough to extrapolate the direction of incoming fire. *Rookie mistake,* she told herself, *I should have known better!*

But that was what happened when you reacted to a threat instead of owning it. The implant did so much to make her a better soldier, but it also enhanced the mistakes she made as well. An oversight at five times the speed of human thought was an oversight made five times worse.

She leapt backwards and away, hoping that SG-1 would see nothing but a weird flicker where she moved. The impact of realization hit her hard. The mission was blown. She had taken too long, her intel had been flawed, and now it was a failure. The machines flailed around, shooting in all directions, filling the air with laser fire as they tried to bring her down. Her legs went tense, the muscles pulled taut with a mixture of fight-or-flight reflex, the time index blaring through her brain. The window was closing. Time to go. *Time to go.*

"No, damn it!" she grated, but her voice was lost in the sound of thrusters as a dozen mismatched shapes fell out of the low clouds and arrowed over the mouth of the canyon in a vee formation. The gunfire halted as the machines and the humans hesitated in the face of the new arrivals. SG-1 would be saved now, and in a few moments whatever remained of the robot guardians would be obliterated.

But she had failed, and now there was no other choice to

make. Turning the cloak to maximum opacity, she holstered the beam pistol on the run and fumbled with the pod's controls without looking at them, just as she had a dozen times before. Somewhere inside her there was a young woman, a frightened and angry young woman who wanted to scream her fury at the sky; but she forced that voice into silence and ran on toward the Stargate.

Unseen by anyone, a haze enveloped the cloaked figure and with a flicker of blue radiation, she vanished.

"What the hell is going on over there?" demanded O'Neill.

Carter ducked back as a salvo of energy bolts shrieked past her face. "Something might be interfering with their sensors..." Sam was just guessing, though. One second the robots had been pinning them down with wave after wave of concentrated firepower, and the next they had been falling like nine-pins. She wasn't one to question a lucky break, though, and the members of SG-1 used the moment to press the attack; but there were still too many of the mechanicals ringing the entrance to the canyon and Carter and the colonel had just about exhausted their stocks of hand grenades.

"Incoming!" Sam heard Teal'c bellow the warning and instinctively turned to look at him. The Jaffa stabbed a finger at the rainy sky, and it was then that Carter heard the noise of engines. She grabbed Daniel and yanked him into the scant cover of the stone sphere, aware of Jack and Teal'c doing the same just as the forms of a dozen aircraft hissed out of the clouds and roared past. Carter's nerves twitched as she recognized the winged-scarab fuselage of a Death Glider, and she hesitated between training her P90 up to target it or stay on the mechanoids.

"Goa'ulds!" spat Jackson.

"No," retorted Teal'c. "I do not think so."

Carter found herself nodding. The Death Glider was only one of several designs of flyer that comprised the formation; there were sleek, swan-like craft, a pair of bug-eyed machines that resembled helicopters without rotor blades, all of them following the lead of a long-nosed ship with tri-fold wings and three pulsing engines. Sam's first impression was one of rough order, like an airborne street gang.

The robots did not wait to establish intent. As one, they gauged the threat level between SG-1 and the new arrivals and reacted in kind. The machines turned their cannons skyward and threw up a curtain of laser bolts. Carter saw one of the swan-ships crumple into a fist of black smoke and crushed wings. The other flyers returned fire, ripping great divots of wet sand from the ground, shattering the robots with pinpoint strafing runs. In a few moments, the line of mechanoids trapping them in place were smoking ruins.

Sam looked up and grinned in spite of herself as the lead fighter described a cocky barrel-roll over the victory it had just scored. "That's pretty good flying."

"Eh," shrugged O'Neill. "I've seen better."

Daniel hauled himself up and brushed flecks of mud from his jacket. "Well, whoever it is, they pulled our butts out of the fire." He gave Jack a pointed look.

Carter watched the fighter settle to the dirt on a jet of thrust. Nearby, two Death Gliders and one of the swan-ships were landing as well. "How do you want to handle this, sir?"

O'Neill carefully moved his P90 into a more casual, but no less ready, stance. "Let's play what we're dealt, Carter. For all we know, this could be a set-up."

Three men approached from the parked ships, the pilot of the lead fighter walking at their head while a fourth ran to check the wreckage of the downed craft. Jack sized them up carefully; like their ships, there was nothing uniform about them. The clothes and gear they wore were a mix of high-tech stuff like ballistic body armor and comms headsets, combined with rough-hewn tunics and leather jackets. The only common denominator was a tattoo on their right cheekbones, a small four-pointed star in faint silver ink. All of them were armed—the 'flight leader' had what was unmistakably a zat gun tucked in his belt—and all of them moved with caution. O'Neill felt a faint smile tug at his lips. These people were as wary of his team as they were of them.

The guy with the zat stopped, his hand close to the weapon but not so much that it looked threatening. "Which of you is in charge here?" The accent was thick, European-sounding; he had the craggy face of a boxer and a shock of red hair. He was a big man, as tall as Teal'c and broad across the shoulders. Jack found himself wondering how he managed to squeeze his bulk into the cockpit of the tri-wing fighter. Jack gave Sam and Teal'c a look that asked *Are these guys Goa'ulds?* Both of them returned a slight shake of the head.

O'Neill raised a hand. "That would be me. How you doin'?"

"We made claim here," said the pilot. "Didn't you see our ships?"

"Not until just now, no."

One of the other pilots, a slender guy with curly hair to his shoulders, indicated Teal'c and hissed something under his breath to the others. Jack caught the word "Jaffa".

"We came through the Stargate," offered Daniel. "The Chaapa'ai?"

"Planetborne," snapped the slender man dismissively. "This isn't their world."

"We were just out for a stroll," Jack smiled politely. "Making new friends."

The big man's wary gaze found Teal'c. "A First Prime of Apophis? What Lord do you serve now? Your god's long dead."

"Yeah, we know," O'Neill spoke before the Jaffa could reply. "We killed him. Teal'c plays for our team now."

That gave the man pause, and for the first time Jack saw a flicker of emotion on the new arrival's face. "You... You're the Tau'ri." He scrutinized the SGC patch on the colonel's jacket. "Of course. I should have recognized the wargear. I've heard of you."

Jack spread his hands and indicated the team in turn. "We get around. I'm Colonel Jack O'Neill, this is Major Samantha Carter, Doctor Daniel Jackson and the big fella is Teal'c."

The man tapped his chest with a thumb. "My name is Vix." He paused. "You are SG-1... I have heard stories..." He gave Jack a long look. "I thought you would be taller."

"These people are Pack," said Teal'c, touching his face to indicate the star tattoos. Vix nodded in agreement. "A community of refugees," continued the Jaffa, "survivors displaced by the fighting between the System Lords."

"Selmak talked about them, in the last Tok'ra intelligence briefing," added Carter. "They're like a kind of gypsy colony, Colonel. They live on a fleet of ships instead of a planet."

"The Goa'uld crave territory and power over everything else, they gather up worlds to hoard like they were jewels," said Vix's companion. "We stay mobile and we stay free of them."

"You're nomads," noted Jackson.

"We are free," retorted the slender man.

"Ryn," warned Vix. "We share a common enemy with these Tau'ri. Show them some respect."

"So, you're in charge of this, uh, fleet?" asked O'Neill. He glanced at the fighters. "I'm guessing that's not all of it?"

"We have many vessels in orbit. And yes, I govern my people..." He glanced at Ryn. "For the moment."

Daniel rolled his eyes and spoke, *sotto voce*. "Jack, don't say it..."

"So then I guess you're the Leader of the Pack?"

Vix nodded slowly. "Was that not what I just said?"

The early tension of the meeting began to recede. "Thank you for your help against those machines," Carter offered.

"We hadn't expected to find any other humans," said Ryn. "The reports that brought us here spoke only of ruins and the possibility of salvage."

"Ours too," said the major. She nodded to the wreckage of

the robots. "Guess we were both misinformed."

"Lucky us," said O'Neill dryly.

Daniel gestured with his hand. "Before, you said you *made claim*. What does that mean, exactly?"

"The Pack is not self-sufficient," noted Vix. "We must trade and take salvage where we can to keep our ships functional."

"Never thought about settling down?" Jack said lightly.

Ryn's expression darkened. "Every one of us is from a world that was laid waste to by the System Lords. Those who allow themselves to take root place themselves in harm's way."

"Wanderlust, huh?" O'Neill added, trying to ease the mood. "I get it."

"Colonel," said Carter, stepping closer. "Seeing as we owe Vix and his people a debt for coming to our rescue, I think there might be a way to, uh, *salvage* something from this outing for both parties."

"Do tell." Jack knew where she was going, and let Sam run with it.

"Vix, you said the Pack are traders? Maybe we could find something that we have that you want."

From behind Ryn, the Death Glider pilot glanced up from a sensor device in his hand. "This sandball looks like a dead end, Vix. We're not going to find anything of value here."

"But you are SG-1, the great Tau'ri," said Ryn in a mocking tone. "What could mere refugees like us have that you might find useful?"

"Those fighters... They might have some technology we could use for the F-302 program. It's somewhere to start."

Ryn leant close to Vix. "They have a Jaffa among their number. Surely we should exercise caution—"

Vix silenced his companion with a hard look. "I concur with Major Carter. What would you rather have me do, Ryn? Return to the flotilla and tell them we found nothing of use, or bring back the Tau'ri with the chance of trade?" He nodded at Jack. "Come. I'll summon a ship for you."

As they made their way toward the parked fighters, Daniel glanced toward the fourth Pack pilot returning from the site of the crashed swan-ship. "What about your other man, the one who was shot down?"

Vix didn't look up. "Gravity took him. He's got no place in the Pack anymore."

The faint blue glow was still enough to light the limestone walls of the Holdfast, catching the pale rock in the places where the radiance from the weak biolume bulbs did not reach. The haze of color flickered around the edges of the broken Stargate, dissipating from the snapped-off edges of the giant silver hoop; and then she was there, back again, in the gloom.

Tekka was waiting for her, and it wasn't until she shrugged off the cloak and looked him in the eye that her failure hit her with its full and unyielding weight. The scrawny, pale-skinned Pangaran tried to force a smile, but it stalled on his lips and he reached out a hand and touched her on the forearm. "Jade," he said quietly, "I'm glad you're safe."

She swallowed down the post-transition discomfort and gave a bitter chuckle. "No one else will be. I ruined it, Tekka. Another chance, and I burned it. Everyone was counting on me, and I—"

"No, no," He led her away from the chamber, toward the huge oval doors that sat rusted open across the entrance to the Holdfast's interior spaces. "It's not like you were the first. We all knew there was a chance of…" He hesitated. "That it wouldn't come together. Even the Commander understands."

"Did he say that to you?"

"Of course," he responded.

Jade smiled briefly, with a dart of genuine warmth that faded quickly. "You're such a bad liar."

Tekka frowned. "All right, I admit he didn't say it to me as such, but I have no doubt that he thinks that."

She looked at the floor. "If that's true, then he does a good job of hiding it."

The corridors beyond were more regular than those of the natural shapes of the gate chamber, the striated walls cut by laser drills arching overhead like the cloisters of the cathedrals she'd seen in picture books and vids. It was warm and damp down here, in stark contrast to the chilly, frostbitten surface a mile or so over their heads. Jade had only been up there a few times; the twin suns in the daylight sky and the belt of snowy rings by night were just more reminders that this place wasn't really home.

In rooms off the passage she glimpsed groups of people at work in the stark light of the machine shops, or training in stiff silence on the practice decks. She saw Sebe'c leading a group of his Jaffa in hand-to-hand duels, and he made brief eye-contact with her. The warrior inclined his head in greeting, but Jade could see the question in his eyes, the small judgment. Wherever she looked, to the faces of the soldiers, the taciturn cadre of Langarans who tended the hydroponics, even the children in one of the teaching rooms, all of them seemed to look at her and know. They were still here because of her, because she had failed. The gloom of the corridors clung to her like the smell of smoke.

The eyes of the children were the worst; there were so few of them now, and none of them had the artifice of the adults, none of them had the ability to mask their questions and disappointments. Jade felt a stab of self-loathing; a mix of disgust at her own mistakes and at her weakness for wallowing in it. She smothered the churn of emotions and looked back at Tekka.

"Do you need to clean up before you debrief?" he asked, sensing the tension in her, giving her an out. "I can tell him you—"

Jade shook her head. "No. I have to explain what happened, and I have to do it now. Time's the only thing we can't afford to waste."

They halted and the Pangaran rapped on the steel door of the Commander's office. From within she heard the old man's voice, gruff and sharp. "Get in here."

Tekka gave her arm a supportive squeeze, but she was already walking away, forcing down her emotions, becoming soldierly once again. The door thudded shut behind her.

He was lit by the blue-white glow of a datapad, the holographic panels of text and graphics hanging ghostly in the air before him. At once she noticed the clutter around the edges of the desk; a used rejuve-nanite injector yet to be discarded, a scattering of papers. The gun that never left his side, and a tumbler with maybe an inch of scotch in it. The Commander gave her a long, steady look, eyes boring into her from a face of heavy lines framed by wispy, steel-gray hair. "What went wrong?" His voice was level, but it was as much a demand as if he had shouted it.

She hesitated, unable to meet his gaze. "The point of arrival was incorrect. I was supposed to have more—"

"Show me the pod." He cut her off and held out a hand. Jade unclipped the device and gave it to him. He opened it with practiced ease and glared at the readout. "Power feed's unstable. You knew that. You should have compensated."

"I thought I had, sir."

"Clearly, you didn't," he said firmly. "Is that it? Is that your explanation?"

"No, sir," Jade bit out the words, bristling. "The intel on the threat forces was way off beam. There were two, maybe three times as many of the mechs as I was told to expect."

"Maybe? Which was it, two times or three times as many? Give me specifics."

"Three," she snapped, feeling her color rise. "The threat force was more than I could handle alone. I had no choice. I had to abort."

With a terse flick of his wrist, the Commander let the pod roll away across his desk. "More than you could handle." And there it was, the accusation. "You know why you were sent. Because you assured me, against my better judgment, that you could deal with the mission parameters."

A nerve in Jade's jaw jumped and she pressed her lips

together, resisting the urge to reply.

"You know how important this is, what we risk each time we go. We can't afford any more mistakes!" His voice rose to a growl.

"I'll go back," she blurted out. "There are other windows, I can try a different approach."

"No." The refusal came like a bullet. "You haven't forgotten what happened before, all the people we lost when things went to hell. No." He shook his head. "I told you what would happen, and even if you could try again, this thing won't allow it." He angrily stabbed a finger at the pod.

"Dad, please." The words slipped out of Jade's mouth before she could stop them, and in return he looked her straight in the eye for the first time since she had entered the office. "Sir," she amended, but it was too late. The line had been crossed. She had ignored the unspoken rule between them.

The Commander's expression became stony. "There's no other option now. We're going with the backup plan. Get yourself cleaned up and ready to go in ten hours."

"It's too dangerous," she insisted. "There's too much that can go wrong."

"You think I don't know that?" He glared at her. "Don't you get it, girl? We're past the point of no return now. There is no other option." He looked away. "I gave you a last chance to do it your way and you blew it. Now we'll do this my way. Prep your gear and be ready." Her father returned to the holograms. "You're dismissed."

Jade saluted, furious and dejected all at once. "Yes sir," she replied, and left without looking back.

CHAPTER TWO

Vix summoned a Tel'tak cargo ship to ferry the team from the surface, and Carter positioned herself carefully behind the control console so she could observe the pilot's actions. The pilot was a woman with an Asian cast to her features, who introduced herself as Suj. Sam couldn't help but be aware that the cargo ship had a couple of extra crewmen whose sole purpose seemed to be to look menacing and carry large weapons.

"An honor guard," said Daniel, from the side of his mouth. "I feel almost royal."

"We'd be doing the same thing to them if they were on our turf," noted Carter. "Just smile politely and look non-threatening."

"I excel at that," Jackson noted.

The transport ship trembled a little as it pushed out through the atmospheric envelope of the desert planet and into the airless void of space. Sam became aware that Suj was watching her through a reflection on the viewport. "I've never met a Tau'ri before," she said. Her voice had a soft, almost musical quality. "Is it true what they say about your planet? That it is a fortress, guarded by an armada of Asgard warships?"

"Oh, those little gray guys," said O'Neill. "They're wacky."

"We defend our planet if we need to," said Sam, skirting the question. "Of course, we try not to let it come to that."

"You prefer to fight your battles on other people's worlds." There was the slightest air of reproach in her words.

"In conflict, one can rarely choose the arena in which to meet the enemy," said Teal'c. "A warrior must be able to wage war when the fray comes to him."

"Yes," said Suj mildly. "I suppose a Jaffa would see it that way." She worked the controls and brought the Tel'tak around in a languid turn to starboard. "What brought you to Golla

IX?"

"Is that what you call the planet below?" asked Daniel.

"*We* call it P5X-404," said the colonel. "Okay, so I'll admit it doesn't trip off the tongue..."

"We're exploring," continued Jackson. "Some of our people heard rumors that there might be artifacts of interest there."

She nodded. "The spheres. We have encountered them on other worlds in this quadrant. We also have heard tales of abandoned technology here... But those mechanoids were something unexpected."

"I'll say," agreed Daniel.

Sam saw glints of light from the hulls of the fighter squadron off to the sides where Vix's ships were flying in echelon with them; and out beyond the near-orbital region she could pick out a shoal of objects lit by sunlight reflected from the surface of the planet. As they closed in, definition layered on to the shapes. At first, Carter thought she was seeing an oblate, asteroidal satellite—something like the Martian moon of Phobos—but it began to resolve itself into detail. It rotated slowly, turning about its longest axis. Craters on the object's surface were lit with brilliant, city-bright clusters of color, and dozens of towering black spines extended from it in all directions. Around the construct there were slow-moving groups of more recognizable vessels. She identified a pair of Goa'uld motherships amid dozens of others that ranged in shape from winged lifting bodies suitable for atmospheric transit to oddly proportioned ships made from collections of saucers and rods.

"Those motherships are from the war fleet of Khepera," Teal'c noted quietly. "An ally of Ra who perished in battle many decades ago. Apophis believed that all such vessels had been obliterated..."

"Yeah, well, he never was as smart as he thought he was," said O'Neill.

Sam made some swift mental calculations based on the relative size of the giant craft compared to the motherships; it had to be several miles long, at the very least. *It's as big as*

Manhattan Island, she realized. *A self-contained city in space.*
The construct had an unkempt, slightly scruffy look to it that
she saw reflected elsewhere in the Pack, in the hodgepodge of
gear and ships with Vix and his men and again here on board
the Tel'tak. The shuttle wasn't standard-issue System Lord
hardware; Carter could see clear indications where parts of the
ship's mechanisms had been gutted or replaced with technology of completely different origin. Everything about the Pack
had a junkyard feel to it, as if they had taken off-cuts and dis-
cards from a hundred different worlds and hammered them
together into something new. The ingenuity and cunning of it
was amazing, in its own way. Her gaze went back to the viewport in time to see a formation of smaller ships fall away as
they changed course.

"Looks like a UFO convention out there," said the colonel.
"All those boats are yours?"

"The Pack draws its membership from hundreds of worlds,"
Suj explained. "We have been free for more than a generation."

"The largest ship…" Sam began.

Suj nodded. "We call her the *Wanderer*. She was the first,
and she remains our heart. She was once an orbital colony in
the Calai system, until the System Lord Heru'ur began a cam-
paign to subjugate the people there. Some among the Calaians
retrofitted the colony with a hyperspace generator and used her
to escape the Goa'uld. As they sought to flee the reach of the
false gods, they came across others in similar straits and the
first elements of the Pack were formed. Now wherever we go
there are those who come to join us, seeking their own freedom."

"Are you from there? From Calai?" asked Daniel.

She shook her head. "My birth world was in the Pasiphae
Marches, before it was ruined in the wars between Cronus and
Morrigan. I've spent half my life aboard *Wanderer*. She's my
home now."

"Gypsies," opined the colonel. "With a space caravan as

well."

"It's not surprising really," considered Daniel. "There are plenty of nomadic cultures on Earth who exist as essentially rootless societies. There's no reason why a tribal populace couldn't survive on an interstellar level…"

"Ah, no offence, but I'd rather go for the whole 'mud under your feet, wind in your hair' lifestyle, thanks. Being cooped up in a tin-can with recycled air and no sunlight would get real old for me pretty fast," said O'Neill, glancing at Suj. "Not that your big rocky spaceship isn't impressive…"

"I understand your reluctance, Colonel," said the woman. "Some of those who join us do find the transition difficult. But then there are many of our number who have lived all their lives in space, children who have never known mud or wind. To them, it is planetborne like you who appear worse off. In our flotilla, we live in a controlled environment where we never need fear the whims of nature."

The Goa'uld cargo ship shifted and turned, passing through the outer layer of the Pack fleet. Sam couldn't resist the urge to stare at some of the designs of the vessels that flashed past, mentally taking notes. There were a fair few that looked distinctly non-human in design, craft like clutches of eggs on a rope or slender gold needles.

"But all these different people from all these different worlds," Daniel was saying, "isn't it difficult to hold them together? We can't keep the nation states on Earth from squabbling with each other and we've got a whole planet to spread out over."

Suj shot him a look that Carter caught. "We all have a common enemy, Doctor Jackson. You'd be surprised how strong a bond that builds between our people." She turned away, back to the controls. "And Vix leads us well. We draw our principals from those among us who are best suited to the roles, the strongest and most intelligent."

"It's an impressive undertaking, there's no doubting that." Sam spoke up, the questions pushing at her thoughts. "But I have to ask you. How have you managed to stay alive? I mean, the Goa'uld aren't exactly known for their generous and forgiving nature. Why did they let any of you escape?"

Suj sighed. "At first, we were too small in number to draw much of their attention, and they were too busy battling with each other and jockeying for position to pay us any heed... However, in recent years they have tried to eradicate us." She paused, turning the ship toward a landing bay on the surface of the *Wanderer*. "But we refuse to give them what they want, Major Carter. We do not stand and fight. The Pack remains elusive, forever one step ahead of the System Lords." Suj nodded to herself. "There will come a day soon when they wipe themselves out, and we will still be here, outlasting them."

"Amen to that," noted the colonel.

She forced a smile. "I'm sorry. What impression must I be making upon you?"

"You're not what I expected from a shuttle pilot," admitted Jackson.

Suj looked at him again. "That is not my only duty for the Pack," she replied. "Each of us has many skills we bring forth for our people. I am first and foremost a ethnohistorical documentarist."

O'Neill blinked. "You're a what now?"

"A cultural expert," said Daniel slowly. "I get it. You're not flying this ship just because you know how to pilot a Tel'tak. You're doing it so you can get a feel for us, right? You're studying us."

The shuttle slowed and began a slow decent into a shallow crater. "The Pack hasn't survived this long without being cautious, Doctor Jackson," smiled the woman.

The colonel spread his hands. "Well, this is us on our best behavior. You can pretty much take us as you find us."

"I imagine we will," said the woman, as the ship settled on to a landing pad.

The Pack made no attempt to disarm them as they ventured aboard their vessel, although Teal'c could sense the tension in the men that formed SG-1's adjunct. He was aware that he alone generated more of the hard looks and sideways glances than any of his team mates. It was not a new sensation for the Jaffa; since be broke ranks with Apophis, on many worlds Teal'c encountered men and women whose hatred of the Goa'uld transferred to him. He did not allow it to concern him; as his mentor Bra'tac had instilled in the warrior, Teal'c was content to allow his actions to speak for him. If the Pack wished to misjudge him, then that would be their error.

He studied the motion of the guards who walked with them. They lacked the order of Jaffa warriors, or the watchful discipline of Tau'ri soldiers; they moved with the easy arrogance of men used to fighting, but they lacked—for want of a better term—the *grace* of a career warrior. These Pack, he considered, would likely fight with a feral intensity born of instinct, not skill. Teal'c filed that conclusion away for later consideration and turned his attention to their weapons. Like the male who called himself Vix, one of the guards carried a zat'ni'katel, while the other had a dual-barreled ballistic weapon of unusual design; both men exhibited enough confidence to convince Teal'c they knew full well how to use them.

The female named Suj led them through a series of anterooms and Teal'c noticed a subtle change in the pull of gravity through his boots. The mammoth vessel did not use the technology of artificial gravitational generation like most craft with which he was familiar; indeed, the interior of the *Wanderer* was dissimilar to the mechanical, clean corridors of Tau'ri or Goa'uld ships; they were carved out of stone, more akin to the cave warrens he remembered near his village from his boyhood on Chulak. Presently, the party arrived at a set of shallow, broad stairs and Suj hesitated on the threshold.

"I ought to warn you," she began, "we are about to enter the great atrium, and some newcomers find the sight of it rather... Unsettling. If you begin to feel disoriented, look at the ground."

"We'll be fine," O'Neill smiled. "Lead on."

"As you wish." The woman hid a smirk. Teal'c tightened his grip around his staff weapon, ready in the event that this 'revelation' was a prelude to an attack upon them.

They climbed the stairs, and at the top Suj spread her hands to the air. "Welcome to the heart of the *Wanderer*."

The Jaffa hesitated as he took in the sight laid out before him. "Impressive," he allowed.

Daniel reached the top of the stairs and looked up. And up. *And up*. He felt his head swim a little and his balance fluttered. A firm hand pressed into his shoulder and he glanced back to see Teal'c providing the support. "Thanks," he said lamely. "That last step is a doozy."

To be honest, Jackson hadn't really known what to expect. He'd been inside lots of big spaceships before, and one set of corridors looked pretty much like another, right? Granted, the mix-and-match tunnels-and-technology look of the *Wanderer*'s passageways was something new, but this space, this *atrium*... For a moment, it took his breath away. Daniel had imagined they would come out in some sort of room, maybe like a reception chamber or a hall for audiences. He had not expected to find himself standing in the middle of what looked like parkland, having emerged from the side of a shallow hill. For long moments his brain registered a kind of disconnect. The scenery was one of sparse grasses and low, wide trees. The first Earth-like analogy that sprang to mind was the African veldt, a savannah that went off to the horizon—or at least, it would have if there had actually *been* a horizon. Jackson swallowed hard and let his eyes follow the line of the landscape, over the gentle, rolling hills, finding roads and regular, oval lakes, the patchwork of what looked like farmland and clusters of buildings that were bright white stone in the even daylight.

But where the view should have gone to the vanishing point, the land did something very different. It folded up and away, and Daniel tried not to get dizzy as he walked his gaze up it, around and along until he saw the curvature coming together miles over his head. "Whoa."

Suddenly, like one of those weird optical illusion pictures, the sight *popped* in his brain and Jackson's sense of perception caught up to what it was he was actually seeing. "On the inside," he said to himself. "It's inside out. An inside out planet."

"Is that what it is?" said O'Neill. "Oh good. That makes a lot more sense than trees stuck to the ceiling."

Suj, still smiling in faint amusement, held her hands palms up in front of her. "Imagine a map, flat on a table. Then take it and fold it into a tube." She put her hands together. "We are inside that tube, standing on the map. Look up," and she pointed into the air, "and you see the rest of the map arching overhead." Suj inclined her head. "Do not the Tau'ri have similar colonies in their star system?"

"Only in theory," admitted Carter. "I'm familiar with the concept, though." Sam glanced at Daniel and the others. "Back in the Sixties, a scientist called Gerard O'Neill posited the idea of building a huge cylinder in space, or hollowing out an asteroid and setting it to spin along the longest axis." She made a turning motion with her fingers. "The centrifugal force created on the inside surface of the cylinder mimics Earth-normal gravity..." Her voice tailed off. "Never thought I'd ever see one, though."

"O'Neill, huh?" said Jack. "Cool." He gave Suj a look. "No relation, in case you were wondering."

"It's incredible," Daniel took in the scope of the construction. He made out the forms of thin steel towers rising up from the surface like the spokes on a wheel, to meet at a series of spheres along the midline of the massive open chamber. "What are those?"

"The effect of gravity lessens the closer you get to the center of the *Wanderer*," explained Suj. "At the hub there is no effect at all. We maintain artificial solar generators up there to create the illusion of a night and day cycle."

"It's a hell of a lot of real estate to keep in a can," noted Jack.

"The *Wanderer* has been the heart of the Pack since the day of the first escape," said Suj, a little defensively. "Please, if you'll walk with me."

They followed a path down to the nearest of the townships, which lay clustered around the base of one of the steel towers. Close up, Daniel saw that the buildings had an organic feel to them, as if they were made of coral. He wondered if they were grown rather than assembled.

The locals matched the look of Suj and the Pack from the planet. Clothing, technology and the people themselves were an eclectic mixture. This was a magpie culture, he reasoned, tribes of people who had lost their worlds and their identities in the wake of Goa'uld oppression, and then come together to forge a new whole from the fragments. Jackson felt the same rush of excitement as he had on the planet with the stone orbs, the promise of studying something strange and undiscovered; and these were living, breathing people with a vital, ongoing culture, not simply the memorials of a civilization long dead.

In the central square of the township they came upon Vix and Ryn, along with a handful of other men and women who all wore patient and vigilant expressions.

"Hey," said Jack, giving them a jaunty wave. "Nice digs you have here. Love what you've done with the place."

Vix accepted the greeting with a nod. "O'Neill." He turned to his companions. "These are the Tau'ri of Earth. I have brought them to parley."

Ryn said nothing, but an older, dark-skinned man in a heavy tunic and robes stepped closer. "Not what we expected, Vix. Not what we expected at all. Where is the salvage our scouts spoke of?"

"Yeah, about that," offered the colonel. "If I can field that one, I'm thinking that your folks and ours were led on a wild goose chase in that regard."

"There are only war machines down there," explained Vix. "Guardians, I suspect, placed there to protect the stone monoliths. Our sweeps detected nothing that we could use."

The other man frowned. "Our needs—"

"Are known to me," finished Vix bluntly. "Do not question that. This is why I have brought these people to our home. They talk of trade."

"Words cost little," grumbled Ryn.

"Damn right they do," O'Neill broke in. "So, what do you say we see if there's something more tangible we can chat about?" He spread his hands. "We're not the snakeheads, kids. We're here to, uh…" Jack glanced at Sam. "Carter, what was that phrase?"

"Make in-roads, sir," she replied, pulling up the expression from a dull briefing document from the International Oversight Advisory that all of them had been forced to read. The world governments who knew about the Stargate were forever applying pressure for concrete rewards from the program.

"In-roads, right." Jack nodded sagely, and Daniel was struck by the fact that he gave a good impression of knowing what he was doing. "You guys saved our butts back on that pool-table planet. Helluva good way to make new friends."

For the first time, Vix cracked something like a smile. He was warming to them. "You and I will talk, Colonel." He beckoned him closer. "I have chambers where there is food and refreshment."

Ryn sniffed. "Where you can create secret deals with the Tau'ri to strengthen your own position?"

The other man's outburst made the moment turn awkward. "I will seek only what is best for the Pack," said Vix, at length.

"Then there will be no impediment to my presence as well," retorted the other pilot, darting a look at Suj.

"Ryn is correct," said the historian. "The codes of conduct allow it. One of the Pack for each visitor. But this means O'Neill must have a companion as well."

"Oh, I getcha." Jack nodded. "Teal'c? Come with. We can

get a snack."

"What about us, sir?" said Sam.

"Make nice," replied the colonel. "But don't wander too far."

As they departed, the dark-skinned man gave Sam a small bow. "Forgive me, I am remiss. I am Koe, and the Pack's welfare is my remit. Perhaps you and your associate would join me while our leaders talk? I would be pleased to show you some of the *Wanderer*."

"If it pleases you, healer," Suj broke in. "Might I speak with Doctor Jackson? It appears we have some common interests."

The two members of the Pack exchanged glances and Daniel saw a subtle communication pass between them. "Of course," said Koe.

Sam gave him a nod as they parted company and tapped the radio on her gear vest; the message was clear. *Stay in touch—just in case.* Daniel nodded back, and for a moment he felt a slight tinge of disappointment. They'd barely met these people and already they had defaulted to the assumption that the Pack were untrustworthy. It made Jackson feel glum; but then SG-1 had learned through bitter experience that seemingly-friendly faces were often far from it. *The Shavadai, the Eurondans, the Aschen, the Bedrosians... We've had more of our fair share of knives hidden behind smiles.* He sighed and gave Suj a weak grin. *For once,* he hoped, *it would be nice to find the reverse was true.*

O'Neill took the proffered tankard from Vix's hand and gave it a careful sniff. It had an odor that was somewhere between root beer and stale cheese. "And this is?"

"Laerua," explained the other man. "A fermented brew made from Calaian herbs and the milk of a riding beast." Vix drained a hearty draught from his tankard and watched Jack expectantly.

He glanced at Teal'c; the Jaffa was standing by the door of the chambers, doing his usual stoic-impassive thing. Close by, the Ryn guy was on the same bench as Vix, close to the edge of the seat and obviously tense. If Vix noticed his companion's body language, he didn't show it.

Jack took the plunge and sipped at the drink. It made his tongue prickle as it went down. "Smooth," he managed, after a moment. "It's like a tequila-flavor milkshake."

"Is it not to your taste?" Vix asked. The question seemed to be genuine; this didn't appear to be one of those haze-the-new-guy things where they gave him a glass of rubbing alcohol and waited to see if he went blind.

"Sorry, I don't mean to seem rude. I just have a thing about, uh, foreign food. One time on Argos I ate this cake and…" He caught himself and halted. "Well, never mind. So. We're talking here, right?"

"I am interested in how the Tau'ri will repay the debt they now owe us," said Ryn. "You and your people would be dead if not for our intervention on the planet."

Jack nodded, ignoring the man's borderline-snide tone. "Oh sure, you betcha. But then we've been in deeper crap than that and made it out." He tapped his chest. "I've been killed, y'know? You wouldn't think it to look at me, though."

"Understand us, Colonel," began Vix. "The Pack is a society based on debts and obligations. We do not freely give without expecting recompense in return. We intervened because it was felt you might present a better opportunity to us alive than dead." He nodded at the other man. "It was Ryn who made the suggestion."

O'Neill was genuinely surprised at that, but he hid it well. From his first impressions, Ryn didn't seem the overly charitable type. "Well, that's mighty nice of you. But now you're looking for us to pay the bill, right?" He looked up at the Jaffa. "Teal'c, you bring your wallet? I forgot to hit the ATM before we gated."

Koe had maybe ten or twelve years on Sam, and he had a kind of manner about him that reminded her of Janet Fraiser;

thoughtful, intelligent, and compassionate with it. As they walked slowly through the township, he pointed out different homes and told her about the people who lived in them. He mentioned the names of a dozen worlds Sam had never heard of, cultures and nation states that were meaningless to her. Koe caught her studying him and he inclined his head; the gesture seemed common among the Pack. "Is something wrong?"

"No," Carter shook her head. "It's just, you remind me of someone. A friend, someone who looked after *our* welfare. She died a little while ago... She's been on my mind recently."

"I am regretful for your loss," Koe bowed his head a moment. "She was your cleric?"

"A medical doctor. A healer." Sam hesitated. "I'm sorry, when you spoke about your people's welfare, I thought that was what you meant."

Koe's lip curled in a slight smirk. "Are the two things so far apart? My duties are to maintain the Pack's spiritual well-being as much as their physical health. Both test our mettle, Major. The Pack's mix is an eclectic one, and that crosses over into physiologies and philosophies. We are as much a multi-culture as we are a culture in its own right."

"Oh." She nodded. "On Earth, we tend to keep our medicine and our religions separate. It works out easier in the long run."

"Curious," Koe tapped a finger on his lips. "I find it hard to imagine a situation where one would not go hand-in-hand with the other." They crossed an oval area of greenery where a small marketplace had been erected. "The Tau'ri are not a secular people, then?"

"Some are, some aren't. Earth has a lot of belief systems. In our past the Goa'uld took advantage of that."

"You disapprove?"

"Of parasitic aliens pretending to be gods? I'd say yes, pretty much!"

Koe smiled. "No, Major, I mean of religion. The Goa'uld's pattern of invasion and subjugation has been repeated across the galaxy, and there are some who say that they would have been less successful if the System Lords had not had the masks of our deities to hide behind."

"There's some truth in that, I suppose." Sam felt uncomfortable with the direction the conversation was taking.

"But does that make it wrong to reject belief in the wake of its abuse?" Koe gave her a level look. "If I may ask, Major Carter. What do you believe in?"

She knew the question was coming, but when he asked it, it still wrong-footed her. Sam had to think for a moment to frame her reply. "I'm a scientist," she began. "I'm in the business of seeing the rationality of the universe. I suppose, if I had to define it, I would say that I believe there's a structure to existence and I have faith that one day science will help humanity understand it…" She smiled self-consciously. "That sounds a little pretentious, maybe…"

Koe smiled back. "Not at all. If I have learned anything living among the peoples of the Pack, it is that faith in something is better than faith in nothing."

They moved on. Many of the locals threw welcoming nods to Koe, and Carter noted that she wasn't drawing as many stares as she was used to on a first contact mission. It wasn't difficult to rationalize; the Pack was a fluid society that took in new arrivals as a matter of course, so a new face in different clothes didn't faze them. She watched a group of children playing a game with bats and colored balls close to a small canal that cut around the town's perimeter. "How many people are there?" Sam asked as they crossed the canal's bridge. "In the Pack, I mean."

"An accurate census is difficult to gauge," admitted Koe, "but we estimate that there are more than sixty million souls, spread out over roughly one hundred vessels of various sizes."

"The population of a major city," she noted. "That's—" Carter's words were drowned out by a rumble of breaking stone and the thin, high scream of a child. Sam and the healer spun in time to see part of the riverbank slide into the dark green waters in a cloud of dust; one of the game-players, a fair-haired boy who couldn't have been more than eleven years old went with it, vanishing under the surface.

"The verge gave way!" Koe snapped.

Sam reacted without conscious thought, tearing at the clips on her gear vest and shrugging it off. The boy scrambled briefly to the surface of the fast-flowing canal and then went under again in a cloud of bubbles. She thrust her weapon and her equipment into Koe's hands and vaulted over the side of the bridge, her fatigue cap flying from her head. The other man shouted something after her, but Carter was already dropping towards the water.

They took the road out of the township and Daniel tried his best to take in as much as he could with his video camera. The images on the fold-out viewfinder screen seemed flat and sparse; they couldn't compare to the actual sight of the countryside arching away into the sky. "It's like, no matter where you stand, you're at the bottom of the Grand Canyon."

"What is that?" asked Suj.

"A place on Earth, the planet where we come from. A huge gorge created by millions of years of geological motion and erosion." He made a this-big gesture with his hands.

Suj nodded. "I've seen such things on sorties from the flotilla. I prefer a more controlled landscape for my home."

"I guess." On the road, Jackson had questioned the Pack historian ceaselessly, drawing out as much as he could about the nature of their culture. As far as he could determine at this stage, they were an unusual merging of rootless nomadic society with a collective tribal mindset. Parts of their ethos resembled those of the Tuareg or the Apache, and others the traditions of the Romany of Eastern Europe. "So tell me more about Vix and the others. You said he's a good leader?"

She nodded again. "Vix has been our pathfinder for several terms, and each time his stewardship is reconsidered he has been elected once more by his peers."

"So you're a democracy, then?"

"Perhaps not as you would define it," she admitted. "Challengers are free to oppose the Pack's seniors if they feel they could do better. If the peers can be swayed, then Vix would be forced to step down. It would be true to say that many roles are hotly contested."

"Uh-huh," said Daniel, "and let me guess. Your man Ryn back there, he's interested in taking that seat for ·himself, right?"

"Ryn is not 'my man', as you call him, Doctor Jackson. He has followers just as Vix has his."

"Call me Daniel, please." He halted as the road forked. One branch led away toward another township, while the other turned toward the farmlands. Jackson aimed the camera in that direction and frowned as the view came into focus. There seemed to be a strange shimmering between them and the fields, like a wall of heat-haze. "What's that?" He started toward it.

"Perhaps we ought to head back," suggested Suj. "I have a library of records in the settlement. I could show you images from the earliest days of the *Wanderer*…"

"In a second." Daniel's interest was piqued. From a distance, the farmlands had all seemed oddly uniform to him, as if they were too perfectly cut, like the manicured lawns of a golf course; but now he was noticing differences in them. Something that his grandfather had told him as a boy came to the front of his thoughts. *Learn to read the land, Daniel. Half of archaeology is knowing where to dig.* "I just want to take a look over here."

Suj's hand shot out and grabbed his elbow. "No," she said, and now her voice was firm and serious. "I think it would be best if we go back."

Daniel shook off her grip. "Fine. You go first, I'll catch up with you." Without warning, he broke into a jog and split away from her. He had to get a closer look; the curvature of the colony interior had masked it at first, but now he was sure. The fields looked *wrong*, and Jackson was going to find out why.

Carter hit the murky water feet-first and felt the shock of
the cold cut through her like electricity. The canal was deeper
than she had expected, black with churned sediment. The swift
current pressed into her and dragged the major down; it was
a side-effect of the Coriolis force, the spin that produced the
Wanderer's gravity.

She pushed against it and turned, casting about for the boy.
In the dimness Sam saw a flailing shape and swam towards it,
hands knifing through the water. Air pressed against her chest
as she metered her breathing to stay under as long as she could.
Closer now, and she recognized the pure terror of raw panic
on the boy's face. Breaths chugged out of his mouth in great
plumes of bubbles, and the frantic terror of drowning was stark
in his eyes.

Sam ignored the pounding behind her ribcage and caught
the boy as he tumbled past her, grabbing at his arm and his
torso. By reflex the child thrashed against her, lashing out, but
she was ready for it. Carter's water survival training came back
to her with perfect, detached clarity; granted, this wasn't the
same as surviving a post-ejection landing in offshore waters,
but drowning was still drowning, no matter if it took place
in the Atlantic or in a paddling pool. The harsh undercurrent
turned and dragged at them both as Sam gathered the boy close
to her and held him tightly. She felt her boots bounce off something buried in the riverbed muck, and in her chest there was
a ball of acid as her lungs tried to drag in oxygen that wasn't
there. Carter kicked hard, and the pair of them rose with what
seemed like agonizing slowness until finally they burst
through into the daylight.

Together they gulped in lungfuls of air and Sam pushed
to turn them toward the banks of the river. She blinked water
from her eyes to see Koe and a couple of other men from the
township scrambling hip deep in the current. Strong arms took
the boy from her and then guided her to safety.

She was cross-legged on the path that followed the canal when she shook off the adrenaline rush. Her fatigues felt like they were made of lead, heavy with the water. Unsteadily, Sam got up and walked to where Koe was hunched over the boy's slumped form. She could hear a familiar noise; a metallic buzzing. The boy was coughing, bringing up water and thin bile. "Is he…"

Koe threw her a look over his shoulder and Sam instantly fell silent. The sound was coming from the device in his hand, a brass disc that fitted around his palm projecting a warm orange glow over the boy's heaving chest. "That's a Goa'uld healing device!" Carter's hand darted to the Beretta automatic holstered at her hip. "How can you use it?"

"No, Major, please!" Koe pleaded. "Please, I will explain… But I must save this child first!"

Sam nodded, fingering the pistol. "Do it, then." In truth, she had her doubts about whether the gun would fire readily after the dunking she had just given it, but she didn't want to dive for the pile of her gear where her P90 and vest lay a few feet away.

After a few moments, Koe let the boy sit up. The youngster's tear-streaked face was pale and drawn, his breathing was ragged—but at least he *was* breathing. Koe gestured to one of the other men. "Take him home. Make sure he's fed and put to bed." The healer stood up slowly and opened his hands to Carter, revealing the device. "You understand how this object works?"

"The Goa'uld tag those things with a genetic marker," Sam replied warily. "Only someone with a symbiote can use them." She hesitated. That wasn't strictly correct. "Or someone who *had* a symbiote in them."

"Yes. The parasites key their technology to their gene code… But we discovered a way around that." Koe replaced the device in a pocket. "Some of our scientists created a process to duplicate that marker artificially. It does not work for all, but if the patching takes, one can use Goa'uld devices as easily as turning on a lamp." He managed a wan smile and revealed a small scar on his wrist. "I think it is fitting that we can put their machines to better uses."

Carter's gun didn't waver. "I've seen Goa'uld hide their true nature before today. How do I know you're not doing the same thing?"

Koe nodded at the P90. "If the Pack desired your deaths, we have had more than enough chances to kill you already." He picked up her gear and offered it to her. "Are we not trying to build trust between our peoples, Major Carter?"

After a moment, Sam frowned and holstered her pistol. "You're right. I'm sorry. It's just that we've had a lot of bad experiences in the past. It makes you think the worst of people."

Koe chuckled and nodded to the canal. "You risked your life without hesitation for that boy, for one of us, even though we have only just met. I find myself, Major, thinking the very best of you." He beckoned her. "Come. We should return to Vix's home. I will arrange for fresh clothes to be provided."

"Daniel!" shouted Suj. "Doctor Jackson, I must insist you stop!"

She seemed pretty annoyed, but that only served to stimulate his interest further. He jogged down the sloping road and saw several things at once. Along the line of the strange haze there were tall rods of white metal extending into the air—he was reminded immediately of street lights—and the mirage-like shimmering appeared to hang between them in a curtain. "Or a fence," he said aloud. Off to the sides he saw slow-moving machines not much bigger than a motorcycle, ambling along the line of the rods on six robotic legs. Now and then they paused and shot a fan of green laser light from an aperture on their bodies, like a snake flicking out its tongue to taste the air.

But the haze-wall drew his attention. Through it he saw the amber expanse of crops, moving in gentle waves in the wind;

only there wasn't any wind right now. The whole sight seemed off somehow. Daniel stepped right up the flickering fence and reached out to touch it. His fingertips tingled. "What is this?"

"A barrier," insisted Suj. "Nothing for you to be concerned with."

"What are you keeping out?" He asked. "Or should I be asking what you're keeping in?"

"Doctor, please! It's nothing dangerous, nothing for you to be concerned about."

"Oh," Daniel threw her a smile. "Then it'll be okay for me to take a look." Before she could stop him, Jackson stepped into the haze and felt a tickle across his skin. Suj cried out and tried to grab him again, but it was too late. He was through.

What he saw in there made Daniel stop dead. The historian came after him, fuming. "Are all of your people so disruptive?"

"Most of us, yeah..." His attention was captured by the sight of the fields. From the other side of the shimmering fence they seemed bountiful with grain and acres of crops; but from inside it was a very different story. Instead of rows of stalks in rich bloom, there was nothing but ploughed lines of dead, rust-colored earth. Here and there, Daniel saw a few pathetic sprigs of greenery, but these were limp, blackened things that seemed diseased. He dropped to a crouch to examine the earth. It was powdery and lifeless. "What happened here?"

Suj sagged and sat down heavily. "Why didn't you just listen? This isn't any of your business." He waited, and after a moment she sighed. "We call it the blight. It is a disease of plant life. All our best efforts to find a way to protect our crops from it have failed."

Daniel pointed at the metal rods. "But what's with the screen? What is it, some kind of hologram?"

She nodded. "It is important to keep information about the spread of the blight contained. Much of the Pack's food staples are grown on the *Wanderer*. There would be panic if our people thought that was in jeopardy."

"And is it?" He came closer. "How far has this blight spread?"

"Far enough," Suj said ruefully. She got up and took his hand. "Now you have seen, will you please come back with me? And I must have your promise you will not speak of this. Vix would be furious to learn that a planetborne has learned of the blight." She led him back through the image-fence. One of the machines approached and ran its beam over them. "The tenders ensure no blight microbes spread beyond the contained areas," explained the woman.

As they made their way back to the township, Daniel frowned. "Suj, listen. I'm sorry if I put you in an awkward situation, but we might be able to help. On Earth, we've made great strides in agricultural science, and we know other races with other technologies. We might be able to help you stop this."

She gave him a wary look. "You think so?"

"We can try, can't we?"

Jack looked up as the guy with the robes—*what was his name, Koy? Cole? Koe?*—entered the meeting hall with a slightly bedraggled Sam Carter in tow. He blinked. The major wore a kind of dress-jacket thing that reminded O'Neill of an Indian sari crossed with Arab robes. Somewhat incongruously, she had her webbing vest on over the top. Teal'c raised an eyebrow, which with him was practically a shout of exclamation. "Carter," said Jack, trying to keep a smirk out of his voice, "that's a new look for you."

Sam fumed quietly. "I took a dip in the canal, sir."

Koe laughed. "She did much more than that. Major Carter rescued a youth from drowning. She saved his life."

Vix accepted this with a nod. "Koe, see that the child's family provides her with reimbursement for her actions."

Carter shook her head. "There's no need for that."

"There is," said Ryn firmly. "This is the Pack way. Just

as you will compensate us for our intervention on the planet, Major Carter will be compensated for her deeds, in trade or in favor."

"My mom always used to tell me that virtue is it's own reward," noted Jack.

"How generous," sniffed Ryn. "If your people give with no expectation of remuneration, then you must be wealthy indeed."

Carter held up a hand. "Sir, I don't want to make an issue of this…" She fingered the garments she was wearing. "How about… You dry out my uniform and I keep these clothes, and we'll call it quits?"

Koe nodded. "A very reasonable exchange."

Jack's smirk finally emerged. "Hey, what do you know? That looked like an agreement to me. We're off to a great start."

"Then we should continue," said Vix, taking another draught from his drink. "We've heard many stories of the Tau'ri and their exploits. Sokar, Hathor, Apophis, and many other System Lords are dead at your hands. I have heard tell that you obliterated entire worlds and made parley with the Asgard."

"Yeah," Jack smiled. "We like to keep busy."

"Then it would not be unreasonable for us to ask for some measure of your strength in payment for your rescue."

"If indeed your prowess is as great as we hear," added Ryn. "I would be disappointed to learn that these stories have no basis in truth."

"The Tau'ri are staunch enemies of the Goa'uld," Teal'c said firmly. O'Neill could sense the annoyance under the big guy's words. "Of that, you may have no doubts. I have stood with them and fought the false gods for seven years."

Ryn caught the implication at once. "And we have not? Is that what you are thinking, Jaffa? Do you consider us cowards for fleeing the wrath of the System Lords?"

"I have said no such thing."

Carter flashed him a look and Jack clapped his hands together; he had to defuse the moment before Ryn tried to pick a fight with Teal'c, something he knew would end *very* badly for everyone. "So, then. Let's talk trade. What are you guys in the market for? Toaster ovens? An X-box?"

The door to Vix's chambers opened once more, this time to admit Jackson and the woman from the shuttle, Suj. Immediately, O'Neill sensed something between the two of them that made his danger sense flare. He raised an eyebrow in an expression that said *Do we have a problem?*

"I think I can answer that, Jack," said the younger man, and he glanced at Suj. "I saw something interesting out in the fields."

A nerve jumped in Ryn's jaw. "You let a stranger see the crops?" He gave the woman an acid stare.

Suj nodded. "Don't blame her," Daniel broke in. "It's my fault."

Jack felt the conversation getting away from him. "Crops?"

"The farmlands outside the township," supplied Carter. "We saw them from the hillside."

The Pack leader was silent for a long moment, and then Vix set O'Neill with a heavy gaze, as if he had made an important decision. "In truth, Colonel, we did not come to Golla IX in search of salvage. We came looking for food. There is a crisis building aboard the *Wanderer*, and it threatens to tip our people into a spiral of famine from which we may never escape."

CHAPTER THREE

General Hammond threw a glance at Sergeant Harriman as he strode into the control center. Walter's spectacles caught the reflected glimmer of the open wormhole in the gate-room beyond. "Receiving SG-1's IDC, sir," he reported.

"About time," Hammond said, half to himself. "Open the iris."

Harriman placed his palm on the security reader, and in the gate-room the massive leaves of titanium alloy rumbled open. Five figures emerged from the shimmering vertical pool and the general's eyes narrowed. "Alert Doctor Warner. We may have a visitor for him to take a look at."

Hammond made his way down. It was a point of personal pride with him that any new off-world arrivals should be welcomed by the ranking officer at Stargate Command, and if SG-1 had brought someone with them, he had little doubt they were worth a few moments of his time. To be truthful, it was one of the things that George Hammond liked the most about his job. It wasn't often he got the call to venture to alien worlds, so whenever someone from one of those worlds came here, he made sure he'd get to meet them.

As he got to the foot of the gate ramp he realized that two of the five people were dressed in quasi-African robes, and one of them was one of his officers. "Major, you appear to be out of uniform."

Carter gave a wan smile. "Just picking up some local color, sir."

"General Hammond," O'Neill said brightly, "may I present Suj, from the Pack?" He gestured to the other woman in robes.

She bowed slightly and looked around. "You are the Tau'ri leader?"

"I'm in command of this facility," Hammond replied. "Welcome to Earth, Suj."

"Her folks are kinda like interplanetary gypsies, sir," added O'Neill, "and they have this really funky spaceship."

"I look forward to reading your report, Colonel." He glanced at Doctor Jackson and the young man took the hint.

"Suj, why don't you come with me? We need to be cleared by medical before we can proceed."

The woman nodded, distracted by the scope of the gateroom. "Of course…" She smiled briefly. "Forgive me. This isn't what I was expecting…"

O'Neill made a face. "Oh, this? Well, y'know, we don't go in for anything fancy."

The others walked away, leaving Hammond and his subordinate officer alone. "What have you got for us this time, Jack?" he asked. "Space gypsies?"

"For real, sir," said O'Neill, "and more than that. These Pack guys are pack-rats, they have technology and hardware from dozens of planets, and a lot of it is from worlds without Stargates that we've never even heard of. And they want to trade."

Hammond studied the colonel for a long moment. He trusted Jack O'Neill implicitly, having learned through experience to look past the undisciplined edges of the man's personality to the seasoned soldier inside. "What's your gut feeling?"

"Cautious but optimistic, sir. These folks are proud, but they need our help and they're not too dumb to admit it." He gave a rueful chuckle. "I know I've said this before, but we may actually get something out of this one."

The general gave a wary nod. "Don't jinx it, Jack," he warned.

"This won't hurt a bit," said the woman with the blonde curls, and she pressed the small vial to Suj's bare arm. She felt a sharp stab, like an insect bite.

"Ah." Suj shot her a glare. "I thought you said it wouldn't

hurt?"

The woman gave her a sheepish smile. "Sorry. Force of habit." The vial filled with a measure of Suj's blood and then she removed it, tabbing an adhesive bandage over the wound. "There. All done."

Suj rubbed the sore spot gingerly as another of the Tau'ri approached. *Warner.* She had heard Daniel call him by that name, and like the blonde woman he wore a long white tunic over his clothes. It was clearly some kind of uniform, like the drab green that Jackson and the others wore. Suj began theorizing about the Earthers; perhaps they had some kind of regimented culture, where the color of their clothing delineated their position and status. The leader Hammond wore blue. White seemed to be the signifier for their healers.

Warner took the vial from the woman. "Thanks, Cathy. I'll take it from here." He shot Suj a flat smile and glanced at a portable computer device in his hand. "Can I ask you a question, Miss?"

"My name is Suj."

"Suj, yes," He nodded. Warner reminded her of a farmer she knew in the spinward townships, with a large frame and big hands that belied the delicacy of them. "Doctor Jackson told me you come from a space colony, is that correct? You don't live on a planet?"

"No. The Wanderer is my home."

"Interesting. I'd like to examine you, if you'd be willing. I'm conducting research into the way that artificial gravity affects human bone structure and—"

"Doctor," Daniel emerged from behind a folding screen near the foot of the bed where she sat, and interposed himself between them. "Suj has only just arrived. Could we leave the poking and prodding for later?"

Warner's face fell. "Oh. Yes. Of course." He flashed the same slight smile. "Later then." He moved away.

"Maybe," added Jackson. He sighed. "I'm sorry about that. He doesn't get out much. His social skills are a little limited."

She rubbed her arm again. "Is all this necessary?" Suj's gaze crossed the chamber to where the rest of Jackson's cadre were being ministered to by the white-coats.

He nodded sadly. "Unfortunately, it is. We've been on the sharp end of a fair few invasion attempts in the past... Everything from Goa'ulds secreting themselves inside our people to aliens duplicating images of us."

Suj inclined her head. "It is sad, is it not, that the nature of the universe forces one to be so cautious around new faces and new places?"

"Yeah." She heard the regret in his voice. Suj watched the other Tau'ri, considering them. They were an eclectic mix, to be certain. Jackson, with a keen mind and a searching intellect that burned fiercely behind his eyes and those peculiar lenses he wore across his face; he seemed to be a rogue element among the rest of SG-1. The others had a more martial tone to them. The woman, Carter, shared Daniel's insight but she carried it beneath an aura of soldierly precision where Jackson was more open. She reminded Suj of Vix; she seemed, for want of a better word, *leaderly*. And then there was O'Neill. She still wasn't sure quite what to make of him. On the surface, he appeared flippant and lacking in focus, but Suj was starting to realize that might be an affectation. She suspected he was far more intelligent than he appeared at first glance. *Perhaps it is a tactic on his part*, she mused, *a deliberate attempt to make others underestimate him*. Suj filed that conclusion away to later relay to Vix.

Finally, she settled on the Jaffa, and a dart of old terror made her go tense. The burnished golden brand on the dark-skinned warrior's forehead rang peals of warning deep inside her. This man was a First Prime, the most feared and lethal warriors in service to a System Lord. Even being in the same room as him made her uncomfortable.

Daniel saw her looking at Teal'c. "He's a great guy, once you get to know him."

Suj nodded woodenly. "How... How did you manage to

tame him?"

Jackson laughed briefly. "Tame him? I don't think anyone will ever be able to tame Teal'c!" Then the amusement left his expression as he saw Suj did not share it. "He came to our side of his own volition. He rescued us when Apophis was planning to murder us all. Teal'c turned against everything he had been brought up to serve because he knew it was wrong."

"And yet..." Suj licked dry lips. "His kind were the hammers that shattered our worlds. If not for the Jaffa, the people that form the Pack would have lived peaceful lives."

"Not all the Jaffa serve the Goa'uld. Many of them are free now, they've rejected their false gods like the Pack have." He paused, considering. "You have no Free Jaffa in the Pack, do you?"

She shook her head. "They have not been welcomed," Suj admitted. "The memories of worlds and loved ones lost still burn strongly in much of the Pack hierarchy. Every time we have crossed paths with the Free Jaffa it has resulted in disagreement."

"I understand how you must feel," said Daniel, after a while. "I've lost friends to Jaffa, to the Goa'uld. They took my wife Sha're from me..." He looked away, then back. "But that's true for Sam, Jack and Teal'c as well. We've all suffered because of them."

Suj nodded again. "I do not doubt your words. But it is difficult to look beyond the legacy of a bloody past."

Daniel echoed her nod. "Yes, it is. But what happens from here, between our people and yours, that's going to be about the future."

She felt a smile emerge on her lips. "You're right."

O'Neill and the others got up from the examination beds. "Daniel," called the colonel. "C'mon. Hammond wants us in the briefing room for a chit-chat."

"I have to go." Jackson patted her on the arm. "Are you hungry? Doctor Warner can have someone take you down to the mess hall."

"*Mess* hall?" Suj blinked in mild alarm at the name. "How do you people eat on this planet?"

But Daniel was already on his way out. "Try the Jell-O," he said over his shoulder, "it's a Tau'ri delicacy."

Teal'c took his seat at the far end of the table next to O'Neill. The colonel settled into the chair and drummed his fingers on the wood as Major Carter and Doctor Jackson took their places. The Jaffa eased into the comfortable seat and rolled it back slightly, giving his legs the room he needed in the event an emergency required him to get quickly to his feet. It was force of habit for him, an ingrained faculty that automatically led Teal'c to place himself in the most tactically advantageous place in a room. To be Jaffa, as Bra'tac had taught him, was to always be ready.

O'Neill watched him survey the room and rolled his eyes. "Relax, T. It's the briefing room. We've been here a million times." He nodded at the heraldic standards on the far wall. "I don't think the flagpoles are going to attack us, not after all this time."

It would have been easy for Teal'c to make a list of all the adversaries that SG-1 had encountered which were capable of making themselves invisible to the naked eye, but he chose not to and simply accepted O'Neill's mild admonishment in his usual way; by ignoring it.

At the far end of the table, General Hammond looked up from a spread of printouts and still images that had been generated by the MALP sent to P5X-404. "So, SG-1, another mission that went off at a tangent…" He shook his head. "How did it happen this time?"

"Ah, you know us, sir," began O'Neill, "every day's an adventure."

Jackson manipulated a remote control and directed it at a screen by the far wall. "I took the liberty of cueing up some of the footage I captured on the planet." Images of the rainy canyon scrolled past, quickly followed by shots of the stone spheres. "The information Colonel Dixon and SG-13 brought back from their mission last week led us to believe that we'd find alien hardware on the planet, and at first that seemed to be wrong. There were only these monuments."

"Yeah, until the big honking robots started poppin' up everywhere," broke in O'Neill.

Jackson advanced the footage to a set of blurry stills that showed the brassy mechanoids moving and firing at them. Hammond's eyes narrowed. "That doesn't look like any technology we've seen before. Major?"

Carter nodded. "Yes sir. I mean, no sir, it doesn't seem so." She produced a drawstring bag and pulled out a piece of broken, charred metal plate. "I took a sample of wreckage from one of the machines. Just on first impressions you can see it weighs less than aluminum, but it has the tensility of tempered steel. It's some kind of exotic composite alloy."

Hammond took the scrap from her and ran his fingers over it. "Have Doctor Lee give this a full metallurgical work-up. Let's find out if those machines are native to the planet."

"That shouldn't be a problem. We already have some preliminary geological scans of the area around the Stargate from the MALP. We can compare the results."

"As thrilling as the geology stuff is, I'd like to cut to the chase if I may, General." O'Neill tap-tapped his fingers on the table. "The long and the short of it was, sir, we were about to get our asses handed to us by those Rock-em Sock-ems when these Pack guys intervened."

"Coincidence, Colonel?" Hammond asked. "Or a set-up?"

Teal'c saw O'Neill's lip twist. "Still working on that one. My gut says no, but…"

"Sometimes a fluke is just a fluke," protested Jackson. "I'd like to float the possibility that we might just have been lucky today…" He glanced at the noncommittal faces around him. "Or is this the wrong crowd for that?"

"All right, Doctor Jackson, for the moment let's give these people the benefit of the doubt, and accept that they were there following the same rumors we were."

Daniel nodded. "Apart from the stone spheres, which I will want to take a team back to examine, the rumors of Ancient technology on P5X-404 look to be just that. Rumors."

"We should send out long-range UAVs to be sure, but I'm going to concur with Daniel," added Carter.

O'Neill shook his head. "Dixon's gonna be pissed. Reynolds bet him twenty bucks it wouldn't pan out."

"I think we can all agree that the Pack aren't out to pick a fight with us," said Daniel.

"Indeed?" Teal'c offered. "I sensed a distinct aggressive undercurrent among them."

"Toward you, maybe," said the colonel. "You're a big guy, you intimidate folks. Try working on those people skills some more."

"The Pack exhibit a strong dislike toward Jaffa," Teal'c continued. "Regrettably, I understand their anger. They look upon me and see only the Goa'uld who attacked their birth-worlds."

"That's as may be," said Hammond, "but the Free Jaffa are our allies and if, as Colonel O'Neill says, these Pack are in the market for a treaty, they'll have to accept that." He looked at Carter. "What do they want and what do they have to offer?"

"Food, in the short term," said the major. "They're suffering from severe crop failures related to some sort of plant-based virus."

"Which is why you had me institute full decontamination protocols," nodded the general. "Go on."

"We've agreed in principle to lend any scientific expertise we have to their problem. In return, they're going to let us cherry-pick from the salvage they've gathered on their journeys. We're talking about captured Goa'uld technology, items of Asgard and Ancient origin, maybe more. Plus that genetic 'patching' thing."

"I believe they also have a wealth of tactical data." Teal'c added. "The Pack survive by remaining one step ahead of the

System Lords. In order to do that they maintain surveillance on all the Goa'uld powers. They are likely to possess information about threat forces and territories that we do not."

The room fell quiet as Hammond took in their words and considered them. After a several moments, Daniel Jackson was compelled to break the silence. "So, where do we go from here, General?"

Hammond closed the file in front of him with a decisive motion. "*You*, Doctor, and the rest of SG-1 stay here at the SGC and continue an ongoing evaluation of that young lady you brought back as the Pack's representative. *I* am going to head out to Washington to brief the President and set the wheels in motion for a treaty agreement. This is a formal request, so we have to take it up to the State Department." The general got to his feet and the rest of the team stood up with him. "The IOA are making things difficult back on the Hill. This could be a good opportunity to silence some of the nay-sayers."

Teal'c saw a crooked smile cross the colonel's face. "Don't forget to give the boss a hug from me, sir."

The liquid in the glass caught the light and refracted it around the sparse walls of the chamber. The blue shimmer moved in gentle silence over the undecorated steel-gray supports and the umber walls. As the light from the holographic console changed, so did the reflections. The display unfolded like an opening box, a ghostly wire-frame filled with a slow rain of symbols that moved to and fro, repeating information from all stations of the starship to eyes that were dimmed, that did not see them.

Mirris let the clear liquid in the glass fill her sight. She turned the tumbler in her hands, watching the sluggish motion of the fluid. After a moment she took another purse-lipped sip and felt the warmth of the liqueur spread down her throat. As she lowered the glass from her lips, her eyes happened to fall across the metallic desk in front of her and they snagged on the brushed alloy bracelet that rested there, alone and to one side, isolated across the work surface from the profusion of disposable screens and other devices that constituted the debris of her rank. Mirris felt the urge to reach out and touch it in the tips of her fingers, in a peculiar tightening of the skin. It took an almost physical effort on her part to do nothing, to sit there and watch the hologram without watching it.

A low, resonant chime sounded from the door and she flicked a glance up. Mirris tapped a sensor spot on the desktop and the door slid into the wall to reveal Geddel, who entered with his usual expression of muted discontent. He was slightly too old for his posting aboard the ship, and in the usual manner of things a man of his age should have been in administration of a vessel or installation of his own by now. He was rail-thin and lacking in hair, both traits that Mirris found unattractive in males.

He nodded and gestured slightly with a screensheet in his hand. "Administrator, if I am not interrupting?" Geddel phrased it like a question, but he worked in a small measure of reproach as well.

She turned the glass in her fingers. "What is it?"

"Signals Parsing has received an encrypted communication from the migrant fleet. Your...operative...has provided an update." He held out the flimsy sheet of plastic.

Mirris ignored the disdain in his tone and nodded. "Read it to me."

He didn't want to, but her word was her command aboard the cruiser. "Very well. The operative says that the Tau'ri suffered no casualties, which concurs with our own telemetry. There were apparently some matters of small local import that took place aboard the colony ship..." He scrolled down the page, tutting quietly at what he no doubt saw as a disordered and impatient communication. "The end result, if I understand correctly, is that the Tau'ri are following predicted patterns of behavior."

"Good. We will move to the next phase of the project once the Pack have secured an agreement with them." There was an unmistakable undercurrent of relish in her words, and Geddel frowned openly at it. She eyed him. "Is that all, sub-director, or do you have something of your own to add?"

"Administrator," he began, and he made that little sighing noise that Mirris found so very irritating. "I have concerns. In fact, many of the staff aboard ship have them, although of course as your subordinate I have made sure such dissension has been suppressed."

"Really?" She sipped at her drink. "Do go on."

"We all understand that the nature of our mission requires us to step outside the normal conventions of our culture, but in the dealings with these nomads…" He sighed again. "Does it really serve the interests of our confederation to make such a close association with one of them?"

"You find the migrants distasteful, Geddel."

"I do," he admitted. "But that is not the root of my concerns. I feel, Administrator, that you are allowing yourself to adopt some of their baser traits." The thin man gave the steel band on her desk a pointed look. "During the last communication you had with the operative, you were overly emotional. Quite *aggressive*."

"Aggressive?" She repeated the word mildly. From Geddel's point of view, she would have seemed calm, perhaps the only sign of any distress being the subtle whitening of her knuckles around the glass tumbler. Inwardly, Mirris entertained the sudden, violent fantasy of springing to her feet and backhanding him across the face. For a brief instant, she felt the heat of passion, imagining the experience of his cheekbone cracking beneath her strike, of blood spurting from his nose as he fell wailing to the metal deck. *You loathsome little parasite, with your constant disdain. I know what you think of me. Poor broken woman with her hidden anger, marking time.* She blinked away the giddiness and covered it with another sip. "I think you have misunderstood," she lied.

"These nomads lack sophistication, and in order to bring my operative to heel I must sometimes employ obfuscation and fakery. That was not aggression, Geddel. It was theatre."

"Oh." The thin man sighed again. "I see. Of course. It was quite convincing."

"What use would it have been otherwise?"

"Will it be necessary for you to duplicate this behavior in the future?"

She glanced away. "It may be. As such, I expect no more comments or 'concerns' from you, is that clear?"

He bowed slightly. "Of course, Administrator." And once again, Geddel's eyes strayed to the band on her desk. Mirris knew he didn't believe her, and his look was his ridiculous way of telling her that. "Is that a bonding torc?" he asked. "From your late betrothed, am I correct?"

Mirris found her veneer of calm disintegrating, and covered it with a brusque command. "Ensure the aura-cloak remains at full power and keep us to the edge of the migrant fleet's sensor envelope until I order otherwise. It would jeopardize the mission if they detected our presence in this system. You are dismissed, sub-director."

"Of course." Geddel bowed again and made his way to the door. He hesitated on the threshold and gave her a patronizing glance. "If you will permit me to say so, I feel some sympathy for your loss. Perhaps if you would like my counsel—"

"You are dismissed," she said again, with more force than she had intended. Geddel turned away and the entranceway closed behind him.

Liar, she said to the door, *You are mocking me.* But Geddel would see; all of them would be made to see there would be reciprocity. A payment in kind for what the Tau'ri had taken from her.

There was a sharp noise and Mirris felt wetness on her palm. She glanced down and saw a fracture in the side of the glass where it had cracked in the tension of her grip. With icy precision, she disposed of the tumbler in the chamber's reconstitutor and used a dermal regenerator on the cut in her flesh. She did not look at the torc again.

"Hey, Sam."

Carter glanced up from the screen of her laptop and blinked. Her eyes felt sandy with all the hours she'd been starting at the display, and it took a second for her to focus. "Oh, hey Daniel. What's up?"

"Nothin'," he said, wandering into the lab from the corridor, his hands in his pockets. "I was on my way out and I wondered if you needed a ride off-base?"

"Out?" Sam had taken her wristwatch off earlier and set it aside. She picked it up now and frowned at the timepiece. "Is it that late?"

Daniel jerked a thumb at the ceiling. "Yeah. This place plays havoc with your circadian rhythm, doesn't it? Not many clocks around, no windows. Can't tell what time of day it is." He gave a wan smile. "They do the same thing in the casinos in Vegas."

She eyed him. "You've never been to Las Vegas."

"Sure I have," Jackson said defensively. "That last time we were out at Area 51 in Nevada?"

Sam chuckled. "Playing the one-arm bandits at McCarran Airport does not count as Vegas," she told him, "and neither does losing your pay check to Teal'c on poker night."

Daniel made a dismissive gesture. "Ah, I let him win. You know what he's like, he gets so emotional when he loses." He nodded at the computer. "What's so interesting it's got you working overtime?"

"Preliminary reports on the scrap from the robots on P5X-404," said Sam, turning the screen to show him lines of comparative atomic spectra. "The most interesting thing is that the machines were not indigenous to the planet." She pointed at colored bands on the display. "These here? That's traces of rare earth metals in the alloy I brought back. As far as we can see, those metals don't appear to exist anywhere on 404, and even if they did, it would be in amounts too small to be used in building robots. I'm running some chemical dating tests right now, but I'm willing to bet we'll find they don't match the age of the local rocks either."

"Which begs the question, why would someone go to all that trouble? Bringing war machines by ship or through the Stargate to an unremarkable planet and then burying them in the sand…"

Sam nodded. The issue had been nagging at her since she first realized the differences. "I've already ruled out a bunch of races we've encountered as the builders of the robots, but I could be here for days combing the database and still come up empty."

Daniel folded his arms. "Why would someone want to defend a bunch of giant stone spheres?" He asked the air. "Maybe it's a site of religious significance, and the robots were guarding them against interlopers? Or they could be left-overs from some off-world invasion."

"Or maybe the Pack put them there."

"Ah, so we're going for the *distrust everyone because they hate us and want us to die* conclusion, then?" Jackson shook his head. "I know after so long we have a bit of a reputation out there, but this is bordering on xenophobia."

"I never said that," Sam retorted. "But sometimes it is hard to think the best of strangers."

"Suj said something very similar." Daniel nodded slowly. "And I wish I didn't agree but I do." He sighed. "I think I've been hanging around you guys too much. The military mindset is rubbing off on me."

"Really?" Carter smiled a little. "We could say the same thing about you. I mean, look how much Teal'c has mellowed since he met you."

Jackson began to speak, but his words were flattened by the sudden whoop of an alert siren. "What now?" he yelled.

Unscheduled off-world activation? Sam hesitated a

moment, expecting to hear those words broadcast over the SGC's public address system. Instead, there was a momentary dimming of the lights in the lab, so fast and so slight it was barely noticeable. She didn't need to say anything to Daniel; the two of them tore from the lab and ran for the control room.

Jackson threw a glance out of the big armored windows into the gate-room, expecting to see... Well, *something*. But the chamber beyond appeared completely normal, the Stargate silent and dark. He glanced over the shoulder of the duty technician at the control console as one of the large steel blast doors below slid open, allowing Sergeant Siler and a couple of armed airmen to enter. Siler had a complex device in his hand that chattered like a Geiger counter, and he was waving it around in careful motions, taking readings. The two soldiers panned their assault rifles back and forth, watchful and ready.

Sam was already in urgent conversation with Colonel Reynolds, for the moment acting as base Commander while Hammond was away and Jack was already home for the evening. "What's the problem, sir?"

Reynolds's face was set in his usual perpetual frown, but deeper than usual. "Damned if I know, Major. We got a power spike from one of the monitors and it tripped the alert..." He leant down to talk to the technician. "Well?"

Daniel watched the automated checklist on the airman's screen run swiftly down its length, leaving a trail of green tick-marks. "Uh. Gate systems appear to be nominal, sir," replied the technician. "No errors."

Sam tapped the microphone that broadcast into the gate-toom. "Siler? Anything?"

The sergeant glanced up at the armored windows. "Nothing, Major. Electromagnetic, thermal, ultraviolet, quantum... All scans in here read negative."

"My laptop does this kind of thing all the time," offered Jackson, in an attempt to be helpful.

Carter nodded at the Stargate. "This is an alien construct made of exotic matter and crystalline circuits we still only know a little about, Daniel. It's a little more complicated than that."

"And there's no tech support help line, either," noted Reynolds without humor. "Major, what's your recommendation? I can lock down the base if that thing's going screwy on us."

Sam studied the readouts. "I don't think that's necessary. But we should suspend all gate travel for a few hours while I run a full diagnostic."

The colonel nodded. "Fair enough. We're not expecting anyone back until sun-up anyhow. Do what you need to, but all the same I'm going to bump up internal security to level three."

"I guess you won't be leaving any time soon, then?" said Daniel, as they walked away.

"Guess not," said Carter. He could see her mind racing.

Daniel couldn't help but grin. "You love this stuff, don't you?"

"What?"

"All the techy mystery stuff. The robots, this power surge. You love the challenge. You have this expression on your face, like a kid in a candy store." He smirked. "I think it's sweet, actually."

Sam left him at the elevator doors in the corridor. "Funny," she said over her shoulder, "I saw the same look on your face when you were crawling all over those alien monuments."

"Ah." She had him there. "*Touché*."

Tyke swore loudly when Deano slapped him and he cocked his fist back to smack the jerk in his fat, sneering face. Deano shoved him away and Tyke slipped on the uneven concrete floor of the warehouse, but he kept his balance. "Kick your ass—" he began, his anger rising.

"I said be quiet, fool," Deano grunted. "Listen!"

Tyke realized that the others were all keeping it down as

well. Mag had an unlit joint halfway to his lips and AJ was reaching for his gun. It was then that Tyke became aware that the streetlights outside were acting weird; there was a ripple of flickers, as if they were going to cut out, and then they popped back on like nothing had happened. From nowhere, he felt the hairs on his arms and the stubble on his chin prickle. "What the hell?" It was like when he visited his aunt over in Aurora; the woman had these nylon carpets everywhere and you couldn't take two steps without building up a static charge that zapped you every damn time you touched a doorknob, or something. His skin crawled; and then just as abruptly, the sensation faded.

There was a heavy thud from the floor above them, and a distant scraping sound. "Five-oh?" hissed Mag, eyes darting around the large, dimly lit space.

Deano listened intently for a moment. "Naw," he said eventually. "Pigs come in the front door."

AJ snapped his fingers. He always did that when he was nervous. "Reckon its those jerks from Grove Street. Tryin' to be sneakers."

"Could be," Deano allowed. The truth was, there wasn't a lot of what you could call gang culture in Colorado Springs, but what did exist was just as inclined towards turf wars as the equivalents in cities like Los Angeles, Detroit and New York. It was just a little more low-intensity. But that said, crews like the Two-Eight didn't take any less pride in doing violence toward their rivals. Tyke had been jumped into the gang when he was twelve years old, and it had been his life ever since. If there was a concept he understood, it was the idea of *respect*; and someone talking a stroll around a piece of Two-Eight territory like the derelict house without permission was clearly an act of *dis*respect.

Mag rolled the joint between his fingers, and then finally pocketed it. He had personally been responsible for running a stolen car into the porch of a Grove Street banger's place and the resulting fatalities. "They know this is our set," he sneered.

"They here, and it's on."

"Yeah," AJ grinned.

Tyke strained to listen. Faintly, he thought he heard voices. "A couple of them? Come for a look-see?"

Deano had moved away from the pool of light cast through the warehouse window, into the deep shadows. "Don' matter who it is. Two-Eight lives here." He jerked a thumb at the wall where the gang's graffiti tags were writ large in white spray paint. "What we got issa home invasion, dog." Deano reached inside his jacket and his fist returned with a large-framed, nickel-plated revolver. "Check it, we gotta deal."

"Just four of us," began Tyke, "if there's more of them—"

AJ grunted. "You gonna puss out, Tykey?" He made a tutting noise. "Time to represent, homes."

"Get yo' gats," said Deano. "We got pest control to do."

Jade wiped her mouth and offered the water pack to the Commander. He ignored her, studying the cylindrical pod's energy output display. "Good," he said to himself. "The jump went smoothly." He shrugged off the pack on his back and opened it. "Index is almost dead-on for the co-ordinates we set." He was breathing hard from the shock of transition.

"Where is this place?" Jade took a wary step towards the grimy arched window. Through the dirt-smeared glass she could make out buildings and streets, splashes of color and what seemed like vehicles moving on a nearby highway. "I'm here..." She said it herself, as if it was important to voice the words aloud in order to set the reality of it in stone. "We're back."

The old man made a brusque gesture. "Get over here." He didn't look up from what he was doing. "Where's your weapon?"

"Do I need it?" She tapped the discreet holster on her belt. "There aren't any aliens on-planet..."

The Commander snorted. "There's more than enough to be worried about without things from outer space." Metal creaked somewhere off in the shadows and Jade froze. "More than enough," he repeated, this time in a whisper.

She activated the implant with a thought-impulse and felt her eyes prickle. The colors of the warehouse changed from puddles of darkness and weak light to a thermal landscape of blue and black. Attenuated through sheetrock walls, she saw blobs of white and red moving gingerly forward, keeping low to the floor. "Contact." She subvocalized the word, letting the implant's subdermal comlink broadcast it. Jade took out her gun and thumbed the activation stud. At the corner of her vision, she saw the Commander doing the same. By reflex, Jade found herself looking for the tell-tale glow of a symbiote inside the torsos of the new arrivals, but there were none. These were humans; nothing special.

Their body language changed as the four figures moved into the dull light. "So, what we got here?" The voice was a slow, menacing drawl. Jade saw now that they were just youths, most of them half her age at least, and they moved with affected, cocky swaggers. Each was dressed in similar clothes, sporting hats or neckerchiefs in the same colors; blue, black, white. She knew tribal insignia when she saw it. The one who spoke had a silver pistol in his hand and he made an exaggerated play at studying them. "What we got here? Grandpa and some baby doll?" The other three gave a chorus of rough sniggers. "Hey," he said to the Commander, "if you're going for a little somethin' somethin' here, you ought be inna motel, not Two-Eight's house." Jade kept her gun concealed as he looked at her. "Huh. But you don' look like no working girl."

"Easy marks..." sneered the tallest of them.

"Watch your mouth," said the Commander. "She's my daughter."

Another of the youths cackled, laughing around a crude cigarette between his lips. "Better check yo'sef, Deano. You be rude, dog."

"Shut up, Mag." Up came the revolver. "I don't give a crap what she is, meat." The leader bore his teeth at them. "You got about ten seconds to give me what you got, or else you're dead!"

"I don't think so." The Commander raised his weapon and Jade saw the snake-like curves of a zat'ni'katel. With a metallic snap, the pistol's cobra-head muzzle reared up and activated.

"Yo, AJ." The one named Mag called to the tall youth. "See that? Whas' he got there? That ain't no kinda gat."

"The word," said the Commander, "is *zat*." Without warning he flashed off two bolts from the Goa'uld pistol in quick succession; Deano, with his revolver, was hit first, and then AJ, who had an automatic. Both of them went down to the floor, jerking and twitching from the impact of the alien weapon's lightning-like energy bolts.

The remaining two broke and ran, one slipping and racing the way they had come, the other pounding toward an exit door and the rusting fire escape beyond it. In a single, seamless action Jade pivoted and thumbed her pistol's selector to low yield before releasing a dart of brilliant red light. The beam charge struck the fleeing youth in the back and washed over him, for a second lighting the room with hellish color. He fell like a puppet with its strings cut, the pulse overloading his nervous system before he hit the floor.

The last one, the youngest one, was at the stairwell when he was thrown off his feet, and went skidding down on to his backside. He had collided with something large and invisible; the kinetic impact made the prism-optic camouflage concealing the third member of their team flicker, and for a split second the youth looked up and saw the shadow of a giant insect looming over him. Predictably, he started screaming.

The Commander jerked his head. "Shut him up."

Tyke scrambled backward on his hands and tried to get back to his feet, but the icy wash of terror that hit made his legs turn to water. These weren't any Grove Street bangers out to make points—hell, he didn't know *what* they were! Some old dude and a weird-looking girl, acting like it ain't nothing, and then suddenly they're popping these freak-ass *Star Trek* laser guns... He'd seen stuff like that on TV, but that wasn't what sent him panicking like some grade school punk; it was that *thing*.

Tyke's mind was screaming that it couldn't be real even as he replayed the moment over and over, struggling to make sense of it. He'd broke along with Mag once the shooting started and tried to get away, get some backup. Made it to the stairs, almost out of there. Then he hit something, something big and fleshy, solid as a wall. Something he could see right through; or at least, it was see-through *some* of the time. Where he hit it, a patch of color spread out like an ink stain and for long, horrible seconds, Tyke saw the shape of a something that had way too many legs to be human. He caught glimmers of a fanged mouth, of mandibles, dark eyespots, claws and shiny skin like a cockroach had. Only there weren't any cockroaches that stood eight feet tall and could make themselves invisible.

The youth scrambled backwards and felt a hand on his shoulder. He turned and there was the girl with the blonde hair, holstering that freaky pistol and staring into him with cool, serious eyes. "Don't be afraid," she soothed, "he won't hurt you." Tyke opened his mouth to speak, but she shook her head. "Shh. Just listen. We need your help."

"What?" he managed, fear making his voice tight and high.

The girl brought up her hand and on the tips of her fingers he saw the flicker of light on metal. She had steel pads beneath the skin. "This will feel a bit strange," she told him gently. "Don't fight it."

"But—"

Then she touched him on his neck and Tyke felt his world evaporate around him.

"I have contact," said Jade. She cradled the youth's head with her free hand, his baseball cap falling away to the floor.

The receptor plates in her fingers found the nerve clusters in his neck and set to work. In the half-light, small trails of blood glittered on his skin where the nanite injectors entered his body. She studied him. He was young, still in his mid-teens, and with his breathing turned shallow and his eyes unfocussed, the ganger looked every inch the child he really was. "I'm searching."

"Hurry," said the Commander. "If he doesn't have what we want, we may have to wake up one of the others."

Jade shot him a look. "If I go too fast, I could cause neurological damage."

He snorted. "Kid's probably a crack-head. You couldn't mess him up any worse."

She grimaced and turned her attention back to the boy. Jade let the implant feed her thoughts through the link to the nanites she'd injected into his bloodstream. *What's your name?* Her lips never moved, but the boy heard her as well as if she had spoken aloud.

"Tuh. Tyke."

I won't hurt you, Tyke. I just need your help. My friends and I. We need your help.

"Friends?" Raw fear stuttered down the link and back into her mind, a black backwash of cold sensation. Tyke's eyes flicked to where a shape shimmered in the gloom.

That's just Ite-kh. He's with us.

"Spider!" Bits of Tyke's memories pushed at the implant link, dark and crawling sensations that threatened to overwhelm her. The alien had terrified the boy more than she had realized.

No. He's a Re'tu. I know he looks scary, but he's not a monster. He's been my friend for years. He's not from this planet, which is why we can't see him most of the time. She could have explained about the alien's unique physiology, how his kind existed in a dimensional phase-shift that rendered them invisible to humans, but there was no sense in burdening the boy with information that he wouldn't be able to process.

Jade could see Ite-kh as a glassy haze thanks to the implant's connection to her visual cortex, but she chose to block those images from reaching Tyke's mind. He was already on the edge of panic.

"No," Tyke was starting to slip away from her, falling into a murky pit of fear. "Mom..." Jade felt a sharp dart of sympathetic emotion, of razor-edged loss.

"You're losing him," snapped the Commander. "Disengage."

"No!" She said it aloud, and Tyke whimpered. "I've got it." Jade blinked back a sob in her throat and concentrated. *Your mother's gone, Tyke? I'm sorry. I lost my mom too.* She pressed gently into the boy's surface thoughts, sifting through them. Jade saw blurry images of an untidy house, the smells of cooking, stale cigarette smoke. *Is that where she lived?*

"Belongs to my sister, now. Keesha." he mumbled. "We live there. But Keesha... Never around. She works. Gotta boyfriend."

We need a place to stay, Tyke. Just for a little while. Jade threaded the nanites deeper, guiding them by thought. The microscopic machines resonated on the same subspace frequencies as the mechanism of her implant, and with care she made them block certain receptor sites in the boy's brain, cutting off the production of neurochemicals that induced fear and encouraging those that relaxed him, that made him more suggestible. *We can be friends, Tyke. Will you help us?*

"Oh. Okay." His breathing was even now. "Yeah. I'll help you." Slowly, Tyke got to his feet and blinked dreamily.

The Commander peered owlishly at the youth. "How long is that going to last?"

It was a moment before Jade answered. Direct contact, adjusting brain chemistry on so finite a scale... It took a lot out of her. She could already feel the beginnings of a tension headache at the back of her skull. "As long as he doesn't suffer any shock or serious trauma, it will be a couple of weeks before he snaps out of it."

"We won't need weeks." He glanced up as Ite-kh crossed the room, the Re'tu's invisible claws pattering quietly on the wooden floorboards. "We don't have the luxury of that much time."

Jade frowned. "He'll have nightmares for months after we've gone. It's not a precise science, messing with people's brains."

"My heart bleeds," said the Commander, brandishing his zat. "Now we have him, we don't need these three." He took aim, and Jade's face fell as she realized what he was intending.

"You're going to disintegrate them?"

He eyed her coldly. "They would have killed us without even breaking a sweat. Look at them. You think they're innocents? You never grew up seeing people like them on the streets, dealing drugs and peddling death. Trust me, I'm doing the State of Colorado a favor."

"No." She stood in front of him, and Jade heard Ite-kh rumble a warning noise in his thorax. "Just give me a few minutes. I can use the nanites to unspool some of their RNA, destroy an hour or so of their short-term memories. They'll forget they ever saw us."

"We don't have time—"

"For what?" she demanded. "We don't have time to behave like human beings? Is that what you were going to say?"

The zat retracted and the old man tucked it in a pocket. "Fine. Whatever." He turned and strode away. "Ite-kh!" He called. "With me. Let's take our new pal for a walk."

She watched the old man push Tyke toward the stairs, and felt the faint pressure of air as the Re'tu moved past her. She tuned her sight to make the insectoid visible again and saw him pause, cocking his head. Ite-kh's mouthparts released a series of clicks and hisses.

"I know," she replied quietly. "It's just… I wasn't expecting this. I thought he might be different when we got back here. Back to Earth."

The Re'tu made a rustling sound that signified sympathy and compassion in its native language. Ite-kh had been a fighter in the Commander's service for a long time, and he knew Jade's father as well as any of the men and women in the Holdfast.

"This was a mistake," she admitted. "He should never have come with us."

The alien crossed his arms in a gesture of sign-language that Jade had seen many times before, and she knew the meaning full well. *There's no turning back now.*

CHAPTER FOUR

The elevator deposited O'Neill on the main level of the SGC and he wandered out into the tube-like concrete corridor. He felt a little tired, truth be told. Jack had been up since oh-dark-thirty that morning, not because of years of ingrained Air Force training, but because he'd been unable to stop turning the matter of the Pack over in his mind. It was like one of those *Bugs Bunny* cartoons where he had an angel perched on one shoulder and a devil on the other, each one whispering things in his ears. In this case, on one side Jack had confidence and on the other mistrust. Commit to the Pack or hold them off, be friends or show them the door: the choice rolled around and around. It was a simple thing, really, but it seemed so complicated. It all came down to a question of conviction.

From Ra and Abydos and everything onwards, there were days when it felt like the entire universe was out to get humanity—and even the people they made buddies with were still a bit sniffy, like the Tok'ra. Out of all of the alien folks out there, it was only the Jaffa that Jack felt he could call friends, in any true sense of the word. *If only more people were like Teal'c and Bra'tac.* He blinked in mild surprise at his own conclusion. *Well, okay, not exactly like them. Maybe keep the honorable and trusty parts, but add a better sense of humor.*

O'Neill walked on, throwing nods to other officers as they passed him. *Seven years*, he told himself. *After seven years, am I actually starting to get tired of this?* The idea sat uncomfortably in his mind, and he felt worse about it when he realized that he was taking it seriously. A woman in a white coat—Warner's nurse, that girl called Cathy—crossed in front of him and Jack's thoughts slipped back to Janet Fraiser. It still seemed strange to him to walk into the medical bay after a sortie and not find her there with a clipboard, ready to give them the regulation post-mission exam. Jack missed her quiet, steady presence, and he knew that everyone else on the base felt the same way. *Is that why I'm feeling worn out with it all?* They had lost Fraiser months ago now, but the sense of it was still just there, below the surface. So much of what they did here at the SGC was seat-of-the-pants stuff, snatching victory from the jaws of defeat with barely seconds to spare… It was no wonder they felt like they were bullet-proof. An embattled team of people forming the thin khaki line between freedom and alien invasion, winning at all costs—and then Janet's death had shown them that they were all on a clock that could hit zero at any time. Jack frowned. Where could he go from here? Hammond and the rear echelon big hats at Space Command had been gently pressing him to accept a promotion for some time, and O'Neill's resistance to taking a higher rank felt more like inertia than it did any rational objection—but there was also the unwillingness to step back and leave his people to go into harm's way without him. *Then again…* Yeah, on some level he *was* fatigued; Janet had brought that into sharp focus for him. If he got a star pinned to his epaulets, he might actually get the chance to spend some real time on his favorite planet—*this one*. And maybe he could even think about other things, like prospects beyond the Air Force and the Stargate Program. A normal life, with a family, that kinda stuff.

Geez, listen to me. I sound like my grandmother. He took a deep breath and shook it off. Now was not the time to be dwelling on the future; he had a job to do, here and now. The Pack were still an unknown quantity, and they had to make certain of them.

The smell of fresh-brewed coffee caught his nostrils and drew Jack's attention toward a figure in the corridor. "Siler!" he snapped, forcing the sergeant to halt. Siler had a cardboard tray with two cups on it. "Coffee."

"Observant as ever, Colonel," replied the non-com. "I just came from the mess."

"Uh-huh," Jack nodded. O'Neill hadn't had the chance to

get a drink on the way in, and the scent of caffeine promised to jolt him out of the funk he was on the verge of slipping into. "I'm thinking I ought to take one of those for, uh, inspection."

Siler's face fell. "Sir, not again. You do this to me every morning."

Jack held out his hand. "C'mon, give it up."

"But Colonel…"

"Do you want me to order you to do laps around the base on one leg?"

He grimaced. "Sir, I checked the Air Force regulations handbook. You're not allowed to make me do that any more."

O'Neill gave him a look and finally Siler relented. Jack took the cup and sipped from it. "Mmm. Arabica blend, nice. Carry on." He walked on, then turned to call after the airman. "Hey, who's the other cup for?"

"Me," said Siler. "I got two because I knew you were gonna take one."

Jack smirked. "That's good, sergeant. That shows initiative, forward thinking. You ever think about taking officer training?"

"No sir," Siler replied, "I prefer to work for a living."

O'Neill took another sip. "Wiseass."

"Besides," added the sergeant as he stepped into the elevator, "you're gonna want a stiff drink."

"Now what the hell is that supposed to mean?" he asked, but the doors had shut and Siler was gone.

The answer to Jack's question wasn't long in coming. He turned into the corridor to the briefing room and found himself face-to-face with two hard-eyed men, each with near-identical buzz-cuts, the same sharply pressed dark blue suits, coiled wires from their collars leading to discreet radio earpieces and an obvious bulge beneath their jackets that indicated the presence of a service automatic. He didn't need to see the small pin on their lapels to know these guys were United States Secret Service; and the expressions on their faces were enough for

O'Neill to know that they recognized him. He gave them a level look. "You boys going to do that 'talking into your cuf-flink' thing now?"

The two men exchanged glances. "Yes," said the nearest one, and he whispered into a microphone concealed at his wrist. Jack covered his irritation with another sip of coffee and barged past them, into the briefing room. General Hammond was there, still in his blues from the Washington jaunt, and there were two more Secret Service bodyguards who looked like they came from the same mould as the ones in the corri-dor; but what made O'Neill's heart sink was the sight of the man sitting at the table—and in his chair—with a supercil-ious smile on his face.

No matter how many times he'd tried to shut down Stargate Command, discredit the people who served there, and outright ruin the lives of Jack and his friends, this man still managed to walk away without anything sticking to him; and each time he came back, he acted like he owned the damn place. It was a real effort to resist the urge to plant a fist right in the middle of his face.

"Kinsey," O'Neill said the name like it rhymed with 'scum-bag'.

"Hello, Jack," The utterly false bonhomie in the man's voice set O'Neill's teeth on edge.

"Aw, crap." Siler had been right after all.

"Colonel," warned Hammond. "After my briefing to the Commander-in-Chief, Vice President Kinsey decided that it would expedite matters if he took a more direct hand in the treaty negotiations with the Pack's representatives."

"That's just great, General…" Jack attempted to cover his initial reaction with a half-hearted lie, but it collapsed miser-ably. "Aw, crap," he repeated.

"After consultation with the International Oversight Advisory, the President has decided that we should proceed toward forming ties with these people," Kinsey spoke without looking at him. "These Pack folks are in dire need of our help and we have a God-given duty to provide whatever humanitarian assistance we can." He paused. "Obviously, given previous situations of a similar nature and the manner in which they were handled by the SGC, you can understand the President's reluctance to have this potential diplomatic endeavor go the same way."

"I have full confidence in SG-1's abilities, Mr. Vice President," said Hammond, "as should you."

"Of course," Kinsey sniffed. "but politics and affairs of state are hardly the responsibility of our military." He gave Jack a look. "That's the job of our duly elected officials."

"Yeah, that reminds me," said O'Neill, "whatever happened to that thing about a re-count on your vote ballot?"

Kinsey ignored the jibe. "I'll put it simply, Colonel O'Neill, so there's no room for misinterpretation. I am here, with the full support of the President and the IOA, to keep an eye on you. I know that you people do good work here—"

"We like to call it *saving the planet*," Jack retorted.

Kinsey kept talking as if he had never spoken. "—But you don't make national policy and you certainly don't speak for the United States of America, or for the planet Earth. I, on the other hand, am equipped to carry all those responsibilities."

"That's real big of you," noted O'Neill. "But here's my take on it. I know you, Kinsey. You don't give a damn about providing any 'humanitarian assistance'. You can smell the opportunity the Pack represent, so you want to get your fingerprints all over it. Hell, I'm willing to bet that you've already had a secret briefing with your monkeys over at the NID, to evaluate the possibility of taking the Pack's resources by force instead of trading for them." Jack saw a fractional twitch on Kinsey's face that confirmed he was right. "But mostly you're here because you think that your name on an interplanetary trade agreement would do a lot for your future aspirations. Oval Office, Big Chair aspirations, I mean."

"My fellow Americans have always understood the value of strong and compassionate leadership."

"Yeah," Jack made a face, "Well, I voted for that Martin Sheen guy."

Hammond cleared his throat, interceding before the conversation went any further. "We're going to begin preparations for a signing of the treaty here, at Stargate Command," he said. "Suj has already communicated with their ship, the *Wanderer*, and Vix has agreed in principle. But she wants to meet with the Vice President informally first. I've asked Doctor Jackson to join us as well." He nodded at O'Neill. "And she wants you to be present, Colonel."

"Really?" Jack couldn't resist flashing a smile at Kinsey. "That should be interesting."

As the colonel expected, Hammond's statement wiped the smug look right off the politician's face. "I didn't approve that. Jackson I can accept, as his expertise might have some minor application during the discussion, but him?" He jerked a thumb at the colonel. "General, you are the chosen representative of the SGC, and that should be made clear to this woman. O'Neill is surplus to requirements."

"That's harsh, Kinsey." Jack touched his chest in an oh-you-wound-me gesture. "You know how much fun we have when we get together... And I'd never miss the chance to keep an eye on *you*." He leaned closer and patted the other man on the shoulder. "And Suj? You're gonna get on like a house on fire with her. She's all the things you don't like: she's smart, opinionated, direct." Jack glanced up at the general. "Hey, do you think we could sell tickets?"

All the new arrivals got back on the long blue bus after passing through processing at the outbuilding on the perimeter of Cheyenne Mountain AFB, and it rolled away along the winding road toward the base proper. Jade sat in a window seat near the back of the vehicle, her chin propped on her wrist and her nose close to the glass. All the colors seemed so striking; the browns and greens of the trees, the perfect powder blue of the sky, the clean whiteness of the sparse clouds. She found it hard to connect her own experiences of Earth with the world she watched passing by outside. She felt dislocated by the differences, almost as if it were all something unreal, an illusion.

She brushed a length of black hair from her eyes and tucked it under her uniform hat. Jade's life had always been one of conflict, of running and fighting, an existence built on the pain of what she had lost. But now all around her, she saw people and lives brimming with *so much*, and it made her heart ache. On the way from the city, out past the streets and the teeming masses, she couldn't help but be shocked by the sheer numbers of the people. They looked well-fed and unworried, going to and fro on the errands of their lives; they were laughing and eating and talking and living, and they showed no signs of fear. They were, for want of a better description, so very ordinary; and Jade realized as she watched them pass her by that she envied them. None of them had any comprehension about what was out there, about the magnitude of threats that they lived beneath every day. None of them understood how tissue-thin their comfortable existence really was, they didn't know how easy it would be to have it all taken away from them. To lose everything they loved. To find their world in ashes. *If only I could be like you*, she told them, *if only I could live in ignorance, unlearn all the terrible things I know*. Jade wanted to yank open the window and shout at them, warn them about how precious it all was, tell them to be grateful. To be ready.

Only once in a while did she see anyone who looked like the kind of men and women she had grown up with. She glimpsed them in doorways, or huddled in alleys where they could stay out of the cold. Disheveled people with the feral look of a lifetime survivor, whose lives were nothing but conflict, day after day. People like her father.

As it always did, the thought of her parents lit the cold fire deep inside her. She knew that she should remain focused and undistracted, but being here pulled at her calm, set her off-balance more than she had expected it to. She thought of her mother, of her kind face and her warmth, and not for the first time she wondered how her father would have been if she had lived. His words to Jade, as she gathered her gear in the kitchen of the house they'd appropriated, had been terse.

"Stay on-mission, do whatever you have to. Get the job done. This is the last chance we have, girl. No going back now."

His craggy, lined face was set and firm, but she could see the lie of it. No-one else, not Ite-kh, not Tekka or Sebe'c, knew him well enough to see through the veneer of the old man's gruff façade; no-one but Jade. Coming back here to Earth had stirred up memories in the Commander that he was forcing away, dark and troubled thoughts that she saw at the edges of his eyes. She knew he would never speak of them. He was too damn stubborn, too bitter at life to show it that sort of weakness.

Jade shook off the grim train of thought and glanced down at the USAF uniform she wore. It was new and freshly pressed, and she felt uncomfortable in it; but no-one would have known that to look at her. Jade was adept at hiding her real emotions deep beneath a false mask. It was why she was one of the best operatives in the Holdfast.

The bus turned and rumbled over the spike strip that marked the inner perimeter of the base. Jade craned her neck to see the blunt tooth of rust-colored stone that was Cheyenne Mountain rising up before her.

"You new to the facility?" said a voice. She glanced forward found herself looking at a Lieutenant Colonel with a smooth grin on his lips, sitting in the seat in front of hers. He smelled of cologne. He eyed her rank tabs. "Major...?"

"Wells," she lied, dropping smoothly into the Middle American accent her cover demanded. "Hannah Wells. I've just transferred in from Germany."

"Tom Richter," he said, the grin widening. "Welcome back to the US of A. I bet you're glad to be home, huh? I'd swap bratwurst for steaks any day of the week."

She studied the insignia on his jacket. "You're with

Strategic Air Command?"

"And you're a doctor." He nodded, as if he was approving her. "In all my years in this man's Air Force I've never had a physical from someone as good-looking as you, Major."

"Just unlucky, I guess."

"Maybe my luck will change?" Jade was starting to get annoyed by his grinning and the man's oily attempts at charm. "As you're new in town, I could recommend a great place to eat. Perhaps we could—"

"Are you hitting on me, Colonel?" The bus turned into the tunnel and suddenly they were inside the mountain.

"Am I?" He chuckled. "I always think fraternization gets a bad rap. And as we're probably going to be working together—"

"I don't think so," she replied. "I'm not transferring to NORAD. I'm with the other program."

His manner changed instantly and he leaned back. "Oh. You're with those folks down in the pit, huh?" He nodded at the floor. "Project Star-Gate?" Richter sniffed disdainfully. "What the hell is that, anyhow? Something about astronomy?" Richter's lip curled into a sneer. "I heard wild stories, like you got a bunch of psychics in there, tracking down flying saucers, or some other sci-fi crap."

The bus halted and the other passengers rose to get off. Jade leaned closer to the officer and whispered in his ear. "It's all to do with *magnets*. I can't say any more than that."

The duty orders she had taken from the real Major Hannah Wells told Jade to proceed to a waiting area designated by a red line on the floor. She followed the signs, passing through vast steel doors and multiple chambers designed to protect the inner spaces of the mountain from a direct nuclear strike. There was one last security check, and she casually dropped her duty bag on the conveyor for the x-ray machine before stepping up to a flat slab the size of a household door. There were armed men in the room, each cradling a P90 submachine gun; and more discreetly, they also had sealed oval holsters that looked decidedly non-standard issue. Jade didn't have to see inside them to know they held Goa'uld zat'ni'katels. The guards, and the other people on duty in the security room, were ostensibly dressed in nondescript military fatigues. It was only the presence of two unusual patches on their shoulders that set them aside from the other USAF staff on the base. Jade glimpsed the Stargate symbol for Earth on the insignia and tried not to be obvious about it.

A non-commissioned officer with glasses looked up from a clipboard to Jade and the handful of other people waiting for final processing. "If I can have your attention please. I'm Sergeant Siler, and I'll be your guide today. If you can let me have your identity papers and orders we'll get this all put through ASAP." He beckoned the man in front of Jade. "Go ahead and stand in front of the scanner there, sir."

The officer did as he was asked. They had made a good job of making the scanning device look relatively unremarkable, but Jade knew that inside it were sensors that did much more than just look for concealed weapons or explosives. Then it was her turn, and she glanced at the x-ray tunnel as her bag went through it. Like the scanner, she had no doubt the device did much more than just peer through plastic and metal; but the problem about having countermeasures was that someone who knew how they worked could counter *them*. A small device, originally of Ancient origin, was sewn into the lining of Jade's bag and it would make the contents appear to be nothing but clothes, some toiletries and a few papers. In reality, the bag had a false compartment that concealed items of hardware which originated from worlds all over the galactic disc. A similar masking device was threaded into Jade's hat, blotting out the semi-organic masses of her implant and the nanite colonies inside her bones. *Moment of truth*, she told herself. If she set off the alarms here, the whole mission would be blown before they were even started. The scanner began to hum. Of course, there were other ways into Cheyenne Mountain, hidden access channels and vents that studded the hillside for miles around, but those were just as uncertain in their own way. Impersonating Major Wells was a high risk, high reward option, and as the Commander had said, they were way past the time for the cautious approach.

The scanner made a soft pinging sound and Siler beckoned her forward. "Thank you, major," he said, with a brief smile. "Why don't you head over to the elevator bank and I'll take you down for orientation."

It was only as Jade gathered up her bag from the other end of the x-ray tunnel that she allowed herself to relax a little. Very gently, she brushed a fingertip over a spot behind her right ear, bringing her implant back out of its dormant state to full operational capacity. She had only a few moments to send a signal; once they descended into the SGC, opportunities for communication would become much more sporadic and far more likely to be detected. The implant sent a pulse of warmth through her skin, and she sensed the faint static of the comlink through the bones of her skull.

Status? The Commander's question was blunt and thick with emotion; she could feel it leaking into the esper nanites in her brain tissue.

"I'm in," said Jade in a whisper. Siler was approaching, the last of the checks complete.

She expected the link to be severed immediately, but instead the old man spoke again. *Good luck, Jade.* And then she was alone.

"Step inside, major," said the sergeant as the elevator doors opened. "Trust me, ma'am, you don't want to take the stairs."

Carter nibbled on the sandwich with one hand and manipulated the mouse with another, working the display on her computer to separate the levels of energy distribution into their component parts. To anyone without several degrees in physics, quantum mechanics and a bunch of other related disciplines, the screen would have looked like little more than digitally generated snapshots of a rippling sea, layered one over the top of another; to Sam, they were instantly recognizable as the variant strains of particles given off by the Stargate during its normal modes of operation. Boson interactions rendered in green, neutrinos in blue, white for tau-mesons, red for chronitons... She knew the play and rhythm of energies through the gate as well as she did the words to her favorite song—which was *Strawberry Fields Forever*, although she didn't often sing it—and so it irritated her when she saw them out of balance without a concrete, discernable reason.

She sighed. There was still so much they didn't know about how the Stargates worked. Construction, for starters—how had the Ancients managed to fabricate the rings out of that weird quasi-metal naquadah? How was it even possible for the gates to gather enough power to open an interstellar wormhole, let alone maintain an event horizon and hold the things rigid? By any conventional wisdom, it would take more energy than there was in the entire universe just to punch a gateway through space-time, and yet there were the Stargates, linking worlds hundreds of light-years apart in the blink of an eye. It made her feel a bit giddy if she thought about it too much.

Some days she felt like she had a handle on the gate, and then other times... It was moments like these that made her wish she had someone to confide in, somebody who, to put it bluntly, was as smart as she was. Being the most experienced scientist in a field that was generally regarded by most people in the outside world as pure science fiction could get lonely. The only other person who could come even close to Carter's grasp on the theory of the Stargate was Rodney McKay, and it would have to get pretty serious before Sam would be willing to give that arrogant lab hack a call. But the thing was, the gate was doing things she'd never seen before—nothing that seemed immediately life-threatening, but enough to make her concerned.

She glanced up as she finished her sandwich and saw Teal'c pass the open doorway to her lab. A thought struck her and she called out to him.

The Jaffa loomed in the entrance. "Major Carter. Can I assist you?"

"Actually, maybe you can." She beckoned him over, calling up a new display panel on her screen. "It's a safe bet that you've probably been through more Stargates more times than any one of us, right?"

Teal'c nodded. "Correct. I have used the Chaapa'ai many thousands of times."

"And you've seen them malfunction."

"On extremely rare occasions." He frowned slightly. "Have you encountered a problem with the Earth gate?"

"You tell me." Sam tapped a key and the monitor switched to a low-light view of the Stargate. A date and time-code in the corner of the screen showed that the recording was from the previous evening. Carter moved her mouse pointer over a section of the gate. "Keep your eye on this area here."

It happened very quickly; a flickering glint of light that sparked over the gray metal, and then vanished without a trace. Sam ran the recording again, this time at a third of the speed. "It lasted for less than two-tenths of a second. There, and then gone. It hasn't affected the operation of the gate or any other systems, and there doesn't appear to be any alteration to the machine code of the crystal circuits inside. Have you ever seen anything like that before?"

"I have not," Teal'c admitted. "Did this… flicker originate from the gate itself?"

"It seems that way. I have a theory, but unless it happens again, there's no way to prove it." The Jaffa inclined his head, and Sam went on. "We know that the Stargates have an extra-dimensional component, because they draw energy from differential states in subspace, like the Zero Point Modules. They've got a… I guess you could think of it as a 'shadow', really, like an echo of the physical object that extends slightly into that realm, outside of normal space-time. I'm thinking this tiny surge of energy might be the equivalent of a safety valve linked to that."

"The Stargate harmlessly discharged an amount of energy it did not require."

"Exactly. But the question is, if that's a normal function of the gate, why have we never seen it before?"

"I can provide no answer for you, Major," said the Jaffa. "Perhaps I could send a signal to the Tok'ra and ask them to examine your findings."

Sam deflated a little, losing her momentum after the explanation. "Couldn't hurt, I suppose. I guess I'm just a little worried about giving the okay to resume off-world travel without an explanation. I mean, we rely on that thing week after week, but the truth is we know very little about how it actually works."

"Major," said Teal'c, "compared to the Goa'uld and the majority of the races we encounter, the Tau'ri's level of knowledge about the Stargate is extensive. Many Systems Lords have operated them for centuries without even the most cursory understanding of their function. I have every confidence you will determine the true nature of this phenomenon."

She gave a wan smile. "Thanks for the support, Teal'c, but I have to level with you… The deeper I dig into this, the more questions and the fewer answers I have."

The apple crunched loudly as Daniel took a big bite from it, eating on the move as he wandered through the base toward the laboratory complex. He'd already had to avoid two knots of Secret Service men, both times finding the suited bodyguards in intense conversation with Air Force security personnel over some minor point of protocol. Jackson had learned from Walter in the gate-room that his least favorite senator—no, scratch that, his least favorite *vice president*—was on site and already throwing his weight around. Given that Kinsey was here to grab as much of the credit for the nascent Pack agreement as he could, Daniel knew that sooner or later he would be forced to stand in the same room as the man; and given his feelings toward the politician, to which loathing would be too mild a description, Jackson wanted to make sure that he spent as much time as he could, as far as way as possible from Kinsey's line of sight. So far, so good.

For a moment, he felt a little guilty about leaving Jack O'Neill and General Hammond to deal with the creep. But only for a moment. *Sorry, fellas,* he thought to himself, *but rather you than me.*

Daniel returned to the apple as he rounded a corner to find Sergeant Siler and a striking young woman in a major's uniform coming the other way. Siler was in the middle of giving her a perfunctory orientation. "That's storage ten through twelve, and over there are the maintenance bays for the machine levels below this one," he continued.

But she didn't seem to need it; the woman appeared to know exactly where she was going. Jackson paused and self-consciously rubbed a hand over his face in case there were any apple bits clinging to his stubble. He did it without thinking, reacting automatically to the fact that, well, she was cute. The major met his gaze and a peculiar flash of emotions crossed her face. A shock of recognition, the ghost of a smile, there and then gone. Daniel blinked, suddenly certain that this woman *knew* him, even if he couldn't place her. His mind raced. *Have we met before?* She had a familiar air about her, something that he found difficult to articulate.

"Doctor," said Siler, with a nod.

"Sergeant," he replied. He offered the woman a smile. "I'm—"

"Doctor Jackson, of team SG-1," she smiled back. "It's nice to see you—" She caught herself and blinked. "It's nice to meet you. I found your monograph on the Peñasco Blanco ruins very interesting."

He was a little taken aback. "You read that? Are you an archaeologist? I'm sorry, I saw your uniform and I just assumed…"

"Major Wells has rotated in to join the medical team," explained Siler. "I'm giving her the ten-cent tour."

"I like to read," said Wells, by way of explanation. "In my line of work it's important to keep a broad spectrum of interests."

"Right, sure." Daniel nodded slowly. The more he looked at her, the more he felt like he recognized this person, but on some weird, tangential level. And, he had to admit, she had gorgeous eyes, dark hazel and deep enough to drown in. "I, uh—"

Whatever he had been about to say was interrupted by a rough crackle from a repeater speaker up on the wall of the corridor. Walter Harriman's voice issued out and brought with it the words Daniel had been hoping not to hear. "*Doctor Jackson, report to briefing room. Doctor Jackson to the briefing room.*"

"Oh." That was it; Kinsey had finally decided to yank his leash, and at the most inopportune time. "Well. Duty calls. Nice to meet you, Major Wells. I hope I'll see you around base."

"Call me Hannah," said the woman. "It was good to meet you too, Daniel."

It was only when he was going up in the elevator that Jackson realized she reminded him of Sha're.

"Can I see your clearance?" The Secret Service agent tried his best to be imposing, but Teal'c found the man's manner somewhat trying. When he didn't answer straight away, the agent blinked and spoke again. "We're conducting spot-checks because of the vice president's presence on the base."

Teal'c just looked at him and waited. He had no intention of complying with any minor fiat laid down by a man as offensive to him as Kinsey. All this he showed to the agent without moving his expression the smallest iota. The security operative had halted him in the middle of the corridor, blocking the Jaffa's path.

"The Vice President?" repeated the agent.

Teal'c remained silent. He had learned from a very early age that stillness had a disturbing effect on many people. When faced with it, most would find themselves compelled to say something just to fill the quiet, and frequently they would incriminate themselves or weaken their own positions.

"Ah. I guess you, um, probably have clearance though, right?" The agent blinked. "I mean, you wouldn't be here unless you didn't…"

And still he just looked, and said nothing.

Eventually, the agent coughed self-consciously and stepped aside. "I guess you're probably busy. I'll just, uh, I'll check you next time, okay?"

Teal'c resumed walking. He often found the Tau'ri's web of tactical and judiciary organizations to be confusing and overly segmented. The American nation, for example, had separate military forces for waging war on ground, at sea and in airborne environments, as well as groups dedicated to specific elements of overt and covert security for their citizens and national interests; for the System Lords, there were only Jaffa. They were warriors, law enforcers, whatever authority or military was needed. He glanced back at the agent. Why, for example, was Kinsey's personal guard known as 'the Secret Service' when their identities were clearly visible for anyone to see? He decided he would use the Tau'ri mechanism known as 'Google' to learn more about this apparent dichotomy.

The Jaffa's train of thought came to an abrupt halt as a tingle caught him in the torso. It was just the smallest ghost of a physical reaction, but it brought him up sharply. Teal'c held his breath and froze in place, listening. Like the last traces of a faint aroma pulled on the wind, the warrior's ingrained battle sense made him go tense. Something was not right. Carefully, he looked about the corridor, along the walls and the floor, up to the concrete ceiling over his head and down again. The reaction subsided slowly, leaving him disturbed in its wake.

It was hard for him to frame the sensation; Teal'c did not deal in absolutes, but often in what he had heard O'Neill describe as 'gut feelings'. For Jaffa, their greatest weapon was their instincts, honed by years of training and deadly battle. To some it might have seemed like a preternatural sense, but for Teal'c, it was simply the wisdom of experience — and now that experience was warning him that something was wrong.

He braced for a blow that never came. Whatever it was had passed. Another Tau'ri aphorism crossed his mind: *like someone walking over your grave*. Teal'c had failed to grasp the concept behind those words when he first heard them, but all at once he found himself understanding them perfectly.

The Jaffa became aware he was staring at an access well leading to the maintenance tiers below the level he was on. Without questioning it, letting his instincts take full reign, Teal'c grasped the ladder and followed it downwards.

"On behalf of the people of America, the President of the United States and the planet Earth, welcome to our world." The man proffered his hand and Suj looked at it for a long moment before she understood that he wanted her to mirror the gesture. It was clearly some sort of formal Tau'ri greeting, no doubt a simple way of showing a stranger that one was unarmed — and yet the historian noticed that this Kinsey kept his other hand out of sight behind his back. Suj gingerly shook his hand and found his palm to be distastefully sweaty. "It's a pleasure to meet you, Miss Suj."

"Just Suj," she explained. "Thank you for your greeting, Kinsey." She took her seat again behind the large wooden table.

"*Vice President* Kinsey," he replied, with a slight edge to the words. Clearly, rank and status was important to this one. She considered his clothes. Her theory about the colors of the Tau'ri's dress seemed to be baring out. Kinsey and the men who accompanied him all wore dark tunics open at the chest with a strange dangling piece of cloth knotted at their throats. Perhaps that was another signifier of their caste structure? She glanced across the briefing room at Jackson and made a mental note to question him about it at a later time.

"You greet me in the name of all Tau'ri?"

Kinsey threw a bemused look at one of his adjutants. "Tau-what?"

"Earth-folks," supplied O'Neill dourly. "It's what they call us."

His smile snapped back on. "I do."

"Forgive me, but what guarantee do I have of that? So far, I have seen only the walls of this facility and nothing of your homeworld. For all I know, we may not even be on your planet."

Kinsey arched his fingers and leaned forward. "Politics is about trust, Suj. We've trusted you by bringing you to Earth. You have to trust us by accepting my word."

O'Neill made a strangled coughing noise and reached for a glass of water. "Sorry," he husked. "Don't mind me."

Suj thought for a moment; even a blind person would have been able to pick up on the tension between O'Neill, Jackson and this 'vice president', and the fact that she was being allowed to see it heartened her. Her initial impression of O'Neill and his cadre was one of honesty. They seemed to be very close to the surface in thought and deed, traits that were valued by every clan of the Pack. Kinsey, on the other hand, struck her immediately as enclosed and ruled by artifice. "We have little use for what you might call politics," she told him.

Kinsey blinked. "I'm sorry, I thought you were an ambassador? Is that not a political position?"

"I am a historian," she explained, "a student of cultures and social sciences."

The man's face darkened and he shot a brief but venomous look at O'Neill. "It seems there was a miscommunication." When Kinsey looked back at Suj, his expression was patronizing. "Of course, it's delightful to meet a scientific mind from another world, but I think it might be best if we adjourn until your leaders arrive." He stood up and brushed a hand down his tunic in a dismissive manner.

"Suj is here as an official representative of the Pack," said

Jackson. "She's not a tourist."

"Of course," he allowed, "but there are matters of state which I'm sure can only be discussed leader to leader."

"What do you do?" said Suj, studying Kinsey.

"Do?" He paused. "I'm a politician. I'm an official of the United States Government, elected by a majority to be their representative."

"And what about the minority who did not elect you? Do you speak for them?" Suj leaned forward. "Is that all that you do? Speak?"

Kinsey bristled. "It's a very important role. I don't know how things are in your culture, but—"

"In the Pack, every adult serves several roles in order to keep our fleet alive. I am a historian, but I am also an engineer, a pilot and a tutor."

The other man sniffed. "How do you keep order without a government? How do your people know what to do?" He turned away. "Even the most primitive societies have some kind of law."

Suj smiled a little, ignoring the implied slight. "We trust our people to do what is right. We don't impose upon them. That is the Goa'uld way, and we rejected them."

Kinsey eyed her. "That sounds like anarchism."

"I would call it freedom."

O'Neill glanced at Jackson and threw a nod in Suj's direction. "I'm liking these guys more and more."

Airman Fong backed out of the maintenance room and kicked the door closed with his foot, being careful to keep his cargo of boxes level. They were piled, three-high, from his waist to his neck, full of equipment and too damn heavy. He puffed and turned around, walking stiffly into the corridor. The light levels in this part of the base were lower than those on the upper tiers where there were more active areas and passageways in constant use. It was some energy-saving initiative dreamed up by bean-counters at the Air Force accountancy offices, invented by men who'd never had to lug boxes of obsolete 1950s vintage hardware back and forth, running the risk of tripping over and falling flat on their faces because it was too dim to see places where the floor was uneven. Fong's knees still ached from the last time he'd done it.

The airman blew out a breath and started to make his way toward the elevator at the far end of the corridor. He got about ten feet before he saw the figure. ·

It was a guy, a big guy in a crouch, peering into one of the floor-level air vent ducts. Fong picked out standard-issue olive drab trousers, boots, a black t-shirt and thick, tawny arms. "Hey, uh, what's up?" he managed, pressing his chin to the lip of the top-most box.

The figure turned and spared him a glance. Fong saw the glitter of a gold-colored brand in the middle of the man's forehead. The airman came to a halt when the man locked eyes with him. He had steel in his gaze; it was a look that told him to shut the hell up and stay where he was.

Fong hesitated. You couldn't serve at the SGC, even as a lowly airman first class like he was, and not know who the Big T was. Not that anyone ever would have dared to say that to his face. Fong had only seen the man—well, alien actually, if what he heard was true—now and again, mostly moving through the corridors with cool purpose or sitting in the mess chowing down on enough food for six guys. Richardson over in corrosion maintenance told him that there was a pool run by Master Sergeant Riley down in the quartermaster's office, where the guys could bet on him. Like, if he'd say 'indeed' to someone, or for the big payout, if he'd actually crack a smile. To be honest, Fong never went in for that sort of thing, partly because he was never very lucky, but mostly because he suspected the big man would not be pleased if he found out he was the subject of such activity.

Quietly, the guy got to his feet and ran his fingers over the wall stanchions. Fong could swear that the man was actually sniffing the air, like a hunting dog. The boxes in his hands

were getting heavier by the second, and despite his better judgment, the airman felt compelled to speak. "Uh, sir? Is there
a problem?" Technically, Fong didn't have to call the man
'sir' as he was classified as an allied civilian auxiliary, but he
wanted to stay on his good side.

"Airman," came the reply. "Have you witnessed anything
unusual in this area?"

"Unusual?" repeated Fong. *You mean, aside from you skulk-
ing around down here?* "Nothing, sir. I've been in and out a
whole bunch of times." The airman shifted his load. Was this
a drill, maybe? Or worse, the real thing? Richardson had
all these stories about how weird stuff happened on this base
almost every week, like time warps or alien invasions or intelligent computer viruses, but Fong hadn't seriously believed him.
*I mean, come on. Folks say this guy is from another planet, but
he just looks like a linebacker with expensive taste in tattoos.*

"Curious," said the big man, more to himself than to the airman. "For a moment, I thought I sensed…" Then he shook it
off and came quickly to his feet.

"Is anything wrong?" The guy looked pissed, to be sure, and
Fong wanted to make sure it wasn't anything that he'd done.

"I was mistaken," he replied, and walked away. "There is
nothing down here."

"You got that right," said Fong, breaking into a run to follow him into the elevator. He made it, panting, and let the
boxes down on the floor as the doors closed after them. The
car began to move, and the airman rubbed at his hands. "So.
You're from, uh, outer space, right?"

Teal'c eyed the small man. "Indeed."

She waited a full five minutes until after the airman and the
Jaffa warrior had departed before she moved from her concealment. As the Commander had warned, Teal'c was the most
serious threat to the operation she was likely to encounter, and
for long moments she was afraid to move in case he returned
without warning. Finally, she slipped from the cover of one of

the other storage rooms and returned to her mission. She was surprised how easy it had been to get this far without encountering any serious challenges.

Jade had imagined Stargate Command as some kind of impregnable fortress, unassailable by any intruder or spy intent on doing harm. But the truth was rather less impressive. To be sure, they did have state-of-the-art security systems, monitoring devices, even scanners like the detector up above that used non-terrestrial elements of technology to search out the more exotic threats; but even these were overcome by the equipment she had brought with her.

In many ways, she had an unfair advantage. Most infiltrators would not have had the same encyclopedic knowledge of the SGC's layout that she did. Detailed maps of the corridors and service access channels of Cheyenne Mountain were all there in her implant's data buffer, imposing themselves gently on to her visual cortex. They showed her fields of vision from internal security cameras, the operational ranges of radiation sensors, even the structure of the latching pins in the mechanical locks. She could have found her way around blindfolded.

If anyone had been watching her, they would have seen Major Hannah Wells, now dressed in a more basic duty uniform, batting at the air as if she were swatting at a nagging insect; from Jade's point of view, the space before her was filled with oval display windows, which she could move or manipulate like icons on the primitive computer screens throughout the base. She paused to layer them closed and then walked briskly under the dull eye of a camera. Like the dozen other monitors she had passed to get from the infirmary to the maintenance levels, Jade waited until the sweep pattern turned the camera the other way before she slipped beneath it. The woman planted her fingertips to a data cable feeding from the unit and released a small paste of pre-programmed nanites. There was a faint fizzing noise as the micromachines merged through the plastic sheathing and into the fiber-optic beneath. They would layer a ghost image over the live feed from the camera that would make the corridor seem completely empty.

At the far end she found the open access grille waiting for her. Even with her enhancements, Jade would not have been strong enough to be able to shift it on her own. "Thanks," she said to the air. "This won't take long."

She shrugged off her lab coat, dropped down and slid into the shaft. A warm breeze that smelled of stale machine oil billowed past her, on its way up toward the vents that dotted the sides of the mountain. It was poorly lit inside, but a tensing of her eye muscles made Jade's optic nerves reconfigure themselves to give her a monochrome, low-light view of things.

Working quickly, she opened her shirt and removed the flexible device that she had concealed there. It unfolded into a five-petalled flower, each segment inflating slightly. The five sections were spongy with the fluids inside them. In isolation, the liquids were inert, but in a mixture they became a horribly lethal thermochemical explosive. When triggered, the liquid payload would detonate with the power of a small tactical nuclear charge; this was largely due to the energy-enhancing capacity of a naquadria vial in the center of the device. The refined form of the alien super-metal was quite deadly when applied with care and precision.

Molecular adhesives on the back of the bomb secured it to the inside of the vent shaft. If the specifications of the base were correct—and of course they were—the full detonation of the device would turn an area maybe a quarter of a mile wide into a sphere of boiling gaseous plasma. The resultant thermal shockwave and implosion would then cause the core of Cheyenne Mountain to collapse in on itself, most certainly destroying the SGC and everyone in it. She tapped a touch-sensitive spot on the surface of one panel and it illuminated with a soft white light. A string of Goa'uld alphanumeric symbols appeared, blinking and changing. Jade had a wristwatch but she didn't need to look at it—the implant gave her an innate and always accurate sense of time. She had just over nine hours before the countdown reached zero.

Jade took her hand away from the bomb and found that it was shaking. With care, she extracted herself from the vent shaft and gathered up her lab coat, leaving the access grille open behind her. After a moment the anxiety subsided and she walked back along the dimly lit corridor, staying to the shadows. She was back in the infirmary before anyone had noticed she was missing, just in time for Doctor Warner to request her help with a lieutenant who had tripped and broken his wrist.

Jade gave the lieutenant a winning smile and set to work dressing his injury with slow, deliberate care.

CHAPTER FIVE

"Nice jacket," said Jack, with an arched eyebrow. "Armani?"

Daniel's lip curled. "Are you kidding? On government pay?"

O'Neill frowned at Jackson's neat attire, flicked a fleck of lint from the cuff of his service dress uniform and cast a look around the gate-room. An honor guard of Marines flanked the embarkation ramp, and behind them were a cadre of Secret Service agents. Kinsey had made sure he was directly at the foot of the ramp, leaving SG-1, General Hammond and Suj to one side. Military flags crowded around the edges of the chamber and waiting patiently for Kinsey's word were a media crew with video and still cameras at the ready to capture the moment. "Look at this," Jack said out the side of his mouth, "he's brought the whole dog-and-pony show. I'm surprised he didn't get a brass band down here as well."

"He tried to," offered Carter. "Walter told me. But they couldn't get security clearance in time."

"What? Did they think the Trust would sneak somebody through hidden in a tuba?" Jack blew out a breath. "Hey, I'm pretty good with a kazoo. You think Kinsey would go for that?"

The inner ring of the Stargate rumbled around its axis as gusts of steam puffed from the support brackets. The mechanism ratcheted to a sudden halt and another of the orange arrowheads around the perimeter flared brightly.

"*Chevron six encoded,*" Sergeant Harriman's voice issued from a repeater on the wall.

"Are you rolling?" Kinsey snapped at the camera crew. "Make sure you're rolling. I want a profile shot of me against the Stargate when it opens."

Jack waited until the moment the seventh chevron was rotating into place and called out. "Oh, Mister VP? You've got something on your tie."

Kinsey looked down at his shirt just as the wormhole formed, ensuring that he was facing the wrong way when the dramatic flash of blue-white radiation lit the chamber.

Daniel rolled his eyes. "Jack, I think it might be a federal crime to torment the Vice President of the United States."

"Decorum, people," broke in General Hammond.

"Yes, sir," said O'Neill, coming smartly to attention

Through the rippling pool of the open gate came Vix, Ryn and Koe, along with a couple of vigilant-looking types who had to be bodyguards. Kinsey recovered well and puffed out his chest. "Welcome to Earth," he began.

"Thank you," said Vix, and walked right past him, coming to a halt in front of O'Neill and the others. The Pack leader gave Suj a measuring stare. "We came as you instructed. Have they treated you well?"

Suj nodded. "As well as we would have treated them, if our roles had been reversed."

"A fair comment." He nodded to Jack and glanced around. "This is an austere sight. Not what I expected."

"Well, we've got punch and ice cream in the meeting room. It's not the Ritz or anything, but—"

"Vix!" Kinsey called out the man's name and moved smoothly to interpose himself between the Pack leader and the colonel. "I'm Vice President Kinsey. I'm the senior official here." He shot Jack a poisonous look, which Jack returned as a smile.

Vix looked at Kinsey, then to Suj, who gave him a shallow nod. With her endorsement, he finally gave the politician more than a cursory glance. "You rule the Tau'ri?" He said it with an air of obvious doubt. Vix reminded Jack of a steelworker or a farmhand, one of those big, leathery guys who'd worked every day of his life doing hot and back-breaking labor, while Kinsey seemed thin and spindly in comparison.

"Some of them, in a manner of speaking," came the reply. "I'm here to represent the interests of Earth and her peoples."

"We need grain," Vix said bluntly. "Are you going to trade it to us," and he looked back at the Stargate, "or are you going to waste our time?"

Kinsey showed a plastic smile. "Making new allies is never a waste of time. I'm sure we have much to offer each other."

"Definitely," added Ryn, from behind the other man. "This meeting represents a historic opportunity for the Pack."

"That remains to be seen," said Vix.

Jack's lip curled as he watched Kinsey place a comradely hand on Vix's arm, the gesture ringing falsely. "I asked your people here, because I have a heartfelt hope that we, the people of Earth, can help you overcome the trials that you currently face. And in turn, I believe that you will be able to enrich our culture, and help us in our ongoing battle to rid the galaxy of the threat of the Goa'uld. If I can do that, I will sleep better knowing that I was able to forge a bond between our two nations."

Daniel shot O'Neill a look and Jack knew exactly what he was thinking. *He's already making this look like it was all his idea.*

Kinsey gestured ahead. "Please. If you'll come this way? We can get to know each other better."

"If you insist." Vix spared Jack a nod and followed Kinsey's little circus, with Suj and the other Pack following behind.

"We're not going to let Kinsey have them to himself, sir?" said Carter quietly.

Hammond answered before Jack could frame a reply. "I believe this meeting requires a military presence, no matter what the vice president thinks, don't you?"

"Couldn't agree more, sir," said O'Neill. "I think Major Carter and Doctor Jackson should also bring their insight as well."

"But we'll have to tread carefully," said Daniel. "We can't let Kinsey walk all over this, but at the same time we can't undermine a representative of the American government in front of a potential ally. They'll see it as weakness."

"This *is* going to be a fun day, isn't it?" Jack noted, with fake delight. He glanced at Teal'c. The Jaffa had not spoken since they arrived in the gate-room, and he had kept himself to the edge of things during the arrival. At first O'Neill thought it might be the big guy's attempt to minimize any reactions from the Pack toward his former life as a First Prime, but now he gave him a second look Jack could tell he was distracted by something. He stepped closer to his friend. "T? What's up?"

"I will not join you in the briefing room, O'Neill. I… I have concerns."

"About the Pack and their whole anti-Jaffa thing? I'm not going to have them freeze out one of my guys. Hammond was right before, they've gotta learn to hate the game, not the player."

"No," Teal'c shook his head. "This is a different matter."

Jack folded his arms. "Let's hear it."

Teal'c frowned. Jack knew the look. The Jaffa didn't like it when he didn't have all the answers. "While the Pack are on base, there is an ongoing security patrol in progress, correct?"

"Yeah. The Pentagon set up the directive after that thing with the Ashrak assassin…"

"I will join them."

The seriousness in the Jaffa's eyes gave Jack pause. "Come on, big guy, what's going on here? If you think the base has been compromised, then say it. We'll get Hammond to lock this place up."

There was a long moment before Teal'c spoke again. "I am not certain. I have…a 'gut feeling'."

Jack frowned. "All right. You go do what you have to do to get your head straight, or go get some Pepto Bismol from Doc Warner, whatever works. I got enough to worry about today without adding a jittery Jaffa to the list."

"It is probably nothing," Teal'c said as he walked away; but O'Neill had known the man long enough to realize that his 'nothing' often meant 'something'.

The airman with the rifle waved her to one side as the procession of new arrivals came down the corridor, and Jade dutifully stepped into a doorway to allow the group to pass. The Secret Service agents and the handful of USAF military police officers buffered the members of SG-1 and the four representatives of the Pack. She scanned the faces of the people from the *Wanderer*, blink-clicking still images for storage in the implant's memory core. Later, if the opportunity presented itself, she might take the time to go over them one by one, and compare their identities with what data they had back at the Holdfast. Hard information on the Pack was sketchy, and after what had happened in the chaos of the collapse, there had been little time to investigate them. She tried to turn away before she caught sight of the others, afraid that she would stare; she was too slow. Daniel Jackson glanced at her and he gave Jade a nod and a half-smile. She returned it, slightly surprised that it came so easily and so truthfully. Jade covered by staring down at the clipboard in her hand until the rest of SG-1 were gone. A tingle of fear churned in the pit of her stomach. She had the horrible sensation that she would be discovered if they looked at her for long enough, if they stared at her and *concentrated*. It was the secret terror that lurked in the heart of every spy, that somehow her false disguise would peel away beneath their combined scrutiny. It took a distinct effort for Jade to walk away and not look back to Jackson and the others. She wanted to *know* them, to be able to speak with them and see them for who they were; but extended contact risked exposure, and exposure meant failure.

Jade walked on, back to the infirmary. The bomb would explode in just over four hours, timed to coincide with the conclusion of the treaty meeting.

Sam found herself sitting directly opposite Ryn, and she tried her best to give the man a polite smile, but he had a look about him that made her wonder if he was really paying attention to the meeting at all. Ryn's manner seemed different from the first time they met, his brusque and slightly arch tone now muted. She put it down to nerves. After all, previously they had been on the Pack's turf, and now they were on SG-1's. Perhaps Ryn was just one of those people who couldn't hack an away game. She sighed inwardly. *Great. I'm picking up the colonel's habit of making ice hockey references.* Carter glanced around and caught Koe's eye.

He nodded to her. "The boy from the canal is well," he said, in a low voice. "I thought you would like to know."

"Yes, thank you. I'm glad to hear it."

At the head of the table, in the seat that General Hammond usually took as his own, Kinsey tapped his finger on the wood and cleared his throat. "Ladies and gentlemen," he began, addressing the camera crew by the window as much as the rest of them, "today marks a historic moment. The coming together of Earth and the tribes of the Pack."

"We prefer to be known as clans," said Suj.

"Clans, of course," Kinsey smiled, moving smoothly over the woman's correction. "Our explorers have told us of your incredible technological marvels." He nodded off-handedly at O'Neill, Carter and Jackson. "We hope you will be willing to share them with us."

Before he could take another breath, Vix dug in a pocket and produced a flat oval plate that shimmered with strings of text. "These are our needs and our offer." He slid the device down the table to Kinsey, who looked at it with mild alarm.

"I see," said the politician, although to Carter it was clear he couldn't.

"You *can* read the Goa'uld language?" asked Koe.

Kinsey pushed the device towards Daniel. "I have people to do that for me," he replied.

Jackson picked up the plate and Sam leaned closer to get a better look at it. It resembled a palmtop computer, but the construction of it was an odd mix of metallic frames and flexible membranes. Daniel found control icons and paged through the data. "It's soft," he said to her. "Feels like it's made out of some kind of gel."

Carter spotted bubbles moving through the matrix behind the screen. "It's got a liquid component." She looked at Vix. "You use fluids in your computing devices?"

"Some," he replied. "That unit is of Calaian origin, and liquiform processors are a Calai technology."

"I've never seen that before," Sam admitted.

"Fascinating," said Kinsey, drawing the room's attention back to himself. "We have much to learn from one another."

Jackson was silent for a moment as he reviewed the data. Suj had already given them a rough idea of what the Pack wanted and the slow nodding of Daniel's head told Sam that he wasn't finding anything that raised a red flag; but Carter couldn't keep her eyes off the data device. If this was an example of the hardware they had available to trade, she couldn't wait for the opportunity to find out what made it tick.

"So," said Kinsey, steepling his fingers before him, "let's talk about a treaty."

The elevator doors rumbled open and Teal'c stepped briskly forward, one hand resting on the grip of his P90, the other directing a flashlight beam into the darkened corners of the maintenance level.

Three men in duty battle gear followed him warily. They carried their weapons at rest, although the tension radiating from the Jaffa warrior was clearly making them apprehensive. The patrol leader, Lieutenant Everitt, drummed his fingers on the holstered Beretta pistol at his belt and looked at Teal'c without trying to make it too obvious.

The Jaffa stopped and turned to face him. "You have a question, Lieutenant."

Everitt nodded. "Yeah, I do. We already ran a sweep of this tier an hour ago, and it was clear, no-one here but an airman shifting boxes. With all due respect, you pulled us off our patrol pattern to come back here."

Teal'c detected a slight air of annoyance in the man's tone. He was well aware of the effect he had on members of the Tau'ri, that some of them found him difficult to accept because he had no rank or official status within their hierarchy; but he did not have the time or the inclination to consider the lieutenant's issues with taking his orders. Almost from the moment he had risen that morning, Teal'c had been ill at ease. An irritatingly indefinable sensation gripped him, a tension, a tightness in his nerves like the echo of adrenaline rush after a battle. Something did not feel *right*, but definition of what that something was escaped him. It was as if there was a shadow just at the edge of his vision, but whenever he turned to give it his full attention, it was gone; a sound heard distantly, too faint to be sure if it were real or just the wind. It nagged at the Jaffa, like a splinter beneath his skin. "Search the tier again," he said firmly, unwilling to voice such ephemeral concerns to the airman.

"But weren't you down here once already as well?" Everitt pressed. "The guy working here, Fong, he said you—"

"Search it again." Teal'c didn't raise his voice, he just gave the lieutenant a steady and unblinking stare.

After a second, Everitt broke his gaze and looked at the other men. "You heard the man. Do it again. Walker, go with him. Albrechtsen, you're with me."

Teal'c was already walking away, musing on his disquiet. In the past, as a host bearer for a larval Goa'uld, the alien symbiote granted him some measure of preternatural acuity, an awareness of threat, a sharpening of senses beyond those of ordinary men. That time was long past now, the creature dead and his body's immune system bolstered in its place by the tretonin enzyme—and yet still a measure of the creature's unique biochemistry remained in him, imprinted on Teal'c's genetic structure. Was it some remnant of that he felt now, pushing at the edges of his mind? The Jaffa forced the thought away. If these feelings of unease continued, he would have no other choice than to submit himself to the SGC's medical team for an examination, to be sure that there was no other influence acting upon him.

He walked slowly and carefully, examining every dark corner, each place where a threat might lurk. Before, Teal'c had ignored his better judgment and walked away. Now he realized that his first instincts had been correct. Something had been down here, something that left a trail he could only faintly detect, and the more he considered it, the more certain he became.

And there. He spotted it instantly, halting in place with such suddenness that the airman following him gave a sharp gasp. There were a series of ventilation grilles set close to the floor, and one among them was resting slightly open. Teal'c moved around it in a semi-circle, dropping into a crouch. The sense of wrongness was stronger here. He could almost smell it. The Jaffa panned the flashlight back and forth, but there were no obvious signs of any tripwires or traps connected to the vent. He lowered himself and leaned close to the securing bolts that should have held the vent in place. The tops had been sheared off by a force of great strength, the steel twisted and torn so that the hatch could be opened. A cursory search would have missed such a small detail. "Get Everitt," he told the airman. "Now."

"What is it, sir?" said Walker.

Teal'c released his grip on the P90 and pressed himself flat to the concrete floor; the grille was just large enough that he could press through the space and into the vent shaft beyond. He heard Walker speaking into his radio as he snaked forward. The Jaffa moved with care until his entire bulk was inside the shaft. Immediately, he was aware of the glow, a small cold pool of color an arm's length above him. Teal'c turned his flashlight on the object fixed there and what he saw made his jaw harden. He extended a hand and ran it over the surface of the flower-shaped device. It was cool to the touch and it gave a little under the pressure of his fingertips. A thin sliver of crystal served as a display, and on it a march of digits were slowly falling.

"What are you doing in there?" Everitt's voice came up through the open vent.

Teal'c ignored the question, a frown deepening on his fore-head. Elements of the device's technology seemed familiar to him, but others were wholly alien. "Inform Major Carter that her presence is required here immediately." The low rumble of the words echoed along the air shaft. "I have located what appears to be an alien explosive device concealed in this chamber."

There was a pause from out in the corridor; then he heard the sound of heavy booted feet at a run.

"But you're not a hundred percent sure if the objects you found actually are of Ancient origin?" Jackson couldn't help but keep a hopeful tone in his voice.

Koe answered his question. "Our knowledge of the gate-builders is admittedly quite sparse, but we know enough to recognize their artifacts when we see them."

"We won't give them up to you for nothing," insisted Ryn. "Trade in equal or greater value is expected in return."

"Naturally," noted Hammond.

"Hey, we have flexible terms, lay-away, that kinda thing," said O'Neill. "Maybe we can work out a 'buy-now, pay-later' deal."

Vix snorted in mild amusement. "A substantial down payment would suit us better."

Carter cleared her throat. "I've taken the liberty of having some goods assembled for you to take back through the Stargate, food packs and medical supplies. You could think of them as free samples…"

Kinsey eyed Sam, and Daniel could see that he wasn't pleased she'd been acting on her own initiative. "Consider that a gift of the United States government," he appended, quick to put his own stamp on the donation.

He glanced at Suj and saw his own expression reflected there. Despite the vice president's continued approach of patronizing the Pack as if they were some tribe of unsophisticated nomads, the woman could clearly see through the man's intentions. She met Daniel's gaze and smiled slightly.

Hammond nodded to himself. "If I might suggest, then, that we proceed to—"

The general's words trailed off as Sergeant Harriman pushed his way past Kinsey's bodyguards and into the room. Daniel saw the look on Walter's face and felt his blood run cold. Harriman moved quickly to Hammond's side and whispered something in his ear; in turn, the general looked directly at Carter. Then he was getting to his feet, a familiar but no less unwelcoming expression of concern on his face. "Mr. Vice President, ladies and gentlemen, if you will forgive me, there's a situation that requires my immediate attention." He beckoned Sam. "Major, you're needed."

"Yes sir." Carter sprang up, sensing the same implied threat.

"General?" Jack's question hung in the air. *What's the problem?*

Hammond threw him a nod. "Look after our guests, colonel."

"General?" repeated Kinsey, his face reddening. "General Hammond!"

But they were already out the door and gone. Jack gave a wan smile that didn't reach his eyes. "So," he said with false good humor, "You guys like sports?"

Daniel looked out over Koe's shoulder to the Stargate beyond the windows, sitting inert and at rest.

Sam used the access hatchway a few levels above the tier where Teal'c had entered the air shaft, climbing through a double set of doors to a mesh plate walkway. A murky light illuminated the interior of the circular bore, the weak, watery glow spilling from buzzing sodium emergency lamps. Carter glanced down and blinked as her eyes got used to the gloom. She saw the Jaffa on another ledge several feet below her, rendered in shadows from the backwash of his flashlight beam.

"Ah, dang." There was no easy way to descend; it would just be hand-over-hand down the maintenance ladder. "Teal'c!" she called out. "I'm on my way to you!"

"Very well, Major," His voice echoed. "I recommend quickness."

"Quickness. Right." Sam started down the rungs as fast as she dared. "And don't look up," she added as an afterthought."

"Why?"

She fumed a little. "For modesty's sake. I'm wearing a skirt." Carter hadn't had the luxury of changing out of her service dress uniform; she'd simply shrugged off the uniform jacket and handed it to Walter before donning a heavily-laden gear vest. The rest of her clothing was hardly designed for this sort of thing. *And I'd just got it laundered as well. Still, that's the Air Force life. Aim High.*

In a few moments she was down with him, the ladder depositing her on the other side of the gantry. Sam had a penlight clipped to her shoulder and she flicked it on, pulling out a portable scanner with the other hand. "How'd you find this?"

"A lucky guess," Teal'c deadpanned.

"Not so lucky," she replied. Sam felt a chill as the sensor unit presented her with data on the energy and chemical components running through the device. She glanced at him. "Bomb?"

"Bomb." He nodded. "I had hoped I was mistaken."

Sam peered at the timer. "If I'm reading this right, we have about, what? Thirty minutes?"

"Closer to twenty-five, Major. Not enough to completely evacuate Stargate Command."

"We can still try." She took a deep breath and toggled her radio. "Carter to Hammond. Sir, I can confirm Teal'c's estimation. We're looking at a compact, high yield explosive device with what seems like an enhanced naquadria component."

She could picture the general's face as he took that in. *"What's the destructive potential, Major?"*

"Major is right, sir. I'd say if this thing goes, we'd lose the SGC for sure."

"Copy that." He paused for a moment. *"Can you disarm it?"*

"I think so…" She peered at the device, watching the ebb and flow of power through its patchwork of circuits. "It's not one of those 'cut the red wire' things, General, but the technology is familiar. Confidence is high, sir." Even as she said it, Carter felt her throat turn dry. This was not how she had expected her day to go.

"Proceed," said Hammond. *"We'll dial the Alpha Site and initiate an emergency departure protocol."*

"Roger." Sam looked to Teal'c and he nodded.

"Carter." The general spoke again. *"I don't want any heroics, Major. If you and Teal'c can't get that thing deactivated in time, I'm ordering you to abandon the attempt and get up to the gate. Am I clear?"*

"As a bell, sir. Carter out." She pulled a set of probes from her pocket and handed the scanner to the Jaffa.

"It will take us ten minutes to reach the gate from here," he told her.

Sam set to work. "Will it?" She gave him a loaded look. "We better work fast, then, huh?"

Gently, Carter levered away a section of the device's outer casing and peered inside. It was a peculiar mixture of seething bio-organic components and elements that resembled metals and crystals. "Who made this thing?" she said to herself.

"A question I will be most interested in learning the answer to," noted Teal'c, *"after* we have rendered it inert."

Doctor Warner crossed the infirmary with a half-smile on his lips and Jade gave him a tepid grin in response. "Is something wrong, Doctor Wells?"

Jade schooled her expression. "I'm not sure I follow you."

Warner pointed at the silent emergency siren and the alert lamp beneath it, high on the wall above them. "You keep looking up there. And I thought I heard you talking to someone earlier."

She looked away, faking embarrassment. "Oh, I'm sorry! It's a nervous habit I have, I talk to myself while I'm working. And the other thing, I was… Just staring into space, really. Sometimes I just drift off when I'm thinking about things." Jade resisted the urge to glance at the lamp again. The first tremors of concern were starting to ripple across her thoughts. If something didn't happen soon, she would be forced to expedite events herself.

"Oh. Fine." He flashed his weak smile again. "Well. We all have our habits, don't we?" He sniffed and patted his pockets. "Ah. I left my watch on the nightstand. Do you know what time it is?"

Warner had barely finished speaking when the alert siren blared, the red emergency condition light strobing into life. He started with a visible shock. Jade threw a look over her shoulder, relief in her eyes. "It's time," she said, although Warner couldn't hear her over the klaxon.

"Attention, all personnel," Harriman's voice issued out of every speaker and repeater across the entire SGC. *"Condition Black Alert Status. Initiate critical systems shutdown. Proceed to evacuation and egress stations immediately. Dialing of the Alpha Site will commence in sixty seconds. I repeat, Condition Black. This is not a drill."*

"What in God's name does that mean?" demanded Kinsey, bolting from Hammond's chair.

O'Neill fought down the immediate surge of alarm that came with the announcement and forced himself to keep a calm expression. "It means we're going to take a walk. Don't worry, it's just like a fire drill."

Kinsey's men were already speaking urgently into their

radios. "In the middle of a diplomatic engagement?" The vice president sneered. "I want an explanation now, colonel, this very second!"

"You and me both," Jack retorted, his thin measure of tolerance for the politician evaporating. "Vix, if you and your people will come with me, we'll get you out of here." From the gate-room beyond, the sound of the dialing sequence reached his ears.

"Are we in danger?" snapped Vix.

"Probably," admitted O'Neill. "Hammond doesn't usually push the red button unless it's a big deal... But trust me, we'll get you to the Alpha Site and—"

"What is this 'Alpha Site'?" Koe broke in. "We agreed to come here, not go elsewhere."

"It's a Tau'ri colony," explained Daniel, frowning. "We have another facility like this one on the planet."

"And what awaits us there? If this is a ruse of some sort..." Koe retorted.

Kinsey was talking over him. "I'm not going anywhere, especially to some alien planet on the other side of the galaxy!"

"Sir," one of the Secret Service agents spoke up, pressing his finger to his radio earphone. "Confirmation. An explosive device has been discovered inside the base perimeter. Sir, we have to get you out now."

"There's a *bomb*?" Kinsey blurted, and Jack felt the tension in the room jump by a factor of ten. Suddenly everyone was talking at once, the vice president quickly backtracking on his not-going-anywhere statement, Koe and Vix and the rest of the Pack contingent snapping at one another, Daniel trying his best to calm them all down.

Then the Stargate opened with a crash of displaced air and an abrupt flare of color. The noise made everyone jump and Jack took the initiative, jumping on the momentary pause. "Hey!" he yelled. "We got a situation here, ladies and gents, and we have a plan for these things! A calm and orderly fashion, you know how it's done." He stabbed a finger toward the open gate. "One exit, no waiting!"

"We demand to be returned to Golla IX," growled Vix.

"Fine, no problem," Jack said briskly, "Daniel, why don't you go with the Pack and make sure they gate to wherever they wanna go once they're safe at the Alpha Site."

Jackson didn't quibble, he just nodded. "Got it." He beckoned the visitors toward the door. "This way, please."

"And as for you, Kinsey…" Jack gave the other man a hard look as the off-worlders left the room. "It's a couple thousand stairs between here and daylight." He jerked a thumb at the ceiling. "If you get started now, you might make it in a few hours, depending on how fit you are."

The politician was a little paler than usual. "O'Neill, if you've rigged this to make me look like a fool…"

"Oh yeah, Kinsey, it's all about *you*, isn't it? Like I'm going to screw over a major diplomatic effort just to get at you…" He made a tutting noise. "If you don't believe Agent Buzzcut over there, then by all means you're welcome to stick around until something goes boom. Otherwise, get your butt through the gate and outta my way!"

"What the hell kind of operation is Hammond running here?" fumed the vice president. "Don't you people know what security is? If this treaty falls apart because of this, I'm going to hold you personally responsible!"

"You know what?" Jack snarled. "You can fix the blame all you want, Kinsey. Right now, I'm more interested in fixing the damn problem." He glared at the lead bodyguard. "Get him out of here."

"O'Neill!" Kinsey's shout followed him down the stairs to the control room, but Jack didn't turn back.

"Intriguing," Teal'c noted. "The device does not match any manufactured Goa'uld weapon I have ever encountered, and yet several elements of the structure use their technology."

"You don't say." Major Carter spoke around a probe stylus

clamped between her teeth, her fingers working through leaves of flexible circuitry.

"I would hazard a guess that the weapon is an improvised offensive mechanism. It appears to use components from a staff weapon for the detonator core, but the power regulator appears Orbanian in origin." He pointed to another area. "These fluid mechanisms are new to me."

"Not to me," said Carter, with a scowl. "At least, not now." She shook her head, as if dismissing the thought. "We'll worry about that later. For now, we have to disarm this thing."

Teal'c nodded. "Major. You are aware that we are at the ten-minute mark. If we are to do as General Hammond suggested..." He trailed off.

"You don't have to stay," Carter replied. "Go ahead. I'm going to stick with this." She worked at something and a spark snapped back at her. "Ah. Nuts."

"I will remain," replied the Jaffa. He tried to study the device with a fresh eye, to see the shape of it rather than the odd mix of parts that made up the whole. "It is a two-stage detonator," he opined. "A smaller explosive charge released to prime a far larger naquadria-based plasma ignition."

Carter prodded at one of two sacs full of runny liquid. "Could be. A binary explosive made up from chemicals that are inert when separated, but lethal when combined. They mix here..." She tapped an empty reservoir chamber. "And start a reaction that ends with an exothermal discharge, which in turn makes the naquadria in this vial go supercritical and... Well, ka-boom."

"Indeed." Teal'c eyed the countdown display. "Nine minutes, Major."

Jack watched the lines of men and women moving swiftly up the ramp and into the glittering pool of the wormhole.

"How are we doing?" Hammond asked.

"Alpha Site reporting one third of base personnel have been delivered," said Harriman. "Doctor Jackson and the diplomatic party are secure."

"Shame we couldn't have sent Kinsey to his own planet," said O'Neill beneath his breath, "one without a DHD, maybe."

The general glanced at him. "Jack, we can do this without you. Go on, go through."

"Funny, sir, I was just going to say the same thing to you." He gave a wan smile. "Carter's an ace at this stuff, General. And besides, the less time I spend near Kinsey, the happier I am." He glanced away again and his eye line crossed a face in the crowd; a dark-haired young woman in a white doctor's coat. Something about her snagged his attention, some odd compulsion that he couldn't explain; but then she was through the Stargate and gone, and the strange impulse faded.

"Here we go," said Sam. "I've traced the linkages back along the conduit. This is the main trigger. Hopefully, if I sever this, the device will go inert."

"Hopefully," repeated Teal'c. "You are not certain?"

Carter shook her head. "Not as such, no. But I'm pretty much at the limits of my ability here. Alien EOD wasn't top of my MOS at the Air Force Academy."

"How can I assist?" he asked.

"Hold that light steady," she told him, leaning in, "and cross your fingers."

Sam took a breath and used a conductive probe to break the circuit. The device released a strangled electronic chirp and the countdown froze.

"Were you successful?"

She was just about to say *yes* when it made the noise again and the figures on the display started moving again, this time so fast she could barely make out the blur of Goa'uld digits. "Oh, that's not good."

"I did not cross my fingers," Teal'c admitted.

The fluids in the sacs began to froth and flow, trickling onto the mix chamber. Each one was covered with a protective membrane that probably linked directly to a detonation sequencer, but now Carter was past the point of no return and her only sensible option had failed. She had only the dumb, brute force approach remaining. "Knife!" she barked, holding out her hand to the Jaffa.

Teal'c snatched his combat blade from the sheath on his leg and flipped it around, offering her the hilt. Sam grabbed it and hesitated, the point touching the surface of the membrane. *If this doesn't work, we're dead.* With a grunt, she stabbed the knife into the fluid sac and tore it down and across. The carbon steel blade slashed through the wall of the reservoir and thick, sticky chemicals spat out in a fan. Carter shielded her eyes, but the liquid gushed out over her gear vest and shirt. It was cold and acrid-smelling.

"Major!" Sam felt Teal'c pull her to the decking as the device gave off a rattling, angry fizz. Some small measure of the chemicals had mixed, and they flared in a brief, brilliant spit of fire.

It was long moments before Carter hazarded a look up at the bomb. It was largely intact, still attached to the inner wall of the vent, but now blackened and warped. The naquadria vial was visible, unbroken and quiescent.

"Okay," she ventured, "Now we're successful." She sniffed. Her nostrils were full of the stink of the chemicals. "Ugh."

"*Carter?*" Jack's voice emerged from her radio, wary and concerned. "*Sam, do you read me? The clock's at zero. Tell me you got it.*"

"We got it, sir," she replied, a rush of fatigue rolling over her.

"*Outstanding, Major. Get back up here, we'll have tea and medals.*"

Sam studied her shirt and her face wrinkled. "If it's all the same to you, sir, I'm going to go find the base laundry."

The tingling rush of the wormhole transition washed over him and Daniel found himself descending the stone steps of

P5X-404 all over again. Little seemed to have altered from the first time he had arrived there; it was still raining, still overcast and dreary. Only the presence of a parked Tel'tak cargo ship in Pack colors marked the change in circumstances. A couple of Vix's men emerged from the ship's open hatch and the warrior-leader threw a brisk gesture in their direction.

"Um." Jackson struggled to find something to say that wasn't a repetition of the apologies he'd been making since they gated from Earth. "I hope this incident hasn't turned you away from the idea of a treaty."

Vix grunted and kept walking toward the Tel'tak. Daniel glanced at Suj, but she wouldn't meet his gaze. It was only Koe who halted to speak to him, as Ryn hovered close by. "Daniel Jackson," said the older man, "put yourself in our position. We hear these grandiose claims of the power of the Tau'ri, of their abilities to wage deadly war upon the System Lords... And then we visit your homeworld and what do we find?" He snorted with mild derision. "An underwhelming edifice as your home base, staffed by an army of ordinary men. Your leader patronizing us. And then you announce that your sanctuary is so poorly defended that your enemies have hidden a weapon in it that could have killed us all." He eyed him. "I ask you. What would you think if our positions were reversed?"

"Okay, I see how this might look bad," Daniel began. "But we don't go in for that 'If you've got it, flaunt it' kind of stuff. We *are* an army of ordinary men...and women. If anything, that makes what we've done even more impressive."

"A good point," said Suj quietly.

"If you think for one second we intended to put you in harm's way, you're absolutely mistaken." He sighed. "The truth is, the Tau'ri have many enemies. Not just the Goa'uld, but threats from several quarters." Jackson knew that O'Neill would be ticked off if he realized that Daniel was being this blunt, this brutally honest, but he could feel the Pack's trust slipping away and suddenly all he could think of were those fields of dead crops, of famine and starvation. "My team neutralized the bomb, and they'll find out who put it there and why. I'm sure we'll discover it was one of the many people we've annoyed over the past few years... But this is precisely why we can't let a chance for friendship between us fall by the wayside! We both know, Tau'ri and Pack, what a hostile galaxy it is out there, right? And if there's anything that my people have learned, it's that with allies we are stronger."

Vix returned from the Tel'tak as the ship's engines whined into life. "Words. Words and words, that is all we have seen from you, Jackson. I begin to doubt the stories I have heard of your warriors. Perhaps you are not as strong as they say, perhaps Apophis, Sokar, the others, perhaps they killed each other and you have merely taken credit for it!"

"I believe him," said Suj.

Vix did not appear to hear her. "We were promised samples, where are they?"

"You cannot blame the Tau'ri for that," insisted Ryn. "We were forced to evacuate before they could transfer them here."

"How convenient," sneered Vix.

Daniel held up a hand. "If you wait here, I'll have the supplies sent through as soon as I get back to the SGC."

"Wait?" snapped the leader. "We have dallied at this world too long as it is!"

Ryn grimaced. "Then what is one more day, Vix?"

"Don't throw this away!" Daniel's voice tightened. "Your people will suffer without our help, and you know it. Don't let your pride get in the way of that."

"Listen to him!" insisted Ryn. "We must go ahead with this treaty! We must! The future of the Pack depends upon it!"

Koe gave Ryn a curious look. "It seems at least one of our kinsmen is convinced."

"So it would appear," Vix agreed. "Quite a change from your more typical stance on things, Ryn."

The other man's eyes narrowed. "I see the logic in this alliance, that is all. Daniel Jackson is correct. We would be fools to throw this chance away."

"I stand with Ryn," added Suj.

"You do?" Koe smiled. "Then this *is* a day for the unusual."

Vix's hands were clenched, and for long moments Daniel thought the man would turn away and leave him behind, go back to the ship and not look back; but then he gave the scientist a hard-eyed glare. "Very well. The *Wanderer* and the Pack flotilla will remain in orbit over Golla IX for the time being. You will return to your world and have the items Major Carter promised sent through the Chaapa'ai."

"And we'll reschedule the meeting to formalize the treaty at the SGC."

"No." Vix shook his head. "I must think of my kinsmen and their safety. You have proven, even if it was through no fault of your own, that you cannot guarantee the security of your base."

Ryn snorted. "Could we make any better claim? Is the *Wanderer* any more secure than their world is?"

"No," repeated Vix, "and so we will choose a third place for the meeting. A neutral location, a world far from any of our mutual foes."

"Okay," Daniel nodded. "That's fair."

"We will communicate the ring symbols to you when we have made our choice." Vix turned away and left him there on the steps. Ryn and Koe followed, leaving Suj to linger a moment.

"Daniel Jackson," she began, "do not judge Vix harshly. He has only the best interests of the Pack at heart. His position is being challenged by some, and this treaty will affect the way that many people will see his leadership."

"Challenged," he repeated, glancing after Ryn. "I got that. Seems like government on the *Wanderer* has its similarities to the same thing on Earth."

She nodded. "I imagine so. And I think we will probably both agree, this is too serious a matter to be left in the hands of politicians." Suj inclined her head in a gesture of farewell and made for the Tel'tak, leaving him to dial his way home.

As a child, Mirris had been given an aquarium by her crèche-parents and for a time she had watched it with rapt fascination, observing the motion and behavior patterns of the fish inside the small biosphere module. At first she had opened a file on her datapad and made notes. She came up with schedules of feeding and a day-night cycle for the animals, but they refused to operate to the plan she set for them. They did not eat when she fed them. They fought. Sometimes they would gorge themselves until they perished. After a while, Mirris tried more invasive methods of control. She altered the water temperature, she shifted the dimensions of the environment, each small change designed to impose her will on the fish. These actions did not bring forth the reactions she wanted either. Eventually, an emotional response took root in her, and in a single afternoon she systematically removed each of the fish from the tank, laid them upon the floor of her room and watched them die, one by one. When one of her crèche-fathers asked her to explain why she had done it, Mirris told him the truth. The fish had refused to embrace order, and so she had been forced to impose the only kind of order upon them that she could: death.

She could still remember the smile upon his face at her cool, clinical conclusion. She had done well that day. She had passed some kind of test.

Mirris stared into the holographic cube and saw the slow, languid motion of the nomad fleet, and thought of the fish in the aquarium. They were not that different, really. Crude, unsophisticated things that reacted only to stimuli, swimming away each time a predator came close, coming together into a shoal with the foolish notion that it would somehow protect them. *How very wrong of them to think that.* Out there they moved and went about their small lives, utterly unaware of how Mirris was imposing her will upon them. The nomads were, after a fashion, just tools. Just the means by which she would be able to bring order to those who so richly needed it.

The holograph chimed and rippled. A signal from the command center demanded her attention, and with a faint sigh she tapped the sensor spot on her desk. The image faded into a view of Geddel, his pinched face staring up at her from the ghostly cube of light. "*Administrator, a signal has been received.*"

She made a dismissive gesture. "Confederation Central again? They have nothing to say I wish to hear."

"*No, Administrator. The communication comes from the migrant fleet. Audio only, and heavily encrypted. Your operative, I believe.*"

Mirris leaned forward. This was unexpected, and she did not like the unexpected. "Route the channel to this terminal, sub-director."

"*As you wish,*" he began.

"A closed line, Geddel," she added. "No transcripts or records to be made of the signal, do you understand?"

"*That is highly irregular —*"

"Yes," Mirris sniffed, "It is."

After a moment, Geddel's face faded away to be replaced by a writhing field of shifting wavebands, the visual representation of the signal itself.

"*Mirris?*" The voice was hushed and urgent, as if the speaker were trying to avoid being overheard.

"This is not a scheduled communications window," she replied. "You have broken protocol. Why?"

"*Circumstances have changed. There was… An incident.*"

Mirris felt the old, animal anger coiling inside her. The woman's fingers drew into her palms. "You were supposed to ensure an agreement with the Tau'ri. If you have not succeeded in this, then you have no value to me and I will not assist you with your personal circumstances."

"*I had no hand in it! It was beyond my control!*" She heard anxiety bubbling beneath the words.

"Elucidate, then." Her fingernails bit into her skin, and the small pain helped her to focus, to maintain an outward air of dispassion.

"*On the Tau'ri planet, there was a security alert, an emergency. We were forced to abandon the accord summit and evacuate through the Chaapa'ai.*"

"Why?" she demanded.

"*An explosive device was discovered.*" There was a pause. "*I believe that someone may have planted it in a deliberate attempt to derail the summit!*"

"That is one possible conclusion," Mirris allowed, her thoughts racing along the same lines. "One of your people, perhaps?"

"*Perhaps. I will investigate further.*"

A cold fury was building inside her. "Do so, if you wish. All that matters to me is the outcome, is that clear? Nothing must be allowed to interfere with the creation of a treaty with the Tau'ri, do you understand?" Her voice was becoming louder, more strident. "Nothing!"

"*I understand, but—*"

"No excuses," snapped Mirris. "No other outcome is acceptable. Your future, and the future of your Pack, lives or dies on this." She stabbed the control surface and the holograph flickered back to the exterior view once again, the teeming shift of the nomad ships.

Mirris watched the vessels for a long time, cupping the hate and fury inside her, letting it burn, basking in the chill fire of it. She thought of the distaste she would see if Geddel were in the room with her now, imagining how he would recoil at such a blatant display of passion. Her face twisted in the uncommon scar of a smile, and she remembered the fish upon the water-spattered floor of a young girl's bedroom, their silent pain as they lay gasping and dying.

CHAPTER SIX

S he flashed Sergeant Siler a polite smile as he walked past her with a tray of food. Jade turned slightly toward the payphone to make it seem as if she were having a conversation with someone on the other end of the line. In reality, all that was coming through the earpiece was a dial tone. The voice she heard was emanating from the implant's communications matrix, resonating directly into her mastoid bone through the molecule-thin bio-alloy channels created by the nanite colonies inside her body. There was nothing better than hiding in plain sight; if she'd been sitting in a room somewhere, having a conversation with thin air would have been a lot harder to explain away if she were discovered.

"Hey Darlene, how are you?" she asked. Darlene was the sister of the real Doctor Hannah Wells, a portly woman who lived in Oregon with a husband, four kids and some cats. She was currently on vacation in Canada, which meant that she wouldn't be calling Hannah anytime soon and risk blowing Jade's cover.

Status? The Commander's voice was terse.

"Oh, fine." Jade kept her tone light. "I'm settling in okay. Thanks for the flowers. Everybody loved them." There was the code phrase that signaled phase one of the operation was complete.

Any complications? Have they figured out where the weapon came from yet?

"Not yet. Soon, though, probably. I'll keep an eye on it." She hesitated. "How are the boys?"

Fine, came the gruff reply. *I'm fine.*

"Oh. Okay." She swallowed, thinking of the youth from the warehouse. "How about, uh, Tyke?"

Him? The conditioning is holding. He thinks I'm his uncle.

And before you ask, our other guest is stable.

"Good." She glanced across the cafeteria and saw Jackson enter. He caught her eye and gave a weary smile.

If things play out the way they should, they'll relocate the meet. You know what we need.

"Sure. I'll get it for you."

Jade. The voice in her head became firm and hard-edged. *I want you to listen to me. The operation is at a critical point now. I know what you must be going through in there, the people you are seeing, the memories they're bringing up for you... But you can't let yourself be distracted, do you understand?*

Jackson was coming closer, and he had two cups of coffee in his hands. She smiled weakly back at him.

The mission is all that matters. You have to do whatever is necessary to complete it. Do not get emotionally involved, you hear me? There are millions of lives at stake. If you have to sacrifice someone for the security of the operation, you can't hesitate. This is beyond us. It's more important than our lives.

"Yes," she said, her voice catching. "Okay."

Don't fail again. Initiate radio silence from this point forward. And then he was gone.

"I won't," she told the dead handset. "It'll work out. 'Bye." Jade put down the phone and blinked. She tried to cover her reaction, but Jackson saw straight through it.

"Are you all right?" He had kind eyes.

"I'm fine," she replied, forcing the lie back into place. "It's just... My sister, you know? Family can be very demanding."

"Oh, yeah," he nodded, and offered her one of the drinks. "I was just going to take a break, do you want to join me?"

She should have said no, right then and right there. It would have been simple to give Jackson a polite refusal and go on her way; but instead she told herself that it would be helpful to the mission if she made a friend of him, that it might make things flow better if she could stay close. It was a thin falsehood, but if Jade didn't let herself think too hard about it, she could almost believe it was true.

Jade took the coffee and they sat and talked, and she tried not to stare at him.

The sadness in her eyes gradually faded away, and Daniel found a smile pulling at his lips each time Hannah laughed. It made him feel better to draw a grin from her. He was trying to keep things on an even, professional level, but there was something about her that made it hard for him not to let his thoughts wander. She was whip-smart and funny in a kind of understated sort of way, and it seemed like she knew more about him than he could even begin to guess about her.

They talked, and he found out she liked the same kind of music as he did, she thought the same way about the same books, she even chimed with his take on contemporary archaeological theory. He felt like the woman was a breath of fresh air, and after the near-botching of the Pack summit that was just what he needed to lighten his mood. It wasn't until nearly an hour later that Daniel realized he'd been largely talking about himself and he gave a crooked smile. "So, how did you get recruited into the Stargate program?"

"I've got a very eclectic skill set," she told him. "Mostly thanks to my father. He was Air Force and I wanted to make him proud of me, so I joined up... But it turned out I was a better, uh, doctor than anything else. And when I was growing up I had plenty of interesting adult company who opened my eyes to a lot of amazing things. We moved around a lot and things were tough, but..." She looked away, a shadow passing over her face, and suddenly Daniel felt like he had crossed a line.

"I'm sorry, I didn't mean to pry."

"No, it's okay," she replied. "It's funny. When I was a girl I knew someone a lot like you. I learnt a lot from him."

"He was a teacher?"

Hannah shrugged. "Kinda. Actually, I had sort of a crush on him. He was quite dashing, in his own way."

"Oh." Jackson swallowed, unsure of where the conversation was heading. "All my teachers were plump, balding men with poor taste in suits."

She laughed, and brushed a strand of dark hair from her face. Daniel was struck by a moment of dislocation, the same sense of not-quite recognition. The gesture reminded him of Sha're again. He blinked and shook off the disquieting thought, the bittersweet pain of his wife's memory there and then gone.

"Is something wrong?"

"It's nothing," he said, and forced a smile. "It's just, you know, I can't remember the last time I had a conversation with someone from my own planet that was actually this normal. I mean, talking about ordinary people stuff instead of space aliens."

"That's a pity," Hannah said evenly, "I was just about to ask you about the Pack, but now I feel bad."

Daniel shook his head. "No, it's okay. Occupational hazard, I guess." He blew out a breath. "Not much to tell. At this stage, it could go either way with them. They weren't best pleased with being hustled off to the Alpha Site."

"I read the briefing document on them. You think there's a chance the treaty could fall apart?"

"It's possible," he admitted. "But right now the biggest question is how base security was compromised."

The woman took this in. "They did have one of their people on the base for what, a whole day before the others arrived? Maybe she was responsible."

"Suj? I don't think so." Daniel shook his head.

"Never can tell," noted Hannah. "The SGC could be catching fallout from some internal struggle inside the Pack."

"That occurred to me. But if that device had detonated, Suj would have been killed along with all the rest of us. She doesn't strike me as the suicide bomber type."

"Some people are willing to do whatever it takes, if the stakes are high enough," she replied. "We can't really know what that must be like until we're in the same place they are."

After a moment, Daniel shook his head and tried to change the subject. "Can we go back to an ordinary conversation again? I like the novelty of it."

"Sadly, no." Hannah stood. "I have to go on duty now." She touched him on the forearm and looked at him intently; once again, he saw the mirror of his wife's expression on her face. "How about this? We should arrange to have a dull and normal conversation the next chance we get, just to break up the monotony of all this amazing stuff going on."

"Sounds good to me."

She flashed him one last smile and went on her way. He tried not to watch her go; well, he didn't try *that* hard.

Jade kept her expression fixed until she was through the mess hall doors, and then she let it drop away like a discarded mask. She flattened the pang of guilt she felt at what she had done. Deliberately emulating the mannerisms of Jackson's dead wife was a callous and calculated gambit, but it had worked. The man had let his guard down even without being aware of it, and from then on it was only a matter of expressing the right emotional cues to make him well-disposed toward her. Jade had done similar things to other men and women on dozens of occasions, on other missions in other places, building on stolen information about them to earn their trust; but this time it made her feel cheap and ashamed. He was a good man, and she had no right to manipulate him.

But there was the mission, and it mattered more than Daniel Jackson's feelings. *The mission, the mission, always the damned mission!* She was starting to think like her father. It made it so much easier to betray the man's trust when she laid it at the altar of *the mission*. It was better to think that way, to see him as just another target in the operational environment, to compartmentalize herself and not get involved. *But you're already involved, aren't you?* Her self-accusation echoed in her thoughts. *Jackson's not just a mark. You care about him. And you want him to care about you.*

She shook off the recriminations with a flick of her head. Jade's fingertips felt dusty and she brushed them against the hem of her jacket. The residue there was all that was left of the transmitter medium from the nanite colony she had deposited on Daniel's jacket when she touched him. Microscopic and virtually undetectable unless one knew exactly what to look for, the molecule-sized machines had been tasked to bind themselves to the threads of his clothing and begin a replication cycle. In a hour, perhaps two at the most, the nanites would form a matrix inside the jacket that that would turn it into a surveillance device. From then on, if she was close enough, Jade's implant would be able to read energy patterns in the air around the clothing. For as long as Daniel wore the jacket, she would be able to listen in on any conversations he had, even view data on screens in his close proximity. Everything was ready for phase two.

Jack rapped on the door and Hammond looked up and beckoned him in. "Get in here, colonel, and close that behind you."

O'Neill did as he was ordered, glancing out through the star chart window of the general's office. "You rang, sir?"

"I just got off the horn with the White House," he tapped the red phone on his desk, "and if you notice I don't have a backside when I get up, Jack, it's because the president just chewed it off me."

O'Neill said nothing. George Hammond was pissed off, and that happened very rarely; but when it did, Jack knew well enough to just let him vent.

"It seems that Vice President Kinsey's first action on returning from the Alpha Site after the all-clear was to contact Washington and present them with his version of events."

"I'm guessing he didn't paint the SGC in the most favorable light?"

"That, colonel, is putting it mildly. He's calling for a full senatorial investigation to be drawn up and is threatening to go to the International Oversight Advisory."

Jack had to work to stop his hands tightening into fists. "Could he be any more of a dick?" O'Neill blinked and looked up. "Sorry, sir. Did I say that or just think it?"

Hammond let out a weary sigh. "No matter how much I may concur with your estimation of the man's character, we don't have the luxury of influence that Kinsey enjoys on the Hill. He's demanding that he be given direct operational authority for the duration of the diplomatic summit with the Pack—"

"Aw, for cryin' out loud."

"And he wants a full and complete security overview for the entire program, expedited immediately." The general tapped a sheaf of papers on his desk. "I've already recalled SG-9, SG-13 and SG-27 to bolster base operations. They were on non-critical sorties, so we won't lose anything there… But I need this bomb issue to be resolved, colonel. I need it done *yester-day*."

"Roger that, sir." Jack jerked his thumb at the door. "I took the liberty of ordering a level one sweep of the base, top to bottom, the whole magnifying glass and tweezers treatment. Teal'c volunteered to co-ordinate the effort."

Hammond nodded. "Good. God knows what kind of mess we'd be in if not for him. It's imperative that we find out how that device was smuggled on to the base and who was responsible. All leave has been cancelled and I'm having Air Force Intelligence run a deep read on all the new intake of staff, just to be certain."

"You think it's one of our guys?"

"Until I have proof positive on that weapon's origins, everyone is a potential suspect, Jack."

O'Neill grimaced. He loathed the idea that someone he served with could be capable of planting a bomb that would have wiped them all out; but the general was right. They couldn't afford to leave any stone unturned.

"Frankly," Hammond continued, "I'm more concerned that there might be other devices we haven't located yet."

Jack shook his head. "I don't think so, sir. To be brutal about it, I don't think we'd be standing here debating the point if there was another of those things lying under a box somewhere. We'd be wispy gas and largely dead."

The general gave a reluctant nod. "True. But we have to operate on the assumption of the worst. If an enemy can plant a weapon of mass destruction inside our key facility at will, then maybe Kinsey has a point about security."

He blinked. "Did I just hear you agree with something Kinsey said?" Jack ran a hand through his hair. "Wow. Things really must be bad."

Hammond's frown deepened. "The vice president will be returning in a few hours to be here when Vix radios in. I'd like to have something to show when he arrives."

O'Neill nodded. "We're on it."

The squad of troopers entered the lab and fanned out. Two men with M4 assault rifles remained at the door while four others swept the room with a variety of sensing devices. Teal'c followed them in and saluted Carter with an alien weapon in his grip. Sam recognized the curved form of a transphase eradication rod. The TER was of Tok'ra design, a combined energy weapon and scanning emitter that specifically targeted threats capable of existing out of phase with normal matter. Having tangled with their fair share of invisible enemies over the years, the devices had come in useful on more than one occasion.

She raised an eyebrow. "You're armed for bear."

Teal'c mirrored her expression. "A bear would be far simpler to locate."

"You think there's an intruder on the base?"

"I am prepared for any eventuality." He hefted the TER. "We will meet any threat with the force required to neutralize it."

"Good to know," said Sam. She was back in duty fatigues now, and on the work table in the center of the lab lay the remains of the explosive device and a chunk of wall which the engineering corpsmen had been forced to burn off to remove it. Elsewhere there was a magnetically sealed chamber holding the naquadria vial and on a third Sam had donated her ruined dress shirt so that Doctor Lee could run an analysis on the binary liquids that stained it. She stood back and let Teal'c's squad do their jobs.

One by one, the airmen called out "Clear!" and retreated from the room. The Jaffa nodded to his subordinate and handed him the TER. "Lieutenant Everitt, proceed with the sweep as planned. I will join you shortly."

Sam returned to the dismantled bomb as Teal'c came closer. "As you're here, maybe you can give us the benefit of your knowledge." She pointed at the petal-shaped segments of the device. "Take a good look. Anything seem familiar?"

Teal'c was silent for a long moment. "I have nothing to add to my initial judgment, Major. The weapon is fabricated from a mixture of extant technologies."

"An alien IED..." said Lee.

"Yeah, we got that." Carter pointed out parts of the bomb with a stylus. "This, this and this, all Goa'uld in origin. This section looks like it could be Tok'ra hardware. And these, these things are new to me." She blew out a breath. "It's like a jigsaw puzzle where all the pieces are from different pictures."

"Such an eclectic mix of machinery does parallel the Pack's technological methods."

"That thought had crossed my mind," said Sam. "The same kind of grab-bag of hardware we saw on the *Wanderer*."

"This could be an internal squabble that spilled over on to our turf," said the other scientist.

Sam sighed. "That's hardly a smoking gun."

"Not yet," Lee threw his comment in from across the room, pausing in his work.

Teal'c continued to study the device. "Have you ascertained how it got through base security checks?"

"I thought it could have been beamed in," offered Lee. "Remember that energy discharge from the Stargate? The two could have been connected."

Sam shook her head. "No, the timing doesn't marry up.

That shaft was checked a couple of hours after the discharge took place and it was clean, which makes it certain the device was planted after that. Besides, even Asgard transporters have a problem penetrating this far underground." Carter pinched the bridge of her nose. "I feel like I'm missing something. We have to step back and think about this dispassionately. It's not just a question of dismantling this thing and reverse-engineering it. We need to see through it, figure out who wanted to put it here in the first place."

"Understand your opponent's intent, and you understand your opponent."

"Exactly." Sam waved a finger at Teal'c and began a slow orbit of the work table. "We're concentrating on what this thing is, how it was put here. Let's come at this from a different approach. What's the payoff? Like they say in a court of law, *cui bono*?"

"*Who benefits*?" Teal'c translated.

"I didn't know you spoke Latin," said Lee.

The Jaffa shook his head. "I do not. But I find many of your legal drama serials very entertaining."

"Right," continued Carter, "so if we look at it another way, the real question is — what would have happened if the bomb *had* gone off?"

"Total obliteration of Stargate Command and probably the Earth gate too," said Lee, scowling at the thought. "Even if the gate survived the naquadria blast, it would still be buried under the collapsed remains of Cheyenne Mountain."

"So that would mean no effective SGC presence in the galaxy for months, probably years. No support for our allies in the Free Jaffa Nation and a dozen other worlds."

"We would not be the only victims," noted Teal'c. "If the device had detonated before we discovered it, the senior members of the Pack would also have been killed."

Sam shot him a look. "Result?"

"At the very least, a cessation of any potential for alliance between the Pack and the Tau'ri. At worst, they might consider ·

us responsible and declare hostilities against Earth."

"And who gains from that?" Carter tapped on the table. "Who wants us and the Pack out of the way, at each other's throats even?"

"You believe there is a third force at work?"

Lee shook his head, thinking it through. "Not the Trust. They hate us, sure, but they'd never blow up the SGC. They'd want it intact. It's the System Lords! It's gotta be! They fit the profile perfectly!" He grinned. "Heh. But which one?"

"Take your pick," Sam frowned.

"I do not agree," said Teal'c. "There is a flaw in your hypothesis." He pointed at the bomb. "This method of attack is highly atypical for a Goa'uld System Lord."

"How so?" said Lee.

"This is a patient and anonymous weapon. I have never known a System Lord to exhibit either of those qualities in abundance. If our invader were a Goa'uld, they would have ensured that we were fully aware of their identity before we perished. Their arrogance would not allow them to do otherwise."

Carter nodded slowly, seeing the merit in the Jaffa's words. "He's makes a good point. The Goa'uld really have a thing about gloating. It's practically pathological."

Doctor Lee folded his arms, unhappy that his theory had been so quickly shot down. "If it's not the System Lords, then we're back to square one."

"Yeah," Sam sighed. "We are."

Daniel caught Sergeant Siler as the airman passed him in a corridor. "Hey, what's the rush? I just saw three squads of Marines double-timing it to the elevator bank."

Siler made a face. "Our distinguished guest has returned, Doctor Jackson. He's on his way down right now, and his advance team demanded that he have a full honor guard."

Jackson snorted. "He complains about base security and then he pulls men off search details to inflate his own sense of ego."

"I couldn't possibly comment, Doctor," Siler replied in a dour voice. "I'm just a non-com and I don't get to bitch about elected officials like you civvies do."

Daniel patted the other man on the shoulder. "Well, thanks for the heads-up. I think I'll keep out of Kinsey's way for the moment." He moved off, taking a corridor at random, and Jackson realized that he was close to the infirmary. Immediately, the face of Hannah Wells popped into his thoughts and he found himself wondering about her. Would it look too weird if he just wandered in to say hi? It had only been a little while ago they'd been in the mess hall, and still he found his attention drifting back to her in odd moments of ellipsis. He hovered in the middle of the corridor, and gave a small chuckle. *What am I doing? This base is in the middle of an alert and I'm getting my eye caught by a pretty face like a teenager in High School.* He shook his head and turned back the way he had come, just as the door to a storage room opened and Hannah stepped out. She had a case of blood test syrettes in her hands and she blinked in surprise to see him.

"Oh. Daniel." She covered with a quick smile. "What are you doing here?"

"I'm hiding out. Kinsey's back."

"Who?" Hannah threw a quick, distracted look down the corridor.

On impulse, Daniel followed her gaze; but she appeared to be staring at nothing. "The Vice President of the United States?" he offered.

"Oh. *Him.*" She smiled again. "I'm not much for politics."

He indicated the case. "Do you need any help with those?"

"How gallant, Doctor. No, I can manage. Warner's been snowed under doing blood tests for everyone on the base because of the heightened security levels." She patted the box. "We were running short."

Daniel started to speak again, but his attention was drawn away as booted footsteps sounded around the corner of the corridor. At first he expected to see more Marines on an urgent call to Kinsey's little circus, but instead Teal'c emerged with a knot of armed airman behind him.

"Corridor A-6-9-Bravo, secure," said the Jaffa into his radio. "Proceeding to A-7-5-Charlie." Teal'c spotted Daniel and Hannah ahead of him, and his eyes narrowed.

"I've got to go," said the woman quickly. "I'll see you later." She was walking briskly away before Jackson had a chance to say anything else.

Teal'c came closer, a cold expression on his face. Daniel had seen that look before, many times, on hostile worlds and in battle situations. "What's up?" he asked.

The Jaffa halted and unlimbered a TER from his shoulder strap. "Stand aside, Daniel Jackson."

"Is there something wrong?" He turned in place, looking up and down the empty corridor.

Teal'c thumbed a switch on the TER and the emitter cone on the Tok'ra weapon began to hum, throwing out a faint vapor of energy. The warrior panned the gun this way and that, frowning. After a few moments, Teal'c deactivated the transphase rod and let it drop to his side.

Daniel gave him an arch look. "Did you do that just to spook me, or what?"

"I am disquieted," rumbled the big man.

"*You're* spooked?" Jackson was slightly surprised at the admission. "By what?"

"I cannot say." Teal'c paused, marshalling his thoughts. "Before, with the explosive device, and on a number of other occasions. I have felt... Uneasy."

Daniel gave his friend a measuring look. "Your Jaffa spider-sense is tingling?"

"I find it difficult to articulate. It is as if I see the shadow of an intruder from the corner of my eye, but it is not there."

"It could be stress," said Jackson. "When was your last tretonin injection or meditation?"

Teal'c nodded slightly. "I am several hours overdue.

With the alert in place, I felt it was not right to engage in kel no'reem."

"Well, no disrespect to your Jaffa grit, but I'd prefer it if you were at your peak condition. Maybe you ought to stand down. Just for a little while."

The Jaffa gave him a frown. "Perhaps you are correct."

"And if nothing else, it gives you a great excuse not to be in the same room as Kinsey."

The control room was, to say the least, a tad cramped. Along with all the people who actually had to be there, like Jack and Hammond, Walter and all his technician crew, there was also the vice president, a couple of his flunkies, those same humorless Secret Service guys and a unit of Marines. The latter were doing their best not to look too bored by it all, and at least the recent emergency had meant that the film crew had been left upstairs at NORAD. O'Neill pushed past a suited supernumerary with a snide "Excuse me," and moved to Harriman's shoulder just as the Stargate flashed open.

Walter already had the massive titanium alloy iris closed, preventing anything from exiting the gate's event horizon. "Incoming signal, General," he reported. "It's the Pack."

"Right on time," Hammond remarked. "Let's see them."

Jack caught Kinsey straightening his tie as the monitor screens flickered, revealing Vix's face. O'Neill recognized the interior of the man's home aboard the *Wanderer*. "*Do you hear us?*" he demanded.

"We do," Kinsey was quick, getting in before Hammond could respond. "And before this endeavor proceeds any further, I would like to extend, on behalf of myself, the President of the United States and the people of Earth, our deepest regrets at the distress you have been subjected to. Be assured that I am taking steps to see that the people responsible for placing your lives in jeopardy will be punished."

With that last sentence, Jack could almost feel the vice president's eyes burning into the back of his head. He had no doubt that on some level, Kinsey had to be loving this, being on the spot to gloat when something went awry at the SGC.

Vix peered out of the screen, unimpressed by the rhetoric. "*We have discussed the matter of an alliance with you and there has been dissent.*" In the background, Jack saw Koe, Suj and Ryn, along with other Pack members he didn't recognize. "*But we have reached an accommodation, for the moment.*"

"I can't tell you how pleased that makes—"

The Pack leader ignored Kinsey's platitude. "*We shall meet and attempt once again to find a common agreement. This I do for my people's sake.*" He motioned to Koe, who moved to the edge of frame and operated a small handheld device. "*The glyph code for a Chaapa'ai is being transmitted to you on a side channel.*"

Walter tapped out a command on his keyboard and O'Neill saw a string of gate symbols spool out to form a dialing address. "Confirmed, I have it," reported the sergeant.

"*These are the coordinates for Kytos,*" said Suj, leaning forward. "*It is an arboreal world, currently unclaimed by any of the System Lords.*"

Vix nodded. "*Our fleet is preparing to leave Golla IX. It will take us two of your Tau'ri rotations to reach Kytos via hyperspace flight. We will expect to find you there.*"

"Vix, I look forward to it." Kinsey gave a plastic smile, but the wormhole hissed out of existence and the link was severed.

"Quick and to the point," noted Jack, with an arch tone. "If only all national leaders could behave in such a way…"

The vice president shot a look at Hammond, pointedly ignoring O'Neill. "General, I'd like a word with you."

They adjourned to the briefing room on the next level up, and Kinsey ordered the Marines and his security detail out into the corridor. Daniel entered, looking distracted, as the politician threw a seething glare at Jack.

"Colonel O'Neill," he growled. "I think in future it would

be best if you kept your thoughts to yourself. Your personal grudges against me are one thing, but I'm not going to have you diminish me in front of potential allies or junior officers!" He tapped the small Stars and Stripes pin on his lapel. "You will show my office the respect it is due, Colonel!"

"I've never been to your office," Jack said innocently. "Is it nice?"

Kinsey's lip curled in a sneer. "That cute insubordination act won't fly much longer, Jack. You may think you're amusing now, but you won't be laughing when I post you to some iced-over airstrip at the ass-end of the Aleutian Islands!"

Daniel sat down and caught his eye. "They get the hockey games out there," he said, in mock comforting tones, "you'll be fine."

"And as for you," Kinsey fumed. "Doctor Jackson. Would you like to spend the next ten years of your life in a bunker at Area 51, sifting through pottery shards with a toothpick?"

"Well, actually…"

Jack shook his head and mouthed a 'no' to the other man, and Daniel fell silent. There was no sense in riling Kinsey any more than they already had. There would be time for that later.

Hammond stepped in. "Doctor, what do we have with regards to background on this planet Kytos?"

Jackson opened a laptop and used it to manipulate images on the briefing room's video screen. Jack recognized some blurry MALP photos and what looked like scans from the pages of an old illuminated manuscript. "Kytos, also known as P3F-964. Surveyed four years ago by SG-2, designated as utterly unremarkable. Gate is located in a tropical jungle region below the equator, local life forms encountered by the survey team were mostly benign. Some signs of former human occupation in the last five hundred years or so, but no apparent sentient life…" He tapped the scanned pages. "It used to fall within the domains of the System Lord Notus, but he was apparently disposed of by an alliance of ships led by Athena and K'tesh. This was a outlying world on the edge of his territory, and it seems like it just got overlooked, just slipped through the gaps."

"Empty, uninhabited," said Kinsey. "Good choice for a private rendezvous." He looked at Hammond. "I want a team sent there, right now, to check it out. I need to make sure these Pack folks aren't trying to play us."

Jack rolled his eyes. "If they were going to try something, they'd have done it before they gave us the gate address, don't you think?"

"You can be as cavalier as you like with your own life, Colonel," Kinsey retorted, "but after your failure to protect the SGC from a terrorist bomb, you'll forgive me for being cautious!" He stood up, and pressed his normal, superior façade back into place. "I have some important matters to conclude before we get to the treaty, gentlemen, so I'll leave you to get on with whatever it is you do. But before I do, I'd like to make this crystal clear, so that we all understand exactly what is at stake here." The politician sniffed. "I'm holding the senior staff of Stargate Command personally responsible for the bomb threat and the disruptions to this diplomatic enterprise. If this treaty encounters any more problems due to your incompetence, if it doesn't go off without a hitch… I will see to it that you take the full weight of the blame and have you reassigned so fast it will make your heads swim." He made his way out without looking back.

"They got any carnivorous jungle cats on Kytos?" asked Jack, after a moment.

"I think so," said Daniel. "Some."

"You think they'll be hungry?"

Jade kept to the side of the corridor as the security detail passed by with the men in suits in the middle of their number. She gave the man at the very center of the group a sideways stare. *Robert Kinsey. Of course.* She recalled him now. That had been a moment of inattention on her part, to allow Jackson to see her slip up on that minor point of background. It would not happen again.

Within moments, she was alone in the passageway. There was nobody to see her, but she prided herself on her tradecraft, and with a convincing misstep, Jade made it appear as if she had tripped on something. The file of paperwork in her hands went all over the floor and she sighed, dropping to her haunches to gather it back up. Once she was in a crouch, she ran a finger over the implant's dermal control surface and let the device in her skull tune into the resonance frequency of the nanites on Daniel's jacket. He was two, perhaps three walls away from her, at the edge of the broadcast range for the microscopic machines. It wasn't possible for them to draw any more power and transmit a stronger signal; anything more than the tiny waveband they emitted might be picked up by the SGC's internal sensors. The implant's software sifted through the incoming material, filtering out bio data and audio pickups, until all that was left was the faint aura of Jackson's computer, glowing in the information void like a dying ember. Jade let the signal filter into her thoughts. The symbols were as familiar to her as the letters of the alphabet, and as the nanite web decoded the electromagnetic patterns of the laptop screen from the air, the constellation runes formed in her mind's eye.

Auriga, Lynx, Orion, Scorpius, Pisces, Taurus...and Earth. Just like that, and she had the dialing address for the new meeting point. Jade mentally sent the code for the nanites to cease operation—they only had a lifespan of a few hours anyway, and the longer they were live, the more chance they might be discovered—and picked up the last of the papers, coming back to her feet.

There were offices on this level, and with care, Jade crossed to one of them and fingered the door handle. The office belonged to Colonel Dixon, an officer whose paternity leave had been allowed to stand in the wake of the alert, thanks to the goodwill of General Hammond. Jade removed a thin rod from her pocket and inserted it into the lock; in turn, the rod—which was actually a kind of gene-engineered mollusk from the Re'tu homeworld—expanded to trip the locking pins and release the latch. In a moment, Jade was inside Dixon's office and closing the door behind her.

The implant automatically adjusted her optical register so she could work without switching the light on. She moved carefully around the colonel's desk, taking care not to disturb the mess of paperwork and files strewn across it. Beside a small collection of framed family photos she found a telephone and dialed an off-base number from memory. She could have used the implant's comlink to convey the intelligence, but that would have violated orders; and like the nanites, the subspace carrier wave it generated might be detected. Each time the device operated, she ran the risk of alerting someone on the base.

Somewhere in Colorado Springs, a handset was picked up after the first ring sounded. Neither Jade nor her father spoke. All the Air Force's monitoring software would hear was the sounds of six numerical tones as she tapped out a number code that corresponded to the gate symbols. She took a breath as she finished, perhaps some small part of her expecting the Commander to say something to her; but then the line went dead and she was alone again.

Jade's eyes focused on one of the pictures on Dixon's desk, of the man holding up a little girl. There was a childlike scrawl of writing on the photo; *Vera loves Daddy!*

She scowled at the image and made her way out of the room, taking care to lock it shut behind her.

"Now that just doesn't make any sense," said Sam, laying her palms flat on the work surface.

"Oh, how many times those words have crossed my mind," Colonel O'Neill stood at the door, arms folded, with a slightly amused expression on his face.

Sam blinked, slightly off-put. "Ah. Sir. How long have you been standing there?"

"Since Lee left. It's kinda fun watching you do your thing, Carter. You know, you talk to yourself? A lot."

She grinned sheepishly. "I'm just free-associating, sir. Articulating my thoughts."

"That's what it's called, huh?" O'Neill wandered into the lab proper. "My mom always said it was the first sign of madness."

"Well, maybe that too," Sam admitted. "It's been a long week."

"And it's only Wednesday." Jack nodded at the remnants of the bomb. "What you got so far?"

"Honestly? More questions than answers. I can tell you more about what this isn't than what it is." She gestured with her hands. "It wasn't made on Earth. It wasn't beamed in. It's not a Goa'uld weapon. It doesn't match anything we have in our databases… and…."

"*And?*" The colonel cocked his head. "C'mon, Major, the *and* bit is always the juiciest part."

Carter scratched her head. Now she came to actually say it out loud, it sounded kind of dumb; but there was the evidence staring her in the face. "Well, sir, as far as I can determine… This bomb is a dud."

O'Neill blinked and sat down on a stool. "Okay, now you're confusing me. I'll grant you, that's not too difficult a thing to do, but it's not funny."

She held up a portable datascreen. "It's really subtle, colonel, so much so that at first I just thought I was seeing the circuitry of the device wrongly. But the more I dig through the layers of the programming, the more it seems right. There are fail-safes built into the device's core detonator, deliberate limits imposed on the explosive yield."

"I thought you said it was a dud."

"Well, a sorta-dud. The binary liquid explosives would have reacted if they'd been allowed to mix fully, and that would have caused a low-level blast. Probably something around the potency of a block of C4."

He toyed with a magnifying lens on a gimbal arm. "That's hardly enough to bring the house down. And if it went off in the shaft, it wouldn't do much damage."

"No, exactly!" Sam nodded. "The blast would have been channeled up and down the air vents, probably blowing out a few ducts, but the energy of the explosion would have dissipated."

"But your report said the gizmo was a two-stage munition. Binary explosive ignites bigger, nastier naquadria plasma detonation." Jack mimed an expanding fireball with his hands.

"That's where the 'dud' bit comes in. The naquadria in the vial would never have reached the criticality needed to vaporize. It's just meant to look like it would."

"With all due respect, Carter, your theory's tweaked. Who builds a bomb that's not supposed to go off? Apart from idiots." He thought for a moment. "Maybe that's it? Whoever made this was just incompetent?"

Sam shook her head. "Actually, I think the reverse is true. Whoever built this device was very smart. They covered their tracks well. Odds are, someone examining these remains after the fact wouldn't notice anything and just thank their lucky stars that they hadn't all been blown into, uh…"

"Wispy gas?" offered the colonel.

"Right." She sighed heavily. "So now we have to ask ourselves, what's the point of planting a deliberately-engineered dud in the SGC, that we were possibly meant to find and disarm?"

Jack stood up, and Carter saw his eyes narrow, all jocularity fading from his manner. "Let's not dance around this, then. The bomb looks like Pack tech, right? If it is this whole bait-and-switch thing you're talkin' about, then what we got here is some misdirection going on. Someone's trying to throw blame on the Pack, stall or destroy any chance of an alliance with them before it even gets off the ground."

"A fake bomb seems like an overly complicated way of making that happen."

"Yeah, isn't it though?" O'Neill peered at the remains again. "I'm going to take this to Hammond. This puts a whole new spin on things." He walked away and sighed. "Remember when we used to just get into fights and shoot at bad people? I miss those days. They were simpler times."

CHAPTER SEVEN

In the kel no'reem, there is no self.

How long had it been since the day Bra'tac had said those words to him? Teal'c had still been a youth, no older than his son Rya'c was now. At the time he had thought himself to be a man, that there was little in the universe that he did not grasp. He had been filled with the self-assurance of the young; and the old Master had quickly broken that from him.

So many years ago, and the lesson Teal'c had learned was that there were no answers, only new questions, new challenges. To his strength, to his soul.

To his mind.

The Jaffa's expression tightened, there in the gloom of his quarters, his tawny skin lit by the thick candles arrayed about him. The faint smell of the tallow connected him to his home; the candles had been made on Chulak, by the hands of artisans in simple workshops. Teal'c held on to the slender thread of sense-memory, but it was elusive. He wanted to let himself drift, to find his center, but the obdurate reality of the walls around him remained at the edges of his thoughts, keeping him here, rooted.

In the kel no'reem, there is only knowing, and the peace it brings.

And yet that peace eluded him. Teal'c found himself wishing his mentor was here with him now, to offer some measure of guidance to his former pupil. The Jaffa healing trance was as much a factor of Teal'c's existence as eating and sleeping were to his Tau'ri friends, but today, in this place, it would not open itself to him. The doorway to the meditative state of the kel no'reem remained beyond his reach, held aside from him by the splinter of disquiet that continued to dog his every waking moment.

At first, he had thought that it might be the unidentified device he and Major Carter had disarmed in the vent shaft, that perhaps something in its makeup was disturbing the delicate balance of his Jaffa equilibrium. But the weapon was inert now, and the creeping unease had not abated. The sensation—it was so faint and so fragmentary that he could hardly justify giving it that name—ebbed and flowed as a tide would upon a shoreline. Down on the maintenance levels, in the corridor with Daniel Jackson, and in other places, for moments it had felt so strong that he had sensed the presence of another at his shoulder, no more than a breath away. Then there was nothing. Just the echo of a feeling. Of a *threat*.

Teal'c's irritation rose to the surface and his lip twisted. He was allowing himself to be irrational, concentrating on phantoms instead of certainties. What advice would Bra'tac have offered him had he been in the room at this moment? The Jaffa imagined a look of fatherly admonishment in the old warrior's eyes. *Walk the line between instinct and logic, Teal'c. Find that path.*

"Yes," He said the word aloud and it resonated in the spartan room. Teal'c's instincts told him that there was danger close at hand, unseen, unheard and so far, undetected. His logic told him that there was nothing out there. The sweep teams had gone over the SGC and found no sign of intruders, nothing but the alien bomb. Between the two, the Jaffa knew that the truth lay hidden. He would have to look inside himself to find it; the alternative was the grim possibility that he was affected by some sort of sickness that was fogging his mind.

Teal'c drew in a deep breath, and let the scent of the tallow fill his senses. "In the kel no'reem, there is only knowing," he said to the air. "And I will know."

A plastic-wrapped package thudded on to the desk in front of Sam, making her jerk up in surprise. Daniel gave her an arch look and smoothed a crease out of the freshly-pressed blue duty jacket he was wearing.

"I believe these are yours?" he said, nodding at the package.

Carter saw her service dress uniform inside, neatly folded. "They got them clean already. Great."

"That's the Air Force for you. Fast jets, faster washing machines, apparently."

"What were you doing in the base laundry?"

He pulled at the cuff of his jacket. "I got something on my fatigues," he frowned. "Some sort of white powdery residue, like dried paint. I don't know where it came from. Couldn't get it off…" Daniel nodded to himself. "You know, they have the biggest tumble dryer I've ever seen over there? Honestly, you could walk inside it."

Sam eyed him. "Uh huh. So you decided to visit the laundry services division and then help them out by bringing me my clean uniform out of some sense of helpfulness…"

"Sure," he began.

"…Not because you're trying to avoid running into Kinsey again?"

"Oh." Daniel shrugged. "Well, maybe."

Carter chuckled. "Thanks, anyhow. As you're running errands for me, how about some coffee and a Danish?"

Jackson narrowed his eyes. "Don't push your luck, Major."

"Seriously," she replied. "I'm starting to think I need an intravenous caffeine drip. I'm going around and around on this thing, and it's making me dopey." Sam gestured at the deconstructed bomb.

Daniel folded his arms and gave the device a hard stare. "Jack told me about the whole 'dud' thing. What's up with that?"

"Wish I knew," Carter responded. "I'm dead-ending on this. I've got nothing to show but more maybes than I had a day ago." She toyed aimlessly with the package of clean clothes.

"You *did* prevent a dangerous explosion, Sam. That's hardly nothing."

"Yeah," she said glumly, "and I ruined a perfectly good

uniform shirt into the bargain." Sam jerked her chin towards the work desk where her chemical-stained blouse lay under a series of Doctor Lee's particle sensors. "That's never going to come out, jet-washers or not..." Her voice trailed off as the words sparked a sudden cascade of thought.

"Sam?" Daniel asked. "I know that look."

All at once it came to Carter in a sudden flood of comprehension. "Stubborn stains. Like they say, you can't just get them out with any old detergent."

"Okay, now you're being weird," Jackson retorted. "Lack of rest is making you talk like someone out of a soap powder commercial."

She came up out of her chair, suddenly energized, and crossed to where the detonator core of the bomb was resting in a set of clamps. "No, think about it. Forget the device for a second, what about the person who planted it? We know it wasn't beamed in, so somebody put it there, somebody who could still be on base. If they'd been holding on to this thing for a while, or even if they had been the ones who built it, there would be residual energetic traces from exposure to the naquadria." Sam halted, her train of thought racing through possibilities. "Doctor Lee, Teal'c and me would all have trace amounts from our limited contact, but the bomber would have twice, maybe three times as high a reading."

"So, we scan everyone with a naquada-specific Geiger counter? Do we even have one of those?"

She shook her head. "A person-by-person check would take too long, and it would let the bomber know we were on to them."

"Then we need to find a way to scan everyone in the SGC in secret."

A slow smile crossed Sam's face. "Or all at once."

"Oh yeah. This doohickey." O'Neill gave the steel-colored rectangular box an arch look. "From Thor, right? Some kinda toaster oven, or something."

"Not quite," said Carter, glancing around the medical lab, taking in Jackson and Warner with her explanation "This was a gift from the Asgard, but we haven't been able to get it to interface successfully with our systems."

"That's an understatement," said Warner. The doctor leaned in and tapped a couple of controls. The box unfolded into a compact computer console. "We tried to integrate this into an experimental program similar to something that NASA have been working on." The device gave off a soft hum and Jack saw strings of Asgard runic glyphs tracing across a display screen. "It's a broad-spectrum biological sensor array. Asgard starships use them to scan planets from orbit. The idea was, we'd set this up here in the SGC and be able to keep an eye on the medical well-being of everyone on base, non-invasively, on a twenty-four seven basis."

"So if someone was injured or fell ill, you know about it immediately?" asked Daniel.

Jack scowled. "It's a little bit 'Big Brother', don'tcha think, Doc?"

"The point's moot," insisted Warner. "We couldn't make it work. The sensors were too sensitive, setting off alarms every time someone reported in with a sniffle or a hangover."

"And the interface to our computers couldn't handle all the data from hundreds of full-body medical scans, constantly updating in real-time," added Carter.

"Not to mention the drain it put on the infirmary's power grid," Warner concluded.

Jack folded his arms. "And you're telling me you can tweak this thing to filter out all that other stuff and just sweep for somebody with naquadria radiation traces?"

Sam flashed him a grin and flipped open her laptop. "Yes, sir."

"You're sure this will work?" O'Neill pulled a radio from his pocket. "I don't want to toss some innocent fella in the stockade just because he happens to be wearing a glow-in-the-dark wristwatch."

"I'm sure, Colonel," she replied.

"Okay then," he said with a flourish. "Find me a bad guy."

"*T*," said the voice from the walkie-talkie. "*Got your ears on?*"

"I hear you, O'Neill." At the colonel's request, Teal'c had cut short his meditation and joined Lieutenant Everitt on the base's mid-levels; in all honesty, he welcomed the opportunity, having found no respite in the kel no'reem.

"*Good. I need everyone on the bounce. If we get a hit off this, we may have to move fast.*"

"Understood." The Jaffa glanced at the officer at his side. "There is only one rule of engagement. No fatalities. We must capture this infiltrator alive."

"You still think there's someone hiding out down here?" Everitt's tone made it clear how much he disagreed with the idea.

"I know it," snarled Teal'c.

Daniel raised an eyebrow as the Asgard device's humming grew louder and deeper.

"Here we go," said Sam, "spinning it up…"

Jack eyed the machine warily. "This isn't like one of those photocopiers, is it? Where you go sterile if you hang out around them too long?"

"That's just an urban legend," said Warner testily.

Jackson's eye was drawn briefly to the open door of the medical lab and the expanse of the main infirmary beyond. He saw figures moving around in there and caught the briefest glimpse of a head of dark hair and a white lab coat.

Carter's fingers skipped across the laptop's keypad as the room's lights dimmed ever so slightly. "Sensor bloom is reaching full radius. Commencing trace scan."

Daniel saw the sweep of the Asgard scanner rendered as a green orb overlaid across a wireframe graphic of Cheyenne Mountain's interior spaces. Hazy patches of white, like blobs of computer-generated mist, speckled the laptop screen. "Getting some false positives. It'll take a second for the software to filter out any noise." As they watched, some of the sensor returns diminished to nothing and winked out.

"A firm detection there, science lab four," noted Warner.

Sam nodded. "That's the naquadria vial and the bomb components. Another, fainter one in the mess hall."

"The good Doctor Lee," said O'Neill. "He's at lunch. Said he was going to try the macaroni and cheese."

"On the mid-levels…" Warner pointed out another. "Teal'c, yes?"

Jack nodded. "Yup. That leaves you, Carter."

The woman blinked. "Huh. Just a moment. I've got to alter the gain. It's reading me as a much larger return. Too large."

"You're right on top of the scanner, Major," said O'Neill.

"That's not it," Sam shook her head, and they all heard the warning in her voice. "The sensor field is being reflected off something. I'm getting a feedback echo."

"We should up the power," said Warner. "Just a quick pulse, a single discharge like we were taking an x-ray."

"Good call," Carter typed a string of new commands into the keyboard. "This, this, and *there*."

The Asgard device thrummed with sudden power and Jackson saw something flicker blue-white in the corner of his eye. He turned back to look to the infirmary and found Doctor Wells staring right at him, an expression of mingled sadness and fear across her face; and he *knew*.

"Hannah?"

"Contact," snapped Sam, "right here, ten meters! But there's something else! I'm reading *two* more targets."

Jack's pistol was already in his hand. "Carter?"

"Energy field… Transphase or optical shift… The scanner output's interfering with it—"

"Mother of God!" Warner's cry cut through the air. "What the hell is that?"

Behind Hannah Wells, a six-legged insectile creature the

size of a man shimmered into solidity, flashes of electrical energy coruscating over its carapace. Daniel saw the woman bolt from the room as the alien brandished a boxy object that could only have been a weapon.

"Down!" Jack threw himself across the room and shoved Warner aside as the creature fired wildly into the ceiling of the infirmary. Daniel heard a woman's scream as one of the nurses caught the trailing edge of an energy bolt.

Sam had her pistol out as well and she unloaded three shots toward the spider-like alien. "It's a Re'tu!" she called. "Intruder alert!"

Daniel slammed his fist into the red alarm button on the wall and immediately the base was filled with the whooping of sirens.

The Re'tu snarled and kicked out with its legs, smashing into a wheeled gurney. The trolley spun away across the room, knocking down an IV stand.

Jack was shouting into his radio. "Infirmary, code red! We have a Re'tu intruder, potential Foothold situation in progress!"

The alien fired again, and this time the spread of shots ripped into the lighting strips on the ceiling, shattering the fluorescent tubes and plunging the infirmary into semi-darkness. Daniel caught sight of the insectoid scrambling away, out and into the base.

"Teal'c!" called O'Neill. "It's loose!"

"*I will find it,*" Jackson heard the terse reply. The Jaffa sounded annoyed.

He followed Warner into the other room and helped the doctor pull the nurse from the floor and place her on a bed. Warner thrust a penlight at Daniel. "Hold this." The woman was pale, and he placed a finger against the carotid artery in her neck.

"Is she dead?"

The doctor's shoulders sank and he blew out a breath. "No. Thank god, no." He leaned closer to the nurse. "Cathy? Cathy, can you hear me?"

She moaned and her eyelids fluttered. "She's just stunned," noted Sam. "Like a zat blast."

O'Neill turned at her words. "That's not their style. Last time the Re'tu were here, they shot up the damn place."

Daniel's thoughts began to catch up with what had just happened. "Hannah… The new doctor, Major Wells. She was with it. They were together."

"They've used human infiltrators before," offered Warner.

Jack grimaced. "What the hell happened? Aren't those creeps supposed to be invisible? How come we could see it all of a sudden?"

"The sensor field," said Carter. "I don't know how, maybe it depolarized the transphase envelope or—" The colonel gave her a hard look that said *not now* and she skipped quickly to the layman's explanation. "We accidentally blew through its invisibility. Until the discharge wears off, we can see it."

Jack seized upon her explanation. "How long?"

"Could be minutes, maybe less."

O'Neill was already running for the door. "Good, great. You're with me. Jackson! Let Hammond know, and tell him to break out the weapons. I want that oversize roach in a trap!"

"And Wells?" called Warner. "If she's an accomplice?"

"Then we'll take her down too."

Daniel stood for a moment, staring after them as they raced away down the corridor, the adrenaline rush of the sudden mayhem tingling in his limbs. Warner's words echoed in his thoughts. *They've used human infiltrators before.* But he'd spoken with Hannah Wells, connected with her. Instinctively, he rejected the idea that she might be a human clone, like the boy they had named Charlie. The child had been an attempt by a peaceful faction of Re'tu to communicate with the SGC, to warn of a terrorist cadre of their species intent on attacking Earth; but the violent faction had been driven off five years ago and ceased to be a threat. Hannah wasn't like the sickly, unfinished boy that had come through the Stargate as an ambassador. She was as human as he was, he could sense it.

Human enough to lie to him.

But Daniel couldn't deny the moment of revelation when their eyes met as Sam's sensor sweep rang true. For a single, unguarded instant, the woman had let her mask drop and allowed Jackson to see the real truth of her. He saw fear there, fear and sadness…and shame.

Jade vaulted along the narrow, high corridor and raced for the T-junction at the far end. Her escape route pushed itself forward to the front of her thoughts, overriding any sense of panic. It was the implant's doing, she knew. The moment she had started to run, she allowed the mechanism to suppress the production of the neurochemicals in her brain that might induce fright. It allowed her to move with cold, clinical control, her thoughts unfettered and locked on her objective.

Or at least, it was supposed to. The problem with having a device as complex as the implant melded to something as willful as a human brain was that the two did not always work in tandem. She flashed on a memory of a covert mission from two years ago, on a world devastated by Replicators; on the extraction shuttle, on the way home, her implant had been unable to damp down her fear index and she had burst into a fit of racking, uncontrollable sobs. But that was the price she was willing to pay, to lie and to fight and to lose a little of what made her human, in order to survive.

Her cheeks were burning. She should have felt nothing, but she didn't. The dreadful churning of emotion that she had felt in the Holdfast came back. Betrayal. *I have betrayed my friends*, said an echo inside her. *I am nothing but a liar and a spy.*

Jade shook her head, as if that would make the feeling go away. She came to the junction and met two airmen coming up it at a swift pace. The first saw her and gestured to halt, his M4 pointed down at the floor.

Jade's autonomic combatant training was flawless. She made a small running jump and kicked off the closest wall, leading with her other foot to come down on his ankle. He yelled as she broke the bone, and she followed with a sweeping punch that connected hard with his temple. The second airman was faster; he had his assault rifle at the ready and he drew a bead on Jade's sternum. At so close a range, one bullet would be enough to tear a fist-sized hole through her stomach.

She was vibrating with tension and barely-caged anxiety. The airman shouted a command at her, but she barely registered it. All she saw was the skittering shape moving inverted along the high ceiling, the shape of a brassy weapon in clawed hands, the actinic flash of a stun ray.

The second man collapsed to the floor in a nerveless heap, and Ite-kh allowed himself to drop from above, describing a roll in mid-fall to land squarely on his six legs. His eyestalks quivered with concern and the alien extended a limb toward her. The Re'tu's mouthparts clicked and scraped.

Jade shook her head, becoming angry. "What are you doing? You know the protocol, we're not supposed to be together! Disengage, escape, evade. Those are the rules." She backed away a step.

Ite-kh made a coarse clattering noise and signed to her. *To death with the rules. You must be made safe.*

She ignored his protests. "You've lost your camouflage, you're vulnerable!" Jade stabbed a finger at the pod on the gear belt around Ite-kh's thorax. "You need to use your pod. It's got enough energy in reserve for a spatial transit. Get up a couple of levels closer to the surface and you'll be able to teleport outside the base perimeter."

The alien shook its crested head in an exaggerated parody of a human motion and offered the device to Jade. His meaning was clear.

"No." She held up her hands. "I'll get out the way you got in, through the air ducts. And if that path's blocked, I'll take the secondary route."

Ite-kh's sensory palps twitched as the sound of heavy boot steps echoed along the passageway. They had little time to waste talking, but the alien would not do as she wished. Finally, Jade drew herself up and tapped into the same hard-edged manner that made her father the unquestioned leader that he was. "I am the ranking operative on this mission. I'm making it a direct order. Now *go*!"

The alien rocked on his legs and chittered; it was the Re'tu's equivalent of a resigned sigh. He brought up one claw and made another human gesture—a salute—and then threw himself down the corridor, directly toward the approaching soldiers. He was going to waylay them, giving her a chance to get a head start on the SGC's security forces.

Jade swallowed hard and broke into a run, heading in the opposite direction.

Teal'c felt the enemy coming before he saw it. His teeth bared in a snarl and he spun in place, bring the fluted shape of the Tok'ra weapon in his grip to bear. The TER's scanning emitter cone hummed with energy, but he didn't need it. The Re'tu was naked, perceptible to normal sight, and that placed the creature on a level battleground with the Jaffa warrior.

Here was the unseen enemy that had been pulling at his thoughts; here was the ghost rendered visible. Teal'c understood perfectly now. These creatures resonated at a different phase from normal matter, giving them the gift of concealment—but their ability also disturbed the delicate metabolisms of Goa'uld symbiotes. When the Re'tu had last crossed swords with the Tau'ri, Teal'c had still been carrying one of the immature serpentine parasites within him, and each time he came close to the spider-creatures, the symbiote's revulsion forced a wave of crippling nausea upon him. Since then, the Jaffa had been freed from his Goa'uld burden and survived thanks to the serum known as tretonin; but clearly some element of the Goa'uld's genetic reaction remained with him. The disquiet, the nagging unease, the sickening agitation—all of it had been caused by this thing, hiding in plain sight. The Re'tu had been here all along, was most likely to have been either the guardian of or the bomber itself. How it had got into the SGC was a question he would answer after he had defeated it.

He heard Sergeant Albrectsen make an incredulous noise, a sound that was half in surprise, half a nervous laugh, as the airman saw the insectoid scrambling along the sheer vertical wall as easily as they moved along the floor. It rattled its mandibles — perhaps as some kind of battle cry — and opened fire.

The Jaffa was already moving, throwing himself aside as the flashing darts of energy ripped through the air where he had been standing. Shooting the TER one-handed, Teal'c bracketed the alien. "Shoot to wound only!" he roared, as the rest of Everitt's team opened up on the creature.

"Aim for the legs?" cried the lieutenant. "The damn thing's got six of 'em!"

The Re'tu caught a glancing round as a bullet scored a gouge in its abdomen, and in return it pumped a direct hit into Airman Walker, the stunning discharge wreathing him in green-tinted lightning. The alien leapt from one wall of the corridor to another, bouncing back and forth over their heads. Teal'c led his target and he was rewarded by a piercing screech from the intruder as a bolt from the TER creased its chitinous torso. The Re'tu stumbled but kept purchase.

Teal'c's fingers tightened around the weapon's pistol grip; at full discharge, the Tok'ra energy gun would have slain the alien instantly, but the Jaffa had deliberately dialed down the lethality. His orders were to capture, not to kill.

Albrechtsen was at Walker's side, dragging the insensate man to his feet. Everitt and another soldier, Boyce, flanked Teal'c as he went after the Re'tu. The arachnid spat and hissed at them before slamming itself into a set of elevator doors at the end of the corridor. Claws drawing sparks from the metal, the alien ripped the doors open to reveal the dark shaft inside. All three men fired, but the intruder undulated and thrust itself through the meter-wide hole it had made, grasping on to the elevator cable and swarming upwards.

Boyce gingerly aimed a flashlight into the gash torn in the

doors. "I can't believe what I just saw! How did something that big get through a hole that small?"

"Just like a spider," panted the lieutenant. "Like those hairy little creeps that come up the bathroom drain…" He threw an apologetic look at the Jaffa. "You were right, sir. Sorry I doubted you—"

But the expression of stony fury on Teal'c face silenced him. The Jaffa spoke a clipped sentence into his radio. "The Re'tu is in elevator shaft three. Moving up."

The SGC security control center was dominated by a wall of color monitors feeding live images from surveillance cameras located all through the base, in corridors and rooms on every tier. Sergeant Siler looked up from over the shoulder of one of the technicians as Jack blew into the room. He was still in the process of loading a P90 submachine gun he'd appropriated from an airman in the corridor. O'Neill wasted no time with a preamble. "What have we got?"

Siler pointed at one of the screens. "Teal'c engaged the Re'tu at intersection D-6-2-Echo, sir. Target was hit but is still mobile. Major Duarte and his team have locked off the shaft it entered. That bug's got nowhere to go."

Jack saw the Jaffa flash past, racing up a set of steel stairs. "What about Wells?"

At a nod from the sergeant, the technician working the console brought up another image on the central screen. "Moving towards air processing, colonel. There." The man pointed and Jack saw a figure moving swiftly and carefully toward the camera's location. The dark-haired woman still had her white lab coat on, and as she came closer to the monitor, he got another look at her.

She seemed relatively unremarkable; just an ordinary person, pretty even, in a nondescript kind of way. At least, that was how it seemed at first glance. Again, Jack felt an odd moment of dislocation when he studied the woman's face, just as he had when he caught a glimpse of her in the gate-room.

Even though he was sure he'd never seen this person before, O'Neill couldn't escape the sensation that he *knew* her.

He frowned and forced the reaction from his thoughts. The colonel took his radio and raised it to his lips. "Carter, come in."

"*Here, sir,*" The major's reply was crisp.

"Wells is heading your way. You know what to do."

"*Roger that. We'll be ready.*"

Siler leaned forward to stare at the monitor. "What's happening?"

Jack glanced up. The woman looked right into the eye of the camera and for one brief second O'Neill thought she was actually going to speak. He saw a nerve jump in her cheek, and without warning the monitor flickered and became a featureless rain of gray static.

"She shoot it out?" said Siler. "I didn't see a weapon…"

"Negative," said the technician, "The camera just went down. I'm losing feeds from all over that tier. Looks like electromagnetic interference…"

"Damn it." Jack spoke into the radio again. "Carter! We've lost video down there, do you read? Sam!"

His only reply was the hissing of a jammed channel.

In the planning stages of the mission at the Holdfast they had discussed the possibility of an abort with the same level of reticence that someone might use for talking about a terminal illness. None of them had wanted to consider what the end result of a catastrophe would be, not at this stage, not on this of all missions. Failure was not an option; they could gauge it only in degrees of success.

At the final pre-operational briefing, the three of them sat in the incongruous setting of Tyke's living room, Jade across the dining table from the Commander as he used the holos of the SGC to reiterate how and where the device was to be placed for maximum effect. She had seen the reluctance in the old man's eyes, the subtle war between father and senior officer taking place behind the lined face. He did not want her to go, but he had no choice. None of them did.

No choice. If felt as if Jade's entire life could be summed up with those two words; and now they had driven her to this, on the run and under the guns of people who in other times would have been her friends, her comrades.

She used the implant to secrete a neurotransmitter to damp down her building migraine headache and let the device's crude dampening field run as strongly as it could. She had little need for stealth now. Only escape was of importance. Jade descended the shallow steel steps to the accessway leading to the air processor vents.

There were three armed people waiting for her.

Carter stepped out of her cover with the P90 submachine gun firm against her shoulder, sighting down the length of the stubby weapon. She hadn't had the chance to pick up a zat gun on the way down; if she had, she would have shot first and asked questions later.

"Hands in the air. No sudden moves," she demanded.

"Of course. I should have assumed you would cover this escape route." The woman held her arms up at chest level, palms out and fingers spread. "I have no weapons, Major Carter."

Sam's eyes narrowed at the spy's unwelcome familiarity. 'Get on your knees, lace your fingers together and place them on the back of your head."

"Major, please." The woman took a slow step forward. "There's no need for this. We can resolve this peacefully."

"*Stand still!*" Sam barked, the command loud in the confined corridor. Carter didn't often get to use her 'officer voice' but she did it now, and in a way that made it clear she was not willing to accept anything but immediate compliance. "I don't know who you are or what you're trying to do here, but your little game of hide and seek is over."

The intruder's shoulders sagged, and when she spoke again

the weariness in her voice sounded almost genuine. "You're right, Samantha. It is a game... But if I told you what the prize was, you'd never believe me." Her hands moved a little and Carter saw something strange, a peculiar discoloration on her fingertips that hadn't been there moments before.

"What is that—" began one of the soldiers at her side.

Sam's finger tightened reflexively on the P90's trigger as the woman turned her hand in a sharp wave. A mist of glittering silver vapor flashed into the air and Carter recoiled. Before she could fire a shot, the spray jetted towards her, shifting and moving through the air like a swarm of tiny mites. The woman was running, doubling back and away as the mist went straight for Sam's gun and attacked it.

The composite plastics and metals of the weapon disintegrated, crumbling apart into dust. Carter instinctively threw the gun away, and as it hit the floor it shattered like glass, scattering components and unfired ammunition. She gasped, clutching her hand, but found her flesh untouched. Only the cuff of her uniform and her wristwatch were damaged, the inert materials becoming powdery like the weapon. With horror, Sam watched the steel staircase buckle and melt like hot wax, preventing them from giving pursuit.

The major backed off as the haze began to fade slowly away, leaving odd striations in the walls and the floor. "Gotta be.. Nanomachines," she said under her breath, her keen reasoning finding a explanation, "they only targeted inorganic matter..."

The airman at her side gestured with his walkie-talkie. "Major! I've got comms back on line."

Carter snatched it from his grip. "Colonel O'Neill. Wells was driven off but we cannot give chase. She's moving back into the base proper, sir."

"*I read you,*" came the reply. "*Teal'c has her spider-boy-friend corralled in the elevator shafts and the base is locked down.*"

"Sir, we're not dealing with an amateur here. She'll have another escape route."

"*Oh yeah,*" he agreed grimly, "*and I reckon I know what it is.*"

O'Neill turned to Siler. "Where's General Hammond and Vice President Pain-in-the-ass?"

"Secure conference room on level six." The sergeant pointed at another monitor, and on it Jack saw the room with the large oval table, and the mass of people crowded into it.

He spotted Daniel and Hammond standing together as Kinsey gesticulated and shouted. That the man was extremely annoyed by the current situation was obvious, and it almost made all the effort worth it. Jack was glad the video feed didn't have an audio component; he had no doubt his name was being taken in vain. "Keep them in there and out of trouble until we have our pest problem resolved." He made for the door.

"Sir, where are you going?" asked the sergeant.

He hefted his SMG. "Playing a hunch, Siler. The way my week's been going, I'm about due for a win, don'tcha think?"

"Where?" snarled the Jaffa, as he ran from the stairwell to the elevator bank. The Tau'ri officer shot Teal'c a nervous glance and pointed through the open doors of a lift; the car was empty. The major pointed again, this time at the elevator car's floor.

"The car's blocking the shaft," he said in a low voice, as if he did not want to alert the intruder. "That thing's scrabbling around, trying to get past it."

Teal'c nodded. He could hear scraping noises and the sounds of chitin on metal as the Re'tu probed the shaft for an escape route. "It cannot be allowed to flee," he said flatly. The Jaffa snapped a fresh stick of ammunition into his weapon.

"Look out!" cried one of the airman, as a scythe-like claw punctured the floor of the elevator car with a screech of steel. Dents in the walls of the lift appeared in rapid succession, moving up the side of the car as something impacted them from inside the shaft.

"It's trying to get on to the roof of the car!" snapped Major

Duarte. "It'll have a clear path up to the NORAD levels…"

"No," Teal'c bounded into the waiting elevator and punched open the hatch in the roof. He heard the Re'tu screech as he gripped the edges of the space and threw himself up through it.

The lift car rocked on its suspension as the big man rolled on to the roof and came to his feet. There was only the scattered light of level markers ranging away up the narrow shaft above, but the dimness was enough for Teal'c to see the shiny mass of the insectoid. It spat at him, angry to see the Jaffa again, angry to be distracted once more.

The alien brought up its weapon, but Teal'c was ready. He released a short, full-auto burst from his gun and a tongue of flame back-lit the two combatants for a brief instant. The Re'tu ducked away, but the shots ripped into the alien's boxy brass weapon, sending it spiraling away down the shaft. With a grinding roar, the insectoid vaulted around the central cable pinion and slammed four of its legs into his chest. Teal'c lost balance and slipped to the edge of the car, for one long moment dangling over the dark abyss. With a grunt of effort he rolled back and smashed the alien's head with the butt of the P90.

The Re'tu punched blindly and struck him in the gut. Teal'c recovered his footing before the creature could hit him with another of its limbs, but it was as if he were fighting three men at once. The arachnid was a whirl of chitin, each talon threatening to cut him open if it struck him wrongly. The Jaffa fired again, bullets glowing as they ricocheted off the concrete walls of the shaft.

It made a crackling noise in its torso and came at him, ignoring a glancing gunshot wound, and Teal'c staggered back as the Re'tu snapped the P90 in two with a twin pile driver punch. His foot touched empty air where the roof hatch was open and the Jaffa felt himself drop.

Teal'c skull rang as he collided with an a-frame. Colors and light exploded behind his eyes.

It was a strain for her to force out a last swarm of nanites. The processors and micromanufactories inside the hollows of

ade's bones were almost bled dry from making the cloud she
deployed against Major Carter, and the jamming field that baf-
fled the security cameras. She was close to running on empty,
he mass of her implant throbbing with heat at the back of her
kull. The rest of her hardware was still back in her quarters
on the upper levels, hidden in her gear bag along with a couple
of refill vials of raw nanofluid. She could have used them now;
but instead Jade was back to operating on a human level, without all the enhancements that gave her an edge.

The cloud dutifully deconstructed the molecular bonds on
he tempered steel bolts holding the panel before her in place
and it slid off its mounting. Jade pulled herself out of the dank,
dirty conduit and dropped silently to the floor, the nanites dissipating harmlessly around her.

She glanced up. Following the maintenance crawlway had
deposited her in the rearmost corner of the embarkation chamber. The conduit, sealed shut since the SGC had taken possession of Cheyenne Mountain's lower levels in the 1990s, was
a forgotten piece of the base's Cold War-era infrastructure. As
such, it was the perfect last-ditch route to reach the Stargate
undetected.

Jade grimaced and threw off her white jacket. The lab coat's
color was more drab gray now, dirtied by wading through
years of accumulated dirt, filth and insect colonies inside the
crawlway. Her skin itched and she felt the sudden and very
ordinary need for a hot shower. Jade pushed the desire aside.
She still had one more barrier to cross before she could let her
guard down.

The woman fished in her pocket and removed an object that
appeared on the surface to be a commonplace stick of lip balm.
Discarding the case, Jade removed a slim rod from inside and
twisted it. A compact microwave transmitter of Tok'ra origin, the rod also contained an extremely large memory buffer
that currently held a few million lines of dense computer code.
Moving slowly, careful to keep to the edges of the vision enve-
lopes of the gate-room's security cameras, Jade moved around

and under the massive clamps holding up the Earth gate. From beneath the supports of the embarkation ramp, she aimed the rod's emitter tip in the direction of the control room beyond, to where she knew the SGC's dialing computer was located. Jad pressed a tiny stud and the device went warm in her grip.

Walter Harriman's hands were nowhere near his keyboard in fact, they were wrapped around a mug of coffee, which made it all the more unusual when the console in front of him began generating a stream of commands at lighting-fast speed "Aw, no," he spat, diving at his controls. "Not this, not again!"

Harriman's fingers danced over the keys, fighting to halt the inputs and falling far short. "This isn't supposed to happen! he complained aloud. "We fixed this, we encoded it! You can' take remote control of dialing without a command code—"

On the screen, a data window pinged open. *Command Authenticity Confirmed*, read the display. *System Recognize Authorization Code—Colonel J. O'Neill, Office Commanding, SG-1.*

"What?" demanded the sergeant. "No! He's not authoriz ing anything!" There was a mechanical whine and with stead: inexorable motions, the heavy steel blast doors fell down ove the control room's windows and across the access corridors to the chamber beyond. Walter's frustration broke and he mashed the keyboard. "Stop it!"

The barriers slammed into place with a dull thud and the or screen display shifted into dialing mode. Alarms ringing, the Stargate's inner ring of symbols began to spin.

Someone was calling his name. Teal'c heard it over a meta lic gnawing and crunching, a tiny little voice issuing from his radio.

"*Teal'c*!" It was the Tau'ri Major, the one called Duarte "*Are you all right, man? What's going on up there?*"

He decided not to dignify the question with a reply and blinked slowly. Fresh blood was gumming the corner of hi ight eye and he could feel a gash open across his temple.

In the dimness, he caught sight of the Re'tu—still visible, so the Jaffa's luck was holding—bent over the cables in the shaft's companionway. It took a moment for him to fathom what the alien was attempting. The Re'tu's powerful arachnid mandibles were chewing into the governor cables controlling the elevator's counterweight. Even as he watched, it bit clean through one of the strands. There was a rattling twang that echoed down the shaft and the car lurched.

Teal'c got up and came at the Re'tu. It fended him off with two legs, kicking out aimlessly. With a two-hand strike, the Jaffa broke one of the limbs cleanly, drawing a snarl of pain from his foe. The alien tore apart the remaining counterweight cable and let it snap.

The Jaffa saw it coming and grabbed on to the steel frame of the car. The slab of cast iron counterbalancing the elevator dropped into the dark and with nothing to hold it in check, the lift instantly did the opposite, slamming upwards as the weight fell. The pulleys screamed and spat streams of fat yellow sparks. Acceleration forced Teal'c down and he fought against it, still desperately trying to engage the alien.

The levels of the shaft flashed past in a blur as the elevator rose like a bullet along a gun barrel. The Jaffa heard Duarte's voice again. "*Emergency brakes!*" he called. "*Manual switch right there! On the roof!*"

He saw it instantly; a lever painted in black and yellow stripes. If he could reach it, he could throw it, halt the rise, stop the creature reaching the upper levels of the base; and then he remembered that the alien seemed perfectly capable of understanding the Tau'ri language.

The Re'tu stamped on his hand as Teal'c went for the switch, blocking him. The Jaffa threw punches at the alien's thorax, and there were satisfying crunches of bony matter where his fists landed.

A backward swipe from one of the insectoid's legs hit him in the ribs and Teal'c felt a bone break. The creature pulled

back, disengaging, and tore a device from its belt. The Jaff[
had seen similar objects before—they belonged to the rac
that had built the Chaapa'ai, the ones Daniel Jackson calle
'Ancients'. The small pod flipped open and he caught sight c
a display, like a signal reading, growing stronger as the elev.
tor came closer to the surface.

Abruptly the pod gave off a strident chime and the alie
growled. The Re'tu flashed Teal'c a last look and then stabbe
a control on the device. There was a flash of blue-white radi.
tion, and the arachnid vanished.

He lurched forward and yanked the manual switch, activa
ing the emergency brakes, and with a hellish screech the elev.
tor vibrated to a halt.

Teal'c lay on the roof of the car, panting and furious.

Jade heard the familiar metallic sound of a gate chevro
locking into place and she broke from her cover, sprintin
quickly around the side of the embarkation ramp. She wa
tired and her muscles were singing with fatigue, but in a fe
moments she would be away. The woman gripped the rails o
the ramp and vaulted over to land at the base as the secon
chevron locked.

"That's far enough, missy." The voice was such a shock th;
she actually reacted with a physical jerk, as if she had bee
slapped.

Jack O'Neill was halfway up the ramp, squatting in
crouch. He stood and in his hand was a P90 submachine gu
aimed squarely at her chest. He took a step towards her an
nodded at the Tok'ra data-rod. "Turn that thing off and giv
it up."

Behind him a third symbol swung into place and the che
ron lit with orange light.

For a moment, Jade's voice fled her and she gulped. Whe
she finally spoke, it was with none of the control or strengt
she'd used on Jackson or Carter. "If you don't move, when th
wormhole opens you'll be caught in the plume."

"This isn't going to get that far, Hannah. If that is your real name."

"*Please let me go!*" It came out in a sudden shout, a cry of pleading.

A fourth glyph locked. "Nope," said O'Neill. "Don't make me shoot you."

Jade shook her head. "You wouldn't fire on me, I'm—" Her voice caught and she hesitated for a second, framing her words. "I'm an unarmed woman," she concluded.

The man took careful aim. "I'm just about ready to do whatever I have to. You put my life, the lives of all my friends, heck, maybe even my planet in jeopardy. I am *so* not in a good mood right now."

She looked up as the fifth chevron flashed into life. "Sometimes we have to do things we don't want to. That's a soldier's duty."

He heard the tone in her voice, the pain and the hurt. "Is that what you are? A soldier?"

Jade felt the fight go out of her; all the energy to resist drained away and she felt hollow and abandoned. "I don't know what I am any more."

The Stargate's sixth chevron locked. "Last chance," said O'Neill.

"Yes," said Jade, raising the data-rod. She tapped the actiation stud and the emitter winked out. The dialing sequence aborted and with it the gate rolled to a silent halt, the chevrons fading into darkness.

CHAPTER EIGHT

"Who *is* this woman?" Doctor Lee ran the hand-held scanner over the overnight bag on the dresser beside the unkempt bed. His voice had an air of awe to it. "And where did she get all these wonderful toys?"

Sam Carter glanced up at him from across the small room. "She tried to use those 'wonderful toys' to blow up the SGC. Bill. Try to keep that in mind."

Lee grinned sheepishly. "Yeah. Sorry. It's just that... Well this technology, it's more advanced than anything I've seen in a long time."

The Major had to admit that the scientist had a point. The search of Wells' room in the base officer's quarters had already turned up a handful of items of decidedly unusual hardware. It was Lee who had detected the presence of an exotic device attached to the inside of the room's door, and thanks to his quick thinking Sam had been able to deactivate it with a low range pulse from a zat. She cast a careful eye over the device; it was Goa'uld, made in the shape of a scarab beetle, with an emitter spot where the insect's head would have been. If they had forced open the door, a DNA scanner on the device would have registered an intruder and unleashed a single-shot, high band energy discharge that would have reduced everything in the room to ashes.

The scarab-guard lay on the room's bed along with all the other pieces of kit they'd found so far. There was a pistol, construct of glass and lightweight silver alloy, probably some kind of coherent-energy weapon. A device that resembled the wireless datapads used at some Air Force research center only much smaller; Sam had toyed with it a little, but there were encryptions blocking access to the pad's memory and she didn't want to chance triggering any security programs that might wipe it. There was the sensor-baffle from the woman's bag, which steadfastly blanked the attempts by every scanner they had to penetrate it. Then the vials of thick, mercury-like liquid. Carter picked one up and held it to the light. The fluid inside moved sluggishly, glittering. At least she could be sure of what *this* was; the tubes contained a suspension of inert nanites, the tiny molecule-sized robots floating in a processor matrix awaiting commands to activate them. They bore some resemblance to Replicator design, but not enough to convince Sam that those artificial beings were behind this. Rather, the nanites looked like a back-engineered copy of Replicator tech, but how they'd been made was beyond her.

"Reloads," offered Lee. "Wells must have been planning to use them to top up her nanite stores when she went off shift." The scientist had already tested the remains of the micromachines that had eaten Carter's P90 and determined that they were the same strain as those in the vials.

"Lucky for us we caught her before that." Sam frowned. "If she'd had a full tank there's not telling what she could have done." She thought of the initial medical scan she'd seen of the spy, and the displays showing the reservoirs for the nanites in her bone structure. Carter's skin crawled as she thought about having those tiny robots scrabbling around inside her.

She put the vial back down and her eyes fell to the biggest of the items, sitting on the center of the blanket, ticking quietly to itself. It was translucent and smooth, slightly warm to the touch, with a striated surface made of clean, careful angles. The object unfolded at a seamless hinge along its surface, coming open like a clamshell. One inner surface was a touch-responsive keypad, another what seemed to be a multifunction display screen. At the moment, the pod showed a gently moving waveform and a stream of text made from blocky alien letters. Carter couldn't read it, but she'd seen the language of the Ancients enough times to recognize it. She held the object up to her eyes. "What is this?" she whispered, on some level hoping it might actually answer her.

"I don't know about you," said Lee, "but I am itching to have a go at that thing with a screwdriver. Metaphorically speaking, I mean."

She shook her head slowly. "Teal'c said he saw the Re'tu use something like this just before it teleported away. I'm guessing it could be a locator for some sort of beaming device, but it seems too intricate just for that."

"Maybe it actually is the transporter, not the beacon."

"Inside something no bigger than a pineapple? That's a bit of a stretch."

Lee gave her a look. "After all the stuff we've seen, you're going to choose now to start thinking small?"

"It's obviously Ancient," she replied. "But I've never seen anything close to this level of complexity in their relics."

"Now you have," said the scientist. "I mean, think about it Sam. All the artifacts the gate-builders created, all the ones we've recovered over the years, they're the commonplace ones. The stuff they made a lot of."

She smirked. "I'd hardly say a Stargate's a commonplace piece of hardware."

"To us, yeah!" said Lee, "But not to them." He pointed at the pod. "Remember that time-loop device you found on P4X-639? We haven't come across any more of those yet. That thing could be something like that, some kind of ultra-rare one of a kind..." He paused. "Well, two-of-a-kind, if the Re'tu had one as well."

Sam watched the lines of text moving back and forth. "I need to show this to Daniel." She carefully closed the device and placed it in a padded case. "When you're done, get all this other gear down to the lab. We'll run some tests, see what we can figure out."

"Where's Doctor Jackson now?" Lee asked as the armed airman at the door stepped aside to let her leave.

"The holding cells," said Sam. "Talking to the prisoner."

She looked up as he entered the room, and the expression on her face was the same one he'd seen in the infirmary

She turned away, suddenly seeming smaller in the feature-less orange jumpsuit they'd dressed her in. "I'm so sorry, Daniel."

Jackson's lip curled and he tried—and failed—to keep an angry tone from his voice. "You're sorry. About what? Planting a naquada bomb on the base or lying to me about who you really are?"

"All of the above. Please understand, everything I've done has been for right reasons. I know you'll find that hard to believe, but it's true."

"Hard to believe?" Daniel repeated, his annoyance shifting to incredulity. "Yeah, I guess when someone I thought I had a genuine connection with turns out to be an interstellar terrorist, I would have a tough time of it!"

"I'm not a terrorist," she retorted.

"Oh, pardon me." He sat down opposite her, across the table that was the room's only other furniture apart from the two chairs. "You're a 'freedom fighter', is that it?"

"In a way," she admitted. "But not the way you'd think of it."

"I'll tell you what you're not." He leaned forward. "You're not Hannah Wells from Kansas City, you're not a US Air Force major or a doctor." Unspoken words boiled at the back of Daniel's throat; he knew he was supposed to be calm and maintain an air of detachment addressing a prisoner, but this woman had cut into him in a way that he couldn't readily explain and now to learn it was all part of some subterfuge... It made him furious. "And you are not... *You are not Sha're.* So you can quit mimicking her body language."

A ghost of surprise passed over the woman's face; then her expression shifted again, and it was as if she had discarded a mask. "You're right. I apologize. I had no right to do that. I know how much you loved her." She leaned forward and ran her slender fingers through her hair, the handcuffs around her wrists clinking as she moved.

Daniel's brow furrowed. Where her fingers traced through

her dark hair they left streaks of henna-red, the coloration altering beneath her passing touch. "How are you doing that?" he demanded.

"Nervous habit," she admitted. "There are photo-molecular pigments in the follicles. I can shift my hair color just by thinking about it."

"Another kind of lie?" Jackson folded his arms. "What color hair were you born with?"

She eyed him. "To be honest with you, I don't remember."

Jackson returned her gaze. He was losing patience with her obfuscation. "You're going to be held here indefinitely. You've been classified as an enemy combatant under the provisions of the Homeworld Security Act. I have some questions for you, starting with this one. Where is the real Major Wells?"

"She's safe. She hasn't been injured. Ite-kh won't harm her, as long as you release me."

"Ite-kh?" He considered the name. "The Re'tu?" Daniel leaned back. "And just who are you and Ite-kh working for?" From the corner of his eye he could see the observation balcony above them, the compartment dark behind a sheath of mirrored glass.

"The same people as you. The people of this planet."

"What are you, an agent of the Trust? Perhaps part of the rogue NID elements we've been tracking?"

"I'm as human as you are, Daniel."

He nodded. "That, at least, appears to be partly true. At first we thought you might be a Re'tu genetic construct, maybe even an android."

"I have had some…enhancements," she admitted, "but that doesn't make me inhuman." She leaned forward. "I am not your enemy."

"You kidnapped an innocent woman and stole her identity, infiltrated this facility in collaboration with an aggressive alien life form, not to mention assaulting several Air Force personnel, plus all the lying and bomb-planting stuff." He took a breath. "You tell me what that is, if it isn't the behavior of an enemy."

Behind the one-way mirror of the observation tier, O'Neill watched with a fixed scowl and folded his arms. The door behind him opened and Carter came in, a sheaf of papers in her hands.

"Colonel," she began. "I have some preliminary intel on the prisoner."

Without taking his eyes off Jackson and the woman, he nodded. "Let's hear it."

"There's a serious mismatch between the files in the base computers and the hard-copy records in Wells's service jacket at headquarters." She brandished two sheets of print-out, one showing an image of the woman in the cell below in Air Force uniform and another of a woman of similar age and build in the same outfit. "Wells, Major Hannah Geraldine, USAF Medical Corps. This is the real person, sir. According to airline records, she flew in to Denver, rented a car and drove to Colorado Springs. At some point between there and reporting in to Cheyenne Mountain she was replaced by that woman." Sam pointed at the prisoner.

"And our files were hacked to make the substitution seem kosher," he said grimly. "Kinsey's going to shut us down for sure when he finds out about this." Jack threw a glance at Carter. "Any clue as to the status of the actual Major Wells?"

"We've got Air Force Intelligence and local law enforcement on the ground in Colorado searching. I also called in a couple of favors with my cousin in the Federal Marshal's office and had him put out a back-channel sweep for anything on Wells or..." She pointed. "Or her."

"You think she's from this planet?"

Sam gestured with the papers. "Doctor Warner seems to think it's likely. She's definitely an Earthborn human, doesn't appear to have any of the biological markers we associate with our off-world cousins. Warner's doing full blood panels and physiological work-ups right now. He should have the results within the hour."

There was an x-ray image in among the papers. Jack tapped it with a finger. "And that?" He gestured to the back of his head, indicating the location of a dark smudge on the scan. "I heard him say something about surgical implants."

"Yes sir," Carter nodded. "She's got an artificial device attached to the inside of her skull, close to the brainstem, and what seem to be nanomachine reservoirs in the hollows of her arm bones. "

"Her head's not gonna blow up, is it? I've had enough of booby traps for one day."

"This room's being blanketed with high-intensity electronic countermeasures to block any incoming or outgoing signals, just in case." Sam frowned. "But she doesn't seem the type to me, colonel."

Jack's eyes narrowed. "They never do." After a moment he looked back at her. "How's Teal'c?"

"Pretty ticked off. Soon as he had his ribs taped up, he was pushing to join the sweep teams outside the base looking for the Re'tu."

"I take it they haven't found it?"

Carter shook her head. "It clearly used the Ancient device to beam out of the base. I'd be willing to bet that by now the pulse effect has worn off and it's regained its ability to become invisible."

"So we'd have a snowball's chance in hell of finding it anyhow. Great. A missing major, our computer firewalls leaking like a sieve, and a giant spider loose in the Colorado Mountains." Jack felt like he was going to spit. "I want to know how it was she was able to breeze through every level of our security like it wasn't even there." He blew out a breath and looked back down at the figures in the holding chamber. "At least we got something to show for this."

"How did you know she was going to go for the Stargate?"

said Sam, after a moment. "There's a dozen other ways she could have tried to get out of the facility."

Below them, the woman looked up and stared directly into the mirrored glass, as if she were looking Jack right in the eyes. "It's what I would have done," he replied.

"If you release me now, I promise you I will return Major Wells to you unharmed."

Daniel flicked a glance at the security camera trained on the woman's face. "Really? Take a look around. I don't think you're in a position to make any deals, do you?"

Her lips thinned. "It's funny."

"What is?" he grated.

"Listening to you as you try to sound like an interrogator. But you can't. You want to look like you're not worried about Wells, but you are. You're afraid for her life, but you don't want to give it away." She smiled a little. "You're too kind a man, Daniel. You don't even know her, and you're afraid for her."

Jackson colored, fuming at her insight. "Can you blame me, after seeing what you and your Re'tu friend are capable of? Hannah Wells has a family, and yeah, I'm afraid that they will have to be told by someone like me that their daughter is dead."

She leaned forward. "Look at me." She met his gaze. "This is me, not lying to you. Hannah Wells is alive and well. Believe it."

And the thing was, he did. Her words didn't have the same kind of slick patina they had all the other times they had spoken. They were raw, unfiltered. He felt as if he were seeing into the truth of her, just for a moment. Then she closed up, and the instant was gone. "We'll find her," he replied. "You can be sure of that."

"Ite-kh's difficult to control when he's on his own." She said carefully. "If I'm not around, he might do something… Unpleasant."

Jackson folded his arms. "Now who's trying to play the tough guy? That's a lie again. See, I'm getting the hang of you. It's not so hard, once you know what to look for."

"You always were perceptive, Daniel," she said quietly.

"And while we're at it, you have me at a disadvantage. You're not Hannah Wells, so what is your name?"

She sighed. "Jade. My name is Jade."

"Jade *what*?"

The woman shook her head. "That's all you're getting for now."

"Why are you here? What's your mission?"

"I won't give that up to you. Ask me something else."

"All right." Jackson tapped lightly on the tabletop, thinking back to what the colonel had told him before he entered the room. "You said you're from Earth…"

"I never said that. But, yes, I am."

"So maybe you can tell me how it is you happen to be in possession of a number of alien artifacts?"

"Don't tamper with my equipment." She shifted in her seat. "If I were you, I'd warn Major Carter to leave anything she doesn't understand alone."

"Is that right?" Daniel's lip curled. "Trust me, Sam's smart enough to understand a *lot*." He took two items from his pocket and placed them on the table; the strange probe-like thing made of bony shell and the data transmitter rod. "This," he held up the organic probe. "Okay, I admit I don't have the first clue what that is. But this thing…" He picked up the rod. "This is of Tok'ra manufacture, and they're not real big on handing out their hardware to all and sundry. I'm thinking that makes you a thief as well as a liar."

She sighed. "The man I took that from had no use for it any more."

"What kind of lies did you tell him?"

"He was my friend!" she snapped, suddenly angry. "I watched him die!" Jackson stiffened at her sudden outburst, and Jade herself was surprised just as much by it. *What the hell was wrong with her?* She'd let herself be caught, and now the ironclad mask she always wore was crumbling in her hands. As much as she wanted to, she couldn't summon the strength inside her to lie to Daniel, to shroud herself in easy falsehoods. It was as if she had become glass, and Jackson could see right through her—but then, hadn't that *always* been true?

Jade glared at him. "I watched him die," she repeated, "him and hundreds of others, over and over. It made me sick. I wanted to stop it. I *will* stop it."

"By attacking us? What does Stargate Command have to with this? What do the Pack have to do with it?"

"Everything!" she spat, and sagged back into her chair. "Nothing," she continued, deflating. "It's all so…complex."

"Not from this side of the table." Daniel put the devices back in his pocket. "Look, you were right, I'm no good at this intimidation stuff." He jerked his thumb at the door. "But outside, there are people that *are*. And there's a man on this base whose conscience will not prick him one iota when he decides to turn them on you."

"Kinsey…"

"Understand this, Jade. If you don't talk to me, you'll have to talk to them." He got up and walked to the door.

"Daniel," she called, her gaze falling to the floor so that she would not have to look him in the eye.

"Yes?"

"It wasn't all lies. The connection, the friendship between us? That's real for me." She meant every word.

The only reply was the sound of the cell door locking shut.

"It's my recommendation that we immediately recall all off-world SG teams, cease gate travel and postpone the meeting with the Pack until we can get a read on this woman's intentions." Jack had barely got the words out of his mouth before Kinsey made a spitting noise under his breath from across the briefing room.

"Frankly, Colonel, I am staggered by the arrogance you display. After the monumental screw-ups you've allowed to occur on your watch, you then have the nerve to sit there and make recommendations to me?" The vice president's face twisted with scorn. "What makes you think that anything you say has any value at all?"

Inwardly, O'Neill was seething, but he maintained an insouciant air of innocence largely because he knew that would annoy the politician. "Actually, I was talking to General Hammond, not you."

"I'm inclined to agree with the colonel," said Hammond. "We need to isolate and contain any fallout from this incursion before we address any other concerns."

"You agree with O'Neill. What a surprise," sneered Kinsey. "Well I don't, George, and seeing as the President of these United States and the IOA have given me oversight in this situation, the colonel's recommendations are irrelevant."

"Technically, that's only oversight over the whole Pack treaty agreement thing," broke in Jack. "Military matters like base security—"

Kinsey's fist pounded on the top of the conference table. "You're going to lecture me on base security when you were the one who let alien terrorists inside the SGC.... *Again!*" He made a sharp gesture of dismissal. "Come on, Jack, why don't you reiterate for the record just how many times you've taken this facility—hell, this whole damn planet!—to the brink of destruction?"

A thousand acid retorts balanced on the tip of O'Neill's tongue, but with effort he reeled himself in. "Well," he said, in a languid voice, "I guess you had to be there, really…"

"Here's how it's going to be," continued the vice president, as if Jack had never spoken. "You and your people are going to clean up this mess, and we will go ahead with the rendezvous on Kytos. The Pack aren't going to tolerate another delay. We postpone this thing now and we can kiss goodbye any chance of a trade alliance with them. Nothing is going to be allowed to stand in the way of this treaty ceremony, is that clear?"

"That's your direct order, sir?" Hammond said in a level voice.

"Oh, you bet your two stars it is."

Sure, Jack thought to himself, *why let a small thing like invisible enemy infiltrators stop you from grabbing at all the prestige you can get?* Kinsey was too far into the Pack deal now to back out, not after he'd made a big show of it to the IOA and the rest of the political hordes in Washington. Even as the new president had been inaugurated, Kinsey had made no secret of his desires to take the Big Chair for himself. They'd barely gotten into the White House and already the politico was trying to cover himself in glory. *No wonder he's got such a bug up his ass about the situation... Well, more than usual.*

"Colonel," began Hammond, "brief your people. I want SG-1 to run point at the meeting site."

"One more thing," Kinsey spoke over the general. "Before I forget." He pointed at Jack. "He's not coming." The politician glared at him. "You want to stay on base, O'Neill? Be my guest, because you're on the bench for this one."

The Commander sat in the deep shadows of the rotting back porch, his leathery fingers curled around a beer bottle. He took a slow sip from the longneck and listened. There were noises coming from most of the other squalid single-story clapboard houses around the cul-de-sac where Tyke's family home sat. A few were boarded up and dark, but the majority threw sticky yellow light out on to the street through windows lined with crude iron security grilles. He could hear the babble of a television set, the wooly sounds of people arguing through walls, and under it all a constant rolling rush of sound like surf, coming from the elevated highway crossing over the projects. In the distance there was the sound of glass breaking and the pop-pop-pop of an automatic pistol. It sounded like a nine millimeter.

The noise of weapons fire made the old soldier tense a little, but he knew that the bullets weren't meant for him. The gang tags on the walls told everyone that this was a contested area, a buffer for showdowns between the idiot tribes of misguided kids that populated the slums.

Just the thought of them out there, these hordes of youths throwing each other's lives away over nothing, set the Commander's teeth on edge. They had no idea what they were doing with their future. They were wasting every second of it, squabbling over meaningless parcels of turf that were so infinitely tiny compared to all that up there.

He glanced into the sky. It was difficult to see many stars because of the light pollution spilling from the highway lamps, but he picked out a couple of constellations: Cassiopeia, The Little Bear. He'd stood on the surface of worlds on the far side of the suns that made up those shapes and looked back towards Earth. He thought about Jade, when she was small, how she asked him to explain what the shapes on the Stargate meant, the glyphs that mimicked the star-silhouettes. He'd found her a dog-eared book on the sky at night and she'd devoured it, cover to cover in a single day.

The old man rubbed the spot on his jawbone where his mastoid communicator was located; it had been quiet for days now. At his feet, in the dark, he had the grubby rotary telephone from Tyke's kitchen, a connecting length of extension cord trailing away from it across the floor and out through the open screen door. Just in case she called; in case she was forced to use conventional comms. But she wouldn't. He'd trained her better than that.

At the corner of his vision he caught a glimmer of movement. A slight impression of a non-shape, of the overgrown grass in the backyard parting in a breeze that wasn't blowing. Instantly, his beam pistol was in his hand, the weapon going warm in his grip to show it had a full charge. The Commander panned it slowly across the yard, and he saw the motion again. This time, there was a shimmering around it and presently he could make out the edges of the Re'tu as the alien adjusted its phase index enough that the old man could see some of it. Ite-kh was hazy, like something made of smoke. He could tell the arachnid was injured, and he fought down a pang of sharp fear. "Status?" he demanded. What he really wanted to do was to shout, "Where is my daughter?"

Ite-kh rasped as he walked, in the Re'tu equivalent of panting. The creature settled low on its legs, moving gingerly on one limb that seemed to be broken. It signed to him with slow, deliberated care, making sure he understood it. *Objective compromised. Mission in jeopardy. Agent captured.*

The old soldier's knuckles went white around the neck of the bottle, and with a single fierce jerk he threw it hard at the concrete wall surrounding the yard. The glass shattered wetly, leaving a fan of beer over the shabby stonework. "I told her to be careful!" he growled. "Didn't she listen?" He glared at the alien. "Why didn't she listen?"

The Re'tu bobbed gently on its good legs. *Rescue dangerous, but possible*, it told him.

The Commander wanted to say yes; so it shocked him as much as it did his comrade when he shook his head. "No." It was strange; for a moment, it was like someone else was making the choice for him. "We can't risk losing someone else. There's only the two of us now. The mission takes priority." The old man snatched up the telephone and went back into the house. "Get inside. We can't chance you being seen."

The Re'tu carefully pulled the door shut behind it and made a low whistling noise.

"Don't give me that face," snapped the old man, without even turning to look at the alien. "You think I like it any more than you do?" He finally turned and shook an age-spotted fist. "For cryin' out loud, she's my only child! You think I wanted to make Jade do this crap? Hell, do you think I even wanted any of this for her?" He gestured around angrily, as if he were taking in all the room, the world, the whole universe.

His voice carried, but no-one else in the house made any issue of it. From the other room, the muted sounds of a television on low volume reached his ears. He could see the shapes of two people on the threadbare couch; the ganger kid staring slackly into the screen, and beside him the Wells woman wearing a shapeless jogging suit that Jade had found in Keesha's closet. They did little but breathe and blink occasionally. Colonies of nanites in their bloodstream were keeping them in something just the right side of a waking coma, docile and suggestible.

Ite-kh used two of the kitchen's shabby chairs to support his thorax and picked at the wounds on his exoskeleton with a length of paper cloth. The alien eyed the Commander, not interrupting him, just waiting for him to work out what was pent up inside.

"It's my fault," said the elderly warrior, for a moment feeling every second of his advanced years. "What was I doing, putting her in harm's way?" He looked at his hands. "I made her just like me. And now I'm going to pay for it."

The alien cocked its head and grumbled. *Risks were evident,* it signed, *best agent for the operation was chosen.*

"I know that," he said hotly. "But I'm her commanding officer. I'm still to blame." He sagged into one of the other chairs. "And now... Now I have to finish this myself."

Ite-kh's manipulator talons were damp with the alien's reddish-green blood, and the Re'tu took a piece of the disposable cloth and used the fluid to mark on it, then slid it across the kitchen table toward the Commander.

The old man picked up the scrap. There were shaky four letters picked out: LNMB. He recognized the military acronym immediately. *Leave No Man Behind.*

He was silent for a moment. Then he crumpled the paper in his hand and stood up. The grim, emotionless mask of leadership had returned to his expression. "We don't have that luxury." He walked away. "Patch yourself up and gather the gear. Make sure the pods are configured for an interstellar jump. We'll piggyback off the Earth gate, save some power..." The old man paused at the threshold. "We do this right, and nothing that's happened up 'til now will matter a damn."

Carter checked the strap on her P90 for a second time and secured the weapon on her gear-vest's fast-release clip. She looked up as Colonel O'Neill entered the staging room, with Daniel a couple of steps behind. The two men threaded their way through the soldiers readying their gear. Jack ignored the junior officers and non-coms as they came to attention, making a bee-line for Sam. She noted he wasn't in off-world fatigues, but the base-side garrison jacket. "Sir?"

He answered the question before she asked it. "I'm not coming with you, Major."

"Kinsey benched him," offered Jackson helpfully.

Jack shot Daniel a hard look. "Do you have to say it like that? In front of the troops? I've got a certain dignity to uphold."

He was playing it lightly, but Carter could see that O'Neill was not pleased about being held back from the mission. "Who's going to handle the SGC detail on Kytos then, colonel?"

"Reynolds," said Jack. "but you're the officer with the most field experience, so I'd think he'd defer to you if things get, y'know, hinkey."

"Hinkey." Teal'c repeated the word, approaching from the weapons racks, his staff weapon at his side. "What is the meaning of that term?"

"It's a real word," insisted the colonel. "Hinkey. Meaning like when everything goes...weird. Like it always does."

"We have taken part in missions that did not result in any weirdness," the Jaffa noted solemnly. "On many occasions."

"Yeah," admitted Daniel, "but those aren't the ones people remember."

O'Neill made a dismissive gesture. "Whatever. Look, the op is this: Carter, you and Teal'c are going to escort that dick — I mean, the vice president — to Kytos. Make sure the meeting goes smoothly, and keep a secure perimeter around Kinsey at all times."

She nodded. "Roger that, sir. I took the liberty of issuing some Transphase Eradication Rods to SG-13. If that Re'tu turns up again, we'll be ready."

"Good call. Daniel and I are going to follow along later, after things have started rolling."

"But you're benched," insisted Jackson, "as in take off your skates and sit down."

The colonel spoke in a low, sarcastic voice. "I've always thought the orders of Robert Kinsey to be more like suggestions than actual commands..." He paused. "Besides. I want a little face time with our guest, one on one, and I'd like it without his security detail looking over my shoulder."

Carter looked to Jackson, who wore an uncomfortable expression, and then back to O'Neill. "What makes you think you're going to get any more out of her than Daniel did?"

Jack's expression softened. "I dunno. Call it instinct, but I think I might be able to get her to open up."

"The woman's behavior indicates she is an experienced clandestine operator," noted Teal'c. "She may require a more forceful application of intent before she yields."

"Let's not go to that place just yet," insisted the colonel. "Carter, you're good to go. Break a leg, or somethin'."

Sam saluted. "I'll try not to, sir."

Back in the tunnel-like corridor, Jack and Daniel made their way down the passageway. The alert sirens were sounding as the detachments made their way through the open wormhole to the Pack's rendezvous point.

"You think Teal'c might be right?" O'Neill asked the question without looking at the younger man.

"What, are we going to break out the thumbscrews, Jack?" The scientist pinched the bridge of his nose. "Come on, I mean 'forceful application'? He was talking about torture.'

O'Neill shot him a look. "Teal'c's been on the wrong end of a Goa'uld pain-stick enough times to know what it's like,

Daniel. And I had my fair share too. It's not something he'd say lightly."

"I can't believe we're even having this conversation." Jackson shook his head.

"I didn't say we were gonna stretch her on a rack, damn it!" The colonel's temper flared briefly. "But we might have to ask some hard questions. I'm thinking we could call in the Tok'ra, maybe use that mind-scanner gizmo they got."

"You say that like it's the gentler option."

Jack stopped and looked the other man in the eye. "Hey!" He snapped his fingers in front of Daniel's face. "Hey, Space Monkey! Look at me! What's goin' on? This woman lied her ass off to you, she tried to blow us all up, and here you are stepping up to defend her? Am I missing something?"

"I…" Jackson faltered, trying to find the right words. "Look, forcing confessions out of people by coercion is morally wrong no matter how you justify it."

"It's not just that, though, is it?" He could see the uncertainty in Daniel's eyes. "She really got to you, didn't she? Jackson, this woman is not what you think. She's a spy, a professional deceiver. Whatever connection you think you may have with her, it's bogus."

"No." The other man shook his head. "You've got it all ass-backwards, Jack. She's not what *you* think she is. I know it. I can't tell you how, it's just a feeling."

The intensity behind his friend's words gave O'Neill a moment's pause. He'd encountered this side of him before, in times when they had been on either side of an argument, and in times when they had stood together on something. "Is this some kind of 'Former Ascended Being' thing going on here? Where you have the power to see into people's souls?" Jack was only half-joking.

"No, it's a 'Daniel Jackson' thing. You told me once you keep me around because I tell you what I really think. Well, I'm doing that now."

And he couldn't argue with that. "Okay. I'll talk to her,

and we'll see what happens." He glanced away. "And for the record? I keep you around because you're such an easy mark at poker."

Ahead of them, Doctor Warner emerged from a side corridor and caught sight of Jack. "Colonel! Colonel O'Neill! I'm glad I caught you! There's something here you really should see..." He bounded up, brandishing a folder full of medical paperwork and printouts.

Jackson cast a eye over the files. "Is this the data on Jade?"

"Jade?" Warner blinked at the name. "Oh. The prisoner. Yes, of course. Yes, it is. Well, not all of it, but the majority..."

"What do you have that's so important I have to see it right now?" demanded Jack. Warner was a good doctor, so people told him, but the man had a tendency to ramble and meander around the point of things. He was a marked contrast from Janet Frasier, whose directness and straightforward manner had always made things clearer. O'Neill felt the slight pang of sadness when Janet's face came to him, and he forced it away. "Give it to me straight, doc."

"The prisoner—uh, that is, Jade—her blood tests and preliminary DNA scans threw up some very interesting correlations. At first I thought we might be looking at a genetic duplicate with chromosomal modifications, but that was clearly incorrect."

"Clearly," said Jack, frowning at the papers and the incomprehensible medical technobabble covering them.

Warner didn't pick up on the irony. "I looked at the possibility of her origin as something alien, perhaps with heavy retroviral adaptation, but that came up negative as well. It's clear she has had some implantation and physiological restructuring in key areas of her anatomy—" The doctor pulled at a CAT-scan and the papers in his hand came apart. Warner grabbed at the folder, trapping them before they could scatter across the floor. "Uh. Sorry."

"Warner." Jack eyed him. "Skip to the end."

"Yes, of course." He gulped. "When I was testing Jade's genetic markers, I came across a pattern that seemed familiar to me... I was sure I'd seen it before, and recently."

Daniel considered this. "Your labs are doing blood tests all the time, as a matter of course when SG teams come back through the gate."

"Looking for infection or alien infiltration, yes." agreed Warner. "So I ran a comparative analysis of Jade's profile with our database of SGC personnel."

"And you found a match?" said Jackson, reading the answer on the doctor's face.

He nodded. "A positive correlation, in the 98th percentile."

"I'm not going to like this, am I?" Jack asked.

"Her DNA matches *yours*, Colonel O'Neill."

In the cool of the evening, only the television chattered in the darkness of the house. The Commander weighed his pod in his hand and watched the sensor display spiking up and down. "Ready?" he asked.

Across the room from him, he heard Ite-kh make a snapping click of agreement. The Re'tu had sheathed itself once more, becoming indiscernible. The old soldier touched the controls of the camouflage cloak at his neck and he too shimmered into invisibility.

"Mom?" The ganger kid spoke thickly, with the diction of a drunk. "Issat you?" Beside him on the sofa, Hannah Wells was dozing lightly.

"Go to sleep, Tyke," said the Commander. "You're dreaming."

"Uh'kay," said the boy.

The pod chimed. "Wormhole's at optimum. Initiate jump." He pressed a sensor spot on the device's surface and the cold rush of transport enveloped him.

Outside on the street, a flare of star-bright light flashed through the barred windows of the house, and vanished.

Harriman looked through the control room window as the last few men stomped up the embarkation ramp and into the shimmering vertical pool of the wormhole. At that moment, one of the other technicians handed him a clipboard with a report that needed his signature, and Walter's attention strayed from the Stargate.

He never saw the flicker of silvery sparks that danced around the rim of the steel-gray ring, so fast and so subtle that to any other set of eyes they would have seemed like a reflection. This time no alarms sounded, no alerts were called. By the time the sergeant had turned back to his console, the wormhole had shrieked closed and the gate had gone dark.

CHAPTER NINE

Advance squads of USAF engineers had already set up a camp of temporary tents in the shallow valley below the ridge where the Kytos Stargate stood. Samantha Carter's first impression of the planet was the humidity; it washed over her as she stepped away from the gate and she shifted, feeling uncomfortable. One of the things they never told you about Stargate travel was the small dislocations that came with walking from one world to another in the blink of an eye. She'd gone instantly from the air-conditioned cool of the gate-room at Cheyenne Mountain to the heart of a steaming alien jungle, and her body reacted to it. The instantaneous transitions of gating were shocking if you weren't used to them.

And Vice President Robert Kinsey certainly wasn't. He emerged behind her with an air of mild terror about him, blinking in the waning light of two orange suns setting below the tops of the tree line. Then he caught Carter scrutinizing him, and he straightened, as if all this was as normal to him as climbing out of a limo at some swanky Washington function. "Carry on, Major," he told her.

"Sir," she conceded, and walked down the cairn of oval rocks that made up the Stargate's podium. Teal'c was already in discussion with Colonel Reynolds near the DHD, and Sam walked on, using the moment to take in the site the Pack had picked for the meeting.

There were some stone ruins dotted around the edge of the football field-sized clearing, blunt stubs mostly overgrown with native creepers. The khaki tents were arranged in a ring, with one larger than the others that was probably to serve as the gathering point. Portable generators were humming, and a group of airmen were erecting collapsible towers for halogen flood lamps. Night would fall quickly out here, and they'd need the illumination. Beyond them, she spied a hexagonal command and control antenna pointing up into the darkening sky.

"Major." She turned as Teal'c caught up with her. "Colonel Reynolds reports that his men detected a faint energy spike in the upper atmosphere just before we arrived."

"A hyperspace transition?"

"Most likely. I suspect the Pack flotilla are already in orbit."

Carter looked at her wristwatch. "That's about right. If they stick to the schedule, they should be here any minute."

"Hmph," said Kinsey, with an arch sniff as he drew near them. "This isn't the sort of thing I'm used to, I must admit." He sipped from a bottle of water. "Handshakes in the middle of a rainforest. But then these Pack folks seem to have a primitive mindset, so I suppose we all have to make allowances." He made a face at the muddy path they walked.

Sam's brow furrowed. "Sir, the Pack society is at least two hundred years in advance of ours…"

"In technology perhaps, I'll grant you," he allowed, "but I'm talking about culturally. Rootless nomads are essentially archaic in nature, Major. You can give them rockets and ray guns, but they're still primitives at heart."

Carter had a few choice thoughts on Kinsey's point of view, but the chance to share them with the man was lost as several fast shapes swooped low over the treetops in tight formation, the sound of their engines arriving split-seconds after the craft had flashed past.

"Painting six airborne targets," called Boyce from in front of them, relaying a radio report from the antenna tent. "Fast-movers, rolling around on another inbound pass."

"Is this an attack?" demanded the politician.

Teal'c shook his head. "If it were, we would be dead."

"They're just making a show," said Sam. "Letting us see their rockets and ray guns, sir."

Kinsey grimaced, but said nothing.

The twin sunset turned the jungle sky a burnt umber color,

catching the shapes of the Pack ships as they swept back in, this time at a higher angle. The craft loitered in the air like circling birds, one by one descending to touch down in the clearing on the far side of the tents. Carter spotted Vix's tri-wing starfighter, a Tel'tak shuttle, another one of the swan-neck flyers and a brace of Death Gliders. The last to land was a peculiar spherical craft arrayed with diamond-shaped solar panels.

Sam and Teal'c led the military contingent as Kinsey and his aides moved up to flank them. Carter gave the vice president a sideways look and saw that he'd returned to his default expression of patrician smugness.

From the parked ships came the familiar faces of Vix, Koe, Suj and Ryn, along with a few other men and women who appeared to be a security contingent. All of the Pack members were conspicuously armed this time, more so than they had been at their other meetings. Even Koe and Suj carried large and very visible guns in holsters at their belts. *I guess we shouldn't be surprised*, Sam thought. *Not after what happened at the SGC.*

Vix ran a hand through his red hair and nodded to Carter and Kinsey. "You came, then? I admit, I entertained some doubts that you would."

"We don't break our promises," Kinsey said smoothly. "I take it you picked up the samples of the supplies we offered you."

"We did," Ryn replied. "If those were a representative sample, then we have good cause to make trade."

Vix made a short noise in his throat. "Trade we can find on many worlds. It is only your assurance that you can help us defeat our grain blight that brought me back to the bargaining table, Tau'ri."

"The circumstances aboard the *Wanderer* and the greater flotilla continue to degrade," noted Koe, drawing a glare from his leader.

"Where are Doctor Jackson and Colonel O'Neill?" asked Suj, glancing around.

Kinsey answered before Carter could speak. "They've been assigned to other duties. I'm going to be leading the negotiations from this point forward."

"You?" said Vix. "The *speaker*? The man with only a single purpose for his clan?"

"That is their way," insisted Ryn. "We spoke of this. We cannot judge the Tau'ri by our own standards."

"Yes," added Koe. "Let Kinsey fulfill his role. If we require the viewpoint of a soldier or a scientist, the major may provide it. The Jaffa may speak also."

"If you wish," Teal'c offered. Sam heard the lack of enthusiasm in her friend's voice.

Vix fixed Carter with a firm, measuring stare. "I will tell you this, here and now. It is the reputation of SG-1 that convinces me to put value to your words. I believe that you, at the very least, have honor. I have little time for speakers and those whose only contribution is to lecture. Am I understood?"

"Vix, my friend," Kinsey smiled warmly, either missing or deliberately ignoring the implied jibe, "I think we're all on the same page here." He gestured to the tent set up for the meeting. "Shall we?"

As they walked, Sam lowered her voice so only Teal'c could hear her. "This is going to be a long night…"

The Jaffa didn't look at her. "Indeed."

"Show it to me again," Mirris demanded, glaring into the holographic display. "Filter out the background clutter and isolate the trace."

Geddel made the sighing noise and his fingers danced over the surface of the control slate in his hands. "One moment, Administrator. The effective range of our sensors is somewhat attenuated by the presence of the aura-cloak field."

"I am aware of that," she told him, irritably. "Compensate for interference by running a suppression protocol. It should not be necessary for me to remind you how to perform your tasks, sub-director."

Geddel sniffed. "I am attempting to perform those tasks as swiftly as I can, Administrator. I would respectfully request patience on your part."

Mirris's hands dropped below the level of her desk and she knitted them together, kneading the fingers and imagining Geddel's soft, fleshy neck in their grip. She did not want to admit it to herself, but as time passed on, she was having greater and greater difficulty in maintaining her outward pretence of control. They were so very close now, and there had already been too many upsets to her plans. To have another problem arise at this moment, just as it seemed events were returning to the pattern she had made for them, was almost too much to bear. "Geddel," she said, a warning tone in her voice.

"I have it," he replied. The holographic tank writhed and changed, becoming two conjoined cubes of ghostly light. One showed the streams of data filtering in from the ship's sensor array, the other gave them a topographical map of an area on the surface of Kytos, a zone several metrics wide around the Stargate. Dots of color indicated the presence of many Tau'ri warriors. As she watched, Mirris saw the time index loop back to a moment just before the alert had sounded and then begin moving forward once more. Small peaks and troughs showed the minute energetic fluctuations of the gate's wormhole conduit as it deposited travelers on Kytos; and then suddenly, on a sub-frequency unconnected to the usual workings of the Ancient devices, there was a brief spike of output. Mirris froze the image and expanded on it, teasing the waveform apart.

"There are actually two distinct signals within the anomalous reading," noted Geddel. "Very close together, operating on almost the same pattern. It's quite fascinating."

"There is nothing else it could be?" she asked him. "Not some sensor reflection artifact, perhaps? There is no possibility that any ships within the migrant fleet detected us as we followed them through hyperspace?"

"Negative, Administrator. We traversed from the Golla system inside their thrust wake." He said it with an air of disdain.

"These nomads do not possess the science to track and locate a craft of this class. It can only be as I described." Geddel tapped another control and the display changed to show a graphic of a Stargate. "The energy pulse, however it was contained, was directed through the open wormhole from the Tau'ri home-world. I doubt the Earthers were even aware of it."

Mirris's annoyance ebbed for a moment, replaced by cool, analytical thought. "A matter stream from a molecular trans-porter. Something came through the Stargate with the Tau'ri. Something moving in stealth."

"Undoubtedly."

She tapped a sensor tab on her desktop. "Signals," she ordered, opening a voice link to the ship's communications grid. "Collate a tight-beam transmission using full emissions security protocols and encoding."

"You're going to contact the migrant operative?" Geddel asked. "That presents a risk of discovery."

"This information cannot be ignored," Mirris retorted. "I must pass on a warning. There are unknown infiltrators on Kytos and I have little doubt that they are part of the same group that attempted to sabotage the accord meeting on the Tau'ri planet." She considered it for a moment. "I suppose I should not be surprised that they would attempt to disrupt it a second time."

"If I might remark, Administrator. Your operative's per-formance to this point has not been noteworthy. What makes you believe that imparting this new intelligence will improve that?"

"What do you propose?" she snapped back at him. "That we deploy an assault force, reveal ourselves to the Tau'ri and the Pack?"

"It is an option," Geddel said in a small voice.

"This is supposed to be a clandestine mission," Mirris replied. "The execution of it hinges on that factor! I will draw our weapons directly only if and when there is no other recourse open to us."

"Of course." Geddel bowed slightly. "I was merely offering all alternatives for your consideration."

"Leave me," she told him, turning away. "Continue your surveillance of the migrants and the planet."

When he was gone, Mirris took a deep breath and spoke into her communicator. "Listen carefully," she began, "There is a threat…"

From almost the instant they had rematerialized among the trees, the cloak around the Commander's shoulders began to malfunction. The device was old and it had been running too much recently, first with Jade on Golla IX and now here on Kytos. The flexible pigmentation cells wavered between dozens of different camouflage settings, some of them wildly inappropriate for the emerald shades of the rainforest. Finally, the old man swore under his breath and flicked the controls to a neutral, olive drab. "Forget it," he growled. "More damn trouble than it's worth." He beckoned the Re'tu toward him. "Stay close. I need you to watch my back while I get this set up."

The Commander shrugged off a small backpack made of non-reflective material and pulled open the seal tab. Inside, a compact cylindrical device glittered dully; the black-and-yellow radiation trefoil on the weapon's flank was the first thing that drew his eye. He realized the alien wasn't responding and glanced up. "Ite-kh!" he hissed in a low voice. "I'm talkin' to you!"

The Re'tu attention was elsewhere. The semi-visible smoke-shape of the insectoid raised a taloned hand in a signal for silence. In his other grip, Ite-kh was carefully manipulating a sensor pack.

"You got something?"

The alien's head bobbed and it pointed into the makeshift camp. It turned the scanner so that the old soldier could see the display.

His face creased in concern. There on the device was a tell-tale energy signature that the Commander had come to know intimately through their long and hard battles with the enemy. Somewhere in that camp, a device of enemy origin was operating.

He wavered for a moment, his hands still on the weapon in the bag, unsure of how to proceed. "Forget it," he said, at last. "It won't matter how many of them are here. We set this up, and the job's done."

Ite-kh threw him a look, and with the same studied motions the Re'tu shook its head. Before he could stop it, the alien shimmered and became completely invisible. Grasses and underbrush shifted as the arachnid raced away toward the camp.

The old man swore under his breath. "Fine," he said to the air. "I won't wait for you. I'm not going to screw this up because you went John Wayne on me!"

His eyes dropped back to the cylinder, and it was as if a shadow crossed his face. The cold reality of what he was going to do settled on him like a shroud. In other times, when he was a younger man, he might have hesitated, he might have wanted some kind of forgiveness for taking measures as drastic as these. Things were different now, though. The war had burned those kinds of emotions from him, taken that away along with all the people he cared about. Their faces floated in the back of his mind as he began to assemble the device; he would do this for them, and for all the billions who had followed them into death.

O'Neill dropped into the chair across the table from the woman and studied her. The first thing he noticed was that she wouldn't meet his gaze; she just kept her eyes down, staring at the scuffed olive-drab vinyl of the tabletop.

"Conundrum," Jack offered to the air. "Found that in my copy of *Improve Your Word Power*. Sums you up pretty good, I reckon." When she didn't speak, he went on. "Jade. Cute name. That your real one, or is it someone else's? I only ask because you seem to like being who you're not."

"It's my name," she admitted. "I wouldn't lie about that."

And strangely, Jack had the sudden impression that she *wouldn't*. He'd dealt with enough liars in his time to have a feeling for the truth, and this seemed like it. Either that, or she was such an accomplished con artist he was being snowed and not even knowing it. "Where's Major Wells, Jade? It would go a lot better for you if you just told us where she is." More silence. "Is she dead?" The colonel asked the question in a deceptively light tone.

"I don't think so."

"We're going to find her sooner or later, you understand that, right? Carter, y'see, she figured out that if we could track the naquadria traces on you, we might be able to use 'em to pinpoint where you'd been hiding out recently."

The woman's brow furrowed. "That's... Clever. I didn't think she knew how to do that yet."

"Oh, she's real smart, Jade. Like you wouldn't believe. Sometimes, the stuff she comes out with, even I have a hard time keeping up with it." He pointed up at the ceiling. "Right now, there's a DOD surveillance satellite floating over Colorado following a trail of radioactive breadcrumbs. You could save me a lot of time and just cut to the chase."

She hunched forward. "I think I've said enough already."

Jack tapped his finger on the table. "Just so we're clear, you *do* understand the depths of crap you're in, right? Acts of infiltration and attempted terrorism on a United States military base? That pretty much negates anything close to legal rights you might have, and that's before we get into the whole 'above top secret Stargate program' part." He shook his head. "Collusion with known alien aggressor forces. You're not going to get a fair trial, Jade. We're going to put you in the deepest, darkest hole on Earth and leave you there." He kept his voice conversational, and that made the menace of the threat seem harsher still.

At last, she looked at him. "You've done things you're not proud of, Jack O'Neill. Things you did in service to the flag or your planet. You've sent men on missions you knew would kill them. You've made choices that keep you awake at night." None of what she said was a question; it was simply that she knew the answers already. "And you'll do it again."

"Comes with the job," he said warily. The girl's sudden insight made him feel uncomfortable. He had the sudden, distinct impression that she knew him, on a level far more intimate than he could fathom. "Are you telling me that's what you were doing? *Just following orders*?" He stiffened. "The difference is, Jade, that I'm a soldier and I wear a uniform. What I am is right here in front of you, I don't hide it behind names I stole from other people."

"I'm just like you," she replied. "It's just that my war is different."

Before he could respond, there was a swift knock on the door and he turned as the guard on duty opened it to allow Sergeant Siler to peer in. "Colonel? We got a hit. Downtown Colorado Springs, a residential district. Doctor Jackson and the sweep team are moving in as we speak."

Jack glanced back at the woman. "Told ya."

The three-vehicle convoy drew to a halt under the highway bridge, just short of the mouth of the cul-de-sac. Daniel was in the trailing car, a black Suburban with smoked windows and government plates. Across from him an agent from the Office of Air Force Intelligence listened intently to a wireless radio headset in her ear. "Copy," said the woman, an austere brunette who had introduced herself as Agent Janine Cooper. "Tactical confirms, positive tracking of anomalous signature is concentrated in the fourth house along." She glanced at the screen of a palmtop in her hand. "Number fifty-two, Ventura Terrace. Residence is listed as domicile for Farrell, Keesha, adult female, and Farrell, Tyrone, juvenile male." Cooper hesitated, then continued. "Be advised, I'm seeing flags here from the local PD. The kid's on their gang unit's watch list." She paused, and Jackson heard the tinny whisper of voices coming from the headset. "Roger that. All units, stand by to deploy on my command." She looked at him. "This Tyrone—he goes under the name of Tyke, apparently—he's been seen in the local mini-mart a couple of times over the past few days, acting strangely."

"How so?"

"Guy at the store said he was ignoring his buddies, shuffling around like a zombie. Just bought stuff, paid for it, walked out. Never spoke."

Daniel squinted though the SUV's windshield and saw the van in front of it. Inside was a strike team of men in black tactical body armor with automatic weapons; nobody was taking any chances today. Jackson carefully unzipped a gear case that O'Neill had handed to him and removed a TER from inside.

Cooper's eyes widened. "My youngest has a water gun just like that," she told him.

"Not like this," Jackson replied. "And believe me, I don't want to have to use it." He thumbed the activation stud and the rod's emitter cone went live.

"Oh-kay," said the agent. "Anything else you'd like to volunteer, Doctor Jackson, before we start kicking doors down? Like why Air Force Space Command have us raiding some no-name gangbanger's crib on the wrong side of the tracks?"

"Need to know, I'm afraid." Daniel replied. He tried to sound convincing, but to be honest, all this cloak-and-dagger stuff had never been his strong point.

"Right," Cooper replied, with a frown. She tapped her headset. "All units. Remember, we're looking for a friendly here, so watch those sight lines." The woman gripped the door handle. "On my order. Execute, execute, execute!"

Jackson had to scramble to get out after her, as the agent moved low and fast toward the single-story dwelling. He swung the TER this way and that, watching for the tell-tale shimmer of a Re'tu, hoping all the while he wouldn't see one. He imagined himself explaining it to Agent Cooper. *Oh, didn't*

I mention there might be a alien monster from outer space hiding in there? Sorry.

The metal gate protecting the front door went down as the men on point used a directed cutting charge on the heavy lock; then two more agents took out the hinges on the door itself with shotgun blasts. It fell back like a drawbridge and the black-clad men boiled inside, fanning out into the rooms of the house. Cooper and Jackson were close to the back of the group, and as the reverberation of the shots died away the next sound to reach Daniel's ears was the incongruous theme music to *Wheel of Fortune.*

"Clear!" called a voice from the hallway. Jackson panned the TER around just in case it actually *wasn't* clear, as other agents chimed in on the same chorus. In the living room, he saw the flickering blue glow of a television set and on it the grinning face of a game show host.

"Doctor!" called Cooper. "Get in here."

Daniel threaded his way past the black-suited tactical officers to the agent's side. Cooper stood facing two unhealthy-looking people on a threadbare sofa. He recognized the real Hannah Wells from her service records. The teenage boy sitting next to her was most likely Tyrone Farrell. He gave the room one more sweep with the TER and then let it drop on its strap. If the Re'tu was here, it would have made itself known by now. "Major Wells?" he asked, leaning down. "Hannah? Hannah, can you hear me?"

The woman blinked owlishly, staring right through him, her glazed expression fixed on the TV. The boy had exactly the same look on his face. A blank, soporific daze.

"Are they okay? Are they on something?"

"Something," repeated Daniel. Both of them had the look of borderline malnutrition about them, and in the flickering light of the television he saw a grainy white residue marking the skin of their necks, in a spot just below the right ear. He thought about the white powder he'd found on his jacket where Hannah… Where *Jade* had touched him.

Cooper snapped her fingers in front of Tyrone's face. "Huh. Looks like whatever party these guys were having, we missed it."

"Yeah," Jackson allowed, rising as another agent entered the room.

"Ma'am," began the other officer, "got some traces in the other parts of the house. Empty beer bottles, utensils and stuff in the sink. We found till receipts from the store, food and drink. I'd say we've had four, possibly five persons in this house for the last couple of days."

"Any signs of weapons, illicit equipment?"

"Nothing yet. We'll give the place the full treatment, see what turns up."

Daniel listened carefully. "You're not going to find the stuff they were using with conventional sensors, Agent Cooper. I'll get General Hammond to send a team of our people to do a sweep."

"Your people?" Cooper replied, arching an eyebrow. "And what about *these* people?" She pointed at Wells and the boy.

"They're going to be coming with me," he replied.

The woman placed her hands on her hips. "Is that right? Well, then, perhaps Doctor Jackson, you might give me some kind of idea of what exactly I'm supposed to put in my post-operation report for this little outing."

"Training exercise?" he suggested. "Believe me, it's best you don't know." Daniel hesitated. "Do you like spiders?" He made an eight-legged shape with his hands, wiggling his fingers.

In spite of herself, Cooper shuddered. "Not really, no. They give me the creeps."

"Then trust me, you *really* don't want to know."

O'Neill came back into the room with a hard look in his eye. The guard inside the room shut the door behind him and locked it, standing across the threshold.

"Bus-ted," Jack told Jade. "Nice digs you had there. Very *Boyz N The Hood*, so Jackson tells me. You gonna start talking now?"

For a split-second, he saw a flash of panic on her face, but then she buried it and schooled her expression. "Major Wells was recovered alive."

"Yup. Her and the kid. No thanks to you." He drummed his fingers on the table. In truth, Jack was annoyed by the apparently cavalier mistreatment of Wells and the Farrell boy, but he couldn't let it show too much. "So how'd you do it? Dope them up with some kind of drugs to keep them obedient, while your buddies hid out in the house and you stole Wells's identity?"

"Not drugs," she admitted. "That wouldn't have worked. I used nanomachines to edit their neurochemical processes, just temporarily."

"Oh, that sounds much more humane," Jack retorted, his irritation poking through.

"It would have been much more expedient to kill both of them," she snapped back. "That they're still alive should tell you something."

O'Neill snorted. "You'll pardon me if I'm not overcome by your kind-heartedness."

She sighed. "Listen to me carefully. A tight-beam electromagnetic pulse on the kappa-band frequency will trigger an automatic shutdown of all the nanites in their bloodstreams. They'll come out of the somnambulant state in about five hours."

"I'll pass that along."

Jade eyed him, and O'Neill felt uneasy under the girl's sudden scrutiny. "The others weren't there, were they? Ite-kh and…" She halted. "They've already gone."

"We'll find your bug-eyed buddy and whoever else was hiding out there," Jack replied. "It's just a matter of time."

She shook her head. "No. They might not…."

Her expression changed suddenly, from a tense, fixed

façade to a sharp look of real, immediate fear. It was so quick and so fluid that O'Neill knew it had to be real.

"You have to release me!" she blurted suddenly.

"Ain't gonna happen,"

"My equipment, then!" Jade snapped. "Bring it to me! It's important! I have to see the pod…"

Jack shook his head. "Nope."

Jade rocked back in her chair and fell silent. After a moment, she spoke again. "All right, then." She convulsed and her eyes rolled back in her head, showing the whites.

"What the hell?" said the guard. A drool of white foam issued out of Jade's lips and she lolled back against her chair, twitching.

"Ah, damn it!" O'Neill got to his feet and punched the intercom on the wall. "Containment room six, medical emergency. I need a doctor down here, double-time! The prisoner's having some kind of seizure!"

The guard was already at the girl's side, reaching for her.

"Careful," Jack began.

"I've got her, sir," said the airman. But he hadn't.

Jade moved like lightning, her eyes snapping back as she did an nearly-impossible pivot on the steel chair and spun her legs around to scissor-kick the guard in the head. The man fell and she was rolling over him, tugging his Beretta M92 pistol for the holster on his belt as she flipped, her jumpsuit making her a blur of orange.

O'Neill pulled his own gun and leveled it as a shot echoed through the concrete room. The colonel felt the sonic pulse as the bullet passed his head and smashed the intercom vox on the wall. Jack shifted, his back pressed flat against the door, and then they were there, the two of them aiming guns at each other's heads.

"Drop the weapon and get out of my way." Jade spoke tonelessly.

"I'm not going to be doing that," Jack's reply was careful.

"I'll kill you," she told him.

The moment the words left her lips, he knew it was a lie. "No. You won't." He looked her right in the eyes. "You *can't*."

She pulled back the pistol's hammer. "I will!"

"This from a woman who planted a bomb that was made to be a dud. Who could have used her nano-deelies to strip Carter's skin from her bones. Who let two prisoners live when it would have been simpler to just roll them in a ditch somewhere." He nodded at the insensate airman on the floor. "All those guys you beat up? You went for disabling hits instead of straight kills. And now you're gonna turn murderer?"

"Get out of my way!" she shouted, her face reddening.

"Seems we had this conversation before," Jack safed his weapon and placed it back in the holster. "Gate-room? Remember? I didn't go then. I won't go now."

Jade flinched as if he'd struck her. Slowly, the woman turned the pistol in her hands, weighing a darker and more final solution to her confinement.

O'Neill used the moment of distraction and grabbed at her, tearing the weapon from the woman's grip before she could use it. "What the hell were you thinking?" he demanded.

Jade sat silently on the table and looked up at him. Her eyes were shining. "I'm sorry," she said, in a small voice, like a child. "I've let you down. I've let everyone down."

Behind him, the door slammed open and in the corridor beyond there was Warner, Siler and a detail of armed men. Jack ignored them and kept his steady gaze on the girl. "Why don't you tell me about it?"

CHAPTER TEN

The Jaffa walked the edge of the tree line, taking care to move as silently as possible, his staff weapon held in the crook of his arm. Although he had made no mention of it to Major Carter, he was glad to have been given the opportunity to slip away from the discussion in the long tent. She was a perceptive woman; Carter only had to glance at him to see the hardness in his eyes and know that Teal'c was, as O'Neill would have put it, "bored out of his skull". She suggested quietly that he check the perimeter and Teal'c was more than willing to oblige.

Listening to Kinsey's pontifications and Vix's grim-faced rebuttals tried his patience. More than once, the Jaffa had entertained the fantasy of bellowing "Enough!" at the top of his lungs and slamming his staff down on the tabletop. What was it, he wondered, that made all races become hide-bound and slow when affairs of state were the matter at hand? Politics—he loathed the idea of it. It was anathema to a man of action like Teal'c, and he hoped fervently that his nascent nation of the Free Jaffa would not fall prey to the same sort of chattering and time-wasting. He had not fought to break the yoke of the System Lords for such things…

He passed around the soldiers from the SGC and the guardsmen from the Pack flotilla, taking care not to disturb their patrol patterns. All seemed attentive and at the ready; he threw a nod to Everitt, who stood at the outer edge of the encampment, and the wary young Lieutenant raised his rifle in a half-salute.

Teal'c hesitated for a moment at the edge of the open clearing where the Pack had landed their ships. Already, an unspoken agreement had formed between the two groups, with the Air Force troopers sticking to their side of the space and the warriors of the Pack keeping out of the tented camp, but Teal'c was Jaffa, and he felt that gave him the entitlement to move wherever he wished. He walked on, around the slightly inclined glade, studying the silent vessels. Most of the Pack's guardsmen were concentrated around a thermal heater at the rear of the parked Tel'tak; the cargo vessel's loading ramp was down and dull red illumination spilled from inside. He noted this with an approving nod — Vix's men were intelligent enough not to ruin their night vision with lights in the normal spectrum.

He continued on his patrol, passing the two parked Death Gliders. They were models he recognized, two-seater Osiris-types with twin fixed energy cannons. Between them sat Vix's personal starfighter. The Pack's leader no doubt had the pick of vessels in the flotilla's inventory, but rather than pilot something showy and large, the man had chosen a compact craft, a well-muscled ship that gave fully half its fuselage to a triad of pulsar engines. Twin beam weapons hung either side of the blunt snout, and the puffs of carbon scoring around them made it clear they were no strangers to being fired in anger. Teal'c found himself wondering what the starfighter would be like to fly; doubtless fast and lethal, but perhaps without the agility of a Glider.

His attention was on the cusp of wandering when an involuntary twinge in the muscles of his forearm brought the Jaffa back to the moment. The sudden bloom of tension flowed through him and settled in a tightness around his chest. *There is a threat here.*

Teal'c's eye line was instinctively drawn across the landing field to one of the other Pack ships, the swan-necked flyer. The craft had an oval primary hull with engines on outriggers and a delicate forward fuselage studded with canards and gun muzzles. *Ryn's vessel*, he remembered. The egress hatch at the rear was open, and as he watched through the bubble-canopy, the Jaffa made out the shape of something moving inside the ship's cockpit. Just the ghost of a motion, a faint shadow; there was something about the movements that struck him as wrong, as covert.

"Intruder…" The word came out in a whisper, a confirmation of what his senses were already telling him. He was feeling the same rough edges of sensation that had brushed against his thoughts back at the SGC. Was it possible? Could the Re'tu saboteur somehow have followed them here, to Kytos?

Part of Teal'c knew that his first action should be a warning to Carter and the others, but that part was drowned out by a hot flood of anger, by the need to face the enemy that had left him beaten and bleeding in the SGC elevator shaft. Keeping low, he skirted around to the swan-ship's aft quarter and slipped through the open hatch.

"No, Doctor Jackson, down here." Siler pointed along the corridor in the opposite direction.

He halted, drumming his fingers on his belt. The rush of adrenaline from the raid on the Farrell house was still tumbling around his system, and the helicopter ride back to Cheyenne Mountain hadn't calmed him any. "This is the way to the base's cells, isn't it?"

"Yes sir," said Siler, "but the prisoner's been moved to medical isolation on Colonel O'Neill's orders."

"She's sick?"

"No, but Doctor Warner…" Siler frowned. "Well, I guess it probably would be best if the colonel filled you in on the whole thing."

Daniel nodded. "Okay. That way, then." Jackson followed the sergeant, musing. He'd relaxed a little after they'd touched down and Warner's senior nurse—Cathy, that was her name, the one who had the nice smile—had taken custody of Wells and the boy. She'd confirmed what he'd begun to suspect on the flight back, that the white residue was some kind of by-product of nanomachine use. Clearly, the nanites she deployed had multiple applications. Perhaps the marks on his jacket had been some kind of tracer; and it was obvious that Jade hadn't tried to dose him in the same way she had the others. He found that odd. Why had she left him untouched?

Siler opened the door and gestured inside. "Here we are, Doctor."

Daniel stepped into the room and saw a ring of medical monitors, a couple of gurneys and assorted other kinds of hospital hardware. Jade was sitting on one of the beds with a dejected look on her face as Jack and Warner stood nearby in close conversation with General Hammond. He couldn't miss the two armed Marines flanking the door, each with an M4 rifle in a ready stance.

The woman looked up as Daniel approached and a glimmer of gratitude lit her face for a brief instant.

Jackson's first response surprised him. "You didn't hurt her?" he demanded from O'Neill, feeling a flare of anger as he recalled their earlier conversation.

"Of course not," the colonel shot back hotly.

"I'm… okay," offered Jade. "I thought it would be best to have a doctor present."

"Present for what?" said Daniel.

"I'm still against this, Colonel," Hammond's voice was low. "Willfully exposing two of my senior staff to this, it's inviting havoc."

Jack nodded at Warner. "The risk is minimal, right?" The doctor nodded back warily. "He knows what to look for, how to pull us out if it all goes screwy. And it's not like we haven't done this kind of stuff before, with those human-form Replicators."

"Sorry, what?" Daniel waved a finger, trying to get a feel for the situation. "I'm missing something here."

Jack kept talking. "I'm going to run the risk, General. We need to know the whole truth, sir, not just scratch around with pieces of it." He pointed at the woman in the orange jumpsuit. "If her way is the only way to do it, then I'm taking that train."

"Perhaps, if I had a couple of days to give Major Wells and the boy a thorough examination, learn more about the nanites."

"There's no time for that," said Jade dully. "Everyone on Kytos is in jeopardy."

"So *you* say," replied Hammond. "For all we know, this could be an attempt to manipulate us into taking you there."

"General," O'Neill's voice was firm. "I know this sounds wacky, but I trust her. Even after everything that's happened, I believe one hundred percent that she is not lying about this."

"I trust her too." It was a moment before Daniel realized that the words had been his. He frowned. "Why do I get the feeling I just agreed to something I shouldn't have?"

"She's willing to give us the skinny on her mission and the reasons behind it," said Jack, "but only to you and me and only through, uh... What did you call it?"

"A neural induction link," Jade replied. "It's like touch-telepathy, but via technological means."

"As in those nanites?" Daniel's blood ran cold.

Warner had one of the vials of silver fluid in his hand. "She'll need this."

Hammond took the glass tube and stepped closer to the woman. "I want you to understand me, miss. I'm agreeing to this against my better judgment. Hell, I'm agreeing in spite of all evidence to the contrary that I should lock you up and throw away the key. The only reason I'm not doing that is because those two men say they trust you." He unlocked the cuffs around her wrists and handed her the vial. Jade pressed it to the back of her hand; with a slight hiss of pressure, the silver liquid discharged into her flesh. "You need to know one thing," the general continued, the normally composed lines of his face hard and serious. "If I even so much as suspect you are attempting to coerce or injure Colonel O'Neill or Doctor Jackson, those two Marines at the door there have orders to shoot you where you stand. Are we clear?"

"Perfectly, sir," Jade replied. "I don't want to see them hurt any more than you do."

"Then let's get this over with." Hammond stepped back as

Jack approached the gurney, beckoning to Daniel.

"C'mon. What, are you chicken?"

"A little," Jackson admitted, coming closer. "I don't want to end up blank-eyed and brain-fried." He tapped his head. "It's my favorite organ."

"My second-favorite, actually," said O'Neill.

"This is different to what I did to Tyke and Hannah," Jade raised her hands, and he saw the shimmer of something metallic on her fingertips. "It only works when you're in physical contact with someone else. I'm going to give you both a direct link into my conscious thoughts. You'll see my memories."

"The truth?" asked Daniel.

She nodded. "I can't lie to you in there. No-one can."

He was aware of Warner taping medical sensors to his throat and temple. Jade's fingers touched a spot behind his right ear and he flinched; it was cold.

"Here we go," she said. "This will feel…a little weird."

The Pack ship was cramped, the interior spaces ranging off a single narrow corridor that ran from the open airlock at the aft right through to the slender cockpit area in the nose. Teal'c belatedly realized that he had practically no room to maneuver his staff weapon inside the close quarters; a zat'ni'katel or a Tau'ri handgun would have served him better. He moved silently forward, spreading his weight as he moved to avoid any tell-tale creaking from the deck plates beneath his boots.

The pressure on his senses was there, the taint of the Re'tu's presence hanging in the air. Light shifted as something rendered barely visible moved in the cockpit section. The shape dithered over a console and then drifted away. The Jaffa studied the panel that had attracted the alien's interest; it seemed out of place, as if it had been retrofitted into the swanship's systems. Where the controls of Ryn's vessel were made of beaten copper or red-enameled steel, this device was of blank, brushed silver. A hologram cube hovered over it, turning slowly. Teal'c's eyes narrowed. It looked like some kind of communications module, and the design was familiar to him, but he couldn't place it.

He moved closer, to the threshold of the hatch that led into the cockpit proper. *There*. He saw the shimmer, like heat haze, where the Re'tu was toying with the ship's navigational logs.

The Jaffa knew that the staff was useless to him in such a confined space. He let it drop with a clatter that drew the arachnid's attention, the Re'tu's ghostly head swiveling to face him.

The creature pushed off at him, spinning around hands of bladed talons, but Teal'c was too fast. The two warriors collided with one another and went down to the cockpit floor, the alien's form shimmering between opaque and glassy invisibility.

There was this one time, out at Nellis for a Red Flag tournament, when O'Neill had learned what the real meaning of the term *flight envelope* was. Aviators use the phrase to describe the graph of capability given to any particular aircraft—how fast it can go, how high it can fly, how many gees it can take before it starts to spit rivets and disintegrate, that kinda thing—and each plane has its own one. Take your aircraft too far toward the upper right-hand corner of that graph, though, and bad things will happen to you. And on this one day, when he was strapped into the cockpit of an F-16C and making it do things that would have caused airframe designers to weep, Jack had learned that the reason it was called an *envelope* was because the upper right-hand corner was the place where they got *stamped*.

The bird just came apart underneath him and one second he was flying, the next he was falling. Ejected, out, tumbling toward a featureless sea of desert. And the rush, the sensation it gave him… Jack had never forgotten it.

What was happening to him now was a lot like that, except this time he didn't have a parachute.

"Holy crap." She hadn't been wrong when she said it

would be weird. Jack felt a dozen sensations all at once, flashing through him with incredible speed. Images and feelings
bounced through his mind's eye so fast he could barely comprehend them. *The fur of a sleeping cat. Ice cream taste on the
tongue, chocolate chip. A dog barking. Screams. Freshly-cut
grass. Falling. A gunshot wound. Wet stones. Music, like wind
chimes. Darkness. And cold. And...*

He shook the feelings away, letting them ebb. "Uh. That
was unpleasant." O'Neill blinked. The cold was staying with
him, not fading like everything else. It was a deep chill, the
kind that made you feel like the ice was getting into your
bones. He shivered involuntarily and looked up. "Oh." He
managed, after a moment. "Wow."

Desolation; the word had more meaning to Jack in this one
moment than it ever had before in his entire life. They were
standing on a road, with stands of dead trees going on for miles
on either side. Cars were dotted here and there along the highway at odd angles, like they were toys abandoned by a child.
The sky was the color of old granite, low and threatening; the
air was the worst thing, though. It was dense with the smell
of decay, old ash and damp rot. He was walking, Jackson and
Jade there next to him.

She wore a slight frown, concern in her eyes mixed with a
sort of sadness that reminded him of doctors. That kind of look
they had when they brought you bad news. *Someone you love
is gone forever. I'm sorry. Are you all right?*

"Are you all right?" said Jade. "Take a moment. The shift
can be difficult if you're not used to it."

"Where..." Daniel seemed to sag under the weight of his
own question. "Where are we?"

"Still in the SGC, still in that room," she explained, "but this
is from my memories. You're getting it first hand. Think of it
as virtual reality."

Jack shuddered. "Too damn real for me."

Daniel peered into one of the derelict cars, a rusting red
Toyota with its nose rammed into the median strip. There was

a skeleton inside, draped over the steering wheel. The rest of the vehicle was full of boxes, suitcases, some torn open, others intact. From where he stood, Jack could see the driver had died of a gunshot wound to the head. The entry point for the bullet through the spider-webbed windscreen was still visible. "This is Earth," said Jackson. "This car has a Colorado license plate."

Jade nodded solemnly. "We're just a few miles outside the Denver city limits." She pointed up along the highway. "There, see it?"

O'Neill squinted in the direction she indicated. For a second he couldn't see anything, but then his eyes adjusted to the gray-on-gray of the landscape and suddenly he could see the lightless towers of the metropolis pushing up against the stony sky. Even from this far away, he could see the dullness of their shapes, the yawing chasms of a thousand shattered windows. Faint black streamers, like smoke, moved in the middle distance. "What is that?"

"Crows," Jade replied. "Some species of birds had a natural immunity, but we never found out why. They're about all that's left at this point, along with the roaches." The wind began to pick up, blowing fines of dust around their ankles. They walked on in silence, listening to the barren world around them.

"This is some sort of alternate reality..." said Daniel, after a while. Jack knew the look in his eyes, that moment when the guy started putting facts together in his head faster than anyone could follow. "I've seen the same kind of thing."

Jade nodded, breaking in. "I know, the Quantum Mirror from P3R-233. I've heard the stories." She shook her head. "This isn't that, Daniel. Oh god, I wish it was."

Jack grimaced. "If you're making this stuff up to scare us, I admit, okay, it's all too creepy for me."

"This isn't fantasy," she insisted. "This is reality. This is fact. This is where I'm from, this is my *now*." Jade sighed. "I'm showing you the last memory I have of Earth, from a little over thirty years in your future."

"Say what?" O'Neill felt ice in his veins. "Where the heck are all the flying cars and robot maids? C'mon on now, it should look like *The Jetsons*, not… Not like this!"

"You're from the future, that's what this is all about?" Daniel fixed her with a hard look.

Jack kicked at loose stone. "Aw nuts. That would be a lot easier to ignore if we hadn't done that 1960s trip ourselves."

She nodded again. "From your viewpoint, in around two decades the Earth becomes a wasteland. Burnt-out, almost nothing left. Most of the population has died off, and those who didn't fled off-world in ships or through the gate before the… Before the collapse. Some of us escaped to safe havens, places like Chulak and Holdfast. Not that it did us much good."

Jade stopped and sat heavily on the hood of a gutted Chevy. It was hard for her to talk about this; the horrible reality of it was pressing down on her. Jack felt the emotion radiating off her like waves of heat. "This is the end result, the legacy of your harmless little treaty with the Pack. This is mankind dying a slow and lingering death." She looked up at him. "This is what I've dedicated my life to stopping."

Teal'c had once heard General Hammond speak of a particular combat engagement as being similar to 'a knife fight in a phone booth', and at the time, the Jaffa had found it difficult to visualize such a battle. Now, with the Re'tu's limbs slashing the air around him and the confines of the swan-ship cockpit pressing in on them from all sides, he found a measure of understanding.

In the rush of the fight, Teal'c was losing himself, switching to pure animal adrenaline and pressing every ounce of his strength into disarming and beating the alien insect. He had already smashed the Re'tu's beam gun from its grip and sent it skidding away, but with such a creature 'disarming' meant snapping the razor-sharp talons or outright rendering it insensate.

He rained punches against the arachnid's softer underbelly, and it grunted with pain. Teal'c remembered where he had hurt it before, pressing into the thing's injured leg and setting it off balance. The Re'tu had cut a swath through the SGC and left him for dead; the Jaffa was determined that this rematch would have a very different outcome.

A double-slash from twin leg-talons gouged his torso, but Teal'c shut out the pain. He could sense the alien was flagging, the will for battle ebbing under his ceaseless attacks. There was a moment he was waiting for, searching for, and it came. The Re'tu let its guard down for one fleeting instant and Teal'c pounced on the moment. His fist curled, the Jaffa sent a heavy punch into the alien's mandibles and the insectoid's crested head flicked back, bouncing hard off a support stanchion. Nerveless and dazed, the Re'tu slipped back down the console and sagged into a heap of chitin and claws, air wheezing from the breathing apertures in its torso.

Teal'c spat out a dribble of bloody spittle. "You are beaten. Submit."

The alien raised its two forelimbs in surrender, cocking its head to the side to look over his shoulder. It was then the Jaffa realized that they were no longer alone.

When Jackson opened his eyes again, it was with a palpable wave of relief as he saw the drab but familiar walls of the SGC medical lab.

"Whenever you're ready," said Doctor Warner. "Let me know when you're going to begin."

"We just did... Whatever it was we did," said O'Neill. "We must have been gone for what, ten or twenty minutes?"

Hammond shook his head. "No, Colonel. The three of you appeared to go into a trance for a couple of seconds, and that was it."

"The passage of time in dreams always seems longer than it actually is," Daniel noted.

Jack threw him a look. "My dreams usually involve ice

hockey, fishing or tropical islands. Sometimes all three. *That* was a nightmare."

"*That* is my world," said Jade.

"I've seen the future, General," said Jack, "and trust me, you'd wouldn't like the décor." O'Neill turned and studied Jade. "Okay. You've got our attention. Why don't you tell us the rest of it?"

She licked her lips. "For the last few years we've been fighting a guerilla war. It's all we could do, really, there were so few of us left. We scavenged whatever we could use in the fight, alien weapons, biological modifications…" She tapped her neck. "That's where my implant came from, the nanomachines too. We had a few victories here and there, but in the end it counted for nothing. The damage had been done, see?" Her hand strayed to her stomach. "We'd already lost, we were already dead. We just hadn't got there yet." The woman nodded slowly to herself. "But then we found the hardware. Our Commander said we were due for our luck to change and he was right."

"What hardware?" said Hammond, throwing Daniel a quizzical look.

"A lab. A storehouse of technology built by one of the Ancients, a guy called Janus."

The name lit a spark in Jackson's thoughts. "Janus," he repeated. "Yes, we've come across his experiments before." He looked at O'Neill. "You remember that weird *Groundhog Day* thing you and Teal'c got caught in on P4X-639? He built that."

"Oy," sniffed Jack, "Don't remind me."

"Time machines," Jade said bluntly. "This genius had been experimenting with the flow of time, and he'd built a lot of prototypes. Big ones, small ones…" She made a shape with her hands.

Daniel suddenly realized what she meant. "The pod. The one we found in your quarters on the base, that was of Ancient design. You saying that's a time-travel device?"

"A DeLorean in a little box?" offered Jack. "That's pretty slick."

Jade shrugged. "Actually, they're bigger on the inside than they are on the outside. Something to do with the compacting of relative transcendental dimensional spaces…" She paused. "I don't understand the complete theory. But there were a few of them, and once we'd figured out how to operate the pods, we knew we had a chance to change the playing field. A chance to re-set things."

Warner waved a hand. "Okay, this isn't my field of expertise, it's Bill Lee's, but I've read the files. Don't you need a solar eclipse or something to bend the gate's wormhole around to make a time-warp?" He made loops in the air with his fingers.

"Solar flare," corrected Hammond. "And he's right."

"But Janus found another way," Daniel looked at Jade. "Something controllable."

"The Stargate," said the woman. "They exist in four dimensions… It's like they have a footprint in time as well as a physical component. From the notes that we deciphered, at first Janus tried to build a time machine inside a small spacecraft, but then he went for a different approach. The gate network has existed since before the beginning of recorded human history. They're unchanging points of reference in time as well as in space. He created devices that could ride on the back of the network, that you could use to transport people to any place, at any point in time—providing it was within a certain radius from an existing Stargate." She blew out a breath, as if the effort of the explanation had drained her. "The gates do all the work. The pods are really just glorified portable beaming devices."

O'Neill's eyes narrowed and he pinched the bridge of his nose. "Does anyone else's head hurt?"

Daniel nodded. It was mind-stretching stuff all right, but no more than many of the strange things SG-1 had encountered on their travels. "Sam's gonna be kicking herself that she missed this."

"The Re'tu used one of the pods to beam out of the base,"

noted Hammond.

"Yes. Ite-kh moved in space but not time. A time jump takes a lot more power. We barely had enough make it back to 2003 again."

"Again?" Jack eyed her.

She sighed. "This isn't our first attempt, believe me. But multiple incursions into the same time period cause all kinds of problems."

"Like meeting yourself?" suggested Warner. "I could see that might be embarrassing."

"Like quantum instability and phase-space break-down," said Jade.

"Will you quit it with the ten-dollar words?" demanded O'Neill. "Okay, let's say we're buying the whole 'time-traveler' thing. If the Pack meeting was such a bad idea, why didn't you just send us a note from the future, or something. We did that once." He paused. "I mean, I did that once. Possibly. Or something." Jack rubbed his eyes again. "Ugh. Where's Carter when I need her?"

"What makes you think we *didn't*?" Jade retorted. "Do you think we would have resorted to something as drastic as this if we hadn't already exhausted every possibility?" She straightened and got to her feet. "If you think of time like a length of string, then this point in history is wound up in knots! We made ten separate incursions, some to make changes, others to undo the changes we'd made when they went wrong! You think you have a headache?" She tapped her temple. "Try figuring that out. You're not even aware that your timeline has been cut, spliced and stitched back together! We barely knew what we were doing the first few times… We made a lot of mistakes." The woman looked away. "And now we're down to our last chance."

"You've come from our future to change your past," said Hammond carefully, sounding out the facts.

"From a future where the Earth's a depopulated ruin," said Daniel grimly.

"You're a soldier, fighting those responsible for that?" The general got a nod from Jade in return. "Which begs the question—Who is your enemy? The Pack?"

She shook her head. "No. The Pack were just pawns. It was years before we found out the truth, and by then every one of them was dead."

Teal'c's labored breathing echoed in the cockpit and he peered at the new arrival. Blood was gumming shut his right eye and dozens of shallow cuts sang with pain across the skin of his bare arms and his torso. "Ryn," he said.

The Pack warrior was quite still. In one hand he held the Jaffa's staff weapon, and in the other the pistol that belonged to the Re'tu.

"This creature was aboard your ship," he explained. "Perhaps... Preparing sabotage."

"Perhaps," agreed Ryn. There was a metallic click and the petal-shaped cowl at the end of the staff snapped open. Before Teal'c could react, an amber bolt of energy shrieked from the weapon's maw and blew a fist-sized hole through the torso of the alien spider. The shot killed the Re'tu instantly, blasting fluids and flesh across the consoles and windows.

"It had surrendered!" Teal'c was furious. It mattered little to him that only moments before the Jaffa and the Re'tu had been trying to slay each other. The creature had shown honor and judgment in submitting to a superior foe, and the thought of butchering a prisoner was abhorrent to Teal'c. "Why... Why did you kill it?"

Ryn seemed distracted, uninterested in the Jaffa's anger. He studied the beam gun, then threw a look at the out-of-place communicator unit and back at Teal'c. "You should not have come aboard my ship. You were not supposed to see that."

Cold emotion glittered in Ryn's eyes and Teal'c saw it coming. He threw himself forward across the cabin, but there was nowhere for him to hide.

Ryn squeezed the trigger bar and put a flare of light into the Jaffa's chest, the impact blowing him backward to the floor. Smoke curled from the discolored patch of flesh on his chest, heavy with a sickly-sweet scent.

With care, the Pack warrior tossed the gun to land at the Re'tu's feet and then dropped the staff weapon at Teal'c's side. It was an inelegant solution, but the only one that presented itself. Ryn moved swiftly to the control console and replaced the enameled cover that concealed the silver communicator unit. Checking once more to make sure it was securely hidden, he took a deep breath of air and ran to the swan-ship's rear hatch.

"Help!" he cried, pitching it at the perfect level of near-panic. "Someone, come quickly! We need a healer! The Jaffa has been hurt!"

Jade looked Jack in the eye. "They call themselves the Aschen."

"Aw, *son of a bitch*!" O'Neill spat out the curse. "That miserable, boring blank-faced gang of losers? Didn't we send them runnin' after that thing with the Volians?"

"Who?" said Warner.

"P3A-194," said Jackson, displaying once again his uncanny ability to retain seemingly-meaningless strings of letters and numbers. "Two years ago. A race calling themselves the Aschen Confederation tried to make a move on us, but I discovered they'd been systematically annexing planets, including a world called Volia. They wiped out the civilization there and turned it into a giant agricultural farm. We held them off, but in the process they captured a laptop full of gate addresses and a US ambassador."

Jack's eyes narrowed. "Faxon. I remember." He felt a sting of guilt at the man's name. SG-1 had been forced to leave the ambassador in the hands of the Aschen; and given that the first gate code on that laptop had been for a planet in the process of being eaten by a black hole, he imagined that Joe Faxon—if he was still alive—would have been the target of any reprisals from the would-be alien conquerors.

Jade was nodding. "They didn't take their defeat quietly, and we found that out the hard way. After you gave them a bloody nose on Volia, Earth and the SGC got put to the top of the Aschen's most-hated list. They saw us as a threat to their plans for galactic expansion and set up an operation to wipe us out. It was lead by one of their top bioscience experts, a woman called Mirris." She looked at Jack. "Remember an Aschen named Mollem?"

"Yeah. Gave new meaning to the word 'dull'."

"Mirris's husband. Apparently, he was killed along with a lot of their top brass when they dialed the coordinates of a singularity that Colonel O'Neill had left in that gate directory. She didn't take it well. Mirris cooked up the plan to do to Earth what they'd done to Volia and a hundred other planets."

"Forced sterilization," said Hammond.

"And then some. The Aschen engineered a smart bio-weapon that infiltrated the human population in a dormant state, spreading out through members of the SGC to their families, to everyone they came into contact with. After a couple of months, it went active, and by then it was global. The pathogen was 98 percent effective. It caused instant sterility in both sexes, immediate termination of all pregnancies."

Warner's hand went to his mouth. "Good grief."

Jade nodded, her hand resting on her stomach. "Yeah. But it gets worse. The virus mutated. Mirris was sloppy... I guess she was too burned up by revenge to realize. The pathogen jumped species, killed plants and animals worldwide. It found its way to other planets and did the same there." The lab was completely silent now; every one of them hung on her quiet words. "Things just fell apart. On Earth, there was chaos. Governments crashed, people turned against each other. Then the Stargate became public knowledge and it got even worse... Those that could escape, did. Those that couldn't...." She looked away. "Here's what it comes down to. Where I come from, there's not enough Earth humans left to make a difference. In less than a generation, we'll be extinct, and the same goes for the folks on a bunch of other planets too. The pathogen's long gone, burnt out and vanished, but the effects are set. Not enough births. Not enough people. And in the meantime, the rest of the galaxy is being torn to bits in the fighting between the Replicators and a freak Goa'uld called Anubis." Jade sighed heavily. "My father... The Commander... He figured out that we couldn't win, no matter what we did."

Jack felt a cold sense of understanding settle on him. "The only way to make it right is to stop it from happening."

Another nod. "Mirris used the Pack as carriers for the pathogen. The treaty, the trade agreement, that was the back door for the Aschen attack. The Pack never even knew it. We think she'd turned someone in their hierarchy, but we never found out who."

Hammond frowned. "And this is why you planted a fake bomb. You wanted to disrupt the agreement, prevent it from ever taking place."

"But we stopped you," said Daniel. "Your Re'tu friend escaped, but you failed in your mission. The meeting is going on right now."

O'Neill's hands knit together. "Why... Why the hell didn't you just tell us all this at the start?"

She shot him a look. "And you'd have accepted it right off the bat, would you?" Jade snorted. "You didn't the first time we tried. Or the second. And when I did get you to believe me, Kinsey overruled your decision not to meet the Pack and it all happened anyway. We couldn't afford to risk any more failures and I couldn't take the chance you wouldn't believe me. This is the last shot."

Daniel chewed his lip. "That has an awfully fatal sound to it."

"This is why we have to go to Kytos," said Jade. "It wasn't just me and Ite-kh that came back this time, the Commander was with us too. He had a fall-back contingency, and I know he must have initiated it by now. He's on Kytos, with a naqadria-fusion device. Unless we stop him, he'll wipe out any chance of Mirris's plan succeeding by nuking the meeting site."

"That's pretty damn drastic," Jack retorted. "You, bug-guy, your pop... Don't any of you folks from the future go for the subtle approach?"

"Why do you think I tried so hard to make my plan succeed?" Jade snapped. "If I hadn't failed in my assignment, the charge would have gone off, nobody would have been hurt, the Pack would have left and all you'd be left with was the fallout from a failed diplomatic mission. I wanted to do this without hurting anyone."

"Kill a few dozen people on Kytos and save billions of lives in the future," said Daniel. "It's very logical, in a cold kind of way."

"I'm not letting anyone get nuked," growled O'Neill. "Not even Kinsey." He shot a look at his senior officer. "General?"

"You have a go, Colonel," said the general. "I want this mess untangled."

They were making for the door when Warner held up a hand. "Wait," he said, "there's just one other thing that I don't understand."

"Only one?" said Daniel.

"The results of the bio-scan I completed," said the doctor. "If she's from a future time period, why does Jade's DNA profile match the colonel's?"

Jade frowned. "I guess I get that from my father."

Warner blinked. "Your father?"

She nodded. "The last surviving officer of Stargate Command, leader of the Earth resistance... Commander-in-Chief Jack O'Neill."

The colonel felt the color drain from his face. "Say what now?"

Jade gave him a wan smile. "Hey, dad."

CHAPTER ELEVEN

"And this is what, exactly?" Kinsey held up the clear crystal cube between his thumb and forefinger. Sam could see a small green shoot in the matrix of the block, like a tiny sprig of plant life frozen in ice. All eyes in the long tent went to the politician, which was just the way he liked it.

"A dormant meladni flower," explained Suj. "It is a symbolic gesture. The plant comes from Calai, the original home of the *Wanderer*, and every ship in our flotilla has at least one growing aboard it."

"Meladni is the only growth that resists the blight," said Vix grimly, "although we do not know why. It has come to be a symbol of our culture."

Sam suddenly understood; the plant had star-shaped petals, like the discreet tribal tattoos worn by the Pack.

"It's hermetically sealed for the moment, but the flower will bloom on exposure to the air of your planet," Koe concluded. "And thus, a small part of the Pack will live on your world, cementing our alliance."

"That's a very quaint custom," noted Kinsey, handing the cube to one of his aides. "Thank you."

"It was Ryn's suggestion," noted Koe.

Carter glanced around and noticed that the other Pack member was no longer in the meeting tent. She hadn't seen him slip out.

Suj saw the expression on her face and answered her unspoken question. "A matter required his attention. A communication from Ryn's clan-branch, as I understand it."

Sam was slightly surprised. Here they were, about to put ink on the document that would cement a formal agreement between the Pack and Earth, and one of their senior leaders had snuck out to make a phone call? The thought nagged at her until she heard the shouts, and then abruptly she had something else to think about.

Carter caught cries of alarm from outside the tent, voices from men of both factions. She heard someone say the words "Jaffa" and "Re'tu" and the major was immediately on her feet. Colonel Reynolds was doing the same, shooting her a warning look.

"What's going on?" demanded Kinsey.

As if in reply, the flap of the long tent snapped open and there was Sergeant Albrechtsen. "We got a situation," said the airman, his face pale, "It's Teal'c…"

Sam looked back at Reynolds and he nodded before she had to ask. "Go, Major. I want a sitrep, ASAP."

"Sir," Carter bolted out after Albrechtsen and the sergeant led the way. Her blood ran cold as the non-com took her straight to the infirmary tent.

She pushed her way inside and the smell hit her first. The stink was, as disgusting as it was to admit it, horribly familiar to Sam Carter. She'd lost count of the number of times that seared-flesh odor had struck her. All the people she'd seen die under alien energy weapons, and they all left that same stench hanging in the air—a stinging mixture of ozone and burned meat. It brought back a moment of awful sense-memory, flashing to the front of her thoughts, undimmed by the passage of months.

Janet's body on the stretcher as we run with it toward the gate. Her face, slack and empty. The smell, on my hands, in my hair, my clothes.

It took effort to shut the memory out. A medical corpsman was working on the figure lying on the gurney in front of her. Parts of the Jaffa's uniform tunic lay on the ground in wet, sticky tatters where they had been cut away to give access to his wound. Teal'c's ebony features had an unhealthy pallor to them, and his mouth and nose were hidden under the cowl of an oxygen mask.

Albrectsen pointed to a second gurney on the other side of the medical tent. A blue-black shape made up of too many limbs and strange bony curves lay underneath a sheath of thick plastic. "The bug was already dead when we got to it," he explained. "Big man was still breathing, though."

"What happened?" she husked.

"Near as we can figure, the bug was screwing around inside one of the Pack ships and Teal'c caught him off-guard. They shot each other." He smiled mirthlessly. "But the Jaffa are tough mothers."

"Whose ship?"

"The skinny one. Ryn. He found them, came running."

"Teal'c would have died if not for him," said the corpsman. "Hell, for a second we all thought he *was* dead. But the Sergeant's right. Even without a symbiote's healing abilities, a Jaffa body can take a lot of punishment…"

"Will he make it?"

The corpsman's face darkened. "I'm not going to lie to you, Major, he's hurt real bad. It's too dangerous to move him again, so we can't gate him back to the SGC. I stabilized him. If we let Teal'c's natural physiology do its thing, we might be able to send him through in an hour or two. Right now, he has to stay put." He sighed. "I'll do everything I can. Lucky for him, the vice president insisted on having a full emergency medical unit brought through to the encampment, although I doubt he had Teal'c's welfare in mind at the time."

"Lucky, yeah," Sam said quietly. She reached out and squeezed the Jaffa's hand. His loose grip felt clammy.

"I'll let you know the moment his condition changes," said the medic.

Carter nodded, drawing down her leadership face and putting aside her personal fears. She crossed to the dead Re'tu. "How did this thing get here?" Sam ran a practiced eye over the corpse and found the limb that Teal'c had reported he'd broken during the fight at Cheyenne Mountain. "It's definitely the same Re'tu that invaded the SGC."

Albrechtsen's face twisted. The dead alien's body reeked with strange scents. "Had to have come through the gate with us."

She shook her head. "We had TERs set up on the Earth side. If it had been inside the SGC, we would have detected it." Carter thought it through. "It used a beaming device... It could have beamed itself through the open gate, right down the wormhole."

"Is that possible, ma'am?"

"It's here, and Teal'c's in critical condition because of it, so yeah, I'd say it's possible, Sergeant." Her reply was sharper than she'd have liked. "Where's Ryn now?"

"Last I saw, he was giving his ship the once-over, making sure there were no surprises left behind."

Sam nodded. "We should do the same. Get Lieutenant Everitt, tell him to sweep the whole area and make sure it's secure."

"Yes, ma'am." The sergeant saluted and ran out through the tent flap.

She followed, giving Teal'c a last look before she exited. As the major strode back to the long tent, her radio crackled. "This is Carter."

"*Major, Captain Grant here. We have activity at the Stargate. Chevrons are lighting up. We got an incoming wormhole.*"

Sam grimaced. "Copy that, Captain. Nothing's scheduled to come through, so I want all guns and TERs on it."

"*Will do. Grant out.*"

She glared up at the ridgeline where, out of sight behind the thick trunks of the rainforest, the Kytos gate stood. "Now what?" she asked the air.

It took all of Sub-Director Geddel's self-control not to flinch in surprise when the door to the control nexus opened and Administrator Mirris strode purposefully into the vessel's command center. Operators on all the systems consoles did their best to look busy, but he knew that every one of them was just as shocked as he was. Mirris had ventured into the nexus on no more than two occasions during the entirety of this cycles-long mission, preferring to stay in her chambers and govern the ship from there. Geddel composed himself rapidly, wondering if perhaps her poor self-control had finally slipped away. He hoped so; it would mean that he was free to relive her of her posting and take it for himself. While he had a degree of respect for the woman's academic and scientific skills, he had long harbored a belief that she was poorly suited to be placed in command of an operation such as this one. Her obvious desire for revenge was quite distasteful, and behind her back some of the junior intendants showed disrespect that bordered on insubordination. Geddel had turned a blind eye to such things because he, in truth, felt the same way. Of course, when he took governance of the ship, such lenience would be a thing of the past.

He snapped back to the moment as Mirris advanced through the ranks of operations cubicles. "Main display," she ordered. "Planetary sweep."

Amid the flat walls of gray plastic and metal, the holographic table in the center of the nexus opened out of itself to produce the virtual images she had demanded. Geddel saw a topographic scan of the local geography on Kytos. There were the crude shapes of temporary shelters, the darts of fighter craft from the migrant fleet, dots of light indicating the motion of life. He failed to see what she was interested in, and remarked on this to the administrator.

Mirris shot him a glare that was loaded with naked emotion. "The Stargate has opened, depositing three more humanoids on the surface of the planet," she spat, gesturing angrily at a time-indexed long-range replay of the event. "No others were supposed to travel to this location during the treaty session. Something is wrong."

"Administrator," he began, attempting to mollify her with a neutral tone, "we have no evidence of that. You are…" He found the word distasteful to say aloud. "Over-reacting."

"And you are being deliberately obstructive," she retorted. "The prosecution of this mission depends upon the correct unfolding of key events, and as we proceed, more and more of those events have been disrupted." She peered into the hologram. "We must take steps, sub-director. Immediately."

"What do you propose?" He showed her a placid, blank expression.

"Deploy a stealth lander with an inspection unit and have them make planetfall. Their orders are to set up a teleportation terminus on the surface and maintain a closer surveillance on the Pack and the Tau'ri."

Geddel sighed. "That runs the risk of detection—"

"That was not a request," she interrupted. "That was an order. Once we have a beaming terminal established on the planet, we will be free to transport more units to the surface if they are required. Contact the hangar and have them prepare a force of combat drones."

He blinked. "Is that necessary? This is a clandestine mission."

"You were the one who first voiced the option of armed response," Mirris replied. "I would think you would be pleased I am finally listening to your suggestions."

"As an alternative," Geddel insisted. "Only that."

She glared at him. "Carry out my orders and they may not be needed." She looked away. "Do it now." When Geddel didn't immediately move to implement Mirris's commands, the administrator's lip curled in a open expression of annoyance. "Was there something else, sub-director?" Her words were acid.

Inwardly, Geddel sneered. "I had been planning to mention this matter at our next scheduled meeting, administrator, but perhaps it is best if I bypass protocol for the moment."

"Yes?" She loomed up before him, and he could see she was thinking of striking him.

He manipulated his portable display. "Signals received

a directive message from Confederation Central on Aschen Prime. It was an explicit order in your name, requesting an immediate situation report and progress determination on the operation." Geddel allowed himself a moment of smugness as Mirris's ire cooled in the face of his statement. Central doubtless had a morality monitor operative aboard the ship and he imagined word of Mirris's overtly emotional behavior had reached their homeworld. He knew as well as she did that the order to report in was a pretext. At best she would be ordered to disengage and return home; at worst she would be cashiered and relieved of duty.

A sneer threatened to emerge on Geddel's lips. The Aschen were a superior species because they had learned to master their baser natures and become detached and passionless. The longer he served under Mirris, the more Geddel came to think of her as a throwback, wallowing in the crudity of her sentiment over the death of her mate, Mollem. Geddel had known of Senior Administrator Mollem; the man was a fine example of Aschen aloofness and a great loss to their race. He would have been disgusted to think that his bond-partner would be so open about her feelings in front of her subordinates.

But as he watched, a wall of wintry calm descended on Mirris's expression. "Thank you, sub-director, for bringing that to my attention. I will address the directive when a moment permits me."

"It is a prime classification message," he insisted. "Your first duty is to answer it."

"Do not presume to tell me what my duty is, Geddel," she kept her voice low, and devoid of any sign of emotional timbre. "For your own sake, do not presume." The threat, with its icy power, was more disturbing to him than any of the small tantrums and rages he had seen the woman exhibit.

Geddel nodded slowly. "As you order, administrator."

"Whoa!" Daniel had barely made it two steps out of the gate before he threw up his hands and skidded to a halt. Four men, one pair with assault rifles cocked and ready, one pair with transphase rods humming, trained their weapons on the figures exiting the wormhole with swift, lethal intent.

Jack strode past him, apparently unruffled by the display of force. "There's only three of us. Stand down, Captain," he demanded, and the officer leading the group waved the weapons away. "Or did Kinsey tell you to shoot me?"

The captain saluted. "Colonel, sir. I'm sorry, but you weren't expected, and we've just had an incident."

Jack shot him a hard look. "And that means?"

"I don't know the full details, sir, but Major Carter just ordered security up to Threat Red."

"Oh no," Jade was at Daniel's shoulder. It seemed strange to see her in a regular SG team outfit after the bright orange of the prisoner jumpsuit. "We might be too late."

O'Neill considered this for a moment as the wormhole hissed out of existence behind them. "Captain, keep your post here. Jackson!"

"Uh, yes?" Daniel blinked.

"You get down into the encampment, find Carter, find out what's happening, give her the skinny on…" He glanced reluctantly at Jade. "Well, the main points."

Daniel looked at the woman, who was self-consciously fingering her hair, making the henna-red tresses turn purple-black. "Does that include the, uh, daddy-daughter thing?"

The colonel's eyes flashed with anger. "Will you just *get*?"

Jackson did as he was told, and broke into a swift jog. In retrospect, he shouldn't have been surprised by O'Neill's bad mood. Time travel, bio-war, covert operatives, fusion bombs, future incarnations of people. It was enough to ruin anyone's calm.

After Jackson was gone, O'Neill left Captain Grant and his men behind and followed Jade into the tree line. For a moment, he'd considered co-opting some of Grant's team for the search, but if Carter had turned up the dial on security then there had to be a good reason for it, and leaving the gate undermanned was a bad idea.

And besides, if the girl was on the level about this situation, then Jack wasn't really sure he wanted anyone else coming into contact with… with *him*.

He looked at her from out of the corner of his eye, thinking back to those moments in the SGC, when he'd had that feeling, that weird kinda familiarity with her. Was that because he'd been seeing something of himself in her, some tiny fragment of his own face reflected in Jade's? The more he looked, the more he found himself believing it. She had a quality of Jack's mother about her, in the way she carried herself. As a boy, O'Neill had found a shoebox full of faded old photographs from the youth of his parents. He remembered a shot of his mom at a bridge game, taken with her unawares, her face fixed in thought over some hand she was about to play. Jade had that look, the same focus. *Stakes are a lot higher here, though.*

He moved carefully through the tree trunks, one hand gripping a zat and the other a pocket scanner. Jade had one as well, although Hammond had not been willing to give her a weapon.

"I think I have something," she whispered. "Over there."

Jack looked at his scanner. "I got nothin'."

She nodded. "The pods generate a faint jamming field. The scanner won't read it."

"Then how do you know where to look?"

Jade tapped the screen. "Easy. Look for the place where there isn't anything." She smiled briefly. "You taught me that."

O'Neill's reaction was sudden and strong. "Don't talk to me that way. I'm not… Just *don't*, okay?" He was surprised by the potency of the feeling. Jade's face darkened and she nodded, moving on again.

He sighed. *This damn job,* Jack told himself, *just when you think it can't screw with you any more, the game goes up to a whole new level of screwitude.* Jack thought briefly about the guys who had graduated from the Air Force Academy the same year that he had. He was willing to bet good money that the worst they had to deal with were wives who didn't understand them and uniforms that didn't fit as well as they'd used to. *And here's me, crawling through the jungle on some planet a million billion light years from Earth, looking for an eighty-year-old version of myself and staring at the curvatious backside of someone who may actually be my daughter.* O'Neill shuddered. All that talk about promotions, about stepping back a little, now it sounded better than it ever had before…

"Snap out of it," he grumbled under his breath, getting angry with himself. He had to focus. This was mission time now, and that was the priority.

"I see the Commander," husked the woman. "No sign of Itekh. I'd be able to find him, even if he was fully shrouded."

Jack was looking where she was looking but he saw nothing but trees. Jade never blinked, and in the moonlight there was an odd quality about her eyes that he found slightly creepy. "You got a night sight built right into your head, don't you?"

She nodded vaguely.

"Other parent's kids just get a tongue stud."

"Come on." Jade stood up and walked brazenly out of cover.

A shape that Jack had thought to be nothing more than a heap of wind-touched leaves against the bole of a tall tree changed shape and elongated. Suddenly he realized it was a man in a cloak, moving in the shadows. The figure turned in place and the cloak parted, the colors streaming off it until it became a neutral green.

"Dad," she began as she approached.

O'Neill saw a lined but familiar face in the dimness, saw it twist in sudden fury. "Why?" The demand was strident and full of anger and disappointment. "I told you to stay away! *Why don't you ever listen to me?*" He knew the emotions behind the voice immediately. It was his grandfather's voice when Jack had been a troublesome boy; it was his father's when he had been a rebellious teenager; it was *his* voice, thirty years from now.

He moved out of his cover and the other figure went deadly silent. It took a long moment for Jack to find his words. "You and me, old man," he said finally. "We gotta talk."

The stealth lander settled into the trees on silent repulsor-field generators, shedding the last flickers of energy from re-entry as thin waves of shimmering air. As planned, the ship had come down completely undetected by either the migrants or the Tau'ri force. Four landing legs folded out of the egg-shaped craft and from the flat ventral surface a panel slid open to allow an object to drop the last few feet to the jungle floor. The device landed hard and metal grippers snapped open, digging into the spongy loam to steady it. By the time the two Aschen crewmen had disembarked, the unit was showing a circuit of softly glowing power indicators.

The senior crewman left his subordinate to keep watch and crossed to the device. It was a disc two meters in diameter with an arc of metal folding up before it, like a lectern. He ran a quick diagnostic and the unit chimed in return. "Carrier wave established," he said quietly. "Final checks in progress."

Aschen science, while impressive in its scope and capability, had still not mastered the intricacies of point-to-point matter transmission technology. While far more advanced than the comparatively crude 'ring transporters' used by the Goa'uld and their subject races, the Aschen teleporters were still bound by the requirement of having a receiving platform at their destination. Such a requirement made the mission of the stealth lander of paramount importance; however, now it was complete and the beaming conduit established, the Aschen would be free to deposit whatever they wanted on the surface of Kytos in the blink of an eye.

There was another set of chimes. "Transit stream parity is acceptable." The senior crewman pressed a device on his wrist that sent an encoded burst signal to the ship hidden in high orbit. "Sub-Director? Forward terminal has been established. Ready to proceed."

Geddel's voice was tinny over the comlink. "*Confirmed. Standby by to receive support units.*"

He stepped away as a glittering column of energy began to form on the small dais. When it faded there was a brass automaton standing on the platform, with hoop-shaped wheels where a man would have had legs. The blank-faced drone rolled off the terminus and the energy reformed, bringing a second machine with it. In a few moments, there were five of them, waiting patiently in the shadow of the lander.

The subordinate glanced at his scanner unit. "Indeterminate life sign readings several metrics from the Earther encampment." He pointed. "That way."

The senior scout accepted this with a nod. "Take three drones and investigate."

"You brought *him* with you?" The disappointment was thick in the old man's words. "Are you deliberately trying to make this mission fail?"

"Hey!" Jack broke in, feeling a sudden urge to defend the girl. "Ease up on her. It's been tough all round."

The other man ignored him. "You shouldn't have come here, Jade. You have to get a ship, get away." His face became an angry snarl. "Just go, while there's still a chance!"

"No-one is going anywhere," Jack retorted, coming closer. He kept up a good front of calm, but behind it his thoughts were racing. Until this moment, O'Neill had entertained some kind of vague hope that there would be another, easier explanation for all the shenanigans—but now he was looking the old man in the eye and he knew that all of it, every damn bit of that future crap Jade had told him, was true. "She says there's a bomb somewhere around here. Why don't you save us all a lot of trouble, pops, and show us where it is?"

The other man—the *Commander*—shot Jack a hard look. He was hard-faced, grim and he sure as hell didn't look like he was pushing eighty-something. "*Pops*?" he repeated, with withering scorn. "And to think, I used to imagine that glib joker stuff was clever."

"And to think, I used to imagine that I would be fishing and writing my memoirs at your age. I guess we're both disillusioned." O'Neill stepped forward, feeling his temper building. "I mean, come on. Tell me she was wrong about all this. Tell me that Jade made a mistake. Tell me that you... That Jack O'Neill is not about to detonate a nuke that'll wipe out innocent people, people who are my friends!"

The old man looked away, his face turning to shadow in the folds of the cloak. "You don't know what the hell you're talkin' about, pal."

Jack's hands bunched into fists, and he straightened. "Fine. You wanna be a hard-ass? Your choice, grandpa." He snatched up his radio. "I'm calling Grant. I'll get him to gate to the SGC and come back with enough men to go through this jungle with tweezers."

"Bad idea," growled the other man, and he said it with such certainty that O'Neill paused with the walkie-talkie at his lips. "The device has a sensor trip switch keyed to the Stargate's DHD. Anyone who dials out will automatically trigger it."

Jack pressed the 'talk' switch and spoke in a steady, clear voice. "Grant, this is O'Neill. You are not, under any circumstances, to dial the gate. This countermands all other orders."

"*Uh, roger that, Colonel,*" said the officer. "*Sir, are you all right?*"

"I'll get back to you on that, captain. O'Neill out." He glared at the old man. "Don't make me ask you again."

"Or what?" growled his elder self. "You think there's anything you could do, anything you could say that would threaten me, change my mind? After all I've been through?" He glanced at Jade. "Did you show him? Earth, the war?"

She nodded.

It took a physical effort for Jack to moderate the fury he felt inside him. "I understand what you're trying to do," he began.

"Sure you do," said the old man. "It was all your idea. My idea."

"But you have to know it's wrong! For cryin' out loud, man, you're talking about killing men and women you've served with, who trusted you... Us... Whoever!" He shook his head, barely able to take it in. "Teal'c, Daniel, *Sam*!" Jack stabbed a finger at Jade. "Your own daughter, and hell, me too!" He tapped his chest. "How's that gonna work out for you? Kill me now and you'll never live to be doing this in the first place!"

"I never listened to that time paradox crap," grated the old soldier. "I only care about stopping the Aschen."

"Like this?" Jack retorted. "I could never condone this insanity! You can't be me. I'd never agree to do it."

"But you did," snarled the Commander. "You did, you will! Because it's worth the price, Jack! Billions of lives, thousands of planets, more deaths than the Goa'uld and the Replicators caused combined..."

Jack met his own gaze and he felt sick inside. He saw something of the man he had once been, in those dark months after his son had died in the accident that nearly broke his spirit. He remembered being in Charlie's room, catching sight of his own reflection in the window. That coldness, that same dislocation... He saw it in the old man now. "What happened to you?" The question slipped from his mouth.

"The war happened to me." Every word was a razor. "The famine and the pain and the death happened to me. Every one of them, gone..." He fixed Jack with a chilling glare. "Bonner, Dixon and Whitman. Sheppard. Everitt and Allan. Ellis. Mitchell. And hundreds of others. Nothing left of them now except names on a wall in the Holdfast." He snarled. "I'm doing this for *them*!"

"It's revenge..." whispered Jade.

"That's all this fight has ever been about," said the old man.

But Jack wasn't listening any more. There was something at the tree line, shapes that were moving too fast to be human. "Company!" he snapped.

"Life signs located, three humans," Mirris stood behind Geddel as the sub-director's fingers danced lightly over the control console in his cubicle, following the communication from the scout on the planet. *"Confirming tribal identifiers as Earth origin, not Pack."*

"A patrol," said Geddel. "They must not be allowed to report your presence. Terminate them, immediately."

Mirris's gaze swept the cubes of holographic imagery relaying from the optical sensor bands of the drones. The view bobbed as they trundled over the ground towards the three figures, tracking for a kill shot from their particle weapons. Energy fire was zipping past the viewpoint; the leading drone saw an immediate threat and turned its focus to the Tau'ri firing a Goa'uld pistol at the Aschen machines. With its low-light scanners, the view of the small jungle glade was rendered in bright green and white; target cues leapt out and framed the man with the gun as the drone took careful aim.

Mirris saw the face of the shooter as clearly as if he were in the command nexus with them, and she let out a wild hiss of shock. *It's him!*

Geddel flinched at her outburst and jerked around. "Administrator? What is it?"

She ignored him and snarled into the comlink. "Orders rescinded!" Immediately, the drones hesitated. As mission leader, any command from Mirris overrode all others. "I want him alive!"

"And the others?"

"Make the attempt!" Her teeth bared in a feral grimace as the drones began moving again, weaving into hand-to-hand range.

"Administrator, I do not understand," said Geddel. "Why did you countermand me?"

In one of the holo-cubes, a female came into view and fired

at a drone, blinding it. In a second, the display from another of the machines homed in on her. Before the woman could react, the second drone clubbed her with the heavy gun pod on its arm. Mirris saw the unconscious female spin away, tumbling down a steep incline in a cloud of fallen leaves and debris. The drone's audio monitors caught the sounds of the other men crying out in dismay. Mirris grinned. She was causing him pain. *Good.* It was just the beginning.

"Administrator," Geddel began again.

She silenced him with an acid glare. "It's him, Geddel. The war criminal." Mirris tapped a keypad and the view from the drone folded into the front of the hologram. A human male wearing a cap, face set in determination. "Colonel O'Neill. The man who murdered my bondmate."

The sub-director was lost for words for a moment, his jaw working. When he finally spoke, it was with mild surprise. "Of course. It was a high probability that he might be on site… But I did not assume we would encounter him." Beam fire tailed off over the open channel. "A very high-value target indeed," Geddel concluded.

"The Confederation can have what remains after I have finished with him." A strangled cry issued out of the comlink. Her fingers formed into fists as she saw, at last, O'Neill and the cloaked figure go down. "Take them to the terminus. I want them transported aboard immediately." She turned on her heel and strode towards the nexus's door. "I'm going to the beaming chamber."

"The… The female," Geddel added, attempting to take some control of what had just happened. "Should I have her body recovered?"

"Don't waste my time with trivia," Mirris snapped, working her hands. A strong and long-nurtured hate was streaming to the surface, and the Aschen woman realized she had not felt so alive in months.

Sam slumped back in the folding chair and looked past

Daniel to the rest of the operations tent. Jackson had asked her to empty it for the duration of their conversation, and now the half-dozen computers and monitor units ranged around the room were unmanned, with Boyce and the other operators standing outside in a grumbling, wary knot.

She shook her head again. Carter had been doing that for so long, it seemed like it would fall off her neck. If she had to use a single word to describe her mindset right now, it would be *incredulous*. "Are you really Daniel Jackson?" she asked, half-joking. "Are you sure you're not some shape-changing alien from the Ancient's version of *Candid Camera*? Because that's pretty wild stuff."

"Sam," the scientist's face was fixed. "I couldn't be more serious."

"This is a lot to assimilate all at once," she retorted. "Individually, I buy it. The Aschen on a revenge kick, yeah, because they dropped off the radar after Volia and I'd been wondering when we'd run into them again. Time travel, well…"

"Been there," said Daniel, "done that."

"I remember the kaftans."

Jackson frowned. "What I don't get is, after that jaunt back to the Sixties, when we overshot on our way back and ended up in the future, there was no sign of any epidemic apocalypse having happened."

Sam nodded. "True. But from our point of view, that's only one possible future. Timelines branch at every decision point we make. That wasteland future you saw is just as likely to occur as the one where we met Cassandra as an older woman."

"Ugh." Daniel looked at the floor. "Jack was right. It's giving me a migraine."

Carter turned Jackson's earlier words over in her mind. "It's not difficult to imagine something like this happening. Members of a future SGC trying to retroactively alter their own past to negate an incorrect timeline. We'd probably do the same thing if it happened to us." She sighed. "It's just…"

"Just what?"

"One thing that boggles my mind." She eyed him. "Jack has a daughter?"

"*Will have.* Her name's Jade." He paused. "And no, I don't know the answer to the obvious question."

Sam felt a little color rising in her cheeks. "Oh. Okay. It's just that the colonel's separated from his wife and… Well, he doesn't, uh…" She trailed off into a sigh. "Anyway, that's not important right now. What do we do about the Pack?"

"Jade said they don't know who the Aschen agent is. It could be any one of them. We let on we know there's a rotten apple, and we run the risk of alerting the person we're looking for."

"So what do we do? We can't gate home on the colonel's orders, Kinsey's climbing the walls, the Pack are sharpening their knives and now you tell me there are likely to be Aschen and time-travelers running around out there as well." She gestured to the jungle outside, her manner turning brusque. "Any input, Daniel, would be welcomed."

Jackson, as usual, was perceptive enough to see through to what was really gnawing at her. "Any news on Teal'c?"

Sam shook her head. "Koe offered to take a look at him, did what he could. But there's been no change."

"He's tough," said Daniel. "He'll make it."

Carter didn't answer him. She didn't want to think about what might happen if Jackson was wrong. Covering the moment, she toggled her radio. "This is Major Carter. Captain Grant, any further contact from Colonel O'Neill yet?"

"*Negative, Major,*" Grant seemed distracted. "*We just heard something off in the distance. Sounded like weapons fire, but I can't be sure. Shall we investigate, over?*"

Sam weighed the request for a lone moment and then replied. "No, stay put at the gate, and stay alert." She switched to a different channel. "Colonel, this is Sam, do you read me?" Faint static hissed back at her. "Colonel O'Neill, are receiving?"

The channel remained resolutely silent.

She entered the ship's transportation chamber and forced her way around a pair of security drones and a contingent of intendants. O'Neill was on his feet, pulling the other man in the cloak to a standing position. Her crew had already stripped them of their equipment, piling the crude hardware on the deck. Mirris's skin felt hot and tight across her face, as if her anger was on the verge of ripping out of her.

"Administrator?" One of the subordinates offered her a screensheet, but she ignored it. She could not take her gaze off the Earther. "There is an anomaly. The matter stream bio-monitor registered a peculiarity during the transportation process, which almost caused an abort."

"What are you talking about?" she growled, and the younger woman recoiled visibly.

"The two prisoners… They share identical genetic profiles. Closer even than clones. It is as if they are the same man."

Mirris stalked forward and pushed past O'Neill, ignoring his shout of "Hey!" The human stumbled, still dizzy from the effects of the drone's stunner. She tugged back the hood covering the older human's head and saw something remarkable.

"You're alike," she said quietly. "Older, but alike. How is this possible?"

There was a flash of recognition in the eyes of the elderly man, as sudden and as hateful as the emotion she had felt in the command nexus. Mirris took cold satisfaction from it. "It's you," he said. Abruptly, the old man leapt at her, his fingers curling into claws to tear at her throat.

One of the drones blocked his path and hit him across the legs, dropping the elder man to the deck. Mirris turned her gaze on the colonel. "The Aschen believe in logic and science," she began, stalking toward him. "We dismiss ideas of fate and luck." A lethal smile emerged on her lips. "But if such things do exist, Colonel Jack O'Neill, then they have clearly decided to favor me today." She chuckled, and it was a hollow sound. "I don't yet comprehend how that one comes to be here with you, but I will happily exploit what he represents."

The Tau'ri made a play at looking unconcerned. "I'm sorry, have we met? 'Cos your face isn't ringing any bells with me."

Mirris shook her head, basking in the desire to kill him where he stood. "No. But you knew my partner. And I remember very clearly the gift you gave him."

Understanding crept across his face, flattening his swaggering manner. "Ah. Mirris, right? Listen, about that laptop…"

She turned away and made for the door; she knew she had to, because it would be important to wring O'Neill dry of every vital piece of intelligence she could compel from him, and if she stayed in the chamber any longer she would not be able to stop herself from murdering him. "Place them in secure holding," she told the intendant, and strode out into the corridor.

Her hand strayed to her wrist, to the place where she had once worn the bonding torc that Mollem had granted her. *He will pay,* she told herself, *O'Neill, and every last human on his blighted, backward planet.*

CHAPTER TWELVE

It turned out that 'secure holding' was actually a featureless white chamber somewhere on the lower levels of the Aschen vessel. The room was oddly proportioned, with a small footprint of floor but a very high ceiling that extended up for two levels. There were a group of cube-shaped cages made from bars of a clear blue plastic sitting in a square on the floor. One side hinged open as the security drones hustled them forward with the muzzles of humming energy guns. Jack didn't want to feel the sting of the weapons a second time. In the good light of the alien ship he could see the machines clearly, and it confirmed his suspicions. These were the same kind of robots that SG-1 had engaged back on P5X-404. The designs were not exactly the same, but the art deco bullet-head look was unmistakable; he filed that bit of intel away for later consideration.

The Aschen themselves had been quite happy to let the tinheads do the heavy lifting with their prisoners. Mirris's junior officers seemed afraid to get their hands too dirty, like they didn't want to get too close to Jack and... And the other guy. O'Neill halted in front of the open cell, and the robot gave him a shove toward it. Another machine pushed the old man toward a second cage.

"Okay, okay," Jack retorted, "I was just wondering if you had anything with a sea view, maybe." He saw a flat panel extruded from one inner wall that had to be a sleeping pallet, and a weird-looking thing in a corner that could have been a toilet or a shower, or maybe both. O'Neill hoped he wouldn't be in here long enough to have to find out.

He walked into the cell and the wall dropped down again, sealing it seamlessly. Jack automatically put his hands on the bars and tested them. They gave a little under pressure; not so much that they might break, but maybe enough that he could bend them… Escape plans began forming in his head the moment the machines turned and rolled away through the hatch to the corridor beyond. In the neighboring cell, the old man sat on the pallet and leaned back, ignoring him.

"Hey," Jack hissed, "Pops. These bars are pliant. Might be able to get—"

He never got to finish his sentence. Something hummed underneath the two occupied cube-cages and they rose into the air on a column of invisible force. O'Neill baulked and watched the floor recede away from him until they were a good thirty feet off the ground. The cells stopped and floated there, as immobile as if they were cemented into the walls.

"Go ahead, skinny out," said the other man. "Reckon you could make that drop without breaking your neck?"

"Ah, bite me," Jack retorted, and began feeling around the seams of the cage, taking the measure of his new confinement.

It was Everitt who brought them running; the lieutenant burst into the command tent with a grim look on his face. A patrol of men from SG-3 had recovered someone out in the jungle surrounding the encampment. Injured, he told them.

Sam and Daniel came out to meet them at the edge of the clearing, two of the men carrying a third figure in SGC fatigues between them.

"Jade!" blurted Jackson, recognizing the woman. Carter saw the pale cast of shock on the woman's slack face, her skin marked with the new bloom of bruises and abrasions.

Williams, the corpsman from the medical tent was right behind them with a folding stretcher. In moments, they had her on the steel frame and were marching her into the camp. Williams kept with them, checking Jade on the move. "Minor concussion," he said to himself, "no apparent signs of blunt trauma from ballistic weapons or burns from energy attacks."

"Found her at the bottom of a shallow ravine," said one of the SG-3 troopers. "Far as I can tell, she lost her footing up top and came down head first. She was lucky, could have broke her back on rocks or tree trunks."

Daniel bent over her. "Jade? It's Daniel. Can you hear me?"

Sam saw her eyes flutter. It was odd; Carter had hardly been aware of the woman when she had been masquerading as Major Hannah Wells, but now she knew who—and what—Jade really was, Sam suddenly found herself seeing faint ghosts of Jack O'Neill's face in the semi-conscious woman's appearance. There was a part of her that was searching for elements of another face as well, but she pretended not to be aware of it.

Williams yanked open the flap on the medical tent, and Jade coughed and drifted to the surface of consciousness as they hauled her inside. "Where…?" She managed.

"You're in the camp on Kytos," explained Sam. "You're safe."

Jade tried to shake her head. "No… Not…" Her gaze fell across Teal'c's silent form and found the broken insectile shape on the far side of the tent. "Ite-kh?" Her voice cracked and she tried to get up from the stretcher.

"Easy, now," said Williams. "Stay put."

The woman didn't hear him. Sam saw her eyes shimmer as she understood what had happened to her Re'tu companion. "No…" she repeated, her voice fading.

"Jade, I'm sorry," said Daniel; but she slumped back into the carry frame and passed out, a few tears streaking the caked dirt and blood on her cheeks.

Sam shot Daniel a look and he knew she wanted them to leave. Williams got to work and they exited with the men from SG-3. Carter sent them back out to bolster Captain Grant at the gate, while he followed her through the camp.

"The men who found Jade, did they say anything about Jack, or… Uh, Jack?"

Carter shook her head. "Both MIA." She sighed. "The colonel will contact us when he can."

They approached the long tent. "If he can," Jackson said grimly.

Predictably, inside the meeting pavilion things were not a model of peaceful diplomacy. The raised voices of the Pack members, of Kinsey and his staff, and the occasional attempted interjection from Colonel Reynolds came to them even before they entered. While Sam gave the colonel a run-down on the current circumstances, Daniel found himself standing next to Suj, who wore a frown that ruined her pleasant features.

"Ryn is aboard his vessel, in communication with the *Wanderer*," she said without preamble. "Word of the chaos here has reached our flotilla and the people there are distressed. There's talk of a combat deployment being prepared to come and extract us."

"There's no need for that," Jackson said quickly, "This isn't chaos… It's just, uh, a concern." He knew how lame his denial sounded and Suj's expression showed she knew it too.

"One of our guardsmen saw your warriors returning with the woman. Is it true that she was the interloper who disrupted the meeting on Earth?"

Daniel's first reaction was *How did they find that out so fast?* and he failed to hide it from her. He gave a reluctant nod. "Yes. But I'm afraid the situation is more complicated than that."

"It is her?" Koe broke in, picking up the thread of the conversation. "So, we are in danger here on Kytos, then, as much as we were on the Tau'ri homeworld!"

"No!" Jackson retorted. "Well, maybe. We're still trying to determine that."

"In our codes and laws, we have the right to demand she is turned over to us for a criminal hearing," said Suj. "The Pack hold claim to Kytos and she is on the planet. Technically, she is already our prisoner."

Daniel was still trying to frame a good reply when Kinsey's voice brayed. "No one is claiming anything or anyone unless

I agree on it!"

"So you dare to take control here?" Vix growled. "This is not an enclave of yours, Tau'ri. You have no right to come into our territory and enforce your edicts on us!"

Jackson groaned and caught Carter's eye. She looked like he felt; frustrated and annoyed.

Teal'c was aware of voices and movement, but they seemed to come to him from a great distance, as if the Jaffa were at the bottom of a deep well. He was conscious of the cage of his own flesh, the edges of a great burning pain across his chest , the searing of his skin. With effort, he tried to open his eyes, but they only fluttered, giving brief and cloudy impressions of the medical tent around him. He could smell blood and chemicals, the acrid tang of disinfectants. Teal'c saw a man in fatigues and at his side, stepping closer, a familiar figure in the patchwork garb of the Pack.

Ryn. The one who had tried to kill him.

Teal'c wanted to cry out a warning, but his lungs sucked at air and his muscles would not respond. He was trapped, pressing against the wall of his own agony.

I will not submit, he told himself, and began to marshal his concentration. *There is no pain. I will rise. In the kel no'reem, there is no defeat.*

"Is this the intruder?" Ryn kept his tone level, almost chatty.

The Tau'ri healer shot him a look, irritated by the distraction of his arrival. "Can you remain outside, please? I'm busy."

Ryn ignored the order. "Will she live?"

The healer sighed heavily, turning back to work on the woman, who moaned softly. "Yeah. If I can tape up the ribs she broke without any interruptions, she should be okay."

The Pack pilot let a slender silver rod slip from his sleeve into his hand. Like the communicator matrix in his ship, it was a gift from the Aschen. The body of the device held a revolving magazine with five vials of fluid, two of which were already spent. Ryn had made good use of them, removing obstacles to his ascension up the Pack hierarchy. He did not understand how the liquid worked, only that it left no traces and turned the inherent weakness in any man's body against himself.

He had hoped to use one of the vials on Vix; but the big warrior was wily and there had never been a moment when Ryn could have done so without alerting others. Under different circumstances, he would not have considered using the rod at all, but a cold flood of panic was building in his thoughts and Ryn's options were limited. The Jaffa had not died when he was supposed to, and so there was the risk that he would awaken and reveal what he knew. Matters were now clouded further still by the arrival of the woman. Mirris's warning had been curt and unequivocal; the newcomer was a threat to the entire scheme. She had the potential to bring Ryn's duplicity into the light before he could cement a position at the head of the Pack. She could not be allowed to live.

Ryn had an inelegant solution, but it was the only one that he could employ. He had to make the kills quickly and silently, then use the confusion that followed to press his advantage.

"I need you to go," said the healer, without looking at him.

"The same can be said of you," Ryn replied, and stabbed the sharp end of the rod into the other man's back. The device discharged instantly and the Tau'ri stiffened, the muscles on his neck standing out in cords. Ryn pushed him into a folding chair and the healer choked silently, wracked with sudden paralysis. He watched the other man until the healer stopped twitching.

Reloading the rod was a simple matter of working a thumb wheel, setting another vial in place for the injector mechanism within. Ryn hesitated at the woman's side, clutching the Aschen device like a dagger. His nerves tingled and he fought to stop his hands from shaking. "To the heart, then," he said quietly to himself, making a decision. He raised the device over her chest and she blinked into wakefulness, her face creasing in fear.

Ryn stabbed out, but the downward arc of the needle-tipped rod halted inches from her skin as an ebony skinned hand locked around his wrist and held it there.

Teal'c's vision was blurry and he fought off the effects of the drugs in his bloodstream, forcing himself to stay focused. The effort of propelling his body off the gurney sang in his muscles. Dimly, he was aware of the corpsman slumped in the chair, not moving, not breathing. He saw the flash of silver in Ryn's hand and knew it for what it was: *a weapon*.

The Jaffa pulled every ounce of his will together and snatched at his target. Ryn gasped as Teal'c grabbed him, pulling the glittering rod away from the injured girl's chest. The Pack pilot's eyes were wide with manic intensity. He struggled against the Jaffa's brute strength, shaking his hand as he attempted to break Teal'c's iron grip.

At any other time, this poor excuse for a fight would have already been over, but Teal'c's body was still rising through the fog of sedatives, weakened from the fights in the cockpit and the SGC. He felt slow and ponderous.

"Curse you!" spat the other man. "You'll die!"

"Eventually," he managed thickly, "but by your hand, not today."

The woman stirred, trying to push herself away from the two combatants, and Ryn shouted wordlessly, throwing all his might into shifting Teal'c's grip. The tip of the silver rod described loops in the air as it veered away, toward the Jaffa's injured torso. With a final, forceful shove, Teal'c broke the momentum of Ryn's attack and reversed the turn.

Before he could stop himself, Ryn's thrust impaled him on the rod, the metal disappearing into the flesh of his stomach. Teal'c heard a faint hiss from the inner workings of the device and Ryn's cheeks flushed red. A strangled scream escaped the man's lips and he fell away—slowly, so it seemed—to crash into a heap at the Jaffa's feet.

Teal'c head swam and he staggered a step. Then there were

arms holding him up. He turned to see Daniel Jackson at his side, alarm clear on his face.

"He was a spy," Teal'c gave a slow nod toward the Pack warrior. "And a killer."

Eventually, the Commander's voice drifted across the gap between the two floating cells. "You're wasting your time. I've been in these things before. There's no way out unless the power's deactivated. The cells are made of a bio-plastic. It seals itself shut like bones knitting, or something."

"How'd you get out last time?" Jack demanded.

A shadow passed over the old man's face. "Sam rescued us."

The way he said Carter's name gave Jack pause. Regret and anger oozed out of the word. He found himself unable to stop from asking the question. "Where is she in... Where you come from?"

The Commander turned on the pallet and glared at him through the transparent bars. "She's dead, okay? *Very* dead. Not Ascended-dead or any of that other stupid new age crap, dead like Charlie-dead, like Fraiser-dead—"

"That's enough!" Jack shouted, his anger from the confrontation on Kytos returning. "You hateful son of a bitch." The words slipped out of him in a rush; normally, he would never have had such a harsh and immediate reaction to being goaded, and it cut into him. He felt a powerful loathing uncoil in his chest. "What the hell are you made of?"

The old man made a disgusted spitting noise. "Look at you. You make me sick. I'm embarrassed to think I was like you once." He got up and came to the bars, closing the distance between them. "You... I... We never used to be this weak. Back in the day. Afghanistan and Libya. Kuwait City. That thing outside of Gdansk? Remember those days, Jack? The things you did under cover of darkness?"

O'Neill's blood ran cold. Each of those places, and more that the other man left unspoken, conjured moments from his tours with the Joint Armed Forces Special Operations Division, memories of missions so secret—so *black*—that many of his colleagues at Stargate Command had no idea of their existence. "I put all that behind me," he said quietly.

That got him a sneer in return. "After Charlie, yeah. As if that would make things better. But you couldn't help wondering, could you? If his death was payback for it all? Like scales being balanced?" There was accusation in the tone.

For a long moment, buried emotions pushed at O'Neill's thoughts and threatened to rise up and swamp him; but then he met the old man's gaze and held it. "That's not who I am anymore. If you're really me, you'd know that."

"Yeah," agreed the Commander. "You lost that for a while, that edge." His voice softened. "The gate... It was redemption, in a way. Until the Aschen and the war, at least." His eyes glittered like chips of granite. "That brought it all back. Had to be that man again, ruthless. You get me? Dosed up on alien tech to keep me tickin', using everything we had to fight them. Tactics we never would have conscienced before.... But I couldn't afford to be the good guy any more. Had to make choices, take a hard road." He gave a soft, humorless laugh. "Black Jack came back."

"In God's name, are you deliberately trying to provoke a war?" Kinsey had given up all pretence of maintaining a calm and considered façade, and now the vice president's face was red with fury. "You're all as bad as O'Neill, nothing but a bunch of cowboys!"

"Ryn killed Williams in cold blood," Sam retorted hotly, "Teal'c saw him do it! It was self-defense."

"I cannot accept that," Koe shook his head gravely. "Ryn was no stranger to battle, yes, but to commit murder..." He looked up across the long tent to Vix and the rest of the Pack delegation.

"He stabbed Williams in the back," Teal'c's voice was a rough growl, still leaden with pain. "He attempted to kill me, and shot down the Re'tu after it had surrendered."

Koe grimaced. "Forgive me, but the word of Apophis's First Prime is difficult to accept."

"I am Free Jaffa!" Teal'c roared, startling everyone in the tent. "I do not lie! Whatever enmity lays between my people and yours, do not let it blind you to the obvious truth!"

Vix's stony expression was rigid. "Why would he do such a thing, Jaffa? What proof do you have beyond your declaration?"

Daniel pushed forward and tossed something on to the long table. "How about this?" The silver rod rolled to a halt before the Pack. "The murder weapon."

Koe's eyes widened and he gingerly picked up the device. There was still blood on it. "A medical injector..." He noted.

"It's not of Goa'uld or Earth manufacture," Sam added. "It's Aschen."

She saw recognition creep across the Pack healer's face. Koe nodded slowly. "Yes. Yes, the major appears to be correct. This is indeed of Aschen origin."

"You know of them?" said Jackson.

Vix nodded once. "We have encountered the Aschen... And their works." His manner betrayed the low esteem the warrior had for the aliens. "They offered us membership in their Confederation of worlds if we would settle in their space. We declined their offer and the refusal did not sit well with their emissary."

"Was her name Mirris, by any chance?" Daniel asked.

"It was," Vix eyed him. "How did you know?"

"Educated guess." He glanced at Carter, who gestured for him to go on. "That's not all the Aschen kit that Ryn had. Teal'c also found a communications device in his ship. Now, unless the Pack have recently salvaged any Aschen vessels—"

"We have not," Suj broke in.

"Then Ryn was likely working with Mirris," Sam finished. 'He killed the Re'tu to stop it raising the alarm and Teal'c was in the wrong place at the wrong time. He just didn't reckon on Jaffa strength."

"Ryn came to silence me while I lay injured," continued Teal'c. "He would have killed Jade as well if I had not been able to stop him."

A grim silence settled over the Pack side of the room as Vix, Koe and Suj exchanged glances. Finally, the historian-engineer spoke. "Ryn made no secret of his plans to challenge you for leadership, Vix. When we refused the Aschen offer all those cycles ago, perhaps he did not." Her face was troubled. "Many of us wondered why they did not simply force us to submit to their rule. Now we know why."

"They always said they were a patient people," Koe admitted, "and it was only after our encounter with them that the grain blight came upon the *Wanderer*. I never dared suspect the two might be connected, but now…" He trailed off and looked up to meet Teal'c's gaze. "Forgive my earlier words, Jaffa. I see I may have been in error."

With a sudden rush of motion, Vix came up from his chair, startling all of them. The big man's craggy hands balled into fists. "Ryn was my rival but I gave him commerce, the free trade of ideas and trust! Now I hear this, and curse that he is not here to answer to it!"

"Mistakes were made," Kinsey ventured; Carter could see that the situation was getting away from him again, and he wasn't willing to let it go. "The important thing is, we're still talking. We can still walk away from this with something tangible."

Vix glared at the politician. "The matter has gone beyond questions of trade and treaty, Kinsey. We skirt issues of honor now!" He took a menacing step forward. "Every man, woman and child in the Pack is free from the yoke of the System Lords. I will not stand by and let them be manipulated by the Aschen instead!"

"I… Couldn't agree more," replied Kinsey, clearly daunted by the other man's passionate rejoinder.

There was a commotion at the entrance to the long tent and Sam blinked in surprise as the door flap was flung open and the woman Jade entered. She was sallow and drawn, but her face was set with determination. "I have to be heard!" she snapped, shrugging off Lieutenant Everitt's hand on her arm.

"It's okay," Sam told the officer. "Let her speak."

Colonel Reynolds nodded agreement, speaking up for the first time. "The major's right. If you've got something to say, now is the time."

Jade threw a look at Daniel and he gave her a supportive smile in return. *She looks like hell*, he thought. *It can't be easy for her to be here, to have had to go through all this.*

"I'm the one who sabotaged the assembly on Earth," she said bluntly, "I did it to stop the Aschen using your people to take revenge on mine... But things have gone beyond that now."

Kinsey sniffed. "I appreciate your confession, young lady. When we return to the SGC, I promise you there will be plenty of blame to be apportioned."

Jade shot him a withering glance. "We're not going back to the SGC, Mr. Kinsey, not unless you listen to me! I failed in my attempt to prevent this meeting and now other contingences have been set in motion!"

"Why do I not like the sound of that?" said Reynolds.

"Somewhere out in the jungle is a naquadria-enhanced fusion device primed to detonate, probably on a timer." Jackson heard the shock at her statement roll around the tent. "It's got a failsafe that will trigger it early if anyone dials out from the Stargate. I can disarm it, but we have to find it *now*."

"You admit your part in this subterfuge with one breath and then you ask to prevent it in another?" Suj snorted. "Now you wish us to trust you as well?"

"My father activated it before he and... And Colonel O'Neill were taken by the Aschen's drones. I'm the only person who knows how to defuse it."

"You must find it first," said Teal'c.

Sam gasped as a thought struck her, and she pulled a small hand held sensor device from her pocket. "If she can give me the energy pattern, I can track it down."

"Are you sure?" Kinsey demanded.

Daniel saw Sam look right past the vice president to Colonel Reynolds. "Sir. Permission to execute EOD sweep?"

Reynolds gestured sharply. "Don't wait for my say-so, Major, go, go!"

Daniel caught her arm as she turned to leave. "Sam! What about everyone else?" He lowered his voice. "There's not enough ships down here to get everyone off the surface if you can't find that bomb."

Carter glanced at Jade, then back at Jackson, and he felt her eyes boring into him. "You said you trusted her, despite everything that's happened. Now we'll get to see if you made the right call."

The two women headed out toward the tree line, and into the darkness.

O'Neill watched his counterpart's craggy, age-scarred face. He was caught between pity and fury at the old man. "So you brought your war here? You made your own kid a soldier, you played it like a coward, like a terrorist?" He shook his head. "I look at you and I'm supposed to accept that you're what I'm going to become? A man who sneaks a nuke into a peace conference. Someone willing to sacrifice the lives of his closest friends and the men he served with for a mission objective."

"The end justifies the means. The camp gets wiped out, the treaty's gone and the Pack collapses, Mirris and the Aschen get caught in the fallout." His lip curled. "Earth goes on, the SGC goes on. Millions live instead of dying. The war never happens."

"There's gotta be a better solution!" Jack snapped. "Stop this! We'll help you find Mirris, we'll go after the Aschen and hit them first."

The old man shook his head. "Doesn't work out. We tried it that way and that jackass Kinsey screwed it up even worse, started a goddamn interstellar conflict." He sighed. "This is the best tactic. Quick and clean. No survivors. Just like in Libya."

"This is nothing like that, and you know it," O'Neill retorted hotly.

A crooked finger tapped on the bars. "Out there, thirty years from now, thirty damn years of hell, with everyone dead and the rest of us barely hanging on, the human race goin' over the edge to extinction… All of it's ruined, Jack. The whole galaxy, on fire. This is the only way to stop it."

O'Neill pushed away and turned his back on the old man. "To hell with you. I don't care if you're me or the Ghost of Christmas Future or Santa freaking Claus. I'm not going to trade one set of deaths for another. Not now, not ever. If you won't help me, I'll stop it myself." He knelt at the fresher unit and turned all his attention on the device, looking for something he could use to escape.

"So, is this thing on a countdown, or what?" Sam asked, holding her scanner close to her face, reading the display. A faint trace lit the edge of the sensor envelope.

"Primary detonator will be a remote link. Failing that, after a pre-set period a timed delay will kick in."

"What's the clock on the timer set for?" Carter asked.

"I have no idea," Jade admitted.

"Great," said Sam, "so no pressure, then." She kept her P90 in her free hand, alert for any signs of trouble, but as much as she tried to keep her thoughts on the immediate problem, her gaze kept wandering back to the girl. And without thinking about it, she said the words. "You're Colonel O'Neill's daughter."

"Commander-in-Chief O'Neill, yes," she corrected, and then pointed along the ridgeline. "This way?"

"Yeah." Sam kept close, a step or two behind her. "You're from the future."

"The year 2032, Earth calendar," Jade replied. "I'm not going to be born for another couple of years yet."

Sam fumbled with her next question. "What's it like... then?"

Jade didn't look at her. "If it was good, I wouldn't be here."

She frowned, her thoughts swinging back and forth between questions of the mundane and ordinary, and the scientific and cosmological. Inevitably, the scientist in her won out. "I get what you're trying to do here. Change your own past for the better and everything... But M-theory means you may not change anything. History splits off into branches at every decision point... You may do all this and get home to find nothing is different."

"Maybe," she agreed, "but it's worth the risk. If you saw how we lived, you'd feel that way too. Where I come from, mankind is a generation away from extinction. Even if you're right, if time splits into alternates and our future still happens, at least *you* won't have to live through it."

The simple directness of Jade's statement made Carter shiver involuntarily. "If you succeed, you may cease to exist in this timeline. It's not much of a reward-loss balance."

The other woman laughed quietly. "You're amazing. I'm telling you about the end of the world and you're worrying about me." Jade gave Sam a sideways look. "You're just the same as you were. As you *will* be."

"You know me?" Carter asked, even as a voice in her head warned her to say nothing more. "We were friends?"

The moment of warmth on Jade's face faded. "We were," she replied. Then the scanner beeped, and the woman became all business again. "Do you have it? We must be very close."

Sam saw the bloom of radiation on the scanner. "I read something over there. An energy surge, very faint."

Jade broke into a run. "The device is charging," she called, "we don't have much time, it's on a build up to detonation."

Carter sprinted forward and came upon something that looked like a camouflage poncho heaped over a shallow pit in the jungle loam. Jade ripped it away and the two of them hesitated at the sight revealed. It was similar in mass and design to the unit that Sam had disarmed in the air shaft at Stargate Command, but she could see immediately that this device had a much larger naquadria vial, and far more strands of anti-tampering mechanisms.

A holographic panel showed a stream of tumbling symbols; they had no more than a minute before the bomb went critical. Carter felt sick inside. She had no time to dismantle the weapon, no time to think it through as she had back on Earth. Her hand hesitated on the hilt of her knife, even as she realized her slash-and-hope approach wouldn't work again here.

"Let me," said Jade, bending down to study the keypad. "It's locked with a codeword for deactivation."

"You know what it is, right?" Sam asked.

The other woman shook her head. "Nope."

Carter's knuckles tightened around her weapon. "You told me you could disarm it!"

"That wasn't the complete truth," said Jade, tapping out data strings into the panel. "What I meant was, I *think* I can disarm it." The spool of vanishing symbols was streaming away to nothing before Sam's eyes. "My father programmed this," she explained, as calmly as if they were discussing the weather, "and he's never been that original about coming up with passwords."

Carter's mind raced; she remembered a discussion about the same thing, years ago at the SGC when she'd accidentally discovered Jack was using the name of his favorite sports team as a code key. In the tension of the moment, her mind blanked. "Ice hockey!" she blurted.

Jade shook her head. "I guessed that one when I was twelve, and he stopped using it. And, besides, I tried it already." She hesitated, then typed something else. Sam didn't see the word, but it did the trick. The symbols froze and the device went inert, shutting down.

With care, the two of them pulled the bomb from the earthen

pit and secured it in Jade's backpack. When she was sure it was safe, Carter allowed herself a moment to take a breath. "That was close. Two bombs in a week. I don't want to have to do that again any time soon."

Jade nodded distractedly, staring out into the trees.

"So what was the codeword, then?"

"A name," Jade said quietly. "My mother's name."

A branch snapped out among the trunks and Carter caught the sound of movement over fallen leaves. "We got company…"

A shape, large and metallic in the twilight, rolled forward, picking its way through the jungle. Twin limbs ending in gun pods turned toward the women, thread-thin targeting lasers cutting through the air. "Drones!" snapped Jade.

"Run!" shouted Sam, and she pulled the P90's trigger, lighting up the night with an arc of muzzle flash.

CHAPTER THIRTEEN

In the clean and well-lit chamber, the clinician showed Mirris how the interview chair would operate, demonstrating the unit's restraints and the multiple injector ports along the arm rests and the torso mounts. There were wireless monitor pods that would keep track of blood chemistry, heart rate, neural condition, endocrine saturation and the like to ensure that the subject remained completely awake during the interrogation; medical automata arms lay curled up behind the chair, ready to unfold in the event of a catastrophic physiological collapse. The machine was designed solely to prolong the life of a subject while information was extracted from them.

Mirris kept the device on board her ship with the vain hope that one day she would have the chance to use it, and now, by some odd chance, she found herself wishing she had brought two of them. Confederation Central would be eager to see what secrets the Tau'ri Colonel had to give them, but in all truth Mirris cared little about what kinds of intelligence they could glean from Jack O'Neill; she only wanted him to suffer.

"I would suggest processing the older one first," the clinician was saying. "He will likely not survive an intensive interview. Additionally, his bio-scan shows signs of some interesting cellular reconstruction on the nanometric scale. I deduce he may have used rejuvenating chemicals at some point... After he expires I would like the opportunity to conduct a dissection of his major organs."

Mirris nodded remotely. *Two O'Neills*. She could simply torture one to death and present the other intact to the Confederation; but even killing both would never be enough to bring Mollem back to her...

"With regard to that, I have a hypothesis regarding the origin of the second subject," continued the scientist, "but it is of such a spurious nature I almost hesitate to give voice to it."

"Tell me," she demanded, running her hand over a cluster of needle-sharp injector rods.

"There is residual evidence of exotic particles in the older male's bloodstream, different in nature to those encountered during typical wormhole travel. An energy signature of chronometric nature."

Mirris shot the clinician a look. "You're suggesting a temporal flux effect?"

The scientist shrugged. "It does fit the extant conditions."

"Time travel is impossible," she snorted. "The energy requirements alone are insurmountable."

"As you say, Administrator. It was only a theory."

The door to the chamber sighed open and she turned to see Geddel enter. Her subordinate's face was tight with barely-concealed anxiety. His eyes sought Mirris out and he came quickly to her side, his gray robes flapping around his heels. He took in the room as he approached, the clinician and his staff, the watchful security drone at its post.

"What is it?" she demanded.

The sub-director had a screensheet in his hand. "An alert indicator from Kytos. The induction tracer that was implanted in your operative…"

Mirris felt alarm creeping up inside her. She snatched the readout from his grip and ran her eyes down it. "The signal has ceased."

Geddel nodded, unable to keep an air of smugness from his gesture. "It may be a systems malfunction, but that is extremely unlikely. The most probable options are that the tracer was discovered and removed or that—"

"Ryn has been terminated," Mirris finished, refusing to allow him the satisfaction of saying the words. Her fingers tightened and the screensheet crumpled in her hand, the moving images on the plastic cracking and flickering.

"I believe so." Had he been less Aschen, less rigid about his own emotions, Geddel might have smiled with those words.

"Our presence here has been discovered. The scouts on the ground report enemy contacts. Respectfully, I would suggest that we employ an exit strategy and exfiltrate from this system under cover of aura-cloak. We have the prisoners. We should return to Confederation space and submit them to Central." Geddel allowed himself an arch sniff. "In that manner, the mission will not be seen as a complete failure."

Mirris flicked the crumpled sheet from her hand and it fell to the deck, to be recovered and tidied away by a small servo mechanoid. When she spoke, the menace in her voice was thick and ready. "Failure will not be considered, sub-director. It appears that the time for patience and subterfuge is at an end." She glared at Geddel. "We will not disengage. Give the order to the control crews. Program all space-capable drones for immediate combat operations and deploy them against the migrant fleet. Have all available ground units transported to Kytos. Their orders are the same—exterminate everything that is not Aschen." Her voice gave a little shudder of pleasure as she gave the command. There was something almost sexual about the release of her hate on so grand a scale.

"We will lose the aura-cloak!" Geddel retorted. "Our ship will be visible, open to counter-attack! And what value is there to engage in direct military action? You have fallen short, Mirris! You cannot hope to rescue this convoluted scheme of yours by so wasteful an action as—" He never finished the sentence. Suddenly Geddel was spinning away from her, stumbling and falling against the interrogation chair. His hand was at his face, pressing at a fan of blood streaming from his nose. "You struck me!" he choked.

Mirris looked down at her hand, at his blood where it marked the knuckles of her fist. "I did. The experience was quite pleasurable. I think I may repeat it."

Geddel stumbled away, holding out a hand to ward her off. "No! No!" He looked around in raw fright, looking for support from the other crew, and when it did not come, he found a measure of strength and sneered back at her. "Such a display... It is beneath your rank, Administrator! You clearly cannot perform your duties with the emotional detachment required of a commander! You should be relieved of duty!"

"And who will relieve me, Geddel?" she asked, not for one moment releasing his gaze. "You? Is there anyone aboard this ship who will dare to disobey me?"

Geddel looked down at his own blood on his hands, and in that moment Mirris saw the weakness inherent in her species. By bleeding their passions from themselves, they had lost something that the Tau'ri had nurtured—a tough, animal refusal to accept defeat. She was pleased she had rediscovered it in herself.

When the sub-director did not respond, Mirris smiled thinly. "I thought not. Now do as I ordered. Deploy all drones. Maximum lethality."

The clans of the Pack fleet had gone about their daily lives for months and never once suspected the silent, invisible predator that lay close to them. The Aschen ship stalked the flotilla, hiding beneath the sensor-opaque mesh of its aura-cloak, behind passing moons or in the lee of solar radiation belts, forever pacing them. The Pack ships were primitive in comparison to the Aschen vessel, and there was not a single crewmember aboard it who did not hold the nomads in utter contempt.

On Mirris's command, the aura-cloak was fully deactivated, and the ship emerged from the shroud of its camouflage like an orca suddenly surfacing among a pod of dolphins.

The Aschen warship had no name—such trivia were the traits of inferior races who foolishly imbued their machines with delusions of character and spirit—it was only one of a number of vessels in service to the Confederation, hybrid explorers and battle cruisers that could serve the Aschen in furthering their scientific knowledge or by turns subjugating client worlds for the greater good of their dominion. In aspect, it presented a simple but lethal silhouette. Long and bullet-nosed, the ship was forged from bare metal in sheets of tarnished brassy gold or dull gunmetal gray. Two thick fins emerged from the fuselage, one on the ventral and one on the dorsal surface, close to the cluster of throbbing sub light engines at the aft. The overall impression generated by the vessel was one of calculated, machined lethality. Not an inch of the Aschen ship was given over to filigree or extraneous detail; Mirris's craft was the embodiment of cold function over form.

Already, some of the Pack's older and slower ships traveling at the rear of the ragged fleet were reacting to the new arrival. Thrusters lit the space over Kytos as the diverse vessels split apart and raced to flee from the invader. The Aschen ship claimed its first two victims when, in panicked flight, a Calai helium tender collided with a converted Goa'uld Al'kesh and both craft destroyed one another. Deeper in the flotilla, combat-capable ships were responding, but slowly. *Too slowly.*

With stately menace, the Aschen turned and presented the length of its hull to the Pack. Hatches recessed seamlessly into the wall of metal opened in their hundreds and released a swarm of automata. Mirris's people found the idea of combat by direct means — that was to say, where one being would fight another face-to-face — to be distasteful. This societal antipathy was the motivating force behind their choices of weapons and conquest, typically through subterfuge and the insidious, creeping death of biological warfare; but on occasion, the Aschen found themselves forced to fight in more conventional patterns. For that they had their drones.

The robot weapons were, after a fashion, self-aware, but only in the limited ways that would make them better killers. Each drone had a virtual mind imprinted on a matrix of crystal-organic components, a basic template that had been drawn from a breed of domestic canine from Aschen Prime. The two factors that defined the minds of the drones were unquestioning obedience and ruthless intent. Guided by a central nexus aboard their mothership, once released upon a target only the commands of their masters would stop the machines from destroying everything in their path.

Each drone was in constant communication with all the others, a shared hive-mind that allowed incredible flexibility on the battlefield. The Aschen did not deploy their killers often, but when they did, there were usually no survivors left to tell others of it.

Energy cannons blazing white fire, the leading edge of the drone swarm powered through the expanding cloud of debris that was all that remained of the Al'kesh and the tender. A solar-ion sailship lay before them, wallowing as it tried to make a turn too sharp for its gossamer ray-wings to manage. The drones killed the ship and moved on without stopping, flowing toward the core of the flotilla and the beating heart of the Pack; the *Wanderer*.

Standing at the edge of the encampment with Colonel Reynolds at his side, Daniel experienced a cascade of emotional states that flashed through him so fast he barely had time to register one before he was hit by another. Anxiety gave way to relief when he heard Sam's voice over the radio; the bomb had been disarmed, and that meant that the camp was *not* about to vanish into a cloud of free molecules at a moment's notice. But then he heard the tension in her voice, and he knew that they had only exchanged one threat for another.

"There!" shouted Reynolds, pointing to the tree line as Carter and Jade exploded out of the undergrowth and raced at full tilt toward them. Sam was hosing fire from her P90, heedlessly shooting spray-and-pray style towards whatever was coming after them. Fear spiked in Jackson's gut as a gunmetal machine burst from the trees, spitting energy bolts at the feet of the fleeing women. Reynolds and his men, two of them armed with heavy SAW machineguns, laid into the robot and Daniel joined in with his pistol, aware on some level that his contribution would probably do little good. The machine was clearly a cousin of the ones they had encountered on Golla IX, and he remembered all too clearly how hard it had been to take those down.

But finally the combined gunfire forced the machine off its spinning wheels and silenced it, and Daniel's shock ebbed away—for about three seconds.

"There's more of them!" Sam called, gasping out the words between gulping breaths of air. "The Aschen must have a beaming point out there, they're dropping them in one after another!"

"But the bomb," Jackson replied. "The gate! If you disarmed the bomb, then the Stargate's free to dial! We can get everyone away…"

"Yeah," Reynolds said grimly, "but we just lost contact with Captain Grant and his men up there guarding it. Wanna take a guess why?"

"Oh, no." Daniel felt the ice-water sting in his veins all over again.

"Major!" Reynolds called out to Carter as he slammed a fresh magazine into his assault rifle. "Give me a threat assessment!"

"Multiple hostiles inbound, Colonel," she replied. "Company strength, maybe more."

Sam barely got the words out before the rattle of gunfire sounded from the far side of the encampment. Daniel caught Sergeant Albrectsen's voice over the radio channel. *"Command, this is post bravo! I have enemy contact along the east perimeter! Engaging!"*

"God damn it," spat Reynolds, "they're trying to box us in!"

"What are we going to do?" Jackson asked.

Carter shot a look at Jade. "You've fought these things before, right? What are their tactics?"

The other woman grimaced. "They're dangerous but not innovative. Expect a brute force attack from all sides at once. They'll just keep throwing themselves at us until we waste them all."

"Or until we run out of ammo," Reynolds replied. "All right." He toggled his radio to the general channel. "Listen up! All units, dig in and secure fire corridors. Stand by for multiple enemy contacts!"

"Where's Vix?" said Daniel. "The least we can do is try to get the civilians out of here…"

"I am here, Doctor Jackson," said the Pack warrior, approaching with Suj at his side. "But I am afraid we must leave you. The flotilla is under attack, and my priorities lie there, with my kinsmen."

"What?" In spite of himself, Jackson looked up into the night sky.

"The Aschen," said Suj. "A warship appeared at the rear of the fleet and launched a large force of drone fighters. We must go to our people's defense."

"Yeah, well we got our own drone problem to deal with down here!" snapped Reynolds. "We need every gun hand we can get!"

Vix's face twisted in frustration. "I will leave you some warriors and our energy weapons, but we are short of battle-trained pilots as it is."

"Colonel, if I may?" Sam broke in. "I'm a fully qualified combat aviator and I'm checked out on a Death Glider. If you'll let Suj take our civilians out to somewhere safe in the Tel'tak, I'll join you up there, see if I can help."

Suj looked to her leader. "I am willing, if you agree to it."

Vix considered the offer and then gave a nod. "Very well. I will have a Glider pilot take Ryn's ship instead. But a Goa'uld fighter requires a crew of two."

"I can handle it alone," Carter replied. "I think…"

"That…" said a new voice, "…will not be required." Teal'c came out of the shadows. "I will serve as your co-pilot, Major."

Daniel's face fell. "Teal'c, far be it from me to dismiss Jaffa bravado, but you can barely walk."

The big man nodded. "Indeed. I would be of limited use in a ground engagement. However, in aerial combat, my skills could be better employed."

"You're sure?" said Sam. Teal'c raised an eyebrow and Carter smiled. "Yeah, he's sure. Why am I even asking?"

Vix gestured to the ships. "We go, then." He gave Reynolds a sharp look. "Good hunting, Colonel."

Teal'c hesitated, and then tossed his staff weapon to Jade. "I assume you know how to use that?" In reply, the woman flicked a hidden switch on the hilt and the beam emitter snapped open, ready for combat. The Jaffa inclined his head. "I will expect you to return it to me after we have won the battle," he said, walking away.

Daniel let out a small chuckle. "Wow. You know, he never lets me touch his staff."

Jade took up a position, aiming as more of the machines ambled out of the trees. "It's all about knowing how to handle it."

O'Neill dropped back on to his haunches and made a face. There were simply no places for him to get purchase with his fingers. Every closure inside the floating cell-cage was perfect, without even the hint of a seam that he could try to dig into. The translucent bio-plastic was strong and resilient; if he marked it with a thumbnail, the material slowly reverted back to its original semi-pliant state. He looked up to the next cell, expecting to see the old man watching him with that judgmental you're-wasting-your-time look, but instead his counterpart was at the far side of his cell, listening intently.

Jack's brow furrowed. "What are you doing?"

"Quiet," came the terse reply. "You hear it?"

"Hear what?" O'Neill held his breath and strained for any change in the distant humming of the Aschen ship's systems; and for a moment, it seemed like there *was* something different, but he couldn't put his finger on it.

Finally the old man nodded to himself. "Power flow sounds have changed. Cloak's offline. We're moving under forward thrust."

"Why?"

He got a shrug in return. "Your guess is as good as mine, junior."

It was, as the saying went, a target-rich environment. The Death Glider cleared the outer edge of Kytos's atmosphere, Teal'c worked the weapons controls and the holographic screens in front of Sam hazed into view. They were dappled with countless numbers of vessel indicators, transients spiking this way and that, some fighting around one another, others fleeing, others attacking. The sweep of the Glider's sensor grid began to pick out which ones were friendly and which ones were not. Tags showing friend-or-foe beacons lit up, and the Pack were in the minority. Red enemy tell-tales dotted the screen like a rash.

Carter threw a quick look through the canopy and saw Vix's tri-wing pacing her, blue flame throbbing from his fighter's drives. She could see his head moving behind the triangular glass panels of his cockpit. "*Suj is away,*" he called, "*I have directed her to take the Tel'tak toward this system's asteroid belt. That is the designated rally point for all our unarmed ships.*"

"Copy that," Sam replied, trying not to think about how the vice president and his staff would be handling a rickety flight crammed into the Tel'tak's cargo bay.

"Weapons are free," Teal'c informed her over the Glider's intercom. "We are clear to engage, Major."

"*All defense interceptors, engage the Aschen,*" said Vix. "*Protect the crèche boats and the* Wanderer."

Carter flexed her fingers and gripped the flight controls. It had been a while since she had flown a 'pure' Death Glider—these days, the SGC had enough of its own breed of F-302 starfighters to go around—but she hadn't forgotten how to put one of the Goa'uld ships through its paces. She thumbed the beam cannon controls from 'safe' to 'ready' and followed Vix in.

"Three drones, quadrant six, attack vector." Her co-pilot

spoke crisply through the communicator tab on her cheekbone. "Illuminating now."

"Roger, I have the targets." Adrenaline tingled through her. "Engaging!"

The triad of Aschen robots dithered for an instant before turning into a three-pronged split, making exactly the maneuver that Sam expected of them. The enemy ships turned tighter than any fighter with an organic pilot could—their machine brains were not as susceptible to the forces of gravitation as a human body was—but the Goa'uld Gliders had structural integrity fields that haloed their cockpit modules, and allowed their fragile, fleshy crew to make turns and accelerations that would crush an unprotected body into a slurry of compacted meat. Carter stood the Death Glider on its tail and rose through a climbing turn, cutting first one, then two of the drones from the sky. The fighter's winged-scarab fuselage described a tight Immelmann that brought it squarely into the last target's rear aspect. Sam pulsed the energy guns once and orange fire tore the leading drone into glittering fragments.

"Nine drones, quadrant four. Six drones, quadrant three," Teal'c reported, glaring at his sensor console.

"They brought friends," Carter began to say, but the Jaffa was still speaking.

"Three drones, quadrant five. Three drones, quadrant one. All targets show attack orientation, Major."

Sam pumped more power to the Glider's sub light engines and extended away from the ball of debris she had created. Carter hazarded a look up and around, and saw the headlong approach of the drone force that dappled the scanner screen. Glaring white bolts of coherent energy flashed soundlessly past the cockpit, and distantly she registered the sphere-shaped fighter she'd seen on Kytos vanishing inside an expanding plume of green fire. Static rumbled over the intership com channel.

Beyond the edges of her immediate arena of battle, the bigger and slower ships of the Pack flotilla drifted with streaks of fire and crystallized gas leaking from their hulls. Hundreds more flashing drones swept and dove around the large vessels, tearing into them. Here and there, heavy wattage beams or plasma flares issued out and swatted at the robot fighters, but with every passing second there seemed to be more and more of them.

Sam spun back into the fray as Vix's fighter shot past her and she destroyed two more drones that came hot on his tail. The Pack leader's ship waggled its wings in a gesture of thanks.

"I read critical failure on a grain lighter in quadrant two," said Teal'c. "It is about to explode."

Carter inverted the Death Glider just as the vessel Teal'c described became a brief, tiny sun. She felt her throat tighten. "How many people were aboard that ship?"

Vix's answer was grim. "*Eighty families, with livestock and hydroponics.*"

The major's jaw stiffened. "Vix, we can't hope to counter all these drones face-to-face. They're being commanded from the main Aschen vessel. We need to target that, cut off the head."

"*We cannot leave the flotilla undefended,*" came the reply, static lacing the words as a Death Glider in red livery imploded nearby.

"You're fighting a defensive battle," Sam pressed. "You're engaging on the Aschen's terms, not ours. We have to turn things around, get in their faces…"

Teal'c grunted in agreement. "Colonel O'Neill has often opined to me that a good offence is the best defense."

"*I won't divert all my interceptors for a fruitless attack on the mothership,*" he retorted. "*We must hold off the drones until the Pack can enter hyperspace. To stay and fight risks death for us all… I must think of the safety of the clans.*"

"The Aschen have been tracking you for months," said Teal'c, "what makes you believe you will be able to avoid them now? Mirris will not allow you to escape."

"Two!" Carter snapped. "Just give me two fighters! You tie up the mass of the drones defending the flotilla and I'll loop around, strike at their command ship. It's worth a shot…" She glared out at the battle as another capital ship exploded. "For all our sakes."

Vix's voice came back a moment later. "*Two interceptors, then.*" He called out on the general channel. "*Noa, Kiq? This is Vix. Form up on the Tau'ri's Glider and follow her orders.*" The warrior's ship crossed over Sam's canopy and she saw him nod in salute. "*Good hunting, Major.*"

"Right," Sam replied, steeling herself. "Time to put your money where your mouth is, Carter." She pushed the throttle bar forward and powered toward the Aschen vessel, with a pair of dart-shaped Calaian fighters riding in on her engine wake.

"Interim report," demanded Mirris, striding through the rows of cubicles in the command nexus. Geddel turned from his operations podium near the hologram dais and blinked at her with watery eyes. She could feel the fear coming off him in waves. The fool's arrogance had made him so bold that he had dared to openly oppose her, and her violent physical response had shaken the sub-director to the core. Aschen never raised their hands to one another; it simply was not *done*. But the pleasure it had brought to Mirris and the lingering after-effect of Geddel's new fear—an echo of the way all the crew now looked at her—made that old thinking seem outmoded and dull. She smiled thinly as she watched him scramble to obey her orders.

On some internal level of consideration, Mirris knew that Geddel had actually been correct. Her dealings with the Pack nomad Ryn, her obsession with the Tau'ri and the hateful sorrow over Mollem's death, these things had gradually worn away the veneer of Aschen detachment bred into her. He accused her of taking on the traits of these inferiors, and she had. Mirris had become like the Earthers in her quest to destroy them; perhaps she should have found an irony in that, but the immediate promise of destruction occupied too much of her thoughts.

Geddel brought a holograph of the combat zone into life. "Uh. Drone attrition within acceptable parameters, Administrator." His voice was more nasal than usual where his nose was swollen from her assault. "The migrants are incurring ongoing losses. I estimate they will have depleted their forces before our own losses reach the midway point. Some smaller tonnage ships are attempting to move out of the engagement area, but these are being tracked and will be eliminated once main threat forces are destroyed." He swallowed. "The planetary attack continues. Ground drones have isolated the Tau'ri encampment and continue to assault it."

She nodded. She was pleased. "This is adequate. Ensure that no-one escapes through the Stargate or into hyperspace. I want no survivors."

Geddel did not acknowledge her order and she shot him a look. The sub-director's attention was on the holograph. "Administrator..." He began, as if he were fearful of bringing something unpleasant to her attention.

"Speak!" she barked.

He pointed into the ghostly image. "A flight of migrant fighters have broken off from the main engagement and are making a high-velocity approach toward our ship." The display reformed to show three small craft, one of Goa'uld design, the other two of Calaian construction. "It could be a probing attack..."

"Three fighters?" Mirris's scorn was withering. "Have the drones obliterate them."

"I cannot," Geddel winced as he replied. "All drone units have been deployed to other targets."

She bared her teeth. "Then bring the beam cannons on line. I want them turned into *vapor*."

"I read multiple power nodes, transmission antennae and energy conduits," said Teal'c, running his gaze down the scan results coming in from the Aschen mothership. The Death Glider's targeting grid highlighted the vital systems inside the alien vessel, but the profusion of them was so vast that he could not be sure of the best place to strike. He relayed this to Major Carter.

"Yeah, Aschen use a centralized network for all their main systems," said the major. "I noticed that when we took a look around their harvester back on Volia. All their power infrastructure channels emerge from a core location, but they modulate the pattern so it merges into the background clutter on a scanner."

"I take it you have a method of defeating this concealment?"

She nodded. "After Volia, the Pentagon wanted some tactical analysis in case the Aschen decided to show up again, and I came up with a way to isolate and track their power grid."

The Jaffa paused, framing his next words. "Major. You are aware that if Colonel O'Neill and his…counterpart were captured by the Aschen, then it is most likely they are on board that vessel." It was a statement, not a question.

"Yeah, I know it. And I know what his orders would be right now if I could ask him." He heard the slight catch in her voice.

"We must proceed," he replied.

Carter nodded and toggled a control on her panel. "I'm broadcasting this to everyone. Tune your sensors to this subfrequency modulation, and then aim at the big glowy thing."

Teal'c raised an eyebrow as the major's algorithm shifted the scanner's point of view; abruptly there was a clear line of sight to the Aschen ship's central generator.

"*This is Noa, I have the target,*" called the Pack pilot.

"*Kiq here. I see it too.*" The delta-wing fighter peeled off. "*I'm going in.*"

"No, wait!" Sam cried. "We need to concentrate our firepower! It'll be heavily protected—"

"*My mate was on the grain lighter!*" snarled Kiq. "*I do this for him!*"

Carter threw the Death Glider after the Calaian ship, with Noa's fighter right beside them, but they were too late. A blinding wall of white light, so strong that it even penetrated the polarized canopy of the Glider, seared the Jaffa's eyes as the Aschen vessel opened up with its anti-ship cannons. Designed to punch holes in other capital ships, the beam turned Kiq's fighter into a brief sketch of black and gray before it vanished. Teal'c blinked furiously at the purple after-image on his retinas.

"Ugh," managed Carter. "Can't wait. We have to hit them now."

He worked the control console and poured power into the Death Glider's guns. "Weapons at optimum, Major."

"*Noa, ready on your command.*"

"Targeting…" Teal'c saw the gun cues converge over the hot spot on the Aschen ship's hull, even as the anti-ship cannon tracked to follow the fighters. "Now!"

Death Glider, delta-wing and Aschen warship all fired in the space of the same heartbeat.

Raw, unchained energy punched through the brass hull of the mothership and boiled away vital components, severing conduits and spilling vast crackling floods of electricity through a dozen decks; but all of this happened an instant before the anti-ship gun erupted for a second time and disintegrated Noa's fighter, even as the pilot's kill shot left her guns. The backwash slammed into the Death Glider and tossed it away into the blackness, throwing Carter and Teal'c against their restraints and pushing them past the point where the ship's protective integrity field could keep them conscious.

All through the Aschen ship the constant and ready flow of power from the energy core stuttered and dimmed. Lights flickered, life-support became unstable, drives choked on gulps of plasma; and on the vessel's secure holding level, a contragravity generator unit failed completely.

One second they were off the ground, steady as a rock, both men engaged in little more than a grimacing contest, and the next—

O'Neill swore out loud as the cage fell to the deck and cracked open all along one side. He bounced as it hit the floor, rattling around like a dice in a cup, finally tumbling out and across the metal deck in an undignified heap.

Jack ached absolutely *everywhere* as he hauled himself back to his feet amid the flickering lights and the trilling sounds that had to be some kind of alarm siren. Like his cell, the old man's cage had also broken open on impact where the bio-plastic split against the metal floor. As quickly as he dared, afraid that the other man could have broken something, O'Neill dragged him out. He got his cellmate to the edge of the room just as the lights came back on at full strength and the mangled cages rose slowly and unsteadily back into the air.

The old guy blinked and pushed him away. "Get off me."

"Oh, fine. A thank you would be nice."

"For what? You think we're any better off out here than we were behind bars?" He jerked a wrinkled thumb at the cages.

"We're free," the colonel retorted, "that's an improvement from where I'm standing..." He massaged his knee. "*Ow.* Oh, I think I pulled something."

"Free?" said the old man, unconsciously mimicking his action. "This is a class six Aschen auxiliary control craft. Crew of a hundred or so, plus twice as many automated security drones. Getting past them to a teleport terminal would count as being 'free'. Standing around nursing a damn gimpy knee without so much as a butter knife between us, that ain't anywhere near the same."

Jack eyed his counterpart. "You are a sour old bastard, aren't you? Even grandpa had more yuks than you, and he was the meanest cuss I've ever met."

"Bite me," snarled the other man, getting to his feet and limping away.

"Look," O'Neill called after him, "like it or not, you and me are in this situation together and doing nothing about it won't end well for either of us. Maybe you do have a good reason for screwing around with history, and maybe you don't. But whatever happens, I know you don't want to see Jade killed. If you *are* me, then there's no point in lying to... To yourself. Deep down you don't want to see anyone die needlessly, not when we can do something about it." The old man paused, listening, and he continued. "What do you say we get the hell out of here, and try to straighten this mess out before someone we both care about gets hurt?"

The other man turned slowly and gave him a scornful stare. "You've been thinkin' up that speech a while, haven't you?"

"Yeah," he admitted, "a little. I thought it was pretty good. Did you buy it?"

"A little," repeated the elderly soldier, and he gave a sigh like the weight of the world was pressing him down.

Maybe it is, thought O'Neill.

Something that might have been a smirk touched the craggy face of the old man. "A pair of Jacks. Not much of a hand."

"We'll play what we're dealt. That's what we always do."

CHAPTER FOURTEEN

The wheeled forms of the Aschen drones came on regardless, rolling over the sparking hulks of their fallen counterparts, shrugging off all but the heaviest caliber gunfire. The stale smell of spent cordite and ozone was heavy in the damp jungle air and it collected in Daniel Jackson's lungs, tight in his chest like acid heartburn. Close by, Colonel Reynolds dropped back into cover behind a plastic equipment crate and detached the ammunition magazine from his M4 carbine. Daniel saw a thin stream of smoke curling from the barrel of the assault rifle, the heat of so many rounds fired dissipating from the weapon. Lasers crackled as they lanced lines of white light over their heads, mingling with the strident chatter of automatic rifles. There was a small war unfolding on the surface of Kytos, confined into the space around the SGC encampment.

"Aim for the wheel hubs," Reynolds was saying into his radio. "If you can't penetrate the brain-case, go for a motion kill instead." The colonel slammed a fresh magazine into place and went back to the ready. "Doc! How's your ammo?"

Daniel looked at the pistol in his hand. He'd fired his last shot several minutes earlier. "Spent," he admitted. "Colonel, we're not going to be able to hold them off much longer. We need a new plan."

Reynolds aimed and shot out the wheels of another drone. "At this stage, I'm open to any suggestions!"

Jade was near, steadily putting blast after whooshing blast from Teal'c's staff weapon into the advancing machines. Jackson glanced at her. "The Aschen have a beaming terminal out there somewhere. If we could destroy it, we'd cut off any reinforcements…"

"Gotta get to it first," said Reynolds, "and if you hadn't

noticed, we're kinda boxed in here, Doc. You'll have to do better than that."

"The only way to stop the drones en masse is to terminate the control interface, and that's aboard the command ship." Jade threw a nod toward the night sky, where silent glitters of light showed evidence of the Pack's battle overhead. "Also impossible to get to."

Jackson ducked as a beam fanned out and cut a burning slice through the material of a tent to his right. "We're not going to win a war of attrition with those things!" he snapped. "There's got to be another way to reach the ship…" Then all at once, he had it. "The pod!" he shouted. "Your time-pod! It's just a glorified personal beaming device, that's exactly what you said about it!" He continued off Jade's nod of agreement. "We could use it to transport someone to the Aschen ship, couldn't we? They're in near orbit, close enough to reach, right?"

Jade nodded again. "Maybe, but it's not going to happen. General Hammond took all my equipment when you captured me. The pod I was using is in Doctor Lee's lab back at Stargate Command."

"Yes, it is!" Daniel said with a tight grin, "but the one your Re'tu friend had on him is here."

"Hell, Doc, you think you can rig that thing to beam someone up there?" demanded Reynolds. "Before we get overrun?"

"I've had extensive experience with Ancient technology—" Jackson began.

"Whatever!" The colonel waved him away. "Just go do it, double-time!"

Daniel broke into a run, and Jade came with him, the two of them racing across the churned mud of the campground as weapons fire hissed and spat all around them.

"Report! Report! Or do I have to beat it from one of you?" Mirris yelled, spittle flying from her lips in open rage. The intendants in the cubicles around her recoiled as if she had struck them, and their behavior made her want to do exactly that. Her hand strayed to the beam pistol holstered beneath her robes and she considered for a moment which crewmember would be least useful, the most expendable, in order to display her towering displeasure. The flickering lights of the command nexus threw a hellish glow across her anger-contorted expression.

Geddel curtailed her murderous thoughts with a strident nasal reply, at last giving her what she had asked for. "Momentary power fluctuation. System parity loss at power core. One of the ship's energy regulator arrays was destroyed by enemy fire. Automatic self-repair is under way, power is re-routing." He gulped nervously. "I read a twenty percent loss overall throughout primary vessel systems."

Mirris snorted. "Some damage was inevitable. Continue on attack axis and bring all guns to bear on enemy vessels." She straightened, her fists clenching. "Close the distance to the migrant colony ship." Then, as an afterthought, she glanced at the holograph. "Where are the fighters that attacked us?"

"Fighter craft have been neutralized," Geddel said instantly, "Confirming, two positive kills, one target crippled and falling away without power. Likelihood is high of crew termination."

"Two positive kills?" Mirris echoed. She peered at the screen, watching the single icon representing the Death Glider spiral away, falling back toward the gravity well of Kytos. "I see only one wreck."

"Yes, administrator," Geddel replied, regaining some of his poise. "The two Calaian fighters were atomized. If you wish, I can turn the main cannon and do the same to the other ship."

Mirris turned her back on the display. "Do not be wasteful," she chided. "They'll burn up in the atmospheric interface. I'd prefer to keep our war shots for bigger, richer targets…" On one of the secondary screens, the rocky shape of the *Wanderer* loomed large. "Like that one," she continued. "Weapons control. Load bio-agent warheads on all ballistic munitions and target the colony ship." Mirris felt a giddy rush of anticipation. "They will answer for Ryn's failure. I want every last nomad on that derelict to perish choking on their own blood."

Like everything else on the Aschen vessel, the hexagonal corridors reflected a bland kind of design that reminded Jack of the dreary, featureless halls of some government institution. *Like they got the DMV to do all their decorating*, he mused. The ship's interior spaces were clean but dull, and only the flickering lights looked out of place; and even those gradually returned to normal functioning as O'Neill followed the old man along the passageway.

"You have some idea where you're going?" Jack said quietly, glancing up and down the corridor. "It's just that I've skulked around the insides of enough alien spaceships to know they never have those 'you are here' maps like they do at the mall."

"Remember who you're talking to," said the old soldier. "And this isn't the first time I've been inside one of these Aschen tubs. They like a basic, uncluttered layout. Every ship they make is built from the same components." He halted at a flat brass panel flush with one wall and tapped it. The panel flipped open to present a display screen, which obediently illuminated.

"What's that?" said Jack, peering over the other man's shoulder.

"One of those 'you are here' maps," came the sarcastic reply, "like they have at the mall."

"Really?"

"Yup," said the old man. "The Aschen are an officious bunch of pricks. You think of the worst bureaucratic crap you've ever seen and times it by a thousand, that's their culture. Aschen Prime is like *The Planet of the IRS*. They're the kind of folks who have 'no smoking' signs posted even though nobody is allowed to smoke. And that's why they have maps of their own ships on every deck. Because of their regulations."

Jack's eyes widened. "How about that? And I thought the Air Force had regs that were redundant." He scanned the corridor;

the trilling alarms had gone quiet, and there were no signs of any security drones coming to investigate.

"I'm tapping into the ship's internal data network," said the Commander. "See what we can see…"

O'Neill's hands opened and closed. Like he'd said before, he was no stranger to strolling through endless corridors, but he mostly had a gun in his grip when he was doing it. Here and now, with nothing to hand more lethal than his bootlaces and some sarcasm, Jack had to admit he was feeling somewhat vulnerable.

"Weapons storage," said the other man, as if he'd read his mind. *But then, I shouldn't be surprised he thinks the same way I do,* Jack told himself. "On this level, two panels down that way," he concluded.

"Let's go, then."

"Not yet." The old man's hands traced over the touchscreen. O'Neill couldn't follow what he was doing, but then he couldn't read Aschen either. His counterpart saw him watching and gave a small shrug, answering the unspoken question. "You know how it is. You pick things up along the way."

A new screen opened and trails of text rolled up it. After a moment, the other man's expression shifted slightly. "What you got there?"

The old man's frown deepened. "We're moving into the Pack fleet, on a combat alert. Mirris has deployed drones in orbit and on the ground." He shook his head. "A stand-up fight. That's atypical Aschen behavior. She must have gone off the deep end."

"All the more reason to stop her." O'Neill insisted. "What else?"

His counterpart hesitated and Jack read a trace of relief there. "No readings of any thermonuclear detonation on Kytos. The charge I planted hasn't gone off." He sighed. "Jade must have got to it first. She's still alive, I know it…"

"That's a good thing," said O'Neill.

"She's all I have left." The words were almost a whisper,

like they came from far away, so quiet that Jack almost missed them.

"You ever tell her that?" From out of nowhere, the colonel felt a sudden surge of compassion for the elderly commander. For a moment, it was like he saw this Jack O'Neill for what he really was; an old and lonely man who had sacrificed his future in a war that had taken everything he cared about.

"Never enough…" began the other Jack, "Never enough time. It's always been about time." Then a shadow passed over the old soldier's face and he turned a fierce glare on his younger self. "Don't you look at me that way, boy! Don't you look at me with pity on that face!" He gave Jack a shove, pushing him away.

"I don't feel sorry for you," Jack told him, "but now I think I understand you."

The commander made a spitting noise and walked on down the corridor. "You don't understand anything, O'Neill. That was always your problem, just skatin' over the surface of things, being glib, playing off your luck, letting Sam and Daniel and Teal'c do the heavy lifting. Lost them one by one, and then it was too late. Now it's down to me, like it should have been."

Cold certainty crept through Jack's bones, a dark and familiar sensation that he had thought long since banished. "No, I get you, old man. I get it all. Now you're the one who's forgetting who he's talking to." He stepped in front of his counterpart, halting him in the silent, empty corridor. "You've got a death wish. After everything you've lost, you just want the pain to go away. You want to make it stop. You'll do whatever you can to make it end."

"You don't know me!" snarled the old man.

O'Neill shook his head. "I'm the only person who ever will. Because it's a place we've been to before, haven't we?" The words came out without any conscious effort, spilling from him. "After Charlie died. That moment, in his room, with that damned gun in my… In *our* hands. Ready to do it. If General West's men hadn't come that day…" The memory of his son's death stabbed him like knives; the accident had been his fault, it had been his pistol, his responsibility. The stark recall hit him hard, undimmed by the passage of time. Just for an instant, he was there again, standing at the edge of that abyss.

"They came to tell me about the Stargate. Reactivate me. I took the assignment."

Jack's head bobbed in agreement. "But even then, it was a one-way trip. A suicide mission. There was nothing to come home for. And that was—"

"That was what I wanted." The old man finished his words for him.

The silence between them went on for long seconds before O'Neill spoke again. "Yeah. I think I understand you, old man. Better than anyone ever could."

"I have a mission," husked the commander.

"Me too," said Jack, "but no-one has to die for it."

Jade followed Jackson into the storage tent. She spotted Ite-kh's gear immediately, the Re'tu's strangely-tailored vest lying in a heap on a collapsible trestle table, his weapon and his equipment piled to one side. There was dark insect blood on the vest and she tried hard not to see it, pushing away any thoughts of her dead alien friend. *We'll mourn our casualties later*, her father would always say at times like this, *when we're done*. But they were never done, and people kept on dying. When the time came when they could mourn, the number of the lost would overwhelm them.

"Here, hold this." Daniel pressed the Re'tu's beam pistol into her hand and picked through the equipment. Her fingers closed around the oversized grip and by reflex she checked the charge and the power setting. Jackson had his back to her, and she realized that it hadn't even occurred to him to think that he'd just given a live weapon to a woman who had been his prisoner only a few hours ago. *He trusts me*. The realization was a small victory among all the mayhem around them. "Thank you," she replied, but he was too intent on his search to acknowledge her.

Jackson removed the Ancient device from an inner pocket in the torn vest and cradled it in his hands. "Identical to the one you had." He ran his finger along the seam and the pod folded open, presenting a glowing sheet of holographic controls. "It follows the same logic pattern as other Ancient technology I've seen. I think, I can…" He drifted off, tapping at the virtual console.

Jade watched him work and felt sad. All the things she had wanted to tell him from the moment they had met in the corridor at the SGC bubbled up into her thoughts, streaming together. *You were always such a kind person When I was a teenager and we were hiding on Chulak you were my teacher I had such a crush on you I never really got over it When Mom died you hugged me and said it was okay to cry Then the Aschen killed you and I was cut adrift I missed you Daniel I'm sorry I had to lie—*

"Jade." His voice brought her out of her reverie with a jerk. "Are you all right?"

"Fine." Emotion thickened her voice. "Can you do it?" She gestured at the pod.

"Well, from what we've learned, items of Ancient technology have some uncanny attributes, including an innate ability to work in unison with *other* items of Ancient technology, sometimes even at interstellar distances…"

"Like the Stargates."

"Yeah. I think I can configure the pod to locate the nearest other pod… Which should most likely be on Mirris's ship, if they took your father." The device chimed and the display shimmered into green hues. "That… That looks like it. I think."

Jade held out her hand. "Give it to me. I'll beam up to the ship and do whatever I can to neutralize it."

He frowned. "I'm not letting you go alone."

"I can't risk—" *Letting you die again.* The words choked her and she stumbled over them. "It doesn't matter. The pods can only transport one person at a time, anyway."

Daniel shook his head. "Nope, that's wrong. The field has an adjustable radius, here…"

"It does?"

He held out the pod and she leaned closer. "Like so, see?" Before she could stop him, Jackson's thumb touched the activation pad and the nerve-tingling dislocation of a transit jump engulfed them both.

Awareness gradually returned with sluggish, unpleasant slowness. There was the coppery metallic taste of blood in her mouth, and the acridity of raw ozone. The stink of air ripped open by electricity filled Carter's nostrils and she suppressed a gag reflex. The action made her head loll, her neck rubbery and loose. Some indistinct object—part of a panel, maybe?—glanced off her face and Sam raised a weak hand to bat it away, failed. She licked dry lips, and tried to take stock of herself. Carter felt the telltale queasy sensation of zero gravity in the pit of her gut, but found herself stuck, rooted to the spot. The straps on her flight couch were tight over her shoulders and chest. With effort she extended her hands, fingers encountering the flickering controls in front of her. Sam blinked and felt blood gumming her right eye. *How long? How long was I out?* Laboring, she drew in a breath of tainted, smoky air.

"Teal'c?" she managed, pushing the word out of her mouth in a slur, her tongue like a lump of old leather. "Y'hear me?"

When no reply came, she tried to turn in her chair, but the exertion was like shifting a sack of wet sand. Abruptly, a knife of light sheared in through the canopy and marched across her, over her lap and up her chest. The glare needled Sam's eyes and made her gasp with pain. After a moment to adjust, she squinted out through the transparent canopy. A streak of brilliant white glow was the reflected light of Kytos's sun, hanging in a diamond ring corona over the surface of the planet's day/night terminator. The gigantic black pearl of Kytos drifted lazily past; the Death Glider was in a spin, turning end over end, caught in a glittering nimbus of vented breathing gases and hull fragments. A jagged, broken piece of plastic skipped off the glass as it passed her.

As Sam watched, the planet fell away, and the light continued its inexorable march up the canopy and down the length of the cockpit. Carter marshaled whatever reserves of strength she still had and pushed it all into one action; bracing her foot against the aerofoil control pedals, she managed to shift herself around enough to crane a look aft.

The shaft of light traced over the ruined cockpit, illuminating tiny pieces of debris suspended in mid-air. It drew over Teal'c, who shifted against the pull of his straps like a stiff mannequin. Only the shallow rise and fall of his chest indicated the Jaffa was still alive. Sam saw dark streaks across his chest where his wounds from Ryn's attack had reopened.

"Hey!" Carter gave a hoarse bark, hoping to get a response. She gasped, and her breath curled away in a pop of vapor. The temperature was dropping rapidly, and with dawning recognition, the major realized that it was becoming harder for her to breathe. Slowly and deliberately, Carter worked at the console before her, ignoring the gradual tunneling of her vision, the grayish fog that began to clog her every move. Lights on the panel steadied and she blew out a sigh of relief as the emergency life support circuits kicked in.

The Gilder's erratic orbit turned it back toward the planet again, and now Carter was sure that the Goa'uld fighter was on a shallow descent course, heading inexorably into the grip of Kytos's gravity well and a fiery death. She worked reluctant controls and made the ship stable, bringing it about to face the battle raging over the planet.

Teal'c coughed and came back to wakefulness. "Major…" He began.

"I'm okay," she lied. "Can you get me mains power? Thrusters and guns?"

"I will endeavor to do so," came the stoic reply.

He was as good as his word; in a few moments the Glider came under its own power and Sam throttled up, angling the craft back up toward the engagement. The Aschen vessel was moving like a slow knife, pushing toward the *Wanderer* through the breaking ranks of the Pack flotilla. As she watched, Carter saw a Goa'uld mothership shatter from within, disintegrating in a plume of nuclear fire.

"Communications traffic," said Teal'c gruffly. "Patching in."

Sam was instantly assailed by a cacophony of voices, some calling out for help, others in blind panic. Amid them she distinctly heard Vix; *The Aschen are opening their missile bays. Can anyone confirm? Are they going to launch?*

"Teal'c?" she asked.

The Jaffa nodded. "Vix is correct. I read several ship-to-ship weapons in pre-firing patterns…"

Carter glanced up. They were powering back into the fray from below Mirris's ship—not that concepts like *up* and *down* made a lot a sense in a space battle—while the majority of the confrontation was concentrated in a higher orbit. She could just about pick out the open missile chambers arrayed along the ventral surface of the Aschen craft's hull. "What are they planning?" she said aloud. "They've got more than enough beam weapons to do the job." The Death Glider's targeting computer saw where the pilot's attention was focused and dutifully enlarged an image of the location for her scrutiny. Sam got a good look at the payloads sitting inside the firing tubes and her blood ran cold.

There were missiles in there, each one the size of a school bus; and where Earth-made rockets would have had a conical cap instead they had a glassy sphere containing a writhing, blue-hued gaseous plasma. Carter had seen the same thing before on Volia, when the Aschen had tried to destroy SG-1. "Bio-weapons!" she shouted, "They're going to fire—"

As one, all the Aschen missiles leapt from their launch cradles and corkscrewed away on fingers of white-orange flame. In a lethal flock, they turned and rose toward the *Wanderer*.

Daniel Jackson had been reduced to his component molecules and reassembled on more occasions than it was probably good for his sanity to consider, with hundreds of Stargate sorties, ring-transport journeys, Asgard beam-ups and beam-downs to his credit; but he wasn't prepared for the sickening, inside-out sensation that the pod forced through his body. When the drab and featureless walls of the Aschen starship solidified around him, it took all of his self-control not to expel the contents of his stomach over the floor. He staggered a couple of steps and lurched against a rack of metal shelving. "Oh," he began, "now I'm wishing I had let you go on your own."

Jade handed him a water bottle and he greedily took a swig to wash the taste of bile out of his mouth. "You think you feel sick now? That was just a point-to-point teleport. A time-jump transition is like that dialed up to ten. I puked my heart out the first time we tried it."

"Charming." Jackson looked around, taking stock of their location. It was a storage chamber, with racks of Aschen hardware in charging ports along the wall. He glanced at the shelving he was supporting himself on and blinked at the barrel of a discarded P90. Beside were a spread of recognizably Air Force issue devices, a radio, a gear vest, a pistol and holster...

"This is an armory," Jade offered, helping herself to another beam gun.

"Here's the other pod," Daniel gathered up the gear, taking the P90 and thumbing off the safety. "Jack's equipment is here as well. Mirris's people must have no idea what the pod is. We're lucky they weren't trying to dismantle it—"

"Quiet!" snapped the woman. "Outside!" She pointed her guns at the recessed oval door that was the room's only exit.

Daniel held his breath and listened; sure enough, there were noises coming from the other side of the hatch, muffled thuds and scrapings. "Drones?" He whispered.

Jade nodded and gestured for him to take up a place on the right side of the doorway. She moved to the left and raised her weapons. Jackson did the same, putting aside the gear and aiming down the spine of the submachinegun. Something chimed faintly and the door shuddered as locks disengaged.

"Get ready," she hissed.

He expected the hatch to roll open at a sedate pace, but instead it snapped back into the wall in the blink of an eye. Sheer adrenaline pushed Daniel on to the balls of his feet and he thrust the P90 into the face of the first person to step through the doorway, even as he found the intruder's gun at his neck. Jade had reacted the same way with a second intruder, and found herself in a similar predicament.

"Daniel?" said the new arrival, with a raised eyebrow.

"Jack?" he replied, not quite catching up to the face of the person before him.

Jade gasped. "Dad?"

An older man went pale. "Jade?" Jackson's jaw dropped open as he recognized *both* of the men as Jack O'Neill; oh sure, one of them looked more like the colonel had that time he'd become a septuagenarian overnight on Argos, but he knew instantly that they were the same man.

Old Jack—as he instantly labeled him—let his gun fall away and pulled Jade to him in a gesture that seemed to shock and delight the girl in equal measure. Daniel saw tears shimmer in her eyes as they embraced. The older man, this Commander, let her go, suddenly hesitant and self-conscious, as if he were surprised by his own actions. "I thought... I'd lost you."

She gave the old man a brittle smile in return. "That'll never happen."

The other Jack—the Now Jack—pushed the P90's muzzle away from his face with a wan look. "Far be it from me to break up this touching, if somewhat unusual family reunion, but what the hell are you two doing on this ship?"

"Good question," echoed Old Jack.

Jade blinked and she was all soldier once again. "We used Ite-kh's pod to teleport aboard, Daniel locked on to the trace from yours."

"Pods don't carry two. How'd you manage that?"

"Actually, it does, uh, Commander," Jackson interjected. "You just need to know how to read the controls to widen the field radius."

The older man nodded to himself. "Huh. We always thought that could be done, just never could figure it out."

"What, you never asked the future me to do it for you?" He asked the question before he'd really thought about it and the uncomfortable silence that followed sent a shiver down his spine.

"Well," Jack broke the tension of the moment, grabbing his gear vest and strapping it on. "Nice to see you both and all, but you should probably beam back out of here. I think one of these nerds we kay-oh'ed hit an alarm…" He nodded at a pair of unconscious Aschen males on the floor in the corridor outside. "This deck is gonna be swarming with them any minute."

Daniel shook his head. "It's a war zone on Kytos, Jack. Reynolds is barely holding the fort down there, and Sam and Teal'c are up to their neck in the fight in space."

"We've got to put the Aschen down hard," said Jade. "Knock out Mirris's control of the drones…"

"And send a message to the Confederation," added O'Neill. "If that black hole wasn't enough, we need to take this ship out, convince them to stay the hell away from Earth and our buddies."

The old man shot his younger self a hard look. "And how do you propose to do that, junior?"

"Actually, I have a solution," Jade replied, shrugging the heavy pack off her back. "Something I picked up earlier…" She unzipped the bag and Daniel saw a skeletal construct of steel and carbon inside.

"That would be your naquadria bomb?" asked Jack.

His elder self nodded. "Yeah. I have to admit, I didn't plan on seeing it again."

"They're coming in too fast!" cried a voice over the com channel. *"I cannot get a vector on them!"*

Sam heard the voices through her bone-induction comlink as the Death Glider's engines shrieked at full power, throwing the Goa'uld ship up past the Aschen vessel and into the flaming wake of the missile swarm.

"*All ships, concentrate fire on the missiles! If they strike, the Aschen poison will be injected into the* Wanderer*'s atmosphere!*" Vix's order was harsh and direct, but even as he gave it Carter knew his pilots had little chance of obeying. The fighters were spread too thinly, too diffuse across the engagement zone in dozens of small dogfights with the drones, unable to simply disengage and go after the bio-weapons.

"Engines are approaching redline," Teal'c told her. "Damage from our attack on the warship has drained the coolant tanks."

Sam saw the glowing alert glyphs on the console in front of her and ignored them. "Guns up," she reported, jinking the Glider into a six o'clock position behind a trailing missile. "Firing!" Carter squeezed the energy cannon triggers and watched three pulses of orange lightning streak out through the dark. The backwash from the blast that had killed Noa had also knocked the Glider's electronics off-kilter, and the major adjusted instinctively by eyeball to move the target cues over the missile. The shots hit home and the rocket exploded, discharging its lethal cargo into the vacuum where it could do no harm. "Splash one," Sam reported. "How many more?"

"Four targets remaining," Teal'c reported, fighting to keep the fatigue from his voice. "Terminal impact on *Wanderer* in ninety seconds."

Carter let the Death Glider slide to port and ranged her weapons. The missiles were fanning out, opening up their separation to strike the colony ship at all points of the compass. The fighter's fuselage rattled and howled around her, but Sam's attention had narrowed to the space around her gun sight. Reacting on pure aviator instinct, she fired again and gritted her teeth as the pulse blasts went wide of her target.

"Engines at critical," called Teal'c. Any other backseater might have suggested that their pilot throttle back, but not the Jaffa; he understood what was at stake. Sam matched velocity with the second Aschen missile and ripped it open with a cascade of shots.

The rocket's motor spat a jet of flame that flicked it out of its programmed pattern and it looped over, narrowly missing the Glider. The missile spun away and collided with another of the death-dealing warheads, destroying both of them in a burst of white fire.

Carter tried to vector away from the detonation, but she was too late. Fragments of metal and ceramic rattled over the fighter, leaving ominous cracks in the canopy and streaking the forward-curved wings. The Glider vibrated as if it had been struck by a colossal hammer and to the pilot's horror, the drive monitors flashed once and went dead. Sam felt the pressure of the ship's engines cease at the same moment. "What the hell?"

"Emergency engine shutdown," reported the Jaffa. "Drive systems have gone off-line."

"Damn it!" shouted Carter, watching the two remaining rockets arc away. With no throttle power, the Death Glider had become an unguided missile itself, unable to change vector or accelerate after the final targets. "Vix!" Sam bellowed into her radio mike. "Stop the last two!"

Behind her, Teal'c's face was stony. "Thirty seconds to impact."

A pilot in a saucer-shaped flyer gave up his life and put his ship directly in the path of the lead missile; unable to turn his guns upon it, it was the only way he had to stop the oncoming weapon. Fighter and warhead met in a globe of gas and flame, and for one heart-stopping moment it seemed as if the fifth and final missile would be caught in the shockwave of the blast; but then the last remaining rocket curved out of the expanding cloud of debris, undamaged, and fell hard into the stone and steel hull of the Calaian colony ship.

The Aschen warhead penetrated the outer decks and polymer plating of the *Wanderer*, finally impacting against a set of support braces with enough force to trigger the weapon's internal detonator. The synthetic diamond sphere exploded along prestressed lines of collapse and released a tornado of bio-plasma into the massive ship's environment. Killing organic matter on contact, every living thing close to the impact point that had not died in the shock of collision perished a heartbeat later; and like a spreading cancer, the lethal Aschen germ weapon began to blacken and consume in a creeping wave of death.

Sam saw the distant flare of contact on *Wanderer*'s hull and her heart sank.

When Vix's voice came back on the radio, the big man sounded as if he had been hollowed out and broken. *"The weapon has struck, but there is still time. This is a clan-wide command—there are lifepods for all who can reach them, but you must go now. Leave everything, and go now!"*

Teal'c bent over his console. "Engine temperature is dropping. I will be able to restore motive power momentarily,"

Carter nodded distantly, unable to look away from the *Wanderer*. "Do you think... Anyone will be able to get away?" Even as she said the words, Sam saw glitters of light as arrow-shaped objects detached from the colony ship's hull in pairs and trios, darting away into the black.

"Anyone who does not is already dead," said the Jaffa, with grim pronouncement.

CHAPTER FIFTEEN

"Sensor probes confirming lethality level," Geddel said tonelessly, his voice carrying over the dull trill of the ship's alert bells. "Estimated total toxin spread through the migrant's colony ship in less than one demicycle." Mirris glared at him, waiting for the sub-director to finish his report. And inevitably, he sighed. "However, we have tracked multiple launches of auxiliary vessels from the hulk, many of which have fled the main conflict zone for open space."

"Lifepods," she spat. The Aschen ship's signals officer had intercepted Vix's earlier transmission. "I want them exterminated. Every last one, found and vented to space. No survivors."

Geddel swallowed hard. "That may be difficult, administrator. Our drones are still engaged in ship-to-ship battle with the remainder of the nomad fleet."

Mirris saw the holograph separate into multiple images from scanners on her ship and others relayed from the prows of their robotic fightercraft. There was a storm of laser fire and explosions raging around them. "Fools. Don't they understand they are beaten?" she snorted. "Why do primitives never show the intelligence to submit?"

"It seems your tactic did not have the desired effect," Geddel added warily. Mirris was surprised that he was daring to be even slightly critical of her, so soon after she had disciplined him. It was clear that she had not done enough to dissuade him from challenging her commands. The administrator's hand slid into a pocket inside her robes as her subordinate went on, looking around the command nexus as if he were trying to garner support. "You said that the Pack would lose the will to fight if we struck at their colony ship, their symbolic home... The reverse appears to be true. Our drones report increased aggression on the part of the migrant pilots. If anything, attacking the *Wanderer* has incensed them."

"They know nothing of fury," said Mirris in a low voice.

Geddel wasn't listening; he was talking for the benefit of the rest of the command staff. "An error on your part, Administrator Mirris. And now I must report another, which can also be laid at your feet." He touched a control and one the holoscreens shifted to show a corridor inside the ship. The image displayed four figures, clearly not Aschen, moving and firing at a patrol of security drones. One of the humans — the woman from the planet, she realized — pointed a staff weapon right into the eye of the scanner and destroyed it, turning the image into a rain of static. "Your prisoners have escaped, and there are intruders on board. I have taken the liberty of initiating a search for them."

Mirris's cheeks flushed red. She felt like she was on fire. Each time the rage came and took her, she thought it could burn no hotter than it had before, and each time she was wrong. The vicious hate flooded the Aschen's mind, wiping away any instant of rationality. Her teeth flared white as her lips peeled back in a pure, animal snarl.

And still Geddel prattled on, unheeding of the towering anger building behind him. "You have compounded your mistakes with poor choices, distasteful displays of emotionalism and physical violence. I have no option or recourse but to relive you of command."

"*Shut up!*" All the vehemence exploded in those two words and Mirris fired her beam pistol into Geddel's back at close range. Some of the intendants at cubicles close by screamed in fright as the sub-director tumbled back over the main console, leaking blood, and fell to the deck. "Shut up shut up *Shut up!*" Mirris dove forward and fired again, punctuating each word with a blast from the gun. Geddel's corpse jerked with each bolt, quite dead but not dead enough to satisfy his commander's murderous fury. Finally she swept around, her eyes alight with madness, and spat out an order.

"Find me the Tau'ri! I'll kill them with my bare hands!"

With an Aschen beam pistol in either hand, the old man lead the way into the anteroom before Jack could stop him. He kept up with his elder self, using his P90 to knock out the security drones guarding the wide oval hatch in the far wall. Jade swung Teal'c's staff like a pro, battering an Aschen technician senseless with the blunt end. Daniel was tail-end charlie, watching the corridor behind them. "Clear," reported Jackson, "but not for long, I think. I heard what sounds like more drones, coming closer."

"Not a problem," said the girl's father. "This is the central processing plexus. The robots don't go inside."

"Why?" Jack demanded.

Jade used the Jaffa weapon to blast the door controls and the hatch retracted. "Take a look and see."

Cautiously, O'Neill peeked inside, leading with his P90. The room was spherical without anything that even remotely resembled a floor. Other similar hatches were visible spaced around the circumference, above, below and on the opposite side from the anteroom. In the very center a wide drum of complex-looking crystalline electronics hummed and glowed green-blue; there were hundreds of cables and rods of varying thickness coming out of ports on the walls, connecting to the unit at the core. Jack's overall impression was of something big, important, and most of all, breakable. "Cool," he opined, "let's blow it up." He took a step toward a ledge just inside the chamber as the Commander called out a warning. The old man's spindly fingers caught the collar of his jacket just as gravity suddenly vanished and O'Neill's legs spun up in front of him. He was hauled ungraciously backwards and dropped to his haunches back in the anteroom.

"It's a zero-gee chamber," said Daniel. "No artificial gravity inside there."

Jack got back to his feet. "Well, now I know that," he said testily.

"The drones have wheels for motive traction. They can't function that well in zero gravity conditions." Jade handed off Teal'c's staff weapon to Jackson and stepped up to the lip of the hatch. "I'll need some cover while I reprogram the detonation sequence. Just watch what I do, and follow me."

"Okay..." said the scientist.

The woman leapt through the hatchway and Jack had to fight off the reflex to reach after her; there was nothing but dead air and a twenty foot drop after the ledge. But Jade moved fast and smooth toward the plexus, like a swimmer crossing a pool, guiding herself by making little pushes off the cables and support pillars. Daniel pulled a face and followed along, with a lot less grace than Jade displayed.

The old man beckoned him. "C'mon, junior," he said, "we'll scoot around the edge, keep an eye out for company."

Jack raised a hand. "One thing. That 'junior' crap? It's getting real old, *pops*."

His counterpart gave him a cold grin. "Ain't it just?" He pushed off into the room and Jack went with him. This time, he was ready for the instant transition, and he used his free hand to find places to pull himself along, keeping the P90 tucked in close to his chest.

He shifted around the cables and stanchions. It wasn't as open as it looked; in fact, there were more obstacles inside the chamber than anything. O'Neill caught a rumbling noise of metal on metal and he glanced around, looking for fire corridors. Abruptly, Jack realized he couldn't see the other hatches any more. "Hey," he called. "I got no joy. Any targets?"

"I see movement," Jackson called back. "Your three o'clock." The scientist and the woman were both crouched on a maintenance ledge jutting out from the main section of the core unit.

"High or low?" Jack demanded.

"High!"

The reply was followed by the sizzle of air molecules as a

white beam slashed past O'Neill's head and scorched a line across the wall. Jack triggered the P90 and the recoil jetted him back against a support brace. Batting away a small cluster of drifting bullet cases, O'Neill moved away as fast as he could.

Daniel panned the staff weapon around, fingers tight on the firing pad. While he'd grasped the nature of the chamber immediately, he still found himself a step behind, thinking in a two dimensional way when he should have been thinking in three. O'Neill had adapted in seconds; *probably his fighter pilot training kicking in,* Jackson thought, but for Daniel it was like being trapped inside a life-size M.C. Escher painting, with upside-down and inside-out walkways all over the place.

"I'm almost done," Jade reported from far end of the ledge.

Jackson nodded and fired off a shot at a figure in Aschen gray threading through the cables toward them. "They must be desperate," he said aloud, "they're actually sending people after us now."

Gunfire rattled around the chamber and beam weapons spoke in return. Daniel pressed back to the throbbing plexus unit, trying hard to look everywhere at once. More Aschen emerged in a group of three, brandishing weapons, and he fired wide shots over their heads, sparking balls of flame off the control cables.

He heard the strident voice of a woman. "Stop them! Kill them all!"

"Mirris," snarled Jade. "She's here."

There was a swirl of robes and he saw her. "There!" The Aschen woman had a cadre of armed men at her side and they all opened fire at once, raining streaks of white light toward him. By reflex, Daniel tried to lunge for the floor, but with no gravity his drop became a slow swan dive. He saw Jade turning, distracted for a lethal second, as Mirris aimed and fired again.

The beam grazed the young woman's torso. She screamed, and the shock of the bolt spun her away from the ledge, trailing lines of flash-burned blood. Without thinking, Jackson threw himself after Jade and shot though the air to intercept her.

Daniel caught her and she shuddered with the impact. The woman's face was pale with pain and the smell of burnt skin made his stomach lurch.

He heard the old man shouting her name. Jade's eyes fluttered and she mumbled something indistinct. Daniel knew the signs; Jade had already been injured once on Kytos and there had barely been time for her to recover, even with the aid of her futuristic implants. She was going into shock.

"Jackson!" O'Neill bellowed across the chamber. "Get her out! Use the pod!"

Daniel's hand closed around the Ancient device and it pulsed with warmth, ready to use. "The bomb?" he called back.

"We got it," Jack retorted. "Just go!"

Daniel nodded, even though O'Neill couldn't see him from his vantage point. More Aschen energy bolts hissed around him, finding their range. Jackson pulled Jade tight to him, crossing the staff weapon over her chest to hold her, and activated the pod. He'd passed the other one to Jack after programming in a return transit back down to the surface of Kytos. "At least, that's what I think I did," he told the woman. "Who knows where or *when* we're going to find ourselves?"

With a flash of strobing colors, the two of them melted into a brief fracture in space-time, leaving a tiny thunderclap in their wake as the air in the room rushed to fill the void they had left.

"Jade!" shouted the old man.

"They're away," Jack retorted, pushing his counterpart out of the firing line. "C'mon, we gotta finish what she started." He stabbed a finger at the core unit, lying below them from their inverted position. "Can you do it?"

"My daughter!" cried the Commander. "God, no, not now! Not after all this!"

O'Neill took the other man's shoulders and shook him hard, bouncing him off a cable trunk. "*She's not dead*! Look at me!"

he growled. "Daniel's got her! He'll keep her safe!"

"Yes…" The word was a gasp. "Yes," he said, with more certainty. "I trust him. You're right. We have to finish this." The old man drew himself up and coiled his legs against the cables, discarding the pistols in his hands. "I'm empty, so you better cover me."

With a grunt of effort, the Commander threw himself down and fell like a diving hawk towards the ledge where Jade's backpack lay tethered to the plexus unit. Jack floated out of cover and switched to single-shot firing. The recoil was easier to handle, and as the Aschen crew bobbed and weaved around him, O'Neill knocked them back with carefully aimed bullets. The Aschen had the numerical superiority, to be certain, but he could see in the way that they moved they were untrained and they lacked the certainty—and the killer instinct—of battle-trained warriors. "Not used to getting your hands dirty, are ya?" he called out, picking off another man as he drew a bead on the Commander.

"*Kill them!*" He heard Mirris screaming at her men. "Destroy it all if you must, but bring me the Tau'ri's head!"

"Whoa," Jack said aloud, "she is *really* pissed off."

In the heartbeats as he tore out a spent stick of ammunition and slammed a new one home in the P90, Jack felt the pressure of the pod in his vest pocket, pushing on his chest. Once the naquadria device was ticking, all it would take was the push of a key and they'd be beamed off the Aschen ship to safety; so Daniel had told him. But nothing about this mission had gone right since the moment SG-1 had stepped through the Stargate to P5X-404, and the grim little nay-saying voice in the back of his mind was telling him, *Why should things change now?*

Jack moved, pushing himself away toward the old man, and from out of nowhere a gray blur barreled into him. The air in his lungs was knocked out in a rattling grunt and he felt the P90 tumble from his grip.

"*Die!*" Hot breath and spittle sprayed over his face and he struck out at his attacker; but Mirris's eyes were wide with wild rage, her reason so far gone that she'd thrown herself at Jack in a vain attempt to kill him. The colonel fought her off, but the Aschen woman was in the grip of a berserk fury. She clubbed him over and over around the head with the butt of her gun, her fingers raked and clawed at his eyes. He landed punches blindly, but she didn't seem to notice. Normally, Jack had reservations about striking women, but he left those behind now, fighting for his life against someone so directed by anger that it had consumed her.

"*Mollem!*" she wailed, calling her dead husband's name in a reedy shriek, "*Mollem!*" The gun spun away, marked with Jack's blood and Mirris's attack continued. He struggled to disengage, but she wrapped her legs about his waist, her robe-tunic flapping open, in an obscene parody of two embracing lovers. Her hands coiled around his neck and locked tight, squeezing his throat, tightening with the hysterical strength of madness. O'Neill fought back, but still his blows did not register. Blood flowed from her broken nose and streams of dark tears lined the woman's face as she leered over him. Jack felt his lungs fighting for breath, the sudden fear gripping him that the horror of Mirris's screaming face would be the last thing he ever saw.

"*Mol—*"

The Aschen woman jerked and stiffened even as O'Neill felt the searing heat of a bullet cross past his cheek. Her hands parted and released him, and Jack coughed in a gasp of air. Mirris fell away, small panting sounds issuing out of her trembling lips, fading. In the center of her forehead there was a single wound blossoming tiny globules of blood.

"Come on, Jack" said a voice in his ear, and he felt a strong hand on his arm. "We gotta jet."

For one dizzy moment, the pain and the lack of oxygen made the face of the man in front of him shift and flow like molten wax. "Pop? That you?" O'Neill gasped through a bruised throat.

"Nah," said the old man, gripping the colonel's P90 in his

hand. "It's just Jack."

O'Neill shook off the fuzz in his thoughts. "Thanks for the assist," he said with a nod. "Now let's blow this tub."

Both of them gripped the pod and held on. Light flashed once again inside the chamber and thunder sounded in its wake.

Her crew panicking around her, Mirris's body drifted down in a slow tumble. She was long dead when the naquadria finally flashed into criticality.

The Aschen ship was split asunder by the detonation. A white glare of sun-bright energy flared through the brass and steel hull plates, turning them instantly to gaseous plasma. Huge pieces of the vessel's prow and aft sections tumbled away from each other, propelled by the shockwave, leaving an expanding sphere of radioactive fragments trailing behind them. The blast rattled on every communications circuit in the orbital region, the static wake like the echoing report of a monstrous executioner's gunshot.

Carter shielded her eyes with the blade of her hand as the stark white flash cut hard-lined shadows across the Death Glider's cockpit. For long seconds the Goa'uld fighter's systems flickered and jumped as the ship's electronics were bathed in a wash of electromagnetic energy. Sam's heart tightened in her chest. "Jack…"

"I am certain Colonel O'Neill has effected an escape," Teal'c said firmly.

Carter nodded and pushed her concerns away as the plume of nuclear flame began to fall back upon itself. Out to the starboard side, she saw two Aschen drones spin around on a drunken axis and collide in a cloud of metallic splinters. "The machines… What's happening to them?"

"Their central control has been disrupted," said the Jaffa, pouring power to the fighter's weapons in anticipation, "command and control systems must have been affected by the mothership's destruction."

Sam gripped the steering yoke and turned the Death Glider to angle after the main flight of drones, dithering and drifting. "Copy that." She toggled the general comlink frequency. "Attention, all Pack combat pilots, this is Major Samantha Carter. The drones have lost their control inputs, they're vulnerable. Concentrate your firepower and take them out! We have no idea how long it will be before their own self-defense programming kicks in, so hit them now!"

She heard a chorus of fierce assent over the hissing channel as she swept in toward the mass of confused mechanoids and triggered her cannons. "Turkey shoot," Carter said to herself.

Daniel made sure he was there when Jade awoke in the Alpha Site's infirmary. He had expected to see Old Jack, but to his mild surprise Regular Jack (it seemed a better name than Now Jack or Present-Day Jack) was there as well. The two men had a pile of playing cards on the table between them, and O'Neill looked up as Jackson entered. "Huh. You know, I've always wondered what it would be like to play Chess with myself..."

Jade's father tapped the tabletop. "Well, this is Uno. And don't expect me to deal you in."

"Yeah," echoed Jack, "you know how you are with cards."

Jade came to wakefulness and frowned. "I feel awful."

"You took a swipe from an Aschen beam pistol," explained the old man. "But you're tough, kiddo. I always knew it."

She smiled and her eyes found Daniel. "Hey," she said.

"Hey yourself," he returned, suddenly feeling the scrutiny of two sets of O'Neill eyes. "Doctors say you'll be fine in a day or so, then you'll be clear to gate back to Earth."

She looked around. "The Alpha Site. I remember this place... Well, sorta."

"A lot different last time we saw it," agreed the old man.

Jack cleared his throat to change the subject. He sounded husky and the unpleasant bruising around his neck wouldn't fade for a good few weeks. "Mirris is gone," he told her, "and her ship to boot. Thanks to you and your father here, the nuke blew the whole thing in two."

"What about the drones?" she asked.

Daniel made a winding-up motion by his ear. "Ah, well, without new input from the Aschen main computer, they got a little confused and started banging into things. Sam helped Vix and the other Pack pilots pick off the space-capable ones and Colonel Reynolds took out the ones on Kytos."

"Good for him," Jack allowed. "Marines. They always need target practice."

"But the Pack?" she pressed. "What happened to them?"

Her father's face darkened. "They didn't do so good."

Carter had her hands knitted together in a ball in front of her, because she was afraid that unchecked, they might wander off on their own and use, say, the pen or one of the small ornamental flags on the table to stab Vice President Kinsey somewhere painful.

He closed the preliminary report folder in front of him with a grimace after less than ten seconds of looking at it, and she could tell that he wasn't even going to pretend to be interested. In the room adjoining this one, Vix and Suj and the healer Koe were waiting on his reply. They had come, along with almost every person who had been able to flee their colony ship and the other vessels destroyed by the Aschen, and built a shanty town tent city along the runway beyond the concrete bunkers of the Alpha Site base. In orbit over the planet were the handful of hyperspace-capable vessels they still had flying, a fraction of the nomad flotilla's original number. She had seen the look on Vix's face when he arrived at the Stargate Command's primary off-world base. After the SGC troops had decamped from Kytos, he and a contingent of his people had remained to perform a solemn, painful duty.

The *Wanderer*, the ship that had been the very soul of their fleet, had been abandoned. Most of the population aboard had been able to escape the effects of the Aschen viral warheads thanks to Sam and Teal'c's actions in shooting them down, but the one missile that made it through had been enough for a death sentence. The colony ship was sealed tight, the lethal bio-weapons on board rendering it uninhabitable. It was nothing but a stone tomb, empty except for the those who had perished from the toxins and the ravaged landscape. Vix had set the vast vessel on automatic pilot to take a final flight into the heart of Kytos's sun, while Koe led prayers.

The loss showed on the face of every member of the nomad clans. They had lost their world, the living symbol of their freedom. Sam had seen that look on others recently as well; on the faces of Jade and her father. She looked up and found Hammond and Teal'c, both men mirroring the fixed, steady concern on her own face.

"I'm supposed to buy this?" Kinsey sniffed, tapping the folder's cover. Like everyone who had been on Kytos for the treaty meeting, he had been forced to divert back to the Alpha Site instead of Earth, on the orders of General Hammond and the IOA, until it was clear that no traces of Aschen bio-agents still lingered. The vice president was not happy about having to wear the same suit for more than one day running. "Time travel? People from the future, invisible giant spiders and some crazed alien woman trying to murder O'Neill?" He smirked. "Okay, I might understand that last part, God knows I've had the urge myself, but the rest? It's pure science fiction!"

"We *are* discussing this on the surface of an alien planet," Carter offered dryly.

He ignored the interjection. "This was all a plot to prevent a bio-toxin being smuggled through the SGC to Earth? That's what it comes down to, General?"

Hammond gave a slow nod. "That is correct, sir. We've since discovered that the plant extract you were given, the so-called 'meladni' flower, was in fact a carrier medium prepared by Ryn on the orders of the Aschen."

Kinsey couldn't help but look down at his hands. Sam

knew he was thinking about the moment in the long tent on Kytos when he'd been handling the cube containing the dormant plant. Luckily for them, the flower's encasement was designed to react and release its load only after exposure to Earth's particular atmospheric signature. Vix had destroyed the flower back on the jungle planet himself when Suj made the discovery.

"It would have destroyed life across our whole world," the general continued. "We have first-hand proof of the Aschen's fondness for bio-weapons from SG-1... And if that's not enough for you, sir, you could step outside and ask those people who've lost their home to the same thing."

"The Aschen way of war is silent and insidious," Teal'c rumbled. "We saw the aftermath of it on Volia, and now with the *Wanderer*."

Carter picked up the thread. "The truth is, from what we can determine the Aschen had *already* started on a plan to wipe out the Pack. The grain blight that spurred Vix and his people to make a treaty with us? Doctor Lee's analysis has shown that it was artificial in origin. It seems clear to me that Mirris created the crisis among the Pack and then used Ryn to further her own plans." She paused, sickened at the monumental callousness displayed by the Aschen in using the clans as their cat's-paw. "They would have starved them to death."

"A tragedy," Kinsey replied, "and clearly one that Earth has been fortunate to have avoided. I'll be sure to include that in my deposition to the IOA's committee, and reinforce my recommendations for a more stringent oversight of the SGC's operations... Perhaps even a cessation until this can be properly analyzed." He pushed his chair back, preparing to get up and leave.

"With all due respect, sir, we're not done here!" Sam blurted out the words, and it was clear to everyone in the room that respect for Kinsey was the furthest thing from her mind. "What about the Pack?"

He arched an eyebrow. "What about them?"

"We have a responsibility here," Carter retorted.

"Yes, *you* do," said Kinsey sharply. "Believe me, Major, I'm well aware of the SGC's culpability..." He glanced up as the briefing room's door opened and his face soured.

"Hey gang, sorry I'm late." Jack O'Neill stepped in and took the empty chair next to Sam. "Hi," he told her. "I miss much?"

"Your input isn't required here, Colonel," Kinsey seethed.

"I beg to differ," said Hammond.

"Oh, don't mind me," Jack continued. "Carter? You were saying something?"

"The Pack came to us with honest intentions for mutual trade," said Sam. "Technology for food and medical supplies."

Kinsey waved his hand as if he was dismissing a nagging insect. "Yes, yes. But since they flew their colony ship into a star and let most of their other vessels get blown up along with all the hardware on board, they really don't have anything to offer us now, do they? Trade implies give and take, Major. Clearly, economics isn't your strong point."

Carter bristled. "The clans of the Pack are in dire need. Are you proposing, sir, that we turn them away? They don't even have enough ships to form a new flotilla."

"That, sadly, is not our concern. They'll just have to find a planet somewhere to settle on..."

Jack clapped his hands together. "Wow. Y'know, that's a brilliant idea. *Brilliant*. And magnanimous too, if I do say so."

Kinsey glared at Jack. "What in God's name are you babbling about, man?"

"A planet." O'Neill made a globe shape with his hands. "Okay, so I know they're gypsies and everything, and they like the peripatetic life, but they could do that on a planet. And we've got plenty to spare, right General?" He flashed a winning smile toward Hammond. "All those worlds we've surveyed, all full of nothing but trees and rocks. Frankly, Mister

Vee Pee, your suggestion about helping the Pack settle on one of them is a gesture of great compassion. I'm sure the President would agree."

The politician froze; Sam tried to follow the train of emotions behind the man's eyes as irritation warred with pragmatic self-interest. Everyone in the room knew that Kinsey had forced his way into the treaty process, because he had expected to return home laden with a treasure trove of exotic alien technology scavenged by the Pack. Now they would all be going back to Earth empty-handed; but the colonel's inspired end-run had backed the vice president into a corner. Now, if he brushed aside O'Neill's suggestion, he would seem as callous as the Aschen. And if he accepted it, Kinsey could return with a moral, if not material, victory. It was no contest; self-interest won out. He schooled his face and stood up, glancing at General Hammond. "George," he began airily, "these people need our help. Find them somewhere to live."

Carter followed Teal'c and O'Neill as the meeting broke up. "That… That was pretty slick, sir," she told Jack. "With your permission, I'd like to break the news to Vix and the others."

He waved Sam away. "Go ahead. And tell them to hold out for one of the good planets," he called after her. "If I know Kinsey, he'll try to palm them off with somethin' made of lava or swamps."

At his side, Teal'c eyed O'Neill suspiciously. "Peripatetic?"

"*Improve Your Word Power*," Jack said sagely. "Honestly, I don't know how I ever got on without it."

A hand caught O'Neill's shoulder and Jack turned to find Kinsey and his cadre of Secret Service minders hovering behind him. The neutral, plastic expression on the politician's face had slipped and Jack was looking at the real Robert Kinsey, furious at being manipulated. "Well done, *Colonel*," he grated, putting hard emphasis on the rank. "I bet you think you're pretty damned smart, playing me like that. Forcing me to waste time and resources on those rag-assed refugees." The other man kept his voice low, so it would not carry to anyone else's ears. "I hope you enjoy your little victory, Jack, because you won't be seeing any more of them. There might have been a time when you could cross swords with me but that time has passed." He touched the Stars-and-Stripes pin on his jacket lapel. "I am the Vice President of the United States of America, and I'm so far over your pay grade that you'd get a nosebleed just looking up at me. No matter how smart you think you are, no matter how much leverage you think you have, I'm here to tell you now it counts for nothing!"

Jack let the man's tirade wash over him. "That's quite a speech, Bob. I wonder what would happen if your buddies on the Hill found out you think that way?"

Kinsey sneered. "And who's going to tell them? Who's going to step in my way, you?" He reached out and flicked at O'Neill's rank tabs. "Just some bird colonel with a big ego?" He snorted. "What can you do, Jack? You just go away and keep playing with your rocketships, your ray guns and your space aliens." He shot a look at Teal'c's grim countenance. "Meanwhile, I'll be back in DC with the other adults, the men whose ranks actually count, making policy." He walked away, leaving his words hanging.

The politician was at the door when Jack called out to him. "Hey, Bob? Listen, thanks."

"For what?" Kinsey didn't bother to turn and face him.

"For helping me make a decision." Jack turned and wandered across to his commanding officer.

"So, sir," he began, thinking it through. "O-7... Brigadier General... What are the perks? You get a good parking space with that?"

"A new world?" Suj said the words as if she couldn't believe them. "You would do this for us?"

"That's the idea," said Sam. "We've got surveys of thousands of planets in this galaxy, many of which are uninhabited. And it's not like we haven't helped people find a new home before."

Vix, his ever-grim expression more dour than before, said nothing, allowing Koe to answer for him. "But a *planet*? When the clans threw off the fetters of the System Lords and the other oppressors who shackled us, we foreswore that kind of life. The freedom of the stars, that is the way of the Pack."

And then the other man spoke. "No. Koe, my good and trusted friend, you are wrong. The way of the Pack is *survival*, no more, no less. When we first fled Calai in ships it was because there was no other way to do it. Now these Aschen have taken that from us... As Major Carter has explained to us, through Ryn's duplicity they would have done it sooner or later... What else can we do?" He paused, and Sam felt a stab of sympathy for the alien leader. "Perhaps this is the path we were meant to follow."

Suj nodded. "The *Wanderer* was our cradle, our safe haven," she added. "Now the universe asks us to step beyond it, to take a world and make that our own."

"Think of it, Koe," said Vix, and she saw a glimmer of a smile on his lips. "A place of permanence, where we could start anew. Somewhere that we could build a memorial to those we have lost, and in its shadow make them proud."

"It will be difficult," Koe warned. "Many will resist. It will challenge every one of us."

Vix nodded. "Yes, clansman, it will. And the Pack will emerge stronger for it..." He glanced at Sam. "With the help of our allies."

Carter felt a grin spread across her face. "So what do you like? Beachfront property, or something with a view of the mountains?"

"This is nice," said the old man, taking a sip from the long-neck in his hand. "I'd almost forgotten how peaceful it could be out here."

"Yup," agreed Jack. He gave the fishing rod on the back

porch a nudge with the heel of his foot, just to put a little play in the lure where it dangled in the mirror-smooth waters of the lake.

"You don't know how lucky you are," continued the soldier. "I saw all this gone, turned to ashes and dust. You won't have to face that now... I hope."

"It's why we fight so hard," Jack replied, taking a draw from his own beer. "For this. To keep it." He leaned closer to the other man. "And I know you won't agree with me, despite my unique perspective on our mutual experiences, but you're pretty lucky too."

The old man gave a cold-humored grunt. "You think?"

Jack nodded at the cabin. "You've got something I haven't. You got a daughter."

"You could have that too. There's still time." He chuckled again, and the laughter was genuine. "Listen to me, talkin' about time. Heh."

Jack looked away, across the still waters. "I don't think so. After Charlie..." He sighed. "It's a deep well to fill, you know?"

The two men were silent for while, both musing on a young life cut short too soon; then the elder spoke again. "I don't want exoneration for what I did here, Jack. I made the only choice I thought I could. I don't apologize for it."

O'Neill's jaw tightened. There was part of him that could never excuse the callous intent that his older self had shown against his friends and his men, but at the same time, as loath as he was to admit it, Jack could touch the edges of understanding the reasons behind such a decision. The most damning truth of all was that he could not honestly tell himself that if he had lived through the same hell as the old man, he would not have made the same choices. Sam had told him something about parallel lines of history, of how the guy sitting beside him on his porch was only a reflection, a relative mirror-image of one potential Jack O'Neill; but he wasn't so sure. Before the Stargate he had taken part in a decade of black operations, many of which had forced him to make choices that would haunt him to his grave. It wasn't so hard to believe that a dark and unkind path might take Jack to the same place again; and in that moment he realized that the real test of his future would be to make sure that never happened.

Daniel watched Jade run her finger over the framed photograph of Jack; it was a picture of him on a snowy mountainside, his cheeks red with cold and swaddled in a thick military parka, but with a grin on his face like he was in love with the world.

"Norway," she said, by way of explanation. "Dad trained with their special forces troops. He told me once he'd never felt so alive as he did out there in the ice and cold."

Jackson smiled. "I get a chill just looking at the picture."

She returned the smile and reached out a hand to touch his wrist. Her fingers were cool from the bottle in her hand. "You've always made me laugh, Daniel. Thank you for being such a good friend." Then her face darkened. "I'm sorry. I had to deceive you."

"I understand what you did," he said carefully. "I can't imagine what pressures you must have been under... Where you came from." Jackson followed her out of O'Neill's small wood-paneled den and into the cabin's living room. He heard the murmur of gentle conversation from the back porch, and saw Jack and Jade's father talking. It was at once both the strangest and most natural sight he'd ever seen.

"I never wanted to lie to you. Do you believe me?" she husked.

Daniel found himself held by her dark eyes, the face framed by hair in ice-blue, copper and auburn shades. "I do. I forgive you."

Jade let out a slow breath. "What you think of me is very important, Daniel. I had to tell you how I feel before we leave."

"Leave?" Jackson was startled. "Where? You can't go back." The thought had never occurred to him. "Can you?"

"What do you think will happen if we remain here?" She looked away. "I know you and General Hammond are on our side, but as long as there are men like Kinsey in power…" Jade frowned. "He won't just allow the pods to be locked away in some vault in Nevada. The technology is too valuable, and my father and me? We know how to work it. Do you think they'll just let us walk away and start a new life in 2003?"

"They might," Daniel said, but the words seemed weak. He stiffened and took the woman's hand. "Jade, listen to me. I don't understand time travel theory, but I know there's a chance that if you try to leave, you'll be… *Deleted* from history. And I would hate to think that would happen. I would hate not to have known you." His brow furrowed. "Don't leave. Not yet."

"How is Hannah?" she asked, deflecting the implied question. For the moment, Jackson decided not to press it.

"Major Wells is fine. Doctor Warner flushed the remaining nanomachines from her blood thanks to your help. She's a bit shaken, but she'll be up and around soon. Apparently, she took it as a 'test of fire'. General Hammond said that if she could handle something like that with good humor, then she'll be a fine addition to the staff of the SGC."

"And the boy, Tyke?"

"He didn't take it so well, but I think you might have scared him straight. Colonel Dixon knows some guys in an Air Force mentoring program who can give him some alternative to a life in the gangs."

"That's good." She drew away slightly and handed him her bottle. "I'm thirsty," she said, "buy a girl a drink, Doctor?"

He forced a smile. "Sure. I'll be right back."

"We've been here hours and not a single bite." The old man finished his beer and eyed him. "There's not a single damn fish in this pond, is there?"

"Nope," replied Jack. "Not a one. It's great, isn't it?"

"Great enough to retire to?"

He took another sip. "Not just yet. I'd been considering it.

Y'know, as an…"

"An option?"

"Yeah. An option. But after Kytos and everything, I'm thinking about staying in a little longer." Jack glanced at his older
self. "Truth is, you got me wondering. I mean, 'commander-in-
chief' is pretty cool and 'colonel' is getting a little tight around
the britches. Maybe I could do more good if…."

"Like the saying goes, 'rank hath its privileges'. Getting a
star on your collar puts you in a whole different league."

"I think it might be worth it."

He got a nod in return. "I appreciate you doing this for us,
persuading George to let us off the base. Just being able to see
Earth, green and whole. It makes me feel like I'm sixty again."

Jack nodded back. He didn't spoil the mood by telling the
old man that there was a Blackhawk with a tactical team on
standby no more then five miles from where they were sitting, just in case something went screwy. He imagined that
the Commander knew full well that they were out there, too.
O'Neill covered the thought with a look at his watch. Ten
past the hour. Sam and Teal'c were running late.

"Got the time, flyboy?" said the old man with a dry chuckle.
He rolled up the cuff on his jacket and showed O'Neill the very
same wristwatch, a USAF-issue Tactical with a dark blue face.
His counterpart's watch was discolored and scratched, but the
hands were still moving smoothly. "Still tickin'."

Jack considered the sweep of the second hand for a moment.
"Okay, so maybe this is a question I should ask Carter, but I
don't want another technobabble explosion." He glanced at
the other man. "We changed history, from your point of view,
right?"

"Right."

"So if we did that, then the future you came from, with war
and all, we made that un-happen. That future, your future, it
doesn't exist any more."

"I sure as hell hope not," growled the old man. "After everything we paid to prevent it."

"So what happens if you use those time-pod gizmos? You don't have that future any more, it's been erased. There's nothing for you to return to."

"Maybe," he admitted. "But like I told you before, I never listen to any of that time-warp, mind-bender, go-back-and-shoot-your-own-grandpa crap."

Jack took a breath. "My point is. You don't have to go. You can stay here, now." He opened his hands. "I'd make sure you and Jade were okay. I'd keep the government off your back."

The other man's eyes clouded over. "I believe you, junior. I know you'd help us, even if it meant breaking the law to do it. But as much as I want to say yes, every time I look around, every face that passes me by, all I can see is all the things that I lost on the road to get here. Too many things, Jack, too many things to remind us of old hurts and losses. Seeing people who I watched die walking and talking again, friends and…" He trailed off, glancing back at the cabin, towards his daughter inside. "And other people."

A question pressed at him—*the* question—and Jack frowned, unsure if he should ask it.

The old man nodded. "She's just like her mother. I see so much of her in Jade, it cuts me like a knife sometimes." He smiled. "I'll tell you who, if you're sure you want to know."

O'Neill was lost for the right words. "I don't… I'm not sure…"

His elder self sat up in the deck chair. "I tell you what. How about you take a walk to the fridge, get us a couple more beers and take the moment to make a choice?"

Daniel opened the refrigerator and scanned the contents. O'Neill had an eclectic collection of brews, both foreign and domestic, inside the big cooler. He reached in and selected a pair at random.

"Nah, not those," said Jack, pushing past him. "Guests get the better stuff. Here." He handed the other man two bottles of Samuel Adams. "Take these."

Daniel eyed the dark ale. "Actually, I like that Singaporean beer, Tiger?"

Jack kicked the fridge door closed. "You drank all mine last time, remember?"

"That was Teal'c."

"Yeah, sure it was." O'Neill popped the caps with an opener. "And another thing. Don't think I haven't noticed the way you've been looking at Jade."

Jackson attempted to appear affronted. "What do you mean?"

"I know that look. You think she's cute."

"She is," Daniel admitted. "Your point?"

"She's my daughter."

"From the *future*," Jackson made quote marks in the air. "She *may* be your daughter, from one quantum standpoint."

Jack's jaw hardened. "Don't you go all Carter on me, pal."

"She's his daughter, not yours," Daniel replied, the humor of the moment fading. "And he's not you, Jack. I hope he never will be."

O'Neill took a draught of beer. "Don't be too hard on him. He got that way because he thought he had nothin' left." Both men turned as the sound of a car drawing up outside caught their attention. Daniel looked and saw Sam and Teal'c stepping out.

Beside him, Jack smiled. "Me? I reckon I've got plenty."

Her father looked up as Jade stepped out on to the porch. He gave her a wary nod and she returned it. "The equipment?" he asked. "The nano-fluid and the guns, the other kit?"

"Destroyed," she replied. Jade waved her hand. "I used the implant and the last of what I had to program a dissembler swarm. The nanites will seek out and turn anything we brought back with us into inert dust. There'll be nothing left for them."

"And the pods?" He stood up, coming closer.

She pulled them out of a pocket in the coat that Major Carter had loaned her. "Here. I managed to steal them from the SGC after we gated back. I used the combined charge from both to build up the power store. There's enough for us to make a return trip."

"Where's the third one?"

"I programmed it for an overload cycle, set it for a narrow-beam transit to the planet where we found Janus's other lab. If I did it right, it will disrupt the Stargate DHD there when it materializes and stop anyone from ever gating in. No one will stumble on the technology like we did."

He smiled. "You thought of everything."

She returned it. "I had a good teacher."

His aged, papery skin touched hers as their hands crossed over the devices. "Are you ready?" said her father. "If we do this, there's no certainty as to where we'll end up."

She saw a kindness in his eyes that had been absent for years and it caught her words in her throat. "We can't stay, Dad," she told him. "No matter how much we want to, we don't belong here." Jade took a final look at the cabin, catching the sound of a car engine approaching. "We have to let them find their own future."

The old man nodded. "Your mother would be proud of you," he said, and he touched the activation pad.

Exotic radiation glimmered over the lake like summer lightning, and they vanished.

With Teal'c following behind, Sam walked toward the back of the cabin. "So, what movie did you bring?" she threw the question over her shoulder.

The Jaffa held up a DVD case. "*Timecop.*"

Carter rolled her eyes and crossed around to the lakeside. She found Daniel and Jack on the porch, each man with two beers in their hands, each with a lost, rueful expression.

"Hey," she called, stepping up to take a bottle from both of them. "Thanks." She passed a beer to Teal'c and the Jaffa raised an eyebrow as he took off his hat.

"Where are the others?" he asked.

Jackson sat down silently and O'Neill nodded to himself. "They… They had to go."

"Where?" Carter looked around.

"Home," said Daniel.

The members of SG-1 sat in silence, taking in the measure of Jackson's statement; finally it was Teal'c who spoke. "Kinsey will not be pleased."

"Oh yeah," said Jack, "like that's a surprise."

"He'll be very angry," Daniel said distantly. "Very, very angry."

"He will," agreed the colonel, "so at least there's one good thing."

Sam motioned to get up. "We should radio in to the SGC, inform General Hammond."

Jack waved her suggestion away. "Nah. They gave us a good day. Let's not waste it."

"If not for Jade and her father, we would have no 'good days'," noted Teal'c.

Sam paused with her beer at her lips, and then held it up in salute. "To the future?" she offered.

"The future," said Jack, "and whatever challenges it brings."

The four bottles clinked together.

ABOUT THE AUTHOR

Along with his stories set in the Stargate universe and fiction such as the Sundowners series of steampunk Westerns (*Ghost Town, Underworld, Iron Dragon* and *Showdown*), *Jade Dragon* and *The Butterfly Effect*, James Swallow has also written for the worlds of Warhammer 40,000 (*The Flight of the Eisenstein, Faith & Fire, Deus Encarmine* and *Deus Sanguinius*), Star Trek (*Day of the Vipers, Distant Shores, The Sky's The Limit, Shards and Shadows*), Doctor Who (*Peacemaker, Dalek Empire, Snapshots, Destination Prague*) and 2000AD (*Eclipse, Whiteout, Blood Relative*). His short fiction has appeared in *Stargate: The Official Magazine, Inferno!* and several anthologies.

His non-fiction includes *Dark Eye: The Films of David Fincher* and books on scriptwriting and genre television; Swallow's other credits include television, audio and video-game scripts for *Star Trek Voyager, Doctor Who, Battlestar Galactica* and *Blake's 7*.

He lives in London, and is currently working on his next book.

STARGATE SG·1™

STARGATE ATLANTIS™

**Original novels based on
the hit TV shows,
STARGATE SG-1 and
STARGATE ATLANTIS**

AVAILABLE NOW

**For more information, visit
www.stargatenovels.com**

SNEAK PREVIEW

STARGATE ATLANTIS: BLOOD TIES

**by Sonny Whitelaw &
Elizabeth Christensen**

"Wait—are you saying that Carson found a link between actual human DNA and the *iratus* virus?"

Rodney hoped irrationally for a rapid denial, or at least an assurance that he was on the wrong track, as unlikely as that might be. Instead he got only a solemn, silent glance.

"Oh, God," he murmured, horrified. "That's it, isn't it? Humans have the virus. We've *always* had it. Oh, *God*."

"Rodney, calm down," Elizabeth advised, "and let Radek finish."

"Research shows that the virus was introduced to the human population at the same time and geographical location as the ATA gene," said Radek. "Not all humans possess it, of course—not even all humans with the ATA gene—but about half the population has fragments of the base code. Under certain conditions, gene therapy being one such condition, mutated versions of the *iratus* virus can become active."

"And something has suddenly triggered the virus in people here, like a kind of *iratus* time bomb?" Elizabeth started to twist around in the driver's seat.

"Eyes on the road!" Rodney barked, turning to face the front. Suddenly the cramped interior of the SUV was too warm, too constricting. He put his head down and tried to breathe deeply, but his lungs didn't seem interested in complying. *Wide open fields...clear blue skies...*

Rodney heard his name dimly, over the hammering of his heart, and couldn't have cared less. "Pull over," he panted. "Dammit, pull over!"

One of Elizabeth's many admirable traits was her willingness to act without hesitation when it mattered. No sooner had Rodney made his plea than the SUV made a swift right turn and came to a halt.

Barely lifting his head, Rodney shoved the door open and flung himself out of the vehicle. He sucked in a lungful of cold air and, ignoring the splashes of half-frozen mud, sat down hard on the rear bumper, trying to get himself back under control.

Other doors opened and closed, and before long he found himself surrounded by his colleagues. He noticed that the faux CDC truck had pulled up behind them. A hand came down to rest on his shoulder. "Dr. Lam's gone to get you something to drink," Elizabeth said calmly, as if this sort of thing happened every day. "Just take it easy for a minute."

"Take it *easy*?" Rodney offered a harsh laugh, still bent low and examining the cracked pavement and dirty slush piled in the gutter. The bracing chill and random snowflakes barely registered when compared with the icy tendrils that gripped his stomach. "That gene therapy worked on me, remember? I probably have some variant of this damned bug. We created a whole group of *iratus* carriers ourselves, and any number of them must be hidden in the human population, just waiting to be switched on!"

Seeing Sheppard's polished shoes approach the huddle, he was about to add something further, but the Colonel, who must have received a similar briefing from Lam, got in first. "I need Ronon and Teyla here," he said, his tone matter of fact. "If there's some sort of clue on M1M-316 as to the Ancient who let this gene loose on Earth, then Rodney and Radek should have been the ones to go there with Lorne. Meanwhile, if we've got Wraith, or Wraith wannabes, on the loose on Earth, I can't track them down without Teyla and Ronon. No offense, Rodney. It's just that Teyla can sense them coming, and Ronon's been taking them on longer than anyone we've got."

"Oh, is that your grand strategy?" Rodney drew another frigid breath, quashing a vague twinge of guilt for not paying more attention to the activities of his other two teammates. "Do you really think you can contain this with a couple of hunting trips? You can't simply round up a few pasty-looking people and call it a day. The virus is in our DNA. It's *part* of us!"

When Elizabeth's fingers tightened, digging into his shoulder, Rodney glanced up and identified their stopping point as a gas station, complete with a line of snowboard-topped SUVs and various travelers. Several were looking in the direction of the 'CDC' van and the cluster of people hovering around him.

"Let's maybe talk about this somewhere less public, shall we?" Jackson suggested.

You're not dead yet, Rodney told himself. *And you're not a Wraith. Deal with everything else one step at a time.*

Lam held out a bottle of some kind of sports drink without comment. Rodney accepted it despite its strong resemblance to antifreeze. After a couple of swallows, he felt marginally human again — although apparently that was a relative concept now.

"Claustrophobia," he mumbled weakly. "Uh, please continue, Radek."

"I have told you all I know at this point," Radek replied, standing there with an infuriatingly masked expression.

Rearing up off the bumper, Rodney insisted, "That can't be all."

The other scientist unfolded his arms and, raising his gloved hands in surrender. "The research was, as you said, one of many projects, and not terribly high on the priority list."

"Not a priority? You went far enough to identify the problem and decided to take a lunch break before investigating a solution?"

"Rodney!" Elizabeth's admonishment was less effective than Sheppard's abrupt grip on his arm, hauling him upright and into the backseat of the SUV, then shutting the door behind him.

Once everyone had belted in, this time with Jackson in front, and they were in motion again, Elizabeth finally spoke. "Rodney, try to remember that not everyone in Colorado Springs has the same level of security as you. Carson notified me of his findings and submitted a report to the SGC last year. At that point we had no reason to think there was a problem. Until these killings, nothing had happened on Earth to suggest that any Wraith traits were present in humans. I did recognize some similarities to the succubus myths and possibly some old vampire tales, but that's all. To be honest, based on the manner in which many other myths have played out, including the existence of Merlin and even Atlantis itself, it seemed reasonable to assume that such legendary creatures existed only in the Pegasus Galaxy."

Rubbing his arm, which was certain to bruise, Rodney asked, "And what are those myths—besides the Hollywood version, I mean?"

Jackson turned around to face him. "Dr. Beckett's report traced the first occurrences of the *iratus* virus to the E'din Valley, between the Tigris and Euphrates Rivers in ancient Persia, the area fabled to be the location of the Garden of Eden—what's now Iraq."

"Still nothing I'd call surprising." Couldn't *anyone* process or disseminate information as quickly as Rodney? "We've already discussed the Ancients' evacuation to Earth ten millennia ago. They made that return through the Egyptian gate. *And*?"

As the SUV coasted to a stop at a traffic light, Jackson slouched back in his seat. "You can't imagine how I've missed working with you, McKay," he remarked under his breath, the words still perfectly audible. More loudly, he continued, "The

Ancients' presence in that region explains the appearance of the ATA gene, but not the appearance of the *iratus* virus. Based on the mythology and what we saw on the tape Woolsey discovered, though, I think I have an idea what might have happened."

In the next car over, a mother leaned into the backseat to hand her young child a juice box. Rodney wondered if they carried the retrovirus and if their bright-faced ignorance would end up costing the entire planet dearly.

"Carson had a theory as well," Radek pointed out. "He believed the Ancients were pursuing a method of manipulating the *iratus* virus, either to disable it in the Wraith population or to make others immune to the feeding process."

"Like Ronon's immunity," Elizabeth said, accelerating when the light turned green.

"Or the Hoffan vaccine." One side of Radek's mouth curled upward in a wistful half smile. "It gave Carson a measure of peace to know that our failures were not unique to us."

Rodney took another sip of his drink, wishing they didn't have to face this issue with the ghost of his friend hovering over their shoulders.

"Dr. Geisler recently discovered records in the city database associated with one specific researcher named Lilith," Radek continued. "A number of planets were referenced in conjunction with the project files—possibly some testing was conducted on those worlds. One file in particular looked most promising, because it appeared to contain several references to Earth long before the Ancients left Antarctica for Lantea."

"Which is why General Landry ordered Major Lorne, Ronon and Teyla to check out M1M-316," explained Elizabeth. "We're hoping they'll locate Lilith's research laboratory."

The name set off a chime of familiarity in Rodney's memory, taking the edge off his terror and giving him something on which to focus. "Lilith is the researcher? That can hardly be coincidental."

The SUV swung into the parking lot of the county sheriff's

office, which looked entirely too sedate and tranquil to contain a morgue. Jackson's head turned toward him. "Since when did you become a scholar of Talmudic texts, McKay?"

That threw him off. "What? I'm talking about the name—I've run across it in the Ancient database. What are *you* talking about?"

"I believe Lilith was also the name of Adam's first wife," Radek contributed, earning a surprised glance from both Jackson and Rodney.

"As in Adam and Eve?" Elizabeth parked the vehicle and switched off the ignition. "There was a first wife?" She glanced over her shoulder.

"And you picked up that piece of trivia *where* exactly?" Rodney followed her gaze and watched as Sheppard's 'CDC' vehicle passed them, heading for the rear of the building.

Radek's response seemed to be directed at Jackson rather than Rodney. "Carson believed the Ancient Lilith continued her retrovirus research after relocating from 316 to Earth. Possibly the virus escaped, or else she intentionally released it into the population."

"I'm beginning to find myself agreeing with John's assessment of the Ancients," Elizabeth declared, sounding drained. "They created some staggering messes and made little or no attempt to clean them up."

Radek nodded his agreement. "Wraith, Asurans, succubus—"

"Succubi in the plural," said Jackson. "And we should include incubi, the male version, since, according to the profiler, a male was responsible for the Colorado Springs murders."

As if the FBI's profiler could have even the slightest clue what they were dealing with here. Rodney climbed out of the SUV and pulled his lightweight jacket tight around himself, uninterested in the details Elizabeth was providing on the profiler and the tall tale they'd be feeding her. He was focused on only one thing. "What do we know about this Lilith so far?"

He'd asked Radek, but it was Jackson who answered. "'*Her gates are gates of death, and from the entrance of the house she sets out towards Sheol. None of those who enter there will ever return, and all who possess her will descend to the Pit.*'"

"Talmud?" Radek inquired.

The archeologist shook his head and started walking. "Dead Sea Scrolls."

Rodney stared at the neatly lettered sign near the front door of the building, helpfully directing coroner business to the lower level. The panic that had earlier threatened to overwhelm him now settled into a tight ball of nausea in the pit of his stomach. He doubted it would disappear any time soon.

STARGATE ATLANTIS: BLOOD TIES

AVAILABLE DECEMBER 2007

For more information, visit <u>www.stargatenovels.com</u>

STARGATE ATLANTIS: BLOOD TIES

by **Sonny Whitelaw &**
Elizabeth Christensen
Price: £6.99 UK | $7.95 US |
$9.95 Canada
ISBN-10: 1-905586-08-6
ISBN-13: 978-1-905586-08-0

When a series of gruesome murders are uncovered around the world, the trail leads back to the SGC—and far beyond…

Recalled to Stargate Command, Dr. Elizabeth Weir, Colonel John Sheppard, and Dr. Rodney McKay are shown shocking video footage—a Wraith attack, taking place on Earth. While McKay, Teyla, and Ronon investigate the disturbing possibility that humans may harbor Wraith DNA, Colonel Sheppard is teamed with SG-1's Dr. Daniel Jackson. Together, they follow the murderers' trail from Colorado Springs to the war-torn streets of Iraq, and there, uncover a terrifying truth…

As an ancient cult prepares to unleash its deadly plot against humankind, Sheppard's survival depends on his questioning of everything believed about the Wraith…

Order your copy directly from the publisher today by going to <u>www.stargatenovels.com</u> **.or send a check or money order made payable to "Fandemonium" to:**

<u>**USA orders:**</u> **$10.82 ($7.95 + $2.87 P&P). Send payment to: Fandemonium Books, PO Box 2178, Decatur, GA 30031-2178.**

<u>**UK orders:**</u> **£8.30 (£6.99 + £1.31 P&P).** <u>**Rest of the World orders:**</u> **£9.70 (£6.99 + £2.71 P&P). Send payment to: Fandemonium Books, PO Box 795A, Surbiton KT5 8YB, United Kingdom.**

Or check your local bookshop – available on special order if they are out of stock (quote the ISBN number listed above).

STARGATE ATLANTIS: CASUALTIES OF WAR

by Elizabeth Christensen
Price: £6.99 UK | $7.95 US
ISBN-10: 1-905586-06-X
ISBN-13: 978-1-905586-06-6

It is a dark time for Atlantis. In the wake of the Asuran takeover, Colonel Sheppard is buckling under the strain of command. When his team discover Ancient technology which can defeat the Asuran menace, he is determined that Atlantis must possess it — at all costs.

But the involvement of Atlantis heightens local suspicions and brings two peoples to the point of war. Elizabeth Weir believes only her negotiating skills can hope to prevent the carnage, but when her diplomatic mission is attacked — and two of Sheppard's team are lost — both Weir and Sheppard must question their decisions. And their abilities to command.

As the first shots are fired, the Atlantis team must find a way to end the conflict — or live with the blood of innocents on their hands…

STARGATE ATLANTIS: ENTANGLEMENT

by Martha Wells
Price: £6.99 UK | $7.95 US
ISBN-10: 1-905586-03-5
ISBN-13: 978-1-905586-03-5

When Dr. Rodney McKay unlocks an Ancient mystery on a distant moon, he discovers a terrifying threat to the Pegasus galaxy.

Determined to disable the device before it's discovered by the Wraith, Colonel John Sheppard and his team navigate the treacherous ruins of an Ancient outpost. But attempts to destroy the technology are complicated by the arrival of a stranger — a stranger who can't be trusted, a stranger who needs the Ancient device to return home. Cut off from backup, under attack from the Wraith, and with the future of the universe hanging in the balance, Sheppard's team must put aside their doubts and step into the unknown.

However, when your mortal enemy is your only ally, betrayal is just a heartbeat away…

Order your copy directly from the publisher today by going to www.stargatenovels.com or send a check or money order made payable to "Fandemonium" to:

USA orders: $10.82 ($7.95 + $2.87 P&P). Send payment to: Fandemonium Books, PO Box 2178, Decatur, GA 30031-2178.

UK orders: £8.30 (£6.99 + £1.31 P&P). **Rest of the World orders:** £9.70 (£6.99 + £2.71 P&P). Send payment to: Fandemonium Books, PO Box 795A, Surbiton KT5 8YB, United Kingdom.

Or check your local bookshop – available on special order if they are out of stock (quote the ISBN number listed above).

STARGATE ATLANTIS: EXOGENESIS

**by Sonny Whitelaw &
Elizabeth Christensen**
Price: £6.99 UK | $7.95 US
ISBN-10: 1-905586-02-7
ISBN-13: 978-1-905586-02-8

When Dr. Carson Beckett disturbs the rest of two long-dead Ancients, he unleashes devastating consequences of global proportions.

With the very existence of Lantea at risk, Colonel John Sheppard leads his team on a desperate search for the long lost Ancient device that could save Atlantis. While Teyla Emmagan and Dr. Elizabeth Weir battle the ecological meltdown consuming their world, Colonel Sheppard, Dr. Rodney McKay and Dr. Zelenka travel to a world created by the Ancients themselves. There they discover a human experiment that could mean their salvation…

But the truth is never as simple as it seems, and the team's prejudices lead them to make a fatal error — an error that could slaughter thousands, including their own Dr. McKay.

Order your copy directly from the publisher today by going to www.stargatenovels.com or send a check or money order made payable to "Fandemonium" to:

<u>USA orders:</u> $10.82 ($7.95 + $2.87 P&P). Send payment to: Fandemonium Books, PO Box 2178, Decatur, GA 30031-2178.

<u>UK orders:</u> £8.30 (£6.99 + £1.31 P&P). <u>Rest of the World orders:</u> £9.70 (£6.99 + £2.71 P&P). Send payment to: Fandemonium Books, PO Box 795A, Surbiton KT5 8YB, United Kingdom.

Or check your local bookshop – available on special order if they are out of stock (quote the ISBN number listed above).

STARGATE ATLANTIS: HALCYON

Series number: SGA-4

by James Swallow
Price: £6.99 UK | $7.95 US
ISBN-10: 1-905586-01-9
ISBN-13: 978-1-905586-01-1

In their ongoing quest for new allies, Atlantis's flagship team travel to Halcyon, a grim industrial world where the Wraith are no longer feared—they are hunted.

Horrified by the brutality of Halcyon's warlike people, Lieutenant Colonel John Sheppard soon becomes caught in the political machinations of Halcyon's aristocracy. In a feudal society where strength means power, he realizes the nobles will stop at nothing to ensure victory over their rivals. Meanwhile, Dr. Rodney McKay enlists the aid of the ruler's daughter to investigate a powerful Ancient structure, but McKay's scientific brilliance has aroused the interest of the planet's most powerful man—a man with a problem he desperately needs McKay to solve.

As Halcyon plunges into a catastrophe of its own making the team must join forces with the warlords—or die at the hands of their bitterest enemy…

Order your copy directly from the publisher today by going to www.stargatenovels.com or send a check or money order made payable to "Fandemonium" to:

<u>USA orders</u>: $10.82 ($7.95 + $2.87 P&P). Send payment to: Fandemonium Books, PO Box 2178, Decatur, GA 30031-2178.

<u>UK orders</u>: £8.30 (£6.99 + £1.31 P&P). <u>Rest of the World orders</u>: £9.70 (£6.99 + £2.71 P&P). Send payment to: Fandemonium Books, PO Box 795A, Surbiton KT5 8YB, United Kingdom.

Or check your local bookshop – available on special order if they are out of stock (quote the ISBN number listed above).

STARGATE ATLANTIS: THE CHOSEN

by Sonny Whitelaw & Elizabeth Christensen
Price: £6.99 UK | $7.95 US
ISBN-10: 0-9547343-8-6
ISBN-13: 978-0-9547343-8-1

With Ancient technology scattered across the Pegasus galaxy, the Atlantis team is not surprised to find it in use on a world once defended by Dalera, an Ancient who was cast out of her society for falling in love with a human.

But in the millennia since Dalera's departure much has changed. Her strict rules have been broken, leaving her people open to Wraith attack. Only a few of the Chosen remain to operate Ancient technology vital to their defense and tensions are running high. Revolution simmers close to the surface.

When Major Sheppard and Rodney McKay are revealed as members of the Chosen, Daleran society convulses into chaos. Wanting to help resolve the crisis and yet refusing to prop up an autocratic regime, Sheppard is forced to act when Teyla and Lieutenant Ford are taken hostage by the rebels…

Order your copy directly from the publisher today by going to www.stargatenovels.com or send a check or money order made payable to "Fandemonium" to:

USA orders: $10.82 ($7.95 + $2.87 P&P). Send payment to: Fandemonium Books, PO Box 2178, Decatur, GA 30031-2178.

UK orders: £8.30 (£6.99 + £1.31 P&P). **Rest of the World orders:** £9.70 (£6.99 + £2.71 P&P). Send payment to: Fandemonium Books, PO Box 795A, Surbiton KT5 8YB, United Kingdom.

Or check your local bookshop – available on special order if they are out of stock (quote the ISBN number listed above).

STARGATE ATLANTIS: RELIQUARY

What you don't know can kill you

RELIQUARY

Martha Wells

Based on the hit television series created by
Brad Wright and Robert C. Cooper

Series number: SGA-2

by Martha Wells
Price: £6.99 UK | $7.95 US
ISBN-10: 0-9547343-7-8
ISBN-13: 978-0-9547343-7-4

While exploring the unused sections of the Ancient city of Atlantis, Major John Sheppard and Dr. Rodney McKay stumble on a recording device that reveals a mysterious new Stargate address. Believing that the address may lead them to a vast repository of Ancient knowledge, the team embarks on a mission to this uncharted world.

There they discover a ruined city, full of whispered secrets and dark shadows. As tempers fray and trust breaks down, the team uncovers the truth at the heart of the city. A truth that spells their destruction.

With half their people compromised, it falls to Major John Sheppard and Dr. Rodney McKay to risk everything in a deadly game of bluff with the enemy. To fail would mean the fall of Atlantis itself — and, for Sheppard, the annihilation of his very humanity...

STARGATE ATLANTIS: RISING

by Sally Malcolm
Price: £6.99 UK | $7.95 US
ISBN-10: 0-9547343-5-1
ISBN-13: 978-0-9547343-5-0

Following the discovery of an Ancient outpost buried deep in the Antarctic ice sheet, Stargate Command sends a new team of explorers through the Stargate to the distant Pegasus galaxy.

Emerging in an abandoned Ancient city, the team quickly confirms that they have found the Lost City of Atlantis. But, submerged beneath the sea on an alien planet, the city is in danger of catastrophic flooding unless it is raised to the surface. Things go from bad to worse when the team must confront a new enemy known as the Wraith who are bent on destroying Atlantis.

Stargate Atlantis is the exciting new spin-off of the hit TV show, Stargate SG-1. Based on the script of the pilot episode, Rising is a must-read for all fans and includes deleted scenes and dialog not seen on TV—with photos from the pilot episode.

Order your copy directly from the publisher today by going to www.stargatenovels.com or send a check or money order made payable to "Fandemonium" to:

<u>USA orders:</u> $10.82 ($7.95 + $2.87 P&P). Send payment to: **Fandemonium Books, PO Box 2178, Decatur, GA 30031-2178.**

<u>UK orders:</u> £8.30 (£6.99 + £1.31 P&P). <u>Rest of the World orders:</u> £9.70 (£6.99 + £2.71 P&P). Send payment to: **Fandemonium Books, PO Box 795A, Surbiton KT5 8YB, United Kingdom.**

Or check your local bookshop – available on special order if they are out of stock (quote the ISBN number listed above).

Time is running out for SG-1

STARGATE
SG·1

ROSWELL
Sonny Whitelaw & Jennifer Fallon
Based on the hit television series developed by
Brad Wright and Jonathan Glassner

Series number: SG1-9

STARGATE SG-1: ROSWELL

**by Sonny Whitelaw &
Jennifer Fallon**
Price: $7.95 US | $9.95 Canada |
£6.99 UK
ISBN-10: 1-905586-04-3
ISBN-13: 978-1-905586-04-2

When a Stargate malfunction throws
Colonel Cameron Mitchell, Dr. Daniel Jackson, and Colonel Sam Carter
back in time, they only have minutes
to live.

But their rescue, by an unlikely
duo — General Jack O'Neill and Vala Mal Doran — is only the
beginning of their problems. Ordered to rescue an Asgard also
marooned in 1947, SG-1 find themselves at the mercy of history. While Jack, Daniel, Sam and Teal'c become embroiled in the
Roswell aliens conspiracy, Cam and Vala are stranded in another
timeline, desperately searching for a way home.

As the effects of their interference ripple through time,
the consequences for the future are catastrophic. Trapped in the
past, SG-1 can only watch as their world is overrun by a terrible
invader…

**Order your copy directly from the publisher today by going
to www.stargatenovels.com or send a check or money order
made payable to "Fandemonium" to:**

<u>USA orders:</u> **($10.82 ($7.95 + $2.87 P&P). Send payment to:
Fandemonium Books, PO Box 2178, Decatur, GA 30031-2178.**

<u>UK orders:</u> **£8.30 (£6.99 + £1.31 P&P).** <u>Rest of the World
orders:</u> **£9.70 (£6.99 + £2.71 P&P). Send payment to:
Fandemonium Books, PO Box 795A, Surbiton KT5 8YB,
United Kingdom.**

Or check your local bookshop — available on special order if they are
out of stock (quote the ISBN number listed above).

STARGATE SG-1: ALLIANCES

by Karen Miller
Price: $7.95 US | $9.95 Canada |
£6.99 UK
ISBN-10: 1-905586-00-0
ISBN-13: 978-1-905586-00-4

All SG-1 wanted was technology to save Earth from the Goa'uld ... but the mission to Euronda was a terrible failure. Now the dogs of Washington are baying for Jack O'Neill's blood — and Senator Robert Kinsey is leading the pack.

When Jacob Carter asks General Hammond for SG-1's participation in mission for the Tok'ra, it seems like the answer to O'Neill's dilemma. The secretive Tok'ra are running out of hosts. Jacob believes he's found the answer — but it means O'Neill and his team must risk their lives infiltrating a Goa'uld slave breeding farm to recruit humans willing to join the Tok'ra.

It's a risky proposition ... especially since the fallout from Euronda has strained the team's bond almost to breaking. If they can't find a way to put their differences behind them, they might not make it home alive...

STARGATE SG-1: SURVIVAL OF THE FITTEST

by Sabine C. Bauer
Price: $7.95 US | $9.95 Canada |
£6.99 UK
ISBN-10: 0-9547343-9-4
ISBN-13: 978-0-9547343-9-8

Colonel Frank Simmons has never been a friend to SG-1. Working for the shadowy government organisation, the NID, he has hatched a horrifying plan to create an army as devastatingly effective as that of any Goa'uld.

And he will stop at nothing to fulfil his ruthless ambition, even if that means forfeiting the life of the SGC's Chief Medical Officer, Dr. Janet Fraiser. But Simmons underestimates the bond between Stargate Command's officers. When Fraiser, Major Samantha Carter and Teal'c disappear, Colonel Jack O'Neill and Dr. Daniel Jackson are forced to put aside personal differences to follow their trail into a world of savagery and death.

In this complex story of revenge, sacrifice and betrayal, SG-1 must endure their greatest ordeal...

Order your copy directly from the publisher today by going to **www.stargatenovels.com** or send a check or money order made payable to "Fandemonium" to:

USA orders: $10.82 ($7.95 + $2.87 P&P). Send payment to: Fandemonium Books, PO Box 2178, Decatur, GA 30031-2178.

UK orders: £8.30 (£6.99 + £1.31 P&P). **Rest of the World orders:** £9.70 (£6.99 + £2.71 P&P). Send payment to: Fandemonium Books, PO Box 795A, Surbiton KT5 8YB, United Kingdom.

Or check your local bookshop – available on special order if they are out of stock (quote the ISBN number listed above).

STARGATE SG-1: SIREN SONG

Holly Scott and Jaimie Duncan
Price: $7.95 US | $9.95 Canada |
£6.99 UK
ISBN-10: 0-9547343-6-X
ISBN-13: 978-0-9547343-6-7

Bounty-hunter, Aris Boch, once more has his sights on SG-1. But this time Boch isn't interested in trading them for cash. He needs the unique talents of Dr. Daniel Jackson — and he'll do anything to get them.

Taken to Boch's ravaged homeworld, Atropos, Colonel Jack O'Neill and his team are handed over to insane Goa'uld, Sebek. Obsessed with opening a mysterious subterranean vault, Sebek demands that Jackson translate the arcane writing on the doors. When Jackson refuses, the Goa'uld resorts to devastating measures to ensure his cooperation.

With the vault exerting a malign influence on all who draw near, Sebek compels Jackson and O'Neill toward a horror that threatens both their sanity and their lives. Meanwhile, Carter and Teal'c struggle to persuade the starving people of Atropos to risk everything they have to save SG-1 — and free their desolate world of the Goa'uld, forever.

Order your copy directly from the publisher today by going to www.stargatenovels.com or send a check or money order made payable to "Fandemonium" to:

<u>USA orders:</u> **$10.82 ($7.95 + $2.87 P&P). Send payment to: Fandemonium Books, PO Box 2178, Decatur, GA 30031-2178.**

<u>UK orders:</u> **£8.30 (£6.99 + £1.31 P&P).** <u>Rest of the World orders:</u> **£9.70 (£6.99 + £2.71 P&P). Send payment to: Fandemonium Books, PO Box 795A, Surbiton KT5 8YB, United Kingdom.**

Or check your local bookshop – available on special order if they are out of stock (quote the ISBN number listed above).

STARGATE SG-1: A MATTER OF HONOR

Part one of two parts
by Sally Malcolm

Price: $7.95 US | $9.95 Canada |
£6.99 UK
ISBN-10: 0-9547343-2-7
ISBN-13: 978-0-9547343-2-9

Five years after Major Henry Boyd and his team, SG-10, were trapped on the edge of a black hole, Colonel Jack O'Neill discovers a device that could bring them home.

But it's owned by the Kinahhi, an advanced and paranoid people, besieged by a ruthless foe. Unwilling to share the technology, the Kinahhi are pursuing their own agenda in the negotiations with Earth's diplomatic delegation. Maneuvering through a maze of tyranny, terrorism and deceit, Dr. Daniel Jackson, Major Samantha Carter and Teal'c unravel a startling truth — a revelation that throws the team into chaos and forces O'Neill to face a nightmare he is determined to forget.

Resolved to rescue Boyd, O'Neill marches back into the hell he swore never to revisit. Only this time, he's taking SG-1 with him…

Order your copy directly from the publisher today by going to www.stargatenovels.com or send a check or money order made payable to "Fandemonium" to:

USA orders: $10.82 ($7.95 + $2.87 P&P). Send payment to: Fandemonium Books, PO Box 2178, Decatur, GA 30031-2178.

UK orders: £8.30 (£6.99 + £1.31 P&P). **Rest of the World orders:** £9.70 (£6.99 + £2.71 P&P). Send payment to: Fandemonium Books, PO Box 795A, Surbiton KT5 8YB, United Kingdom.

Or check your local bookshop – available on special order if they are out of stock (quote the ISBN number listed above).

STARGATE SG-1: THE COST OF HONOR

Part two of two parts
by Sally Malcolm
Price: $7.95 US | $9.95 Canada |
£6.99 UK
ISBN-10: 0-9547343-4-3
ISBN-13: 978-0-9547343-4-3

In the action-packed sequel to *A Matter of Honor*, SG-1 embark on a desperate mission to save SG-10 from the edge of a black hole. But the price of heroism may be more than they can pay...

Returning to Stargate Command, Colonel Jack O'Neill and his team find more has changed in their absence than they had expected. Nonetheless, O'Neill is determined to face the consequences of their unauthorized activities, only to discover the penalty is far worse than anything he could have imagined.

With the fate of Colonel O'Neill and Major Samantha Carter unknown, and the very survival of the SGC threatened, Dr. Daniel Jackson and Teal'c mount a rescue mission to free their team-mates and reclaim the SGC. Yet returning to the Kinahhi homeworld, they learn a startling truth about its ancient foe. And uncover a horrifying secret...

Terror stalks the team at night

SACRIFICE MOON

Julie Fortune

Based on the hit television series developed by
Brad Wright and Jonathan Glassner

Series number: SG1-2

STARGATE SG-1: SACRIFICE MOON

By Julie Fortune
Price: $7.95 US | $9.95 Canada |
£6.99 UK
ISBN-10: 0-9547343-1-9
ISBN-13: 978-0-9547343-1-2

Sacrifice Moon follows the newly commissioned SG-1 on their first mission through the Stargate.

Their destination is Chalcis, a peaceful society at the heart of the Helos Confederacy of planets. But Chalcis harbors a dark secret, one that pitches SG-1 into a world of bloody chaos, betrayal and madness. Battling to escape the living nightmare, Dr. Daniel Jackson and Captain Samantha Carter soon begin to realize that more than their lives are at stake. They are fighting for their very souls.

But while Col Jack O'Neill and Teal'c struggle to keep the team together, Daniel is hatching a desperate plan that will test SG-1's fledgling bonds of trust and friendship to the limit...

Order your copy directly from the publisher today by going to www.stargatenovels.com or send a check or money order made payable to "Fandemonium" to:

<u>USA orders:</u> $10.82 ($7.95 + $2.87 P&P). Send payment to: Fandemonium Books, PO Box 2178, Decatur, GA 30031-2178.

<u>UK orders:</u> £8.30 (£6.99 + £1.31 P&P). <u>Rest of the World orders:</u> £9.70 (£6.99 + £2.71 P&P). Send payment to: Fandemonium Books, PO Box 795A, Surbiton KT5 8YB, United Kingdom.

Or check your local bookshop – available on special order if they are out of stock (quote the ISBN number listed above).

STARGATE SG-1: TRIAL BY FIRE

By Sabine C. Bauer
Price: $7.95 US | $9.95 Canada |
£6.99 UK
ISBN-10: 0-9547343-0-0
ISBN-13: 978-0-9547343-0-5

Trial by Fire follows the team as they embark on a mission to Tyros, an ancient society teetering on the brink of war.

A pious people, the Tyreans are devoted to the Canaanite deity, Meleq. When their spiritual leader is savagely murdered during a mission of peace, they beg SG-1 for help against their sworn enemies, the Phrygians.

Initially reluctant to get involved, the team has no choice when Colonel Jack O'Neill is abducted. O'Neill soon discovers his only hope of escape is to join the ruthless Phrygians—if he can survive their barbaric initiation rite.

As Major Samantha Carter, Dr. Daniel Jackson and Teal'c race to his rescue, they find themselves embroiled in a war of shifting allegiances, where truth has many shades and nothing is as it seems.

And, unbeknownst to them all, an old enemy is hiding in the shadows...

Order your copy directly from the publisher today by going to www.stargatenovels.com or send a check or money order made payable to "Fandemonium" to:

<u>**USA orders:**</u> **$10.82 ($7.95 + $2.87 P&P). Send payment to: Fandemonium Books, PO Box 2178, Decatur, GA 30031-2178.**

<u>**UK orders:**</u> **£8.30 (£6.99 + £1.31 P&P).** <u>**Rest of the World orders:**</u> **£9.70 (£6.99 + £2.71 P&P). Send payment to: Fandemonium Books, PO Box 795A, Surbiton KT5 8YB, United Kingdom.**

Or check your local bookshop – available on special order if they are out of stock (quote the ISBN number listed above).